THE
LIVES
OF
RACHEL

THE LIVES OF RACHEL

Joel Gross

NAL BOOKS

NEW AMERICAN LIBRARY

NEW YORK AND SCARBOROUGH, ONTARIO

Copyright © 1984 by Joel Gross

All rights reserved

For information address New American Library

Published simultaneously in Canada by
The New American Library of Canada Limited

 NAL BOOKS TRADEMARK REG. U.S. PAT. OFF. AND FOREIGN COUNTRIES
REGISTERED TRADEMARK—MARCA REGISTRADA
HECHO EN HARRISONBURG, VA., U.S.A.

SIGNET, SIGNET CLASSIC, MENTOR, PLUME, MERID-IAN and NAL BOOKS are published *in the United States* by New American Library, 1633 Broadway, New York, New York 10019, *in Canada* by The New American Library of Canada Limited, 81 Mack Avenue, Scarborough, Ontario M1L 1M8

LIBRARY OF CONGRESS CATALOGING IN PUBLICATION DATA
Gross, Joel.
    The lives of Rachel
    I. Title.
PS3557.R58L5   1984   813'.54   84-6866
ISBN 0-453-00467-9

First Printing, October, 1984

1 2 3 4 5 6 7 8 9

PRINTED IN THE UNITED STATES OF AMERICA

Designed by Kathryn Parise

For Linda Rachel

I have set before you life and death, the
blessing and the curse; therefore choose
life, that you may live, you and your seed;
to love the Lord your God, to hearken to His
voice, and to cleave unto Him; for that is
your life, and the length of your days.

DEUTERONOMY 30

A thousand years in Your sight
Are but as yesterday when it is past
And as a watch in the night.

PSALMS 90

Prologue
May 1982

Rachel Kane arrived in Jerusalem after a sleepless eleven-hour flight from New York, and insisted on going directly to the Western Wall. Her husband, glowing with vitality after ten hours of dreamless sleep in the adjacent seat, insisted on first going to the hotel. "I don't like how you look," he said. "You've got hollows under your eyes, your skin is dry, and you're walking like a drunk. The doctor was very clear that you could go almost anywhere and do almost anything, as long as you don't exhaust yourself."

Rachel was about to respond with a fake clutching of her pregnant belly, but decided against it. This was their first child on the way, and this was *his* first month as much as it was hers. So she simply said to the cabdriver, "You can drop my husband at the King David Hotel, and then I'm going on to the Jewish quarter."

The cabdriver, who had spent the last forty minutes of the trip to Jerusalem from the airport explaining how this car, this road, this country, and this sunset were all the best of their kind in the world, was aghast. "You're going to let your wife go the Wall by herself?"

They effected a compromise: their luggage was deposited at the hotel, and the driver took them to the Dung Gate in the Old City's wall, from where it was a short walk to the Western Wall, the last remnant of the Second Temple, and the focal point of Jewish longing for nearly two thousand years.

1

The floodlights had not yet been illuminated as they hurried past the security booth to the vast plaza before the Wall. Rachel's elegant shoes raised a clatter before the approaching stillness of night. The sky was opening above them, raising its distant cap of clouds to a series of multicolored ribbons; pink and blue strands of gentle fire glowed from an unimaginable distance, from an unknowable source.

"Hold on to me, darling," said her husband, who had offered his arm, and then finally took hold of Rachel by the shoulders. It had grown suddenly cold in the absence of sunlight, and a light wind whipped about the empty spaces before the Wall. Separate groups of men and women prayed together in its shadow, their eyes shut, their bodies swaying to an interior rhythm as old as history. There were tourists too, squinting through expensive camera lenses, separating themselves from the experience by futile attempts to record their presence; electronic flashes burst in irregular beats of time from among them, shoddy reminders of the present against the blackening landscape.

"I want to touch," said Rachel, extricating herself from her husband's grasp. Close to the Wall, a partition was erected, separating the men from the women in accordance with the religious customs of Orthodox Jews. Rachel's husband watched her hurry through the knots of the devotees, women shaking and wailing and raising their shut-eyed faces from the Wall to the heavens. He didn't join the rabbis and students and soldiers on the larger, male side of the partition; he was unable to take his eyes off his wife's figure, even as it diminished in the dark and the distance.

But Rachel felt nothing of her husband's concern. At that moment she was driven by a pure impulse, simply to touch the Wall, to feel the cool ancient stone flush against her hands, to rest her hot forehead where an endless stream of pilgrims had rested theirs at the end of their journeys. She was not a religious woman, nor did she have a prayer ready to mumble through quivering lips; but she was of a family whose ancestors had been in this land, had stood in this place, and to answer some inchoate inner call she rushed for the stone like a lover reaching for her beloved.

It was at that moment that darkness fell.

Not in the sky, for all about her the setting sun still lit the tattered prayer books, the colorful costumes of Near and Middle East, the separate spectacles of ecstasy and sorrow, of joy and lamentation;

but through her wide-open eyes came no light, no shadow. The presence of the stones, of the tiny bits of paper stuffed in its cracks —prayers and wishes from the faithful—faded to black. Rachel felt her heart race, felt a fever rise up from under her skull and spill through every pore in her face. There was heat, there was fear, and her lips moved as she intoned the ancient prayer:

"*Shemah Yisroel, Adonai Elohenu, Adonai Echad,*" she said, the words familiar to her from religious school six thousand miles and fifteen years away; but familiar beyond that. "Hear O Israel, the Lord is God, the Lord is One," she said, but not in English, and not in the badly accented Hebrew of her Connecticut teachers. Rachel said the words fluently, till the syllables slipped together, till the prayer was no longer a string of words but a single incantation, till the incantation was without any other meaning than a sigh or a caress or a love beyond reason.

"*Shema Yisroel, Adonai Elohenu, Adonai Echad,*" she repeated, again and again, and the tears came to her eyes, and without realizing it, her body was swaying, even as she held on to the cool stones, even as she turned her heart into the past, through the blackness, until there was a moment, a moment whose duration was beyond measurement, big and small, round and flat, a piece of time and a thread of fancy—and then there was an end to blackness. She could see quite clearly the white stones, reflecting the brilliant sun of midday, and beyond them, and above them, the towering Temple secure and serene on the Temple Mount, and through it all was a music, familiar and sweet and gentled by the wind, and in the heart of the moment she strained to hear the words, to taste them even if they were harsher than poison, to touch them even if they were etched in flame.

"Rachel," said a voice.

But whether the voice was her own, or that of another, calling to her through time, she couldn't know.

"Rachel," said the voice, and then the name was repeated, again and again, a whisper and a memory and a promise.

Part One

Judea, 168 B.C.

Chapter
1

Rachel could barely see the Holy City through the dust. Like the Pillar of Cloud sent by the Lord to guide the Children of Israel in their flight from Egypt, this dust hovered over the road to Jerusalem like a beacon. Above the road, above the indistinct city walls, above the dust raised by ten thousand feet, above the chatter and song, above the tumult of beasts of burden, of lambs to be sacrificed and chickens to be slaughtered, above the joy and fear and sorrow in the hearts of the pilgrims rose the famous Jerusalem sky. An hour before sunset, it had already begun to fracture the diminishing light into opalescent rivers and meadows and seas. Rachel could well imagine how the pagans had peopled the sky with their silly gods: gods who drew fire through the air, who painted the canopy of heaven with lust and jealousy like the humans who'd invented them to explain the unexplainable. And certainly no sky, not in the king's capital of Antioch, not even in far-off Greece, home of the pagans' gods and seat of their faithless culture, could be more exciting to the imagination. It seemed less a sky than a dome of many colors; it seemed like gold stretched and beaten to an impossible thinness, waiting for the hammer of night, the puncture of starlight; it seemed like a head covering, blowing wildly askew from some preternatural wind, revealing glimpses of heavenly hair, lustrous lines of purple and magenta twisting below a pallid orange sun.

"You're smiling," said Saul, shouting the words at her through the din.

"Yes, my husband," said Rachel. "In spite of the pigs, in spite of the men without faith."

"In spite of the priests who said no one would come," said Saul. He was twenty-four and had been her husband for six years, marrying her on her fourteenth birthday, when the promise of her beauty had been as clear and as certain as prophecy. Saul had married her over the weak protests of his father, and the stronger protests of his uncle, both of whom had wanted a girl of more distinguished lineage for a son of the priestly line. But Saul's infatuation had been stronger than any protest, and no one in his family expected the hot-tempered young man to be a likely candidate for the intricacies of the priesthood, or its yet more delicate affiliate craft of diplomacy. He had become a trader in gold and gems, married to a childless woman goldsmith, and his family was content to ignore him.

Some of the pilgrims had been walking for a day, others for a week or more; a few had been traveling for months, making the dangerous pilgrimage from Egypt or Persia or the distant settlements along the Hyrcanian Sea. But whether they'd traveled the coastal road from Antioch, or gone overland from Alexandria, or left some nearby village nestled in the hills of Judah, all had ascended the last miles, all had begun to breathe the magic crystalline air unique to this high place.

Jerusalem, the city of David, the center of life for the Jewish people in Judea, in Tyre, in Egypt, in Persia; even for those Jews born across the Mediterranean Sea, Greek-speakers who knew little Hebrew and no Aramaic, this city was the symbol of their home, their religion, their nation. King David, who had lived and died before the First Temple was built, had sung of it in the psalms that every boy and girl in Judea had by heart: "If I forget thee, O Jerusalem, let my right hand forget her cunning," he had written. "Pray for the peace of Jerusalem," he had said eight centuries before, and for all the years after that, after Solomon had built the great Temple, after Nebuchadnezzar had driven the Jews into exile in Babylon, after Cyrus had allowed the exiles to return to their city and rebuild the Temple nearly four hundred years ago, after Alexander the Great had conquered their city, after the descendants of his generals had quarreled over it like gluttons anxious for a last sweet,

David's words remained. "As the mountains are round about Jerusalem, so the Lord is round about his people forever."

The outer walls of the city had been recently fortified, and the smooth-cut stones reflected the waning light with an unfamiliar harshness. Rachel had never seen such white stones around the city of her birth. When she'd left Jerusalem almost four years before, the walls had been in bad repair, the gates sloppily guarded, the leering mercenaries of the king too contemptuous of the men of the city to regard them with fear. That had changed, of course. The mercenaries still laughed at the shabbily dressed members of the Pious sect, still followed the city's lovely women with insolent eyes, but they were no longer casual about the walls and the gates. Only weeks before the king's appointed high priest had been deposed by a Jewish force headed by the former High Priest Jason. The mercenaries had chosen not to intervene in the local intrigue; but the choice had been based on their surprise at Jason's strength. The deposed High Priest Menelaus had been despised by most of his Jewish constituency; for the four years he'd taken charge of the Temple and the Holy City, many Jews had stayed away from Jerusalem, unable to bear his admixture of Greek rites with their own ancient rituals. More zealous members of the priestly class, like Saul's uncle and father, still stayed away from Jerusalem. Jason was better than Menelaus, but he was still another pretender to a position that was not his birthright. None of the Pietists could forget that it was under Jason's administration of Temple and city that the cursed gymnasium was built, where Jewish young men, many of them from the ranks of the priesthood, were seduced into the Greek way of life.

"We will make a child tonight," said Saul, reaching for Rachel's hand as they approached the gate.

"If it's the will of God," said Rachel.

"And why wouldn't it be His will?" said Saul, reaching from her arm to her neck with his smooth hand. "With the stars in our eyes, with the fruits of the harvest ready for His Temple?"

"Your mother told me that my childlessness was almost certainly due to your blasphemous tongue," said Rachel, but she couldn't help moving her tired neck more firmly into his embrace.

"I could give you back," said Saul, pulling her closer. "I could find myself an expert in the Law and get back my hard-earned bride money."

9

They were not the only ones kissing as they entered the gates of the city. The Holiday of the Harvest—Sukkot—had little of the solemn weight of other pilgrim festivals. In thanksgiving for the Lord's bounty, the Jews brought part of their harvest to the Temple; in memory of the Israelites' forty years wandering in the desert, they spent the week-long festival living in flimsy fruit-and-leaf-covered booths which they flung up hastily all about the city. Sukkot, being the festival of the harvest, arrived in early fall, when the sun-dried hills no longer held on to the heat of the day for the first hours of darkness. After an evening and a night of bright-burning torches, enormous candelabras blazing in the courts of the Temple, soul-stretching songs chanted above the haze of light, into the cold and overwhelming blackness, the pilgrims would look to love as a solace against the force of the unknown. With the hymns and the pomp and the majesty of the Temple rites lingering in their cold bodies, they would hurry across the windswept high places of the city, searching out their ramshackle booths, eager to huddle together beneath the low roofs, whose branches and boughs were deliberately spaced to let in the pale glow of moon and stars.

But as they passed under the gaze of the Syrian mercenaries at the gate, the reality of the city began to work away at any sense of frivolity or festivity that might have prevailed in former years. A group of spearmen with boyish faces and thick limbs stood at attention, fronting two officers in full armor: one of the officers had a metal breastplate, shot through with a gold design of poor workmanship. The other officer wore gold on his sandals, in two armlets, in a ring so large that it must have hampered his swordsmanship; but at least his breastplate was leather, and thus not for show. He could move if he had need to, and it seemed to Rachel that the deep stains in the heavy shoulder straps that held up breastplate and backplate were of blood. Antiochus, the young king who paid these soldiers and who ruled the Seleucid empire from Antioch in Syria, had not yet returned from Egypt; Jew and Gentiles alike had heard the rumors of his death. Indeed it was the possibility of this that had emboldened the followers of the new High Priest Jason to take over the Temple grounds, and drive out the king's man, the High Priest Menelaus. If King Antiochus was dead, rebellion would be sure to break out in a dozen cities; the dream to conquer Egypt and Parthia and Bactria, to bring back the glorious age of Alexander to this shaky empire would end in a confusion of tiny wars, fought for small reasons. Even little Judea would rise up; Jerusalem would be armed by Egyptians, anxious to undermine Syrian rule. The soldiers of a dead king would be suddenly leaderless, adrift in foreign parts, destined for slaughter or slavery.

"We go left, my husband," said Rachel, taking Saul's thick wrist in her work-hardened hand. "Such a memory you have," she added. "Like a scribe who can't remember his child's name."

Rachel spoke in Hebrew, making her words more palatable to Saul. In Aramaic, the common language of the Jews of Judea— and in its various dialects, of much of their part of the world—her familiar tone might have been shocking; many of those same pilgrims who no longer understood the Hebrew of their ancestors had no sense of humor about the relationship of man and wife. The husband was the master; indeed he was most commonly called "my lord" or "my master" by a dutiful wife in both the Hebrew and Aramaic languages. Directing or chiding a husband, much less mocking one's lord and master, was not only wrong, it was a sin; but of course these rules didn't apply to every level of society.

She led him swiftly away from the mob of pilgrims heading up the first of the two great hills on which the city was built. Rachel could see past the new soldiers' quarters, the crude brick huts sheltering the prostitutes and the sellers of cheap wine that came and went with each new group of conquerors, to the old quarter of merchants' homes, sheltered from the wind by thick-walled courtyards.

"What can't I remember?" said Saul, pulling at the silk mantle he'd brought her from Tyre last year, when he'd gone to buy Cyprian jaspers. The wind blew at her head covering, and now he pulled this away, letting her thick red hair fly about her face as if she were a siren.

"You've missed me then?" said Rachel, looking at her bare shoulder, and then slowly, teasingly pulling up the silk over her flesh and tightening the gold-clasped girdle at her waist, she added: "How many girls did you have in Egypt then?"

"No girls," said Saul. "Only camels and baby elephants, and once a little black boy from the Nubian mines. Such a wife. Your father won't be happy to have you back!"

They had brought two slaves and a single donkey, and now this trio ground to a halt behind them in the alleyway that had taken

11

them away from the noise and the confusion of the masses. Slaves and donkey stood silently as husband and wife embraced. They saw nothing as Saul pulled away at the silk mantle, exposing his young wife's shoulder, and brought his lips to shoulder and neck. "A little present," said Saul, and the slaves heard nothing, did not dwell on the fact that their master had been absent from his home for more than four months, and that on the day of his return he had been forced to join the pilgrimage to the Holy City, a distance of eight hours on foot—no young pilgrims, no matter how rich, could disgrace themselves with a litter among the foot-weary climbers to Jerusalem—without even taking an hour to lie down with his wife.

In the diminishing light Rachel saw the gleam of gold against ivory, felt her husband's smooth hands pull away the hair at the back of her neck, and then he brought his lips to hers gently, briefly, and pulled away, still holding on to her thick hair and holding up the jewelry in front of her green eyes.

It was a hair jewel, flat and elegantly simple, its gold clasp twisted into a Herakles knot, its only jarring note the large ruby inlaid into the center of the gold.

"For your hair," he said unnecessarily as he opened the clasp and closed it over the hair he had gathered in his fist.

"The ruby is for my tribe, I suppose?" said Rachel.

"Even a little girl knows to say, 'Thank you, my Lord.' "

"Thank you, my unfaithful husband—with the smooth hands," and Rachel kissed these hands now, and then unceremoniously pulled open the clasp of the jewel and fixed her hair quickly in the gathering dark. Beyond the slaves came the sounds of hurrying feet, and Rachel thanked Saul more properly, and then urged him to come along. It seemed absurd to her that they were discussing the merits of inlaying precious stones in gold when all about them was the impending majesty of the festival rites, the threatening currents of repression and rebellion. But she was a goldsmith, in spite of being rich and above manual work, in spite of being a woman, and a married one besides. Saul's smooth hands came from a life of business and trade, and his trade was in gems, and he thought less in terms of the dangers to his priestly caste if the Romans grew into the new power in the region than he did about the change in taste it would bring in the marketplace. The Romans loved gems inlaid in gold; the Greeks—and nearly the entire civilized world called themselves Greeks or Hellenes—thought it terribly gauche to ruin the purity of gold with a gaudy addition. It was only the well-known fact that the tribe of Judah's representative gemstones in the Temple treasures were rubies that prompted Saul to bring home such an unsophisticated bauble for Rachel. For in spite of her love of Greek craftmanship, she was devoted to her people—to their Temple, their sacred Scrolls of Law, their history.

Coming out of the alleyway, they entered a brick-paved street, where some of the pilgrims had begun to set up their booths. Torches had already been lit, and the wind whipped the flames dangerously close to the roofs of branches and boughs. Long before the Temple rites would be over that night, the street would be lined with the booths, the smooth brick of the walled courtyards serving as a common fourth side to the makeshift structures.

"You're very beautiful," said Saul, as he prevented his wife from covering her head.

"I must cover my head," she said. "Do you want to be kicked by a Pietist?"

"Don't be ridiculous, Rachel. Jerusalem is far more sacrilegious than sacred, even with Jason as high priest. You have every right to uncover your beautiful hair."

"As it pleases my master," said Rachel smiling. They were close enough to the home of her father and brother, neither of whom had much use for the God of their ancestors. Shimon, Rachel's brother, had been one of the first of the young men of the city to take exercise in the Greek gymnasium, and he was planning to take part in the Greek games at Tyre later that year as both runner and wrestler. When the pressure of Saul's family forced the young couple to leave Jerusalem at the beginning of Menelaus's administration as high priest, Shimon refused to believe that their move was based on anything other than political expediency. Saul's family was powerful, and had connections from Alexandria to Babylon: Shimon simply could not conceive that his lovely and intelligently educated sister could have left Jerusalem sharing a futile protest over the importation of civilization.

In the few times that he'd made the sixteen-mile journey to Modein from Jerusalem, he had been more upset at seeing his sister working at goldsmithing without the proper complement of trained slaves than he had been at the benighted opinions of Saul's family. Shimon knew that Rachel had married into the Judean aristocracy, and that for all the comforts of his own Jerusalem home—and all the money that had allowed him his private tutors and his year of study in Alexandria—the priestly caste looked down on his father and his father's father as beneath their dignity. This was particularly galling to Shimon in light of the fact that both his father and mother descended from the *Cohanim*, the priestly caste, but because of some murky political intriguing in the time of his great-grandfather, the family had stopped sending its young men to the Temple to be inducted into the ranks of practicing priests. The majority of *Cohanim* were in fact nonpracticing; they were accorded certain dignities in the Temple rites, but were otherwise excluded from the mysteries and the honors and the chance of leadership. Rachel's family was so far removed from any Temple politics that Saul's family did not think of it as part of its class at all. Even a nonpracticing priest like Saul was thought of more properly as a *Cohen* than Shimon, because Saul's family was thought of as a priestly family, a purer part of the larger world of ordinary *Cohanim*. Rachel often thought it was this more than anything else that had driven her brother into a contempt for the religious practices of his people.

The dark and the confusion of booths and the growing chatter and song from the pilgrims made it difficult for Rachel to distinguish the outer wall of the house in which she was born. "Perhaps they've sold the house and moved into a tent," said Saul, holding her about the waist. "Simply in honor of our ancestors' wandering in the Sinai." He held her a bit closer. "Think, idiot. If only we had never left Modein. Think if we were in our bed, freshly bathed, drinking wine from Laodicea, eating Jericho dates, breathing the divine frankincense that I paid too much for in Alexandria only because I thought of sharing it with you." Once again the slaves behind them stayed the donkey and saw nothing as their masters embraced. Even as a large blond man in a purple tunic came up to Saul from behind and threw an arm about his neck, pulled him away from Rachel and hurled him violently to the ground, the slaves saw nothing.

"You miserable wretch," said Saul, getting up slowly, his eyes on his powerful opponent.

"You will stop this at once," said Rachel, speaking without thinking in Aramaic. But Saul had been surprised, and for all his soft hands, he had never loved any sport so much as wrestling, and so he lowered his head as if to butt his opponent's belly, but as he charged, he veered sharply to the left, dropping to his knees and grabbing the man's calves in a felling embrace.

The blond man laughed, even as he fell heavily onto his back, and Saul threw himself across his chest. "So clumsy," said the blond man. "I've never seen such clumsiness."

But Saul had the man pinned to the ground, his own knees firmly holding back shoulders more powerful than Saul remembered. "Clumsy or not, you're on your back again," he said to his brother-in-law.

"Ruining his tunic," said Rachel, helping her husband get to his feet. "Scaring me half to death. You could have been a drunken soldier, Shimon."

"Little sister," said Shimon, as he ignored Saul's hand and stood up in one fluid motion. He bowed to Rachel with a twisted smile, then jerked her forward into his broad chest. "Don't pretend. You weren't scared. No one ever scares my little sister."

He guided them back to the entryway they'd missed in the courtyard wall. A slave with a ring of bells about the neck of his tunic waited for them with a torch. They followed him through a tiny courtyard, much smaller than Rachel had remembered, past a stunted olive tree, and around the back of the house, to the washing room. Here the slave washed Saul's feet, and then proceeded to undo the sandals of his master. To Rachel's astonishment, Shimon pushed his foot directly into the slave's face.

"We have a guest," he said. "Even if she's a woman."

"Yes, master," said the slave, speaking in Greek, as had Shimon. Even when Rachel had addressed her brother in the formulaic Hebrew greeting for a long-absent loved one, he'd answered her in Greek.

"Not a very beautiful woman, but still a woman for all that," said Shimon to Saul, jabbing his brother-in-law in the arm. Rachel watched the slave's face as he carefully removed her sandals and washed her very dirty feet, but there was no sign of resentment or anger in his flat features. She wondered where he was from—too light to be African, too broad-nosed to be from Media, too coarse-haired to be Thracian. But of course now slaves came from all over the world, as pirates had fewer restraints on their raiding, not only on the sea but on land as well. And slaves were mated with other slaves, producing blue eyes in black faces, Asiatic cheekbones in the long-limbed bodies of the barbarian northlands. Even her own people—rebels, or merchants captured at sea, or the children of paupers—were slaves in foreign places.

"How is father?"

"We will talk about father after I tell Saul about what I could have done to him if I had felt like it, sister," said Shimon. "By every god in the sky it's good to see you."

"Why not every pig on the altar?" said Rachel.

"Slave," said Shimon. "Don't be hasty. Massage the lady's feet. She's walked many miles for her primitive festival." The slave did as he was told, putting enough effort into the work to set the bells about his neck jangling pleasantly. Suddenly Rachel was very tired, as tired as she had been as a little girl, always being corrected by her older brother, always being guarded or reprimanded or mocked. Shimon's Greek words came to her now filtered by the haze she had learned to put between herself and her brother since they were small children: "For your information we have no pigs in this house, and no altar to any gods, Greek or otherwise," said Shimon. "Before you start criticizing everyone all at once, you should learn what you are talking about. Being civilized doesn't mean denying your heritage. If I wrestle in the games at Tyre this year, I'll be going as a circumcised Jew, not as a renegade. No one can tell me what to sacrifice to the One God, or the ten gods. Any more than any Jew can tell me that I'm a heathen because I won't cover my head or avert my eyes from a beautiful woman or refuse to absorb the beauty of Greek culture."

"Are you going to lie in a *sukkah* tonight?" said Rachel, using the Hebrew word for the traditional booths that gave the Sukkot festival its name.

"Of course not," said Shimon. "No more than I will go to the Temple and watch the candelabras burn up precious oil." He was only a year older than Rachel, but they hadn't seen him for many months; his words stung. What had once been the charming over-enthusiasm of youth now had the hard cast of an intolerant adult. "I am not a follower of the unknowable."

"But what are you saying?" said Saul, who had always felt himself far away from the Pietists but was still faithful to his God. "That you believe in no God?"

"If he cannot believe in the unknowable," said Rachel, "then that is of course what he is saying."

"Atheism is one of the three false beliefs denounced by Plato, idiot," said her brother happily.

16

"He has a God, and his name is Plato," explained Rachel to Saul.

"Not Plato, but reason. Not piety, but beauty," said Shimon. "Not a fear of the supernatural, but a courage to accept a divine will that no scribe can pretend to know."

"And all this from a wrestler," said Saul.

"It is only among the Pietists that our people have turned from the joys of sport and exercise. Look at yourself. You call yourself a Jew, but you dress like a Greek, you travel around the world without hindering yourself with a thousand pious customs, and when I speak to you in Greek of Plato, you don't look at me with blank eyes. In the days of our grandfather—"

"You've told him," interrupted Rachel. "Our grandfather the Egyptian general."

"Not an Egyptian general. A mercenary general," said Shimon as if this were a point of greater pride. "In the days when Jews were famous for being fighters instead of Pietists. When the nations looked to us for help in war instead of in contempt for refusing to honor their gods along with our own."

"You really thought I was clumsy?" said Saul.

"I could have thrown you in a second," said Shimon. "As wrestler and scholar both. As athlete and wit. As fighter and—"

"Then why did it end with me sitting on your chest?" interrupted Saul.

Shimon snapped his fingers at the slave. "Dry her feet, don't take all day. Father is waiting. And as for you and your wrestling, come to the gymnasium tomorrow and I will show you what wrestling is."

Shimon pushed the slave aside, as if dissatisfied with his performance, and Rachel and Saul followed him back outside. A large *sukkah* had been erected against the back of the house, and near it, a much smaller one, sharing the same house wall. The scent of the freshly cut palm and myrtle and willow was delightful in the clear air.

"Why are there two then?" said Rachel, glad to see that her brother, for all his bluntness and lack of consideration for his slave, had hospitably arranged to have their festival booth built before their arrival. "I thought you said you don't believe in what cannot be known."

"I said, more precisely, that I am not a follower of the unknowable, Rachel," said Shimon. A dark shape appeared on the outside stairway that led from the flat roof's comfortable terrace to the courtyard. A white beard caught the light of the torches. "But father—he's changed."

"Rachel," said the white-bearded man, and his voice was full and without hesitation, the voice that had been a constant since her birth. But as her father Mordecai came more fully into the torchlight, she could see that more changes had taken place besides his having grown a beard: a goldsmith and seller of jewelry to kings, her father now wore no rings, no bracelets, no gold at his belt or in his sandals. His garments were gray, and without a rich border. The hair on his head was long, but hadn't been washed or curled or rubbed with oil. Mordecai had on no scent, and as he stopped to embrace her she could see in his hand a Hebrew scroll. They embraced, and she could taste the tears that were running down his cheeks, and when she pulled out of his grasp to study the pain in his eyes, she could see the greatest change here, as if a demon had taken over the elegant restrained gentleman she had always admired more than she had loved.

"Happy holiday, my children," said her father, turning to take Saul into his arms. Rachel noticed a young man with a thick black beard come out of the dark of the stairway, and was momentarily startled. She and Saul both recognized him. He was one of the children of Mattathias, from their own village of Modein. He greeted them without formality or warmth, and then shook his head gravely: "You should have stayed home, like the priests advised. This is not a season to be offering sacrifice or prayers at the Temple."

"There are priests here, as well as in Modein," said Saul. "If we all stayed away from the Temple until the right man was high priest, we might never get a chance to see it on our lifetimes."

"You may not get a chance anyway," said the son of Mattathias.

Mordecai tapped the little scroll against the knuckles of his right hand. "King Antiochus is not dead," he said, indicating the message scroll that the young man had just delivered. "He is returning to Jerusalem with a great force of men to reinstate his own man as high priest. He has said that he will take a thousand captives as slaves, and slaughter a thousand more besides."

Mordecai looked away from his daughter and toward his young son, as if saving the most horrendous piece of news for him: "And the king has let it be known that he will enter the Temple."

Chapter
2

That night, they joined the throngs of pilgrims climbing to the walls about the Temple Mount. Torches blazed the way, and the pilgrims sang, shaking their branches of palm and myrtle and willow, symbols of the festival. Saul carried a large, perfectly shaped citron, a gift from his mother; while she didn't approve of his visiting the Temple with its current high priest, she couldn't imagine him celebrating Sukkot without this festival fruit, picked by her own hands from among hundreds. Palm, myrtle, willow, and citron made up the Four Species. All were essential to the holiday spirit of brotherhood. Festivals united the Hebrew people, smoothed the differences of class, religious observances, and political affiliations.

The fragrant citron in Saul's hand represented the scholars and scribes, the gentle and good and holy among the pilgrims; the palm, tall and strong, represented the secular men of power; the ever-bending willow represented the poor, the slaves, the lowly; while the common myrtle represented the masses who thought of themselves as neither saints nor sinners, powerful nor meek.

It was clear that the news brought by the son of Mattathias to Mordecai had not yet penetrated these masses. There was no fear in the air. Much wine had been drunk in the hours since sunset, and while the ascent to the Temple was sobering, there was a looseness, even a wildness to the songs that had not been present during the day. Near where Saul and Rachel walked hand in hand,

19

a very old man played an abub-pipe, made of reeds. Old as he was, he danced to his own rhythm, skipping up the road with shut eyes, surefooted amid a crush of family. Other pilgrims played the eight-string sheminit-harp, and the still simpler three-string pandura. Children beat on little drums, freshly made for the holiday. For a few moments, it was easy for Rachel to forget about the threat of the king, and to dwell on her childlessness. She missed Shimon, and Mordecai their father, as she was sure Saul missed his extensive family; at least Saul's family would be offering prayers of thanksgiving from Modein. Shimon had little thanksgiving in his heart; and their father Mordecai knew no prayers that might prevent the slaughter of innocents.

"I am glad you forced me to come," said Saul as they approached the outer wall.

"How could a wife force her lord and master to do anything?" said Rachel. She squatted down now to help remove Saul's sandals, as did all the wives for their husbands—and as the children did for their mothers, if they had children—before the gates. No shoes were allowed on the holy surface of the Temple Mount. "It was my master's desire to visit Jerusalem."

"Your master's desire is to lie with you in the *sukkah.*"

"After all this climbing, my husband, who knows if we shall be able to do anything other than sleep?"

Ahead of them, the outer gatekeepers were refusing entry to a ragged group from Samaria, who were not only not wearing the requisite white clothing, but were filthy and disorderly. The gatekeepers were Levites, descendants of the third son of Jacob and Leah, and were honored since the days of Moses as workers about the Lord's Sanctuary. The priestly caste, the *Cohanim,* were descendants of Moses' brother Aaron, and were yet more honored than the Levites in the traditions of the Jews: only the priestly caste were allowed to enter the Sanctuary within the Temple, only members of the caste who had been inducted into the priestly brotherhood could offer sacrifices in the name of the people.

At the gate, Saul gave his name: "Saul, son of Jehoram of Modein, the *Cohen.*" Neither Saul nor Rachel was plagued with any questions about impurities. They were passed through, walking the cold stones of the Temple Square, blinking in the suddenly abundant light of the candelabras. Here the joyous crowd was subdued, awed by the walls rising beyond the pale of torch and lamplight into the immense darkness. Within the walls, the multitude was made small by the endless expanse of the square. The pilgrims remembered that they were the Lord's Chosen People, here in the Jerusalem that the Pietists called "the navel of the world," here on the Temple Mount that was the central reason of the city, feeling the holiness of the earth beneath the paving stones, facing the walls that surrounded the inner Temple courts and the Temple itself— the center of the center.

"We don't have to separate," said Saul, as they approached the second set of walls. Inside were courts for priests, for ordinary male Jews, and one smaller court at the eastern end reserved for women.

"What do you mean, my husband? Am I to pretend to be both man and priest?" She smiled as she said this, feeling his excitement for her grow through all the mysteries about them. "Of course I am the *daughter* of a Cohen—"

Saul interrupted her: "I mean that we can walk around the walls, not through, and go out without ever letting go of each other."

"We can't do that," said Rachel firmly.

"I want to be with you," he said. "And I cannot wait a moment longer." But Saul had no choice in the matter, for Rachel had already kissed the citron he carried, and now admonished him to bless her, and was out of the reach of his anxious hands, hurrying up the majestic steps to the inner gates.

The Court of the Women was crowded and noisy with prayer. It was possible to edge up to the balcony that surrounded the court, and peer out into the Court of the Israelites, where the men received their blessings from the priests before the actual entrance to the Temple. Members of the priestly caste, like Saul, could approach the Temple more closely than the other Israelites, but only practicing priests could enter the Temple itself. Rachel watched the pilgrims prostrate themselves in unison as the priests intoned the Sacred Name; but the women could scarcely see the priests in their sacerdotal finery as they raised their arms and blessed the people, the festival, the sacred city. As a little child she could remember being held in her mother's arms here, urged to search out the figures of her father and brother in the throng below. Some of the women tried to follow the proceedings among the men: one or two would prostrate themselves, several would strain to join in the chanting of the *Shema Yisroel* prayer. But most were content to be removed from the company of their husbands and brothers and fathers. They prayed after their own fashion, stringing together psalms from memory, listing the names of their children, mumbling the prayer for the new festival: "Blessed art Thou, Lord of the Universe, who has kept us in life, who has preserved us, who has enabled us to reach this season."

Below them the men shook the branches of palm and myrtle and willow, held the fragrant citron to their noses, felt the heat of the burning oil lamps, watched the priests carry the huge pans of frankincense up the steps of the Temple—and beyond, out of Rachel's sight, inside. She wondered what treasures were there. There were vessels of silver and gold, she knew; but she couldn't picture their craftsmanship. There was a table for the Bread of the Presence, but she didn't know if this table was of precious metal, of cedar wood, or all of jewels. There was an altar of gold, she had been told, and a lamp stand of gold and silver, and sacred cups and bowls, and special censers and crowns touched only by the high priest. All that was inside. And in the innermost part of the Temple, reserved only for the high priest, and only on the Day of Atonement, was the Holy of Holies, the most sacred place in the sight of God. Rachel shivered at the possibility that the king, a Gentile, a pagan, could think about entering the Temple. What would stop him from touching what was not to be touched, from looking at what must not be seen, at stepping in his unclean clothes, with his impure body, into the Holy of Holies?

Even without an army, the Hebrew people would never tolerate such an outrage; even her Greek-loving brother would rise up and join with his people, no matter what force was sent against them.

No one left the Temple grounds the way they had entered. Going to the Temple was an aspiration; arriving there was a fulfillment. One could never turn one's back to the chief source of earthly joy. Rachel followed the series of gates that led out of the Temple courts, through the inner walls, and into a vast space where men and women separated by various services looked for each other in the artificial light. Rachel wanted to find Saul very quickly, and hurry home around the Temple Mount, leaving the main roads for the neat little streets and alleys, rising and falling with broad stone steps, the shops and houses arranged like sturdy crops on a terraced hillside. She wasn't afraid, but she was wary; there was something coming to the city that was outside her experience, and she wanted to be held tonight in her husband's strong arms.

"Four months," said Saul, coming up to her.

"I didn't see you, my husband," she said, and they kissed at once, and he brought her close to his side, like newlyweds, and hurried off with her toward the outer walls. Here the Levites asked no questions, simply ushered them out with a holiday blessing and left them to join the crowds leaving the Temple grounds. Rachel felt his hand remove her festive hair covering as she squatted once again to help him with his sandals.

"We must fly to the *sukkah*," said Saul. "Not to have you for four months. I shall break one of the Holy Books' laws if we do not hurry."

"If you hadn't spent all that time in the fleshpots of Egypt, you wouldn't be in danger of spilling your seed," said his wife.

"What fleshpots? If there were any fleshpots, do you think I'd be so crazy now? I am half out of my mind with this waiting and waiting! You're just lucky you're so clever with gold or I'd have long since added a wife or two."

"Why would you need a wife or two with all the prostitutes in Alexandria and Memphis?"

"Rachel, when I am not with my wife, I suffer," said Saul. This was perfectly true from Saul's point of view, for his love for Rachel was sincere, and excessive for a man in his position. Even a man who stayed at home all the time would have taken another wife, or a concubine to bear him children; Rachel had been unable to conceive since she was fourteen, and she was now twenty years old. Certainly it was not unusual for a Jewish gentleman of means to visit a hetaera, one of the Greek-speaking, sophisticated prostitutes that practiced love in an atmosphere of romance and elegance, though in Saul's family of priests this would have been considered an outrage. In Saul's family, it would have been considered proper to divorce a childless woman, if one did not love her; if one did love her, in spite of her shortcomings as a childbearer, one could take another wife. If this were too expensive, a healthy concubine would be the only logical step. What was illogical was to remain childless, not fulfilling the first commandment in the Five Books of Moses: God demanded of his children to be fruitful and multiply.

But Saul wouldn't think of having another woman in his house. Even a concubine would gain precedence over Rachel if she was blessed with bringing him a son while his own wife remained childless. He refused to visit hetaeras, even while traveling, because a

23

visit with a hetaera involved so much more than the sexual act; he wanted to expend no love on any woman other than his wife. Certainly he visited the brothels of Alexandria; indeed he fancied his trips to the north too, along the subsidiary road built by Alexander's men off the Persian Royal Road from Jerusalem to Haran, taking him through Tyre and Damascus. It seemed there was a brothel attached to every inn, product of the flourishing trade in young female slaves between Egypt and Syria. But he never learned the names of the girls he paid for; and if one of them had red hair, and had something of Rachel about her when he had first married her, he never went back to her a second time. There was no sense of betrayal in his heart. From Saul's point of view, his passion spoke for itself. There was no way to be more faithful to his wife than to feel the urge to possess her at all hours, in all climates, wherever he went in search of gems.

"And when I am not with my husband, I suffer," said Rachel. They descended a sharp flight of steps cut into the hillside, where a row of small stone shops clustered together. Rachel remembered the apothecary's shop, where Shimon had taken her to buy powdered antimony, kohl, and alkanet root to prepare eyebrows, eyelids, and lips for her wedding feast. In spite of the expense, they had bought myrrh to delight Saul's senses, and an oil of mastic imported from Antioch, which was supposed to prevent the unpleasantness of perspiration on their conjugal night. "Do you remember how you rubbed the kohl from my eyes?" she asked him suddenly.

"Your eyes need no kohl," he said, pulling her along quickly, so that she laughed at his eagerness. Rachel stopped him in the middle of the quiet street, just before it began once again to rise up in a series of steps.

"I must catch my breath from all this talk of love," she said. Saul pulled her into his arms, and they kissed, and for the first time since he'd come back from his travels both of them felt the foreignness between them dissipate to nothing. It was difficult for Rachel to remain in the small village of Modein, living with her husband's haughty relations, constantly berated for her childlessness, her family's lack of religion, and her unwomanly occupation. But it was her occupation that allowed her peace of mind, for in the twisting and shaping of gold she found an outlet for her spirit that was otherwise denied her. She had no baby, and few friends, but she was creating beauty; with her chisel and long-handled hammer and a sheet of gold, she had a place for the love that needed to be expressed, and was stifled during her husband's long absences. And when he finally returned it took awhile to remember how she loved him, how all the frenzied attention to her art was in part a way of forgetting his absence from her life.

Now as she kissed him, she brought her work-hardened palm to his cheek, and he shut his eyes very tightly, as if to shut out anything else in the world, any other love, any danger, any reason for leaving this place, this moment, this girl.

Then a group of pilgrims, no more than four or five, ran past them and up the stairs, not pausing to shout a holiday greeting, or laugh at their lovemaking, or apologize for intruding so frighteningly in the dark and the silence. As Rachel and Saul pulled back from the embrace, the silence fell apart abruptly.

There was shouting, and it seemed to come from every direction. "It couldn't be the king," said Saul, pulling his wife into the greater dark alongside the wall of a shop. A lone young man, dressed in the pilgrim's white, came running from the opposite direction, his sandals slapping at the stones. Saul asked him to stop, but the young man pushed him aside, breathing out the name of the high priest and nothing else, and rushing off into the dark. But then Saul remembered: Jason, the high priest who had deposed the choice of King Antiochus, had not been in front of the Court of the Israelites tonight. He had not thought about how very unusual that was until this very moment, and now all at once he understood.

"We must get inside—to your father's house."

"What is it?" she said, running with him along the steep alley. Toward the north a blaze started up, either a signal or a first mark of pillage. Saul could imagine it clearly: the high priest fleeing the city, even as the king's troops arrived from Egypt, bearing orders to torch the houses, enslave the population, bring the city to its knees.

"I am not sure," said Saul. "But there is trouble, and we had better be inside, behind stone walls." Because the city's streets were irregularly laid out, twisting and crossing each other in a maze that only a native could decipher—and then only in daylight—they soon found themselves up against a mob, furious at their inability to distance themselves from the Temple. People ran and pushed with great purpose, trying to see past their fellow pilgrims to an exit from the city. Lights that had been burning behind the stone courtyard walls were now extinguished, as if those inside were trying not to excite the wrath of the king's soldiers by mingling with the pilgrims. Most of the *sukkah* booths were behind the courtyard walls, invisible from the dark alleyways, or else lined up alongside the greater houses on wider thoroughfares; but the few booths they passed in the small streets were already trampled, their festive fruits and vines spoiled by men and women, oblivious with terror. Animals joined the pandemonium. Lambs due to be sacrificed at the morning Tamid service were loose now, stumbling on unfamiliar ground amid the booths and broken fetters and household servants looking for their masters. Chickens pecked blindly at the food-littered ground, donkeys bit into sweetmeats and dates tumbling out of sacks set aside for the return from the nighttime services.

Saul's fears were quickly corroborated: the high priest had fled the city, the king's troops were returning in force, just as the son of Mattathias had told them. Antiochus's name was on everyone's lips; that, and the fact that their high priest had left them, had betrayed them by bringing them back to the Temple only to be massacred. King Antiochus, who called himself Antiochus Epiphanes, meaning the "illustrious," and often "Theos Epiphanes," the "God-manifest," was as famous for his whimsical goodness as he was for his cruelty. Throughout his empire he was called Antiochus Epimanes—Antiochus "the madman"—and it was said that he found this insult very much to his liking. Unlike his other titles, it was one that was unique to his name and his reign.

Rachel pulled Saul away from the mob into a yet smaller and darker alleyway, from which she could scent the sulfur used in the whitening of cloth. This was the Quarter of the Dyers, where woolen garments prepared in the villages around the city were brought to be bleached and dyed and sold at five times what they would bring in their natural state. "You know where we are?" he asked, and she nodded, stopping not to catch her breath, but to look at a lovely little *sukkah* booth, glowing from inside its frail frame.

"Look, they're singing the *sukkah* blessing," she said. Saul turned · impatiently to the source of chanting, a quiet rising and falling of melody against the backdrop of the nearby mob.

"Let's go," he said. "Just because they're crazy—"

"They're not crazy," said Rachel. "They're putting themselves in God's hands."

It had to be God's will, thought Saul, that the *sukkah* and its oil lamp had not already been overrun by the mob, thereby igniting the neighboring dyer's hut with its rich stores of woolens. "Blessed art Thou, Lord of the Universe," they heard, "who sanctified our Laws, and has commanded us to dwell in the *sukkah*."

"Come on," said Saul again, but Rachel was rooted to the spot, as if intoxicated by the little space of holiness within the ruined festival of thanksgiving.

"They are not crazy, my husband," she said. "Everyone else is crazy, but they are reciting the blessings, and they are safe in the *sukkah* booth, as we shall be." They were beginning the blessings for the Four Species, and Rachel fancied she could hear the waving of the palm branches through the walls of the booth, even as Saul pulled her through the alleyway, deeper into the Quarter of the Dyers.

"I don't know where we are," he said. "You have to help me." She had an irritating slowness about her that Saul recognized from other times of potential danger, like when years before they'd been accosted on the road outside Modein by a small troop of Syrian-Greek soldiers. The men had been drunk, without an officer, en route to a festival in honor of the emperor's birthday; somehow this birthday was at that time being celebrated once a month, instead of once a year, and part of the celebration of Antiochus's glory was the revelation of his relationship to Olympian Zeus. Saul had been frantic. He had been prepared to draw his sword, to fight till the death, to slit the throat of his wife rather than let her end up raped and sold into slavery. When he spoke to the soldiers, he was harsh, already angry with the determined fury of one who is about to die and has nothing to lose. Rachel had been calmer. She had not addressed the men, but kept her eyes to the ground and spoke softly, in Hebrew. At first, Saul had thought she was praying; but then he had realized that the words were directed at him. "Be gentle, my husband," she had said. "Tell them of the golden breastplate we are fashioning for the glory of the king." But the men had already responded to the Judean's angry tone with their own taunts and threats. One of them pointed at the redheaded Rachel and said something in a language unknown to Saul that brought laughter to the troops. "Trust in God," Rachel had said simply, her eyes still on the ground, speaking so slowly and with so little inflection of fear that it brought shame to Saul. Then he had forced himself to calm, waited until the men were almost upon them before he spoke, flatly and deliberately: in Greek he told them of the golden breastplate that his wife was creating for their king, and of the gold that he was licensed to bring into the king's realms.

"Show us some of this famous gold," one of the men had said. "Show us if it can shine like your wife's hair." But at that moment, a larger troop appeared, with four officers among them in mud-spattered litters, and the troops about the young couple fell back at once and the officers came forward to inquire if any trouble had been caused by their rowdiness.

So now Saul beat back his irritation, trying to discern if his fear was irrational and her faith worthy of emulation.

"I will help you," said Rachel, squeezing Saul's hand, leading him past the back ways of a wineshop, a sandal maker, through a broken-down hall and its desolate courtyard, feeling like a child again, a little girl with the run of the city.

"It's quieter," said Saul, a few minutes later. He no longer saw the blaze from the north, across the valley that separated the two major hills on which the city was built. He had little idea of the route that Rachel was leading him on, only that they were climbing, and then descending, and going into darker and darker alleyways, and the rank odors of poor sewage and poverty made him wonder if they had gone all the way around to the Lower City, in the southeast, where King David had once built his palace but was now the quarter of the indigent.

But suddenly he was walking on crushed marble, and beyond the shadow of a tall tree was a dolphin's head of chiseled stone, bubbling forth water in a wasteful display. This couldn't be the poor quarter, he knew; and following his wife's quick steps, he slipped out of the courtyard into which they'd trespassed and into a large public square.

"Where are we?" he said, half to himself, for now the city's shape started to come back to him. This must be the merchants' quarter, near Rachel's father's house, and what he had mistaken for the Lower City was simply a slave quarters attached to a wealthy home. Torches still burned in the square, as if oblivious of the fate of the festival night. He recognized the huge bronze fountains built under Menelaus's administration as high priest. Nearby stood the monumental statue of Zeus to which the fawning sculptor had given the face of King Antiochus, straddling an artificial pond. He wondered what Rachel must think of it all. For all the years that she had lived in Jerusalem, she had never seen the graven images forbidden by the Five Books of Moses erected in the public marketplace.

"Look, they're still standing," said Rachel, and Saul could see that she was looking past the statue and into the adjacent street, whose tall courtyard walls were lined with *sukkah* booths. The mob hadn't come this far, or at least the panic of the mob had not yet penetrated to this section of the city.

Saul was about to say that they were all deserted, but he could hear singing coming from a booth across the quiet street, an old woman's quavering voice, breathing life into a psalm from a half century of memories: *"They that sow in tears shall reap in joy! They that sow in tears shall reap, praise the Lord, in joy forever!"* For one crazy second it seemed to Saul as if they wouldn't have to flee the city, as if they could sit in their *sukkah* booth for the eight days of the festival, could rise before dawn and offer sacrifice in the lovely festival service, watching the priestly fires rise up to greet the sun.

"We shall lie in the *sukkah*, tonight," said Rachel happily. "My husband, we shall lie in the *sukkah*, and tonight we shall be given the blessing of a child."

He had forgotten how much he had wanted her in the rush to escape from the mob. But now he remembered, and knew that his passion was gone. The mob would reach them, and after the mob, the soldiers of the king. The only choice to be made was where to hide: either in a cave outside the city, toward the north and west, or behind the walls of Mordecai's home, hopeful that his status as a merchant and Shimon's position as an athlete might provide some security.

A slave with a torch waited nervously before Mordecai's house, and when he saw them, he called over the wall, and another slave threw open the gate. Shimon was waiting for them with wine on the rooftop terrace. He hurried down to them. "There are fires," he said. "I've counted half a dozen. What in the name of God is happening?"

"Please," said Rachel to her brother.

"What?" said Shimon. "Oh, yes. I'm taking the Lord's name in vain. The Jews are fleeing from their Holy of Holies and you're quibbling about my choice of words."

"She's right, Shimon," said Saul. "No matter what danger we are in, we are in still greater danger if you profane the Lord's name."

"What," said Shimon, the great muscles of his neck standing out in unattractive knots, "is happening, dear sister, dear brother-in-law?"

Saul told him what he knew: that the rumor of King Antiochus's return had precipitated a rush from the Temple grounds, and perhaps out of the city. Shimon told him that he had heard nothing more since the departure of Mattathias's son. "The fact that the rabble is running means nothing," he said.

"Your people are not rabble," said Rachel.

"My people do not run at the first threat of blood."

"Then perhaps we are rabble too, Shimon," said Rachel, "since we have run to seek safety here in the *sukkah*."

"I have not said that you—" began Shimon, turning apologetically to his brother-in-law. But then what Rachel had said penetrated. "You can't stay in the *sukkah* tonight, my dear sister."

"Where else does one stay on the Holiday of the Harvest?" said Rachel. "Unless of course one is afraid?"

Saul retreated from the conversation, seeking solace in his flagon of wine. It was sweet wine, from Syria, and he tried to beat back the images of a life without wine, without comfort, without hope: the life of a slave. The siblings talked on, and he knew that he would do what Rachel wanted, and that was to sleep in the *sukkah* booth, put themselves in the hands of their God, and ignore fear. But he had seen the corpses of slaves taken out from the Nubian gold mines, where they had been worked until they died; most of them went from health to ruination in less than a year. Still they were worth the five or six minae for which they were bought. Their lives were cheap compared to the gold for which it was exchanged. A conquering general had much more to celebrate if he could sell healthy captives into a short life of misery. No one was exempt from the possibility of such a fate. Romans, Thracians, Spartans as well as savage Gauls and Africans were represented in the mines, either as criminals or as prisoners of war or as slaves. But only men and women made slaves by conquest would be sent to such a fate; it was part of the campaign of terror that a conqueror employed in subjugating a people. Saul had seen frail children, no older than nine years of age, taken out dead from the gold mine; they were the only ones small enough to drag the gold-veined quartz from the hellish tunnels. He had seen the wrecks of men sitting naked and chained in their own filth, charged with breaking this quartz down into small bits for the spar-mill. The Egyptian overseers of the mines used women to turn these spar-mills; two or three of them pushed at a time, dragging their feet in an endless circle, whipped at the slightest sign of slowing down. Used worse than any beast, these women often died in a matter of weeks, their naked, broken bodies thrown into open pits like so much refuse. This was how gold was mined, how it was brought into the world for the sake of commerce and trade, but it had never struck Saul to be a sign of a society that ate its own people, that paid for its noble values in human suffering. No, he had taken a simpler lesson from the Nubian mines: it was better to be dead than a captive slave.

"This is not a question of fear or bravery, my dear," said Shimon with exasperation. "Saul, please—you understand me I'm sure. I had no intention of sitting in some primitive desert hut when I have a comfortable bed in my own home. I certainly have no intention of doing so now, simply because some marauding soldiers may have the pleasure of burning up half the booths in the city tonight."

"I have seen no soldiers," said Rachel. "And we're not asking you to join us. We'll just take some food—"

"The slaves have prepared a feast in the banquet room."

"Well, thank you," said Rachel. "But the tradition is to eat in the *sukkah*." She turned to Saul for confirmation.

"Of course," said Saul. "We're not afraid."

"I'm not afraid!" said Shimon. "Are you accusing me of being afraid?"

"You'll do whatever your spirit tells you to," said his sister. She pushed him down into his cushions, and drank to his health with a great draught of wine. Shimon was so childishly angered by his younger sister's implication that he could hardly speak. "What about father?" she said pleasantly. "I have not seen him go into a *sukkah* for a long time."

"The slaves have left him a supper in his booth," said Shimon. "But father will certainly not go there tonight. He's meeting with the merchants of the city, Greeks and Syrians as well as Jews. They're already trying to draw up a plan for the return of the king and his choice of high priest. Even if he was crazy enough to risk his life in the *sukkah* tonight, he would not be able to do it. The meeting will go on and on, and soldiers will escort all of them safely home behind their walls."

"So you think father will be afraid too?" said Rachel. But then she had to run quickly across the terrace, before her brother could strike her, and Saul hurried after her, laughing in spite of his fear.

"I am not afraid," said Shimon. "For the last time, I am not afraid of anything."

The *sukkah* booth's position within the courtyard walls, as well as the absolute quiet around them, relaxed Saul. He resigned himself to ignore fear, and let fate take its course. The laughter with which they had fled Shimon had been beneficial too, and when the slaves entered the lovely *sukkah* booth, carrying platters of meat and bowls of wine and baskets of fruit, it was simple to take hold of Rachel's belief, and share it. When the slaves left, Saul took up the chanting of the *sukkah* blessing, and when it was finished, his wife brought some grapes to his lips, and then she kissed him. Saul extinguished all but a single low-burning lamp, and brought his green-eyed bride to the cushions that covered the pebbled ground.

"We shall make a son tonight," he said.

"Yes, my husband," she said. "If it's the will of God, we shall make a son tonight." When she brought her hands to his chest beneath the loose tunic, his body remembered the passion that had been stilled by fear. Through all his fatigue, all the sensations of the day, came the sharp desire to possess this woman; to enter her, and fill her with what threatened to engulf his heart. He wanted to explain to her what he felt, but the words wouldn't come, only the urgency to strip away her garments; and when he did this, he wanted to make her understand that the love that his body felt for her was but a shade of a much greater love, the love of a weak spirit for one impossibly strong. Saul searched for words, but only endearments came to his lips: how lovely she was, how her hair sparkled in the lamplight, how brave she was, how right she was to be unafraid. "Wait," she said. "Wait a moment, my beloved," for he was too full of lust to feel the tranquility of her mood. Saul looked at her parted lips, at her wide-open eyes, and he would have waited for an eternity. She had only to tell him what she wanted, and he would give it to her, whether it was to eat the swine of the Greeks or walk through the fires of the pagans' underworld.

"Don't you remember?" she said. "We are to hold each other, and look up through the branches at the stars."

And so he held her then, he held her until he thought his chest would break for the pounding of his heart; but then Rachel turned to him, bringing the warmth of her breasts over his nervous frame, bringing her knee up against the inside of his thigh so that he shut his eyes, extinguishing the stars, the branches, the fruit and the leaves and the festival itself. She brought her lips to his briefly, straddling him, and whispered: "It will be all right this way, my husband. I have spoken to Leah, the midwife, and she has told me how to conceive without a doubt." Saul allowed her to guide his penis, shutting his eyes against the blissful welcome of being inside her. She was on top of him, but lighter than air. He had never made love with his wife this way. Only with the young, practiced girls of the brothels had he tried any other positions than what was traditional for a man and his wife. But the shock was momentary. She was innocent, following the midwife's instructions. In the mutual blackness they found each other's lips, and his lips moved to her shut eyes, and her hands pressed back his shoulders as he moved slightly higher, as she slowly turned from side to side, drawing him deeper and deeper as Leah the midwife had told her. But soon the joy of being with him overwhelmed all her instructions. She had no idea of where she was, on top of him, under him, floating through the air or rolling over and over like a dizzying top; all she could sense was the fleetingness of the moment. There was a rush, but she couldn't understand why this must be so. There was a frenzied movement in her body that was outside her control, urging her pleasure forward, faster and faster, so that her heart raced, and sweat broke out on her forehead, and her limbs shivered. But Rachel wanted to hold this back. The pleasure was too intense, because of the speed; it ran on past any comprehension of it, and she wanted to know this joy, she wanted to let it fill her heart and soul, not simply ravage her body, and leave her like some child, recovered from a fever. But then in spite of herself, the urge to understand left her. She forgot that the moment was too short, that she must hold on to a part of her sanity or forever be in thrall to this madness. But she gave in, and willingly, saying Saul's name over and over again, and what it meant was that she loved him, that she had joined with him, and that whatever he did, she forgave him, wherever he went, she was with him, she was his wife.

Much later, they woke to a slight rustling in the blackness about them. Neither was afraid. It was as if they'd woken not into the threat of nightmare, but into some purer part of their lovers' dream. Wordlessly, they moved closer together, listening to the wind move through the *sukkah* booth. Then the rustling grew louder, and beyond this, a low voice of sweet timbre singing.

It was the festival palm branch, being shaken, and with it a prayer. Mordecai, Rachel's father, had entered the adjacent little *sukkah* in the hour before dawn, accepting the rites of tradition.

There was no doubt in Rachel's mind that God had heard her prayer. She was pregnant. She would bring Saul's child into the world.

Chapter
3

The mercenaries came an hour after dawn, on the fourth day of the festival of the harvest, officered by a fat relation of the king. There was no surprise, no attempt at a battle plan, for everyone in the city had known of their approach, and no one had a means to oppose the conqueror. After all, the city was already in the hands of the king's men. The gates were manned by soldiers of the king, the garrison was filled with his mercenaries, the men with spears who walked the tops of the walls were Syrian Greeks. The only insurrection had been at the Temple, and there it had been Jew fighting Jew, until Jason had usurped power, and Menelaus, the king's choice as high priest, had fled. But now it was Jason who had fled. The king's soldiers stationed in the city had taken no punitive measures, choosing to wait for the reinforcements coming from the battles in Egypt. That reinforcements were coming in force was enough to inspire terror. The king had no need of extra men to hold Jerusalem. It was part of his empire, as was all of Judea. The mercenaries were sent as a punishment, an affliction; or to take more than the inhabitants of the city would willingly allow.

Even three days before, when Rachel and Saul had gone back to the Temple to offer sacrifice at dawn, most of the priests had fled. Those *Cohanim* who had supported Jason had gone off into the Judean wilds, afraid of the vengeance of Menelaus. Menelaus's supporters had not yet returned to the Temple, prepared to wait there for the wishes of their leader. The priests who remained were either old men, who knew no life outside the Temple brotherhood, or those priests who were adherents of the Pietists, and were more than willing to meet death in the defense of the Lord's Sanctuary.

One of these Pious priests officiated at the morning Tamid services. Rachel watched from a surprisingly crowded balcony of the Court of the Women. While the Court of the Israelites was nearly deserted, the women were still well represented, causing Rachel to wonder if she and they were more true to the faith, and more willing to let go of their span of allotted years in a world of men. But she had no reason to be critical of the men in her life that morning, for Saul had brought the sacrificial lamb accompanied by both her father and brother. While Shimon had refused to remove his sandals and replace his resplendent tunic with a pilgrim's white mantle, he had accompanied his loved ones where he himself had no desire to go. Though he wouldn't walk onto the Temple Mount, on a day when pilgrims were fleeing the city, he stationed himself near the gates of the Temple, waiting to bring home his family.

Mordecai had donated a small silver shovel in honor of the festival, and the Pious priest used this in removing the ashes from the altar fire that had burned throughout the night. Ordinarily, numerous priests drew lots for the various honors at hand: one to go outside and wait for the rising sun to fully illuminate the eastern horizon; one to bring in the lamb; two to open the gates to the Sanctuary; two to sound the trumpets; two to light the candelabras; one to slaughter the animal; one to prepare its limbs for the altar. Other priests remained before the people outside the Sanctuary, to lead them in reading from the Holy Books, and in singing songs of praise to the Lord. On this day, the priests weren't numerous. Lots weren't drawn, and only one priest remained outside the Sanctuary to lead the congregation's prayers. Two priests emerged from the Sanctuary, bearing golden pans of incense, and the lone priest who had been leading the congregation joined the others inside the Sanctuary, where Rachel knew that the offering was being fired. A few minutes, later, the priests who had officiated at the sacrifice emerged on the Sanctuary steps and blessed the people.

Rachel and the other women on the balcony got to their knees and then prostrated themselves fully, their foreheads resting on the cool stones. A half moment later, the men below did the same, just as the priests intoned the Lord's Holy Name. Hearing this Name, with its familiar, intimately resonant three syllables, thrilled her more than the incense, than the trumpets, than the cymbals that now began to sound the conclusion of the Tamid service. Half a dozen Levites began to sing as the men below got to their feet, shaking off the sense of homage in a retreat from worship.

But Rachel could barely stand, so full was she with the Name's power. She was not allowed to say the Name herself, of course, as that was reserved for the priests, and only during the services. But she could feel the Name in her heart, long after it was intoned; it glowed, not with letters, but with a sense of memory. She felt as if the syllables of the Name had always been in her heart, that they had been placed there in her mother's womb. It was the primeval nature of the memory that was so touching; she was certain that all men had this Name within them, had always possessed this Name, because all men were the Lord's creation. Indeed, she fancied that the Name that lived within her was what was most alive, was what brought warmth and emotion to cold flesh and inert bone.

Rachel thought of the Name often; not of its contours, not its shape in letters or in sound, but of the fact of its existence within her. When she heard the news of the soldiers having entered the city, she felt the presence of the Name like a reassurance: there was something in her that could not be taken away by captivity, by torture, or death.

"Come into the house," said Shimon, after he had brought them all the news. Mordecai had joined Rachel and Saul in the larger *sukkah* booth for the first meal of the day. Rachel didn't fully understand what had made her father turn back to traditions he'd abandoned since the death of his wife, Rachel's mother, more than a decade before. Since she hadn't seen her father in all of four years, what she witnessed seemed a sudden transformation. But Mordecai's disaffection with Hellenism had been anything but sudden. All his life had been lived with reason. Reason had turned him away from the strictures of the Pietists; studying the Greek rationalists had brought him closer to the camp of the enemy.

But the philosophy of Athens was not the same as the practices of the Hellenizing conquerors. For all his love of Athens, Antiochus lived as a tyrant. During the years of Menelaus's administration of the Temple, Mordecai had seen that what the government wanted was not reason for all men, but uniformity and conformity. King Antiochus had an enormous, disparate realm, and he wanted everyone within it to speak the same language, pray to the same gods, define themselves as one subject people. But Mordecai and others could not abide this. Rachel's father wanted the beauty that the Greeks preached, the beauty of the body, and the beauty of the spirit; he wanted the love of learning, philosophy; he wanted poetry that spoke of things beyond the scope of man's relationship to God.

But Mordecai was not willing to give up the fact of belonging to his nation. Even if he had turned from some of the strictures of the scribes and Pietists, he had not turned from the basic sense of the Hebrews as the Chosen People. Indeed, the years under the rule of the Hellenists had intensified the feelings of having been separated from other nations. While the Greeks prayed to a score and more of gods, it was clear that their prayers were childish, self-centered, like Antiochus himself: all their devotions were beggary. They asked for self-aggrandizement. Each god represented something that they wanted more of for themselves, whether it was beauty or manly strength or wisdom.

Even if one prayed to a hundred gods, the prayer was simply a plea to possess their godly attributes. Antiochus sacrificed to Zeus and to Herakles, and all the while thought of himself. For a Jew, even one who admired Greek culture, this was anathema.

Mordecai sacrificed for the first time in years at the Temple of the Jews, and all his thoughts were directed at praising his God. With one God for the Jewish people, the Jews made Him their center. What He was was ineffable, unapproachable, unattainable. He was not an ideal of manly strength or beauty, a bigger-than-life version of a human king. He was their Lord, their Judge, their Shepherd. They would not find him come down to earth to surprise them by running or wrestling in an athletic contest. If He tested them, or punished them, or rewarded them, He would do so in a way outside their comprehension. Most Jews believed, and Mordecai had come to agree, that the riddle of human history was decipherable only to God. God understood the reason for pain and suffering and death. God understood why empires rose and fell, and why His Chosen People were glorified or humiliated, ignored or exalted.

Prophets and scribes had chosen to interpret the ways of their God as outside human ken, but for one lone fact: the Jews were His people, and therefore at the center of the events in His world. Nothing happened to the Jewish people without His knowledge and desire. When Alexander rose and conquered and died, it had an effect on the lives of the Jews; Jewish prophets explained this, and all other world events, as God's way of dealing with His people. In the face of such divine compliment, all the Jews could do was praise His Name. Even in the face of death, their death prayer was a sanctification of the Name of the Lord.

"Come into the house," said Shimon. "The mercenaries are through the first gates."

"Praise the Lord," said Saul and Mordecai at the same time, without thought. They didn't stop to ponder that their words meant their acquiescence to a divine intelligence, to a special role that God had ordained for the Jews in this city, and the mercenaries about to ravage it. It was simply an automatic response, a prayer, a blessing that encompassed their world.

"They won't touch the merchants' quarter," said Shimon, hurrying them out of the *sukkah* booth. "But it would be best to be behind stone walls anyway."

"Is there a massacre?" said Saul.

"I don't know," said Shimon. "I don't imagine there's any fighting. The *idea* that they would wait for a full hour of daylight before entering the city . . . They don't seem to think it necessary to surprise us. We'll be terrorized without any cover of darkness, or charge of elephants, or spiked chariots."

"Don't be so sure," said Saul. "Just because it's light doesn't mean they won't use what they have. I heard that Antiochus had two elephants in the battles in Egypt. There was talk that his cavalry troops outnumbered his infantry. That there were many chariots, squadrons of them. If he has the arms, he will use them."

"Use them against what?" said Shimon. "If everyone is inside their houses, or huddling inside caves, where will the chariots attack?"

"They will attack what they always attack," said Mordecai, taking his daughter's arm to lead her from the *sukkah* booth. "The defenseless. Come—Shimon is right. We must go into the house."

And that was the end of the festival of the harvest. It had been one thing to ignore rumor and fear and sleep in the *sukkah* booth before the soldiers had come. But it would not have been in keeping with the traditions of the Holy Books to wait to be slaughtered. Even within the elitist circles of the Pietists, there were those who believed that one should profane the Sabbath by lifting arms in self-defense. Among more secular men like Mordecai, there was

39

no doubt that the sanctification of God's Name did not preclude the right to break certain of His laws in order to preserve one's life. Rachel wondered if the Pietist priests at the Temple would remain in place; if their Pietist congregations would remain in their shaky booths, eager for martyrdom.

The mercenaries skirted the quarter of the merchants, the quarter of the foreign traders, and the area about the Temple Mount. They remained in the city for four days. The first troops to arrive were spearmen. On the first day, they marched through the main thoroughfares, slaughtering anyone on the streets. There were Gentiles of Antioch and Alexandria who died that day. Greeks too were cut down, their nationality irrelevant to their murderers. They had come in the day before to trade with the pilgrims, and had turned out to watch the parade. But there had been no parade. The spearmen had come from a difficult time in Egypt. Their long bronze-tipped ashwood spears had been of little help against carefully trained Egyptian bowmen. Even in the great victories of their king, they had played little part. The glory had gone to the charioteers, and the Indian elephant trainers. Finally, the spearmen had met an enemy that suited their warriors' abilities.

Pilgrims were not in the streets to witness a parade. They were at the Temple, or in their booths. Those who had remained in the city were either Pietists or their opposites: Jews who had come to the festival to enjoy the wine and the women and the abandon of a metropolis. While the Pietists remained to fulfill the Lord's commandment to honor the eight days of the festival, the sensualists remained to fulfill their lust. In the few *sukkah* booths that had not been hastily abandoned days before, there was both prayer and revelry, pious dissertations on the Holy Books and tireless lechery with weary whores. The Pious refused to flee the Holy City and its Temple, declaring that their fate was in the Lord's hands. Their rakehell coreligionists were too drunkenly satisfied to imagine that their lives were in jeopardy because of something that had happened between religious parties in the Temple.

The spearmen went after both types of pilgrims with equivalent relish. Spears that had proven clumsy against the Egyptians worked very well against men armed with daggers or palm leaves or citrons. Too long to be hurled with much accuracy, these heavy spears were excellently suited to breaking down the shaky walls of the booths, impaling runaways through their backs, herding captives with the prodding of their ornamental hilts. There were women and children among the pilgrims, and these slowed down the warriors' progress, for some were too kindhearted to spear an infant, and many were too preoccupied with rape to get on with their soldierly functions. In spite of these difficulties, the mercenaries succeeded very well in their first day in the city: all the *sukkah* booths outside the walls of courtyards were burned to the ground; the corpses of hundreds of men, women, and children littered the avenues, and a hundred captives had been taken.

But the main force of mercenaries didn't arrive until the second day.

This armed force included bowmen, and a small squadron of charioteers, with the bulk of the forces made up of ordinary infantrymen, armed with curved broadswords and a shorter version of the long spears used by the special troops of spearmen. More importantly, this force was well led. A battle-weary general, Phillip, took charge of the troops already marauding aimlessly about the city. Phillip was a Phrygian, and a perfectionist. As a mercenary, he honored all the wishes of the man who paid for his expertise. Looking at the mess of corpses in the streets, the wasted animal carcasses slain by drunken spearmen, the bulk of the population still secure behind their stone walls, he grew furious.

"Get me the king's fat relation," he is reported to have said.

King Antiochus's cousin, who had been placed in charge of the spearmen's attack, could not be found for several hours. But Phillip's men did not give up the search easily, for Phillip believed that only men who were weak failed. When the king's cousin was brought to him—or so the story ran in the merchants' quarter a day later—he was too drunk to stand, and the general's men held on to him from each side.

"Let the fat idiot drop," said Phillip.

At once, his men did as they were told, and the tall, erect Phrygian got up from his chair and walked over to where the fat officer was trying to get to his feet. Even without the heavy weight of his bronze-covered leather cuirass, the man would have barely been able to rise; with it, and a too-tight wildly decorated helmet, the man would have writhed there on the floor for hours.

"What were your orders?" said Phillip, drawing his sword.

"Excuse me, sir," said the fat man, in the heavily accented Greek of Antioch. He had no idea of what the general was saying, so intent was he on observing his sword.

"I don't excuse you," said Phillip. He slipped his sword under the straps holding up the man's heavy armor and tore it through. "I kill men who don't perform their duty."

"I am the son of Appollonius," said the terrified man. "He is first cousin to—"

Phillip now attacked the straps that held up the bronze greaves protecting his fat calves. "Some kind soldier must have taken trouble to dress you so smartly," he said. His sword tore into the man's tunic, then at the strap of his helmet, then through the thongs of his gold-clasped sandals.

"Please, sir, I am the king's cousin—"

"Get up," said Phillip. He stuck his sword into the man's half-clothed behind, and as the son of Appollonius struggled to get up, the torn-apart tunic and undergarments fell to his feet along with the stripped-away armor. "You're no one's cousin. You're naked, and you've disobeyed your orders. The king has given me ultimate authority to see that his orders are carried out. You're not the king's cousin now. You're a fat, naked criminal."

"Sir," said the son of Appollonius, but at that moment Phillip slashed his sword across the man's chest, drawing a line of blood.

"Don't move," said Phillip, as the man threw his hands to his chest, trying to move back clumsily, as if he could somehow prevent the will of this general. "If you move, I'll kill you." Now Phillip slowly raised his sword, and brought the point of it against the pit of the man's stomach. "What's the price of a female slave of fifteen years?"

"I don't know, sir," said the son of Appollonius, angering Phillip some more, so that he drew the sword tip from the pit of the man's stomach down alongside the man's groin, and then turned the blade, so that the sword was resting on an inner thigh, poised to cut into his testicles. "I'm sorry, sir. Five minae, sir. A pretty slave girl is about five, maybe six minae."

"And how many minae make up a talent, you fat idiot?"

"Sixty, sir," said the man with the sword at his genitals, stupidly proud that he knew the answer to an idiot's question.

"How many slaves does it take to make up a talent, then?" said Phillip. "How many, before I rip off your penis and shove it up your asshole."

This was too much for the son of Appollonius. He would have needed considerable tranquillity to divide sixty into five parts, but with Phillip's threat ringing in his ears, all he could think of was his own death, and the dishonor faced by his corpse, certain to be left to rot in a foreign land.

"Sir," said the fat officer. "I don't know numbers very well—"

Phillip slashed the sword alongside the man's thigh, but downward, sparing his genitals, drawing more shock than pain from the naked man. "Fifteen hundred dead," said Phillip. "Can you understand fifteen hundred, you idiot?"

"Yes, sir."

"Greeks dead," said Phillip, returning the sword to its scabbard, but only so that he would have the use of both hands. "Women and children from Antioch dead," he said, and he slapped the man with one hand and held him in place by the hair with the other. "A Tyrian merchant murdered. A hetaera who was a favorite of your cousin the king raped and left for dead." He slapped the son of Appollonius again, but the pain hardly registered against the humiliation; and the humiliation was welcome payment for the return of the sword to its scabbard.

"I will tell you how many slave girls make up a silver talent: twelve at five minae, and ten at six. Some of these dead Jewish girls would be worth more. Musicians, apothecaries, artisans. But let's say ten to a talent. And among the men we have many who are worth twice that: slaves for the gold mines, swordsmiths, scribes." Phillip had motioned to an aide, who now helped him strip away his own clothes; this aide tried to maintain a serious face, but could not, against the sheer terror in the already naked fat man's expression. The son of Appollonius was not an athlete, but he knew that if Phillip was stripping away his clothes—and his own body had already been exposed by Phillip's sword—that the danger to his life was not at all past. "To be charitable, you fat coward, let's say an average of seven minae for the men you murdered, and three minae for the children." Now the aide was coming to him from behind, and grabbing hold of his hands.

"I'm sorry, sir, what is this—" began the son of Appollonius as the aide strapped an open-fingered glove made of hard-leather thongs onto his right hand. "I am not an athlete, you understand. You do me too much honor."

"Fifteen hundred are dead," said Phillip as he strapped on his own boxing thongs, moving his shoulders as he talked as if to loosen up his anger-tightened muscles. "We were told to kill, but not that many, and not simply the pilgrims. The dead are to be from the zealots, the Pietists, the rebels that live in the Lower City. Fifteen hundred dead instead of in the slave market. One hundred and thirty-three silver talents on the open market. Do you have it?"

"The richest man in Antioch doesn't have fifty silver talents—" began the son of Appollonius. But his words were cut short by the first blow of Phillip's fist.

Rachel didn't know how much the story she heard from her brother's lips was twisted by an athlete's own fascination with sport. Shimon was a wrestler, not a boxer, but he admired the thickset men who were willing to risk their faces and their lives in the most dangerous of Greek games. Phillip had won at Tyre in the games nearly four years ago, and it was said that his opponent had only landed four blows; and all these blows had been allowed by Phillip, as if he had felt it his due to receive some punishment from his battered opponent. But as Rachel heard the story from her brother and as he heard it from a Greek friend and fellow athlete, this time Phillip gave no such advantage.

"Please, sir," said the fat man, holding his face in his hands, the leather boxing thongs grotesquely powerful on his teary and bloodied face. "If you were to tell me what you desire—"

"Fifteen hundred murdered," said Phillip, and he brought his left fist up under the man's chin, breaking three teeth and his jaw. The son of Appollonius fell back violently, and would have fallen if not for Phillip's men. "Fight," said Phillip. "You are about to die. Try to die with some bit of honor."

"Please, sir," said the fat man, his words slurred and painful through the broken jaw. Beyond the pain was a child's hurt, not an adult's fear or humiliation: he wanted to know how it was possible for someone so strong to have singled him out for such punishment. He wanted to cry out, and be comforted, but there was no forgiveness in the general, no chance of waking up from a nightmare of retribution for crimes for which he could not hold himself responsible. "I don't know—" he wanted to say, but now his mouth could no longer open wide enough to articulate familiar sounds. This struck him as sadder than anything else that had yet happened in these terrible moments before Phillip. His body was being destroyed, and there were so many tears in his eyes that the punishing general had become a blurry, dreamlike shape, only emerging into clear focus with each blow, each addition to the sum of pain.

"You killed Greeks," said Phillip, smashing his leather-covered fist into the fat man's nose. "You disobeyed the orders of your king. You brought dishonor to all the troops, and you have no way to bring back to life the fifteen hundred who would have been slaves."

Phillip wanted a moving target, but his men could do no better than hold up the fat man. They couldn't make him fight. With his head lowered into his hands, Phillip punched into the solar plexus; as the man's hands rushed to cover this raw source of pain, the general battered the broken nose, threw right and left hooks at the side of his head, then jabbed repeatedly into the eyes and forehead. His trainer had once told him that he had an aversion to throwing killing blows: Phillip was now trying to kill, and his punches were directed at shattering bone, at destroying the brain beneath the skull.

"Sir," said one of the aides, shouting the words into the air, for Phillip was as absorbed in the work of his fists as if he were in the games at Tyre, or Olympia itself. "Sir, do you want us to continue holding him?"

But Phillip couldn't hear, in spite of the shouting. He had broken into a sweat in the large airy room, and his own mind had long since forgotten the reason for the actions of his body. Like any great athlete he had allowed the concentration on his athletic task to shut out the rest of the world. He was not trying to wring a confession or even death out of the body before him. He was simply trying to punch and jab, strike under the jaw, into the body, snap quick jabs from the wrist, drive straight smashing blows, feint with the left, so that his right hand could appear from nowhere, driving all sense from a body already senseless.

"He's dead, sir," said the aide, and finally, he let go of the fat man, and the other aide did the same, so that the general looked up in shock as the broken body fell to the ground.

"Hold him," said Phillip, but his concentration had been broken. He had caught the sickened look in the eyes of his own men, and stepped back from the body beneath his feet.

"He's dead, sir," repeated the aide, and this time Phillip heard and, looking down at the man, was momentarily shamed. "Would you like the slave?"

"Yes," said Phillip. "And a scribe."

The slave came quickly, bringing a heavy oil to cleanse the athlete's body. Appollonius's dead son was wrapped in a shroud and removed. Phillip would send a messenger to the king to learn

45

whether he wished the body burned, or quartered and left to the vultures. As the slave began to scrape the oil from Phillip's body, using the crescent-shaped cleaning tool, a scribe was ushered into the general's presence.

"Jews of Jerusalem and Judea," began Phillip, feeling his muscles continue to relax under the scraping tool. The scribe, impassive and intent, took down the words of the proclamation. Phillip could smell the heavy odor of musk rising from the inkpot: the primitive inks used by the Jewish scribes were malodorous, and therefore mixed with perfume. "King Antiochus IV, God-manifest of Olympian Zeus, commands your obedience," intoned Phillip. Beyond the smell of the musk, his sensitive sense of smell detected a rankness that was not only offensive, but familiar. He asked the scribe what the smell was, and the humble young man explained that it was the gelatin made from donkey skin that was particularly evil smelling. This was mixed with heavy lamp oil, and together with pine charcoal made a fine black ink.

"Well, your ink stinks," said Phillip to the scribe.

"Yes, sir," said the scribe. Though a Jew, he had a good Greek accent, and there was an unmistakable independence behind the humility in his quiet eyes.

"Commands your obedience," repeated Phillip. The scribe showed no embarrassment at being in the presence of the general while a slave cleaned his naked body. He wondered if the news of the death of the son of Appollonius had already been bruited about. Phillip was about to ask the scribe if he knew that he had just beaten a coward to death with his own hands; but he refrained from asking. This man was a scribe, and his interest and opinions were beneath Phillip's dignity.

"Because of the defiance and rebellion shown by the supporters of the former High Priest Jason against the lawful High Priest Menelaus, the king has ordered an immediate cessation of Jewish forms of worship. Throughout the lands ruled by King Antiochus, the subjects will belong to one people, and that is the people of King Antiochus. There will be no laws and no religions and no gods other than those of King Antiochus, the God-manifest. Burnt offerings, libations, sacrifices, and prayers in the Temple of the Jews are henceforth prohibited. The Jewish Sabbath may not be observed. The Jewish feast days, beginning with the current festival, are strictly forbidden. Altars will be swiftly erected throughout

Judea, and in Jerusalem, centering around the Temple; these altars will be dedicated to Zeus, and on them will be sacrificed swine. Jews will sacrifice to Zeus in honor of the king's name day, and they will partake of the flesh of the swine as an act of obeisance. Jews will cease from circumcising their sons on the eighth day, or on any day. Jews will no longer set themselves apart from their fellowmen, either through circumcision, through the study of the Holy Books, through the celebration of the Sabbath, or the abstention from eating of the flesh of the pig. The penalty for disobeying any element of this decree is death."

Phillip had dressed during the last of his dictation, and as the slave put on his sandals, he looked at the busy scribe, scratching with his long quill over the parchment.

"Where shall that be read, sir?" said one of the aides. "How many copies shall be made?"

"You, scribe," said Phillip, ignoring his aide.

"Sir?" said the scribe.

"What do you think of the proclamation of King Antiochus IV, the God-manifest?"

"I think it is well worded," said the scribe, without hesitation. There was no trace of a smile that Phillip could detect in the man, but he was certain that irony lingered there; that, and defiance.

"Bring some roast meat, the roast meat of a fat pig," said the general, looking all the while at the humble scribe. To his aide, Phillip added these nonwritten orders, but all his attention remained with the young Jewish man.

"Tonight, after the end of the second night watch, in the eighth hour of darkness, the infantry will level the Lower City. This shall be done by fire. As the inhabitants flee, kill all those that resist by force of arms. All others are to be held captive, until fifteen hundred men, women, and children are in chains. Take care to preserve all livestock. All men, women, and children who neither flee the Lower City nor are held among the fifteen hundred to be enslaved, will then be slain. The army is to regard this simple task as an exercise in restraint and order. All those who kill without orders, plunder or rape or run wild through the streets, will be given the death of a criminal, and their bodies left to rot. The honor of the king demands that his will be done, and his will is to punish for rebellion, and to be compensated for the use of his army through the sale of Jewish slaves."

47

So it was that this infamous order, along with that of the king, which denied the right of the Jews to their religion, was placed in the minds of the Jerusalemites against the backdrop of the murder of the son of Appollonius.

But what lingered in the memories of the Jews far longer than this brutal beating of a man who was just as much an enemy of their people was the gentle behavior of the young Jewish scribe. A short while after the general had given his orders, a slave brought wine and roast pork. The smell was delicious to Phillip; indeed he was so suddenly hungry that his mouth watered. But the smell was revolting to the young scribe, a hundred times more malodorous than the smell from his inkpot.

"You will eat of the flesh of the swine," said Phillip, gently motioning for the slave to bring the meat to the scribe.

"No, sir," said the scribe.

For a moment Phillip hesitated, but then he shrugged off this hesitation as irresponsible in a man who leads. The Jews must see what he does here as straightforward, he thought, and not whimsical; they must understand that there is no recourse from the law of the king. He could have ordered the man tortured; in fact, he could have supervised the torture himself, to ensure the man's survival, and the certainty of his giving in to what was demanded of him. But that was weak. The scribe had been ordered to eat of the flesh of what to his religion was an unclean animal. He defied the order of Phillip, and through him, the law of Antiochus. He would be an example, just as the destruction of the impoverished Lower City would be an example.

Phillip drew his sword, and the slave carrying the meat leaped out of the way. With infinite patience the scribe waited, looking gently at the general, for the sword thrust.

It was only in the half moment before the man died, while the blood spurted from his chest and the light dimmed in his eyes, that Phillip knew fear.

It was as if the incomprehensible, pig-abhorring God of the Jews had swept, invisible, through the room. But the general was not superstitious. He shook off this fear like a wet dog shaking water from its back. There was no god in the room, and he had slain an idiot, and the Jews would quickly see that order and happiness would result from obedience and conformity. To resist meant death. Phillip wiped his sword and sheathed it. Then slowly he

48

walked over to the frightened slave and ate the pork and drank the wine.

He could not know that he shivered not because of the coldness of the drink, but because the first martyr in this war against the Jews had been created. Deep within him, beyond all superstition or mortal fears, was a premonition that was yet without a name or a shape. As he drank and ate and smiled at the respect given him by his men, Phillip could feel death and doom rising in him, as slow and steady as the growth of any flower.

Chapter
4

Left alone in her father's goldsmith studio, Rachel found herself dreaming of Modein. She who had longed to be back in the city of her birth now found joy in remembering the most ordinary of village sights: the shabby marketplace with freshly picked fruits and fat chickens, squawking to be selected for the Sabbath meal; the scent of pine logs burning in the mud stoves; the old-fashioned full-length robes of the Pietists, dragging over their sandals and through the mud of the alleyways; the sweet chanting of the Five Books of Moses coming from the square-built house of prayer, every voice familiar, and most of them old.

But mostly she dreamed of the children.

It seemed that Modein was more a village for infants and toddlers than for men and women. Chubby little babies tried vainly to eat everything offered them by a score of aunts and uncles and grandparents; endlessly energetic boys and girls raced about the hilly countryside and through the orchards before hiding in the ruin of a shepherd's hut. She could remember passing by the enormous olive press owned by Saul's uncle at dusk. In the fading light she had seen a half-dozen children, boys and girls, towheaded and fair, black-haired and dark as the queen of Sheba's progeny, crawling over the huge stone machine, laughing and chattering, so young and careless that their lives and dreams were nearly the same.

"I'm going to the gymnasium," said Saul, breaking her revery. She had not heard him enter the studio. This was how he came to her studio in Modein, with the same intense expression, ready to tell her he must leave; that he would not be back for months. But this was not Modein, and he and she both could not leave Jerusalem and go anywhere. All this thinking took up half a moment, and then his words made sense to her: "The gymnasium." Astonishment showed in her face. How could the son of priests go to an unclean place, site of profanities and abominations? Then the astonishment passed. She remembered. They had been in Jerusalem for eight weeks, and for five of those weeks her husband had been accompanying her brother to the heathens' place of games and exercise.

"Be careful, my husband," said Rachel.

"I'll send a slave for the fire."

"I'm not cold," she said, but as he came closer to her for an embrace she realized that this was not true. She was very cold. A wet drizzle was falling outside, a month before its time, and the city's winds whipped the cold and damp through the thick stones of the houses.

"I thought you wanted a goldsmith's fire," he said, bringing his lips to hers. "If it wasn't for your crazy desire to make me an armlet, you would never have been allowed out of bed."

"And who would stop me, my lord?" she said, kissing him, shutting her eyes against the pulling pain along the sides of her abdomen.

"Our son must be kept warm," he said, placing his hand over her still-flat belly. All the other signs were present. Her breasts were full, her menstrual period had refused to arrive, the sight of figs and dates—her favorite fruits—revolted her. But she had no morning sickness, no vomiting, and in spite of occasional fits of exhaustion, she had no nausea, no wild desire to burst into tears. This, the midwives assured them, meant that the unborn child was a boy; therefore, the body rejoiced.

"Why do you go again today?" said Rachel.

"Because I am learning useful things," said Saul. She could see his eyes brighten briefly, as if lit from within by an anger beyond her understanding. He was impatient, and he carried a potential for violence that was frightening to imagine. "Your brother is a good teacher."

"Will the general Phillip be there?"

"Perhaps," said Saul. "What difference does it make? There are

51

always good men to try your skill with at the gymnasium, now that the city is overrun with soldiers."

As dangerous and tense as Jerusalem had remained during the two months of Phillip's occupation, it had been still more dangerous to leave the city and chance the roads. Even the short trip to Modein was too hazardous to take without an escort of the king's soldiers. Mercenaries roamed the countryside, competing with brigands for the chance of plunder and rape. The High Priest Menelaus had returned to the Temple, but neither the worship of the Jewish God nor the worship of Zeus was taking place there; the king's laws against the religious practices of the Jews had not been fully implemented. Phillip had carried out a dozen executions, his victims picked randomly from the city's Pietists, all of whom had refused to eat the meat of the pig. But the executions had stopped. The city waited for the arrival of the king.

Antiochus had been delayed in Egypt. The battle campaigns that had begun to go well, were suddenly aborted. Rumors about the intervention of the Romans were rife. Phillip, of course, knew more than rumor: King Antiochus, on the verge of major victory in Egypt, had been ordered out of the region by a Roman delegate. The order had not been the result of negotiation between equals: worse than the dream of conquest fading to nothing was the utter shame suffered by the proud king. Roman power had grown strong enough to allow its representative to insult this inheritor of Alexander the Great's empire. Barbarians who could barely speak decent Greek seemed destined to take over the lands lusted over by Antiochus.

Phillip knew that the king would arrive in Jerusalem with a need to fill up his pride. He would be able to give him the rule of Jerusalem: the city was cowed, its fifteen hundred captives already sold into slavery, its Lower City decimated, its people in a panic, ready for the yoke of the conqueror.

But it had made no sense to him to keep slaughtering people who would not eat swine. There was no rebellion afoot. Jews were coming forth voluntarily to offer sacrifice to Zeus, Athena, Apollo, even Dionysus. There were Jews who ate swine willingly, who sacrificed fat pigs to the gods as readily as they did bulls and sheep. Jewish merchants had sponsored roadside shrines to Apollo, had paid for the construction of temples in a dozen sites throughout Judea. If Antiochus wanted him to kill every Pietist in Judea, Phillip would oblige him; but he wanted the king to come first to the city, to see how the Jews accepted Menelaus in the Temple, how they allowed the construction of the new fortress in the city's heart, where the palace of their famous King David had once stood. Let the king see the Jewish athletes in the gymnasium, the Jewish philosophers discussing Plato over fine Syrian wine, before he insisted on killing every scribe and reader of the Holy Books.

"Please look after Shimon's temper, my husband," said Rachel, which was another way of reminding him to keep his own. What Phillip perceived as peace and order in the city that he had brought to its knees, Rachel saw as the calm before a storm. The poor who had returned to the rubble of the Lower City, their relatives in chains trudging south and north and west in slave caravans, were not beaten. The merchants who had kept away from the Temple in the past two months were not all converts to the pagan way. The parents who had not held feasts in honor of their newborn sons' circumcisions had still not refrained from the act of circumcision itself; just as the families who no longer paraded in their Sabbath clothes on the Jewish day of rest still were fastidious about its observation in the privacy of their homes.

Rachel's father, Mordecai, had not spent a day in the past eight weeks working in his studio, or delegating work to his artisan slaves. Neither had he tried to enter the Temple, or throw stones at Jews practicing the rites of the heathen. But it was obvious that rebellion occupied his mind. There were notes scribbled in Hebrew passing between him and other men of influence in the city and throughout Judea. The son of Mattathias of Modein had twice more made his presence known in their house, though how he had risked travel between the village and their city Rachel couldn't imagine. For all of Saul's visits to the gymnasium, the heart of all things Hellenic in the city, Rachel knew that his every thought was directed to restoring the Temple to its proper worship. For all her own brother's Greek ways, she was certain that his hatred for having their laws shoved violently on his own people had led him to look for ways to overthrow their power. She too waited for the coming of Antiochus, and with him, an end to the calm.

"Shimon's temper is what we all seek to emulate," said Saul. "It was wonderful to see him pin the great Phillip to the ground."

"Phillip can have you killed," said Rachel.

"These Greeks love no one so much as an athlete," said her

husband. "I am lucky that your brother is so fine a wrestler, and thus gives us entry to our temporary masters." But he had said too much, and tried to make light of his words. "Not that we mean to do anything to these great and noble Greeks, other than beat them at wrestling."

"Phillip beat a man to death—"

"We are not boxing him," said Saul, interrupting his beautiful wife. "We are simply getting to know the man, and his gods."

"Jeremiah said that the gods who did not fashion heaven and earth will surely perish from the earth and from under the gaze of heaven."

These words were beautiful to Rachel, because they expressed a justice that was missing from her world. For a long time after her husband had left her, she thought of the gods who would perish, and wondered if they would die in fire and smoke, or if the prophet meant only that their names would perish—that they had no lives, no substance, other than the vain idols created to represent them by men.

A slave came and started up a charcoal fire. She was Greek-speaking, with dark, closely cropped hair, and when she picked up the blowpipe to heat up the fire, Rachel noticed how slender and shapely her figure was. She asked the slave her name, and she responded quickly, bowing her head as she spoke: "Cilissa, madam," she said.

"I know the name 'Cillas,'" said Rachel. "He drove the chariot of Pelops, I think. You surely know the legend better than I do."

"No, madam," said the slave. "I am badly educated, and never had a mother to tell me the stories of the gods and heroes. What I know is the engraving of stones, and goldsmithing. Your father bought me cheaply, and could sell me at a dear price now, but because he is an honorable man, he will keep me for the full seven years." Cilissa was obliquely referring to the Jewish practice of freeing those enslaved through debt or parental abandonment after seven years of service. Some Hellenized Jews were beginning to ignore this practice—either by selling their slaves before the end of seven years' service, or by ignoring the law altogether, as yet another archaic custom from the Books of Moses.

"Surely my father is lucky to have found one so skilled in gold-work. And it is no special deed for a Jew to simply fulfill what the Holy Book commands."

"I know that I am lucky just to be alive," the slave continued. "There are few so lucky as I am, especially from so poor a place as Syracuse. My mother died when I was born, and there is a custom there to keep the child of such misfortune alive, regardless of its sex."

That was a great deal of conversation from a slave, and Rachel wondered what embarrassment the flood of words covered. Perhaps Shimon slept with the girl, and Cilissa was ashamed about this in front of Rachel. More likely it was fear that the slave girl was trying to hide, fear that her safe little world might end in a sudden uncontrollable horror.

"Did you know your father?" said Rachel, not out of curiosity, but simply to let the girl's fear run out in talk.

"Once I heard his name," said Cilissa. "But he sold me before I was a week old, so I don't know if what I was told was true. My first master, in Syracuse, told me how my mother had died in child-birth, and that I was the last of eight girls she bore. She never had any sons. All the girls but me were exposed."

Rachel took a small square-shaped ingot of native gold and placed it on a workbench. Of course she knew about the Greeks' penchant for infanticide, had even heard Shimon discuss its bene-fits; Saul had grown angrier than she had ever seen him with her brother during their dispute on its morality. Perhaps she was more sensitive than usual, having a child growing within her after six years of longing. But it was more than the miracle of pregnancy that brought her near tears at the mention of the slave girl's seven murdered sisters. It was the idea that the civilization that killed its own infants was intent on forcing its ideals on her own, child-loving people. Even if the Jews rejoiced more at the birth of a boy, they did not drive out the baby girl, expose the frail newborn body to certain death, simply to suit some philosophical ideal. She began to beat at the ingot with a long-handled bronze hammer, slow steady movements that would flatten the gold into a sheet thin enough to work. This simple work was the task of a slave, not an artisan; but Rachel shrugged off Cilissa's assistance.

"You may help me anneal it," she said, looking at the young slave, saved by a superstition from being exposed at birth like her sisters. As Rachel worked the gold she could feel its natural malle-ability harden beneath her steady blows.

"It is hard to believe that parents would allow seven such as

55

yourself to die," said Rachel. "Perhaps it was nothing but a story meant to frighten you, to make you an obedient slave."

"My first master never lied, madam," said the slave girl. She brought over the heavy wood-handled bronze tongs to take the flattened ingot from Rachel, and then carefully placed this in the charcoal fire. "There was no need to tell a story to make me obedient. I am obedient by nature, madam. And of course, it is not unusual in Syracuse to put baby girls to death."

"To expose them, you mean."

"There are some who feel it is kinder to strangle them at once, and have done with it," said the slave girl. She went on to explain how in Syracuse few families had more than two children, and usually these two would be boys. Certainly families did raise females, both rich and poor families, but it was almost unheard of to raise more than one. No one wanted the burden of a dowry, and the chance of rearing someone who might never marry and always be a liability to the family. Boys went off to war, and there was good reason to rear more than one, in case one should die in battle. Females were needed to further the race, but even with infanticide's preference for females over males, there was never a shortage of brides in Syracuse.

"Regrettably, the men there do more honor to pretty boys," said Cilissa. "They marry for money, or for a male heir." The slave girl paused to blow air through her pipe into the heart of the fire. "Will you want to cool this in the air, or in the water, madam?" she said.

"In the air, I think," said Rachel. "I am going to beat it very thin, and stamp in a design from a beeswax impression. It felt brittle very fast."

"But it looks to be good-quality gold," said Cilissa, turning the ingot lazily in the fire. Rachel could see the way her eyes caressed the colors rising from the metal. "Madam knows better than I, but I think there might be more silver in this ingot than usual."

"Then it should not be that brittle once we anneal it," said Rachel, studying the blue of the flame. It took much longer to anneal the gold in the air than by thrusting it directly in water, but there was no great urgency to finish her husband's armlet: it was simply a way to practice her art, and show her devotion to Saul.

"Sometimes such a blueness in the flame comes from a high mix of copper together with a low mix of silver," said the slave girl. Her master, Mordecai, had begun experimenting with alloying metals to the native gold to make it stronger. He had learned to judge the impurities present in an ingot by the way it brightened the fire's steady colors with vivid reds and blues and greens. Of all the artisan slaves, only Cilissa had met with his approval in her ability to discern these colors in the goldsmith's flame.

When the gold had cooled, Rachel allowed Cilissa to resume beating it down with the long-handled hammer. She knew the slave girl wanted to show her what skill she possessed, and Rachel commented favorably on the young girl's confident hammering. "It's becoming brittle," said Cilissa. "If madam would allow me, I'll return it to the fire."

"You needn't be so formal with me," said Rachel. "I can see your skill. We are both goldsmiths."

"Thank you, madam. I have seen your work, and I know how great a compliment that is coming from one of your experience."

Rachel had to smile at this. She knew that at twenty years she was no longer young, but to hear the slave girl talk of her like a venerable old woman was funny; or if not funny, something very much the reverse. Rachel looked at Cilissa more closely, at the thick hair, the smooth skin, and wondered if she were yet sixteen. When all around her were artisans far older than herself, she could still retain the illusion of youth. But Cilissa was younger, her womb ready to bear children. Rachel shut her eyes and silently prayed for her own unborn child to grow strong, for she didn't believe that she would have too many more years to produce a son for Saul.

But the prayer was interrupted. Only moments after she had shut her eyes she heard music, loud but pleasant, and the angry voice of the young slave girl.

"What do you mean by this, Thamyris?" she shouted in Greek, so that Rachel quickly opened her eyes to the astonishing sight of Cilissa threatening a slave boy of her father's house with a bronze chisel.

"Don't hit me, Cilissa," he said. "This gentleman is sent from the master." But the way Thamyris shrank from the tall young man coming up behind him made it clear that he had been afraid to stand in his way.

The slave boy hadn't knocked, or asked Rachel's permission to allow a stranger into their presence; much less four strangers, all of them Greek-speaking men. Cilissa had every right to be angry, but Rachel was too taken aback to join in her attack on the cowardly boy. Accompanying the fresh-faced young man were three musicians, two of them playing horns: one the deep-toned *barbolin*, and the other the happier reed *kalamos*. They kept up their smooth rhythm, shrugging their shoulders and stamping their sandaled feet. The other musician was Greek in appearance as well as in speech; he seemed a cut above the others, and far too dignified to be playing the simple *niktimon* clappers, though these noisemakers were of bone and laced with gold. They flashed as he banged them together, and in his wild eyes, Rachel saw lust and abandon.

"Cilissa," said Rachel, not removing her eyes from the musicians or their master. "Remove the gold from the fire and place it on the cooling stand."

"Yes, madam," she said, dropping her chisel onto a workbench with an unnerving bang. She seemed to be forcing herself to remain silent, as if it were her disgrace, and not Thamyris's, that men had come unannounced and unknown into Rachel's presence.

"What is the meaning of this?" said Rachel quietly, so that the gentleman who led the musicians seemed to incline slightly forward to catch the words.

"Silence, you fools," said the tall young gentleman to his musicians, smiling at Rachel as if he might be her lover. Cilissa held on to the gold with the long-handled tongs, and as she took it from the fire, her anger at the man's insolence to Rachel made her shoulders shiver. "Do you know how unusual it is to find a pretty redhead?"

"You are not to talk to me like that," said Rachel, her words suddenly very loud against the cessation of music. Both horn players had let down their instruments, and when Rachel had finished speaking, the insolent third musician clapped his gold-laced bones together with violence.

"You heard my mistress," said Cilissa, who had deposited the gold on its cooling stand and now turned to the four men with her threatening tongs. "You will not talk to her like that." She jerked her head toward the cowering slave boy. "You, Thamyris—go find the master."

"I am the only master here," said the tall young man. The dusty traveling hat he wore suggested faraway places, unpleasant climates, customs, gods. He wore no sword, no jewelry, no special marks of rank except for the fine cloth of his tunic and the careful pronunciation of his words. "You will be silent, or I will have you killed," he said to Cilissa, so seriously that Rachel thought the pleasant-faced young man must be mad.

"We will all be silent, sir," said Rachel. "These are dangerous times, difficult times, and I am sure you meant no disrespect by entering unbidden into my father's house. But I must insist—"

"For you," said the tall young man, removing his large felt hat and making a little bow in the process. In his hand was a small silk pouch, and when he opened this up there were a scent bag, redolent of sandalwood, and a thick chunk of ivory. "I thought perhaps the slave girl could fasten a bit of gold to this, and make you a hairpin. You see how famous your red hair is, madam. As for the scent bag, it's for me, really. I love the smell of sandalwood, and since I shall visit you when you're hard at work, I should like the chance of seeing your red hair clipped in place by a bit of elephant tusk, and smelling perfume all at once."

"Thamyris," said Rachel. "Go at once and get help." The slave boy couldn't refuse his master's daughter. Not looking at the tall young man or his musicians, he ran for the door of the studio. Slowly, leisurely, the player of the bone clappers raised his leg, so that poor Thamyris went flying across it and slammed himself into the wall. Cilissa no longer hesitated. She grabbed the tongs and swung them before her, making the musicians give way as she ran from the studio. Halfway out the door she was already screaming for help in the common people's Aramaic.

"I hadn't realized so many Jewesses had red hair," said the tall young man, as if Rachel hadn't taken a step back, as if Thamyris was not quivering on the floor, as if Cilissa's voice could not be heard. "Yours is red with gold and honey brown, very nice. May I touch it, madam? I am a friend of your husband's friend, and am told that you make very fine jewelry. Will you take my presents? It is not polite to refuse them."

Rachel slowly opened her hand and extended it to the young man. She had met with madmen before, both in the alleys of the city as a young child, and later, seeing them driven from the streets of Modein by a mob of youngsters. Often refusing them directly drove them to greater madness. Rachel allowed him to drop the ivory and the scent bag into her hand. "Thank you, sir," she said. "But now, I must get back to work."

"Where is your politeness, woman?" said the young man. But he was smiling now, as if whatever he said was nothing but a joke. He turned to his musicians and clapped his hands so that they at once began to play. "No, no!" he shouted. "Happier! Livelier!" Catching Rachel's eyes, he shook his head, as if she would understand at once how impoverished were the imaginations of his musicians. They changed their tune, with the clapper of bone leering at Rachel as if she were a brothel girl.

"Sir, these are very nice presents, indeed, but I must ask you to please leave, as I am a married woman, and as you surely must know it is unseemly for a Jewish woman to be left alone with strangers—"

"Silence, woman," said the tall young man, coming still closer to her, as if he had every intention of crushing her to his chest, either to lavish her with kisses or wring her neck. "You must show more respect. Didn't you hear me the first time? I am a friend of your husband's friend. I have seen the present given my friend by your husband, made by your father's own hands." The young man paused here, looking about the studio, at the stone molds and bronze pinches, at the awls and tracers and hammers and tongs. He ran the back of his hand along the face of a bronze model as if it were warm flesh, the flesh of a loved one.

"I am sorry, sir," said Rachel. "But I don't know you, and therefore I must ask you to leave. According to the laws and customs of my people."

"The laws and customs of your people?" said the madman. "Don't tell me about your silly Holy Books. I know all about your hatred of pigs. It's the stupidest thing I've—" The young man interrupted himself with a laugh. "No. I will not discuss the eating of pigs, do you agree?"

"Yes," said Rachel.

"Why aren't you playing, you idiots?" shouted the madman suddenly. "I am trying to entertain this beautiful young woman before her very athletic husband comes home, and you men aren't doing your jobs."

"Then do you actually know my husband, sir?" said Rachel. She couldn't understand why Cilissa hadn't yet returned with several of the household slaves, or a neighbor, or even a soldier. The madman looked at her suddenly, as if noticing her for the first time.

"Is it possible that you are in love with your husband, madam?"

"In Judea, women are not asked questions like that, sir."

"In Judea!" said the madman to his musicians, waving his hands so that once again the horns began to blow, the clappers beating out the irregular rhythm. "In Judea, even one's musicians must be told to do everything twice. It's quite different in Antioch, and in

Athens, it's altogether another world. In a Greek city you'd spin and weave, you'd dance like a goddess, you'd sing like a bird—but you wouldn't know all these Holy Book customs, you wouldn't hate pigs, and you wouldn't be a maker of such beautiful things of gold."

"I have heard that in Athens there are women who are scholars, philosophers, poets," said Rachel, wondering even as she said the words why she was engaging in conversation with this madman when all she wanted was to make him leave her presence.

"What do you know about Athens? You were never there!" The young man hesitated, as if to draw himself up to his full height required a few seconds of preparatory meditation. "I was born in Athens, madam. In Athens. Athens is my birthplace."

"Well, yes," said Rachel stupidly, for a wild thought had entered her mind, a thought that made little sense, but was yet so unsettling that she felt a weakness in her knees, and with it, a great resolve to remain calm: after all, she had an unborn child growing within her womb, and owed him a restful belly.

"I need a bracelet for my friend, something very rich, stamped with a god, any god that you like, as long as it's not one that hates pigs," said the madman, smiling at the humor of his words. "Zeus, of course, or maybe a half god like Herakles, or even a goddess like Athena, as my friend is very wise, and a lover of women."

"You said you know my husband, sir."

"Your husband knows my friend, madam. He gave him a ring made by your father, a beautiful ring, as light and delicately made as the bones of a bird. And I was told that your father and your husband both value you as a greater artist even than he, the one that made the bird ring that my friend Phillip wears on his finger."

She hadn't known that Saul had given the ring to the general, and this was bewildering enough, and frightening. But that this madman, with his musicians and his proud birthplace, was the friend of the general who had savaged the Lower City, was a hundred times more dreadful.

"I am a poor artist compared to my father, sir. You and he do me too much honor."

"Put that hairpin in your red hair, woman," said the madman. And though a minute before she would have hesitated or at least tried to explain that it needed a clasp, Rachel no longer had a will in the man's presence. She raised her hands, and placed the ivory at her crown, and began to wind thick ribbons of hair about it. He came a little closer. "You will make me this bracelet for my friend, the brave Phillip?"

"Yes, sir," she said.

"I could kill your slave girl for her insolence, you know," said the madman.

"Please, sir," said Rachel. "I will try and make you the most wonderful bracelet." But she couldn't take the murder from his cool blue eyes, and she couldn't stop him from bringing his lips to her forehead as she wound the hair about her gift of ivory. "Please, sir," she said. There was no kiss, just the gentle pressure of his soft, greedy lips on the taut skin of her brow.

"I am to be obeyed," said the madman. "The same as any god, even one who hates pigs. I am to be obeyed, do you understand, woman?"

She was too frightened to speak. Keeping her hands in her hair, she felt exposed to his lips, to his hands, to his power. She tried to stay very still, so that the baby within her would lie quietly, blissfully ignorant of danger.

Keeping his eyes on Rachel, the madman spoke to the slave boy Thamyris, who was still cowering on the floor. "You, slave," he said. "Go to the fire and hold a charcoal in your miserable hand."

Of course the boy didn't know who the man was. He had been frightened enough merely by his size and his aggressiveness. Now he wouldn't move from the floor, and Rachel couldn't move her lips in his defense. "Stop the music," said the madman. "And do it."

The one who played the clappers was the first to grab hold of the slave boy, and Rachel could see this musician's wild eyes just beyond the madman's curly hair. Thamyris's screams ran higher and higher, as one of the horn players helped the player of the clappers to pry open his hand while the other horn player brought over a glowing charcoal with a long-handled spoon. Then the charcoal was clapped into the naked hand, and the screams ran so far up the human scale that they were no longer audible, they were cries of pain heard only in the ears of the one who suffered. All the while, the madman kept his eyes on Rachel, and she kept her hands in her red hair.

Without apology, he told her what she already knew. "I must be obeyed. I am the king, and it is right that my subjects obey me."

"Yes, sir," said Rachel. She knew of no other way to address

62

him. All her words of homage and devotion were reserved for prayer.

"I hope you will enjoy the hairpin, my dear," said Antiochus IV Epiphanes.

Rachel imagined that she could feel how tired he was from his long trip and from his humiliation at the hands of the Romans in Egypt. She wondered if all the wild rumors that circulate about kings were as true as those about this one; there could be no doubt that he was pitiless, and that he acted without benefit of reason.

Antiochus let his eyes rest on the lovely Jewess, the goldsmith that would make his general Phillip a bracelet worthy of a king. "You are very beautiful, and it will give me pleasure to see you enjoy the favor of your king."

"Yes, sir," she said again, even more dully than before. When he finally left her, taking his musicians, it took her a minute to relax enough to take her hands from her head and to find her way through teary eyes to the unconscious slave boy. There was fear and pain and destruction in this place of gold and goldwork. Only the remembrance of the Name within her allowed her heart to calm, allowed her to shake her head against the blackness of the future and dream of her baby in a world no longer mad.

Chapter
5

A cool month in which there was no rain took them into the heart of winter. The dryness was uncharacteristic for the high city in the short days. When the wind whipped through the stones, it was chased by a wintry sun unfettered by the black clouds of the month of Kislev. Rain was seasonal in Judea, and prayed for by the priests; a change to dryness was not only bad for the fields, but suggested a disorder and a displeasure in God's benevolent plans.

"It's fine weather for sport," said Shimon, who stood in the sun-dashed open area of the gymnasium, waiting for a chance to wrestle. Saul had taken him down three times in a row yesterday, and though Shimon still didn't take his brother-in-law's athletic art seriously, he was beginning to doubt the efficacy of art against angry power.

"The cisterns will be empty," said Saul sullenly. "My wife will give birth to a boy in a country without men."

"Shall we go to it, then?" said Shimon, eager to throw off his heavy cloak and let the exercise warm his cold bones.

"Go to what?" said Saul. "I am tired of games, I am tired of waiting. The whole country is waiting, and they wait so long, that when the king walks into the Holy of Holies, no one remembers to be upset."

"This is not the place, Saul," said Shimon, his face twisting into a smile at the approach of Phillip with some of his officers. It had

64

been easy to justify to Saul the need for maintaining contacts with the occupying force. Even the Holy Books spoke of the value of spies: Moses sent spies into the land of Canaan at the express command of his God; King David sent spies into the country of the Ammonites. Clearly there was a value in discovering the plans of the idolaters in the Jews' own Holy City. The way back to power was rebellion, but a rebellion without arms, without knowledge of the enemy, was doomed to failure. Still, Saul had lost patience. He had gifted Phillip with goldwork fashioned by his father-in-law and by his wife; he had wrestled with the man, taking off his clothes in the obscene way of the Greeks. But all he had learned of the enemy was that they worshiped nothing but sensuality and violence, that all they cared for Jerusalem was how best to rape it of its treasures. All this he had known before he had ever set foot in the gymnasium.

"Look, gentlemen," said Phillip to his officers. "The men without penises await a thrashing."

It was clear that he was at least a little bit drunk, and perhaps the minor disturbances in the Lower City the day before had angered his pride. But this was no excuse for talking disrespectfully to fellow athletes. Saul was angrier than Shimon, and not for himself, but for the dishonor offered his brother-in-law as a champion of Jerusalem, training for the great games at Tyre.

"The Lord has promised our seed to be as great as the dust of the earth," said Saul. "That will not come from a people without penises, and you will not be able to insult me by lying in the face of God's words. You will simply anger me."

He spoke quickly, colloquially, reverting to Aramaic, which was as native to Phillip as Greek. But the general walked up to Saul, bringing his threatening smooth-skinned face very close to the young Jewish man's, squinting with exaggerated effort as if he could not quite understand Saul's words.

"Anger you?" said Phillip finally, in Greek. "What if I anger you? How is that different from angering a fly, or a dog, or a pig?"

Saul couldn't utter a word in reply. He was so angry that his movements were stiff as he threw off his cloak and tunic, and the chill air was bested by the heat of his indignation. He agreed with Phillip. What difference did it make what the men of Judea felt? They had allowed King Antiochus IV to build yet another fortress for his troops in the center of the Holy City; they had permitted their people to be led away from their country in chains; they had not rebelled when their holy men had been scourged and burned and beheaded for refusing to eat the meat of the pig.

It was no wonder that the king had dared go where no other Gentile had ever been, not even Alexander.

The pagan king had entered the Temple of the Jews.

Five days before he had been led by the reinstated High Priest Menelaus into the Court of the Israelites, and up the sacred steps to the Sanctuary itself. There was serious talk that the king had entered the Holy of Holies, though no rain of fire had poured from the heavens, no cataclysm had split the earth.

Everyone knew that an old philosopher, a wise man of Athens, had come to the city at the bidding of Antiochus and was engaged in the conversion of the sacred Temple to a pagan shrine. Already altars were being dragged up the city streets to the Temple Mount, brightly colored in the gaudy style of the Greeks; these would serve in the sacrifice of swine to Zeus. The holy altars of the Jews had been desecrated, spat upon by mercenaries, spattered with the blood and offal of pigs. Soldiers ran laughing from the Temple ground, trailing the tattered parchment rolls of the Holy Books. Most of the priests had long since scattered; the zealots among them had been martyred weeks before when Menelaus had returned as high priest, bolstered by the king's soldiers. But even Menelaus's Hellenized priests couldn't bear the sight of the holy vessels running over with urine and excrement, the halls of sanctuary and prayer reduced to temporary brothels for the merceneries and their whores, the scrolls of psalms and blessings and history burning in the open courtyards against the winter night air.

"I don't need the pleasure of looking at your coward's body," said Phillip to Saul. "I am not going to wrestle a gold merchant. I am going to fight your pretty brother-in-law, and for once, we are going to wrestle in the manner of men."

Shimon stripped away his cloak and tunic quickly. "I had thought we had wrestled like men before," he said, his flesh turning red from the cold.

"We wrestled like women," said Phillip. His words were too steady for a drunkard, his movements too easily precise. A wild anger was moving the general, an anger that was somehow related to Saul's: it seemed to be a rage against his self. "We will fight a

66

pancratium, and then you shall see what a fight with a Phyrgian is like."

Saul watched as the general stripped off an armlet fashioned by Rachel and a ring that had been made years before by his father-in-law; all the gifts, all the courtesies suddenly meant nothing. A *pancratium* was an excuse for murder: two men boxed, kicked, wrestled, and strangled until one of them was unconscious, dead, or worse—had surrendered. Only biting and gouging were prohibited. A boxer of great strength like Phillip had nearly as much of an advantage over a wrestler like Shimon in the *pancratium* as if they were trading punches in a boxing match.

Wrestling for the best of three falls was considered an art, a sport where the mind played as big a part as the heart. There were a hundred ways for a clever, practiced man to beat a powerful, un-tutored one; indeed Shimon had easily thrown and pinned the general every time they had fought. But Phillip's game was boxing. He had always wrestled, as almost every able-bodied Greek did for sport; but boxing was the event for which he had gained fame as an athlete, and boxing was practiced by those who disdained the tricks and traps of the nimble wrestler. Some boxers refused to duck or block a punch; they felt it more manly to take the blow, and then strike back. Boxers were used to being hit. Some of them were said to relish the punishment they received as much as that they in-flicted. Like the *pancratium*, the boxing event was for those who were not only unafraid of dying but a little bit enamored of the world-to-come.

"If you're not a coward," said Saul, "you'll fight me. My brother-in-law knows nothing about the *pancratium*."

"All that brother-of-whore needs to know is this," said Phillip, raising the index finger of his left hand—the signal of acknowledg-ing defeat. Shimon started at this. Even if the suppression of his native city had turned him away from the spirit of Hellenization, he was still enough of a Greek to feel the measure of Phillip's insult. A death must follow, his or Phillip's. And if he died, then Saul would avenge both the death and the insult to Rachel. He watched Phillip hand his clothes to the slave. Shimon felt no fear at facing Phillip in the *pancratium*, or in a boxing match, or even in a field with one sword flat on the ground between them. There was no room for fear in the fullness of his anger.

"If Shimon doesn't kill you," said Saul, "I will."

67

"You want to come at me at the same time, you brave Jews?" said Phillip. He swiveled toward Shimon and slapped him twice across the face with enormous speed. At that same moment, two of his officers grabbed Saul from behind and pulled him away from the fight. Neither Saul nor Shimon understood what had come over the normally icily correct general; they could not know of his revulsion during the last terrible hours when a new Jewish martyr had been created by Antiochus. "It's wonderful to see how brave you people are, how quick you are to defend yourselves." Phillip drove his left fist directly into Shimon's chin. The young athlete stepped back, but not with nearly enough speed. He had been slapped, and now he was hit. Tears started up in his eyes. He was astonished at how easily he had been hit, and at the pain.

Shimon tried to clear his head, to remember his training. He had been hit with a fist, and so his own hands were closed, and he was ready to strike. But he remembered that this was all wrong. He was a wrestler, and he must tackle the boxer, bring him to the ground. But before he could crouch low and throw himself onto the man's ankles, another punch hit him under the chin, sending him staggering back from the general and flat on his feet.

"Take him down," shouted Saul in Hebrew, but Shimon's head was unsteady. He thought he saw Phillip smile at him, and with great giddiness, he smiled in return. The general moved in swiftly, slamming punches into the pit of the stomach that forced Shimon to double over, his eyes shut, so that Phillip could take hold of his hair and drag his head up for three brisk punches that left him nearly senseless.

"Very brave," said Phillip. "Too brave to pick up his finger, just brave enough to die like all the rest of them."

But Shimon wasn't dead, and not yet unconscious. He reached gamely for Phillip's right ankle and pulled it with what was left of his force. If only Phillip had fallen down, he could have twisted his legs about the general's neck; he could have drawn an arm up between his thighs and forced him back onto his shoulders; he could have strangled him with an arm, or pressed the heel of his hand under his nose. But Phillip didn't fall. He pulled his ankle away from Shimon's hand and snapped his bare foot into the young man's face. Then he threw himself onto the wrestler's chest and threw his elbow into Shimon's neck.

"Leave him alone, you crazy bastard!" shouted Saul, unable to go to his defense. He shouted at Phillip's officers, shouted that Shimon was dead, that their general was beating a corpse, but all that the soldiers did was try and hold back Saul.

"Very brave," said Phillip, talking to the immobile Shimon. "Very brave of you to give me such beautiful things, from your beautiful sister. Very brave of you to let me break your beautiful face."

Saul broke away at that moment and threw himself on top of where Phillip had Shimon pinned to the ground. He clapped his hands over the general's ears and then drove the side of his hands into his forehead. But then the soldiers took rough hold of him again and pulled him away with violence. Phillip slowly got to his feet aided by his worried chief aide.

"Is he dead?" said Phillip, looking away from Shimon to Saul.

A slave hurried to examine Shimon. Pressing his ear to the man's chest, he pronounced him alive. They brought him wine, but the young athlete couldn't swallow, and when they tried to raise his head, he cried out in pain.

"You had better kill him, and me too, and get it over with," said Saul.

"And just yesterday you brought me presents," said Phillip, wiping blood from his face and drinking from a flagon of wine.

"And today you repay me by calling my wife an unspeakable name, by trying to murder my brother-in-law—"

"I shall be ready to fight you too, Jew, in another moment."After all, there was nothing to do but fight, no way to explain that the mad king had become jealous of Phillip's Jewish friends: these two with whom he exercised in the gymnasium, and who brought him presents from the red-haired beauty who had caught Antiochus's fancy.

"Will all these men be holding me down?" said Saul. "Or will it just be the great general against this poor merchant of gold and gems?"

Phillip could see that Saul had caught the sense of his infatuation with Shimon. The Jews thought of this as an abomination; their Holy Books railed against the sexual union of man with man, forbidding it to the Chosen People. But Phillip hadn't lusted after Shimon, and didn't understand the horror for that imagined lust in Saul's eyes. Shimon was simply beautiful, as so many things were beautiful: the goldwork of his sister, the stones of Jerusalem in the early morning light, the Temple of the Jews, a freshly painted trireme riding its anchor in the port of Athens.

"Let him go," said Phillip. "Do you think I'm afraid of the husband of a whore?"

The insult was gratuitous, but Phillip wanted there to be no mistake in Saul's mind: Phillip was his enemy. He had to tear out any vestige of friendship, for what he was called upon to do in Judea had been made clear that afternoon.

An old man, stooped with age, who would not pay homage to the altar of Zeus, had been found. He was brought to the place of trial set up in a windy square. From the judicial platform one could look up to the heights of the Temple Mount. All about them were market stalls, merchants selling oil and barley cakes and dyed wool as if nothing had changed in their world. It had been the old man's misfortune that the king had come to visit the place of trial, and with him his general, Phillip.

"The Lord is God, the Lord is One," said the old man, speaking the prayer in Aramaic, either because the Hebrew was unfamiliar to him or because he wanted the king to understand that there was no authority on this earth that could challenge his allegiance to his God.

"He is a crazy old man, my lord," said Phillip.

But the king's attention had been distracted by the red hair of a Jewess, and he ordered his men to bring her to him. She came, and with her were two children, and her own old mother, and as the king spoke to them with kindly words, Phillip watched the old man who had refused to pay homage to the altar of Zeus look at Antiochus with the dead eyes of a fish on a wood slab.

"I am your king," he was saying, "just as I am the king of the people of Tyre and of Antioch. And I love you and your children, just as if you were all my children." Phillip had heard the speech before, and hoped that the family, like most families, would be sensible. The king explained that he was the bringer of a great, universal civilization, and that only rabble-rousers and rebels tried to stop the flow of his work. And he offered the red-haired woman the meat of the pig that had been readied for sacrifice on the altar of Zeus.

"Only fools dare to mock sins against the Lord," said the old man, his words directed to the red-haired woman but his eyes remaining on the king.

"He is not responsible for his words, my lord," said Phillip. "He is quoting from his Holy Books."

"The Holy Books are forbidden," said Antiochus. But he had not finished with the woman. He turned his kingly gaze her way and, without saying another word, made his power felt. Phillip could feel the woman flinch. He watched her raise the meat to her lips.

"Let every thing that breathes praise the Lord!" shouted the old man, but his words couldn't stop the movement of the young mother's hand, and her mouth opened to receive the meat. Antiochus praised the woman's common sense.

"You will now feed your children," said the king.

"The Lord is close to all who call upon him, to all who call upon him in truth," said the old man. "I will lift up mine eyes to the hills, from where my help comes." He could not look at the shame of the young woman as she fed the meat to her children, and his eyes sought the comfort of the Temple Mount. Phillip wondered if the old man had any idea of how badly the holy place had been ravaged by the king's men.

"It is very good and fitting that you obey the words of your king," said Antiochus. "And now your old mother, let her taste of the sacrificial swine."

"Daughter of Israel," said the old man. "Put not your trust in princes. Do not do this evil thing." But he could not stop her from bending under the king's will. Women had been thrown from the walls of the city, with their newly circumcised babies in their arms; Sabbath observers had been flayed alive; Pietists had been burned to death for fighting the will of this king. The old woman ate the meat of the pig, and followed her daughter and grandchildren away from the place of justice.

Antiochus was ready for the old man, and asked him whether he would pay homage to the altar of Zeus.

"I spit on the altar of Zeus," said the old man.

"My king," said Phillip. "It will do us no credit with the masses to kill one who is without sense, and therefore incapable of fear."

"He is capable of fear," said Antiochus. "I will show you that anyone is capable of fear."

Phillip remembered how Antiochus had attempted this as he faced the angry Saul on the windswept exercise ground of the gymnasium. By asking for clemency for a Jew, he had risked his own standing with the mad king. Antiochus was a jealous king. He

71

was jealous of Phillip for his friendship with Shimon and Saul, and jealous of Shimon and Saul for their friendship with Phillip. Because he was mad as well as jealous, he could at one moment lovingly treat Phillip with a gift from Saul's wife and at the next moment turn on Rachel in a rage for having created a gift for Phillip that was not made at the king's request.

Antiochus was perfectly capable of calling for Shimon and Saul, and the beautiful Rachel, simply to humiliate them before Phillip.

And in the presence of the mad king, and before the men with whom he had wrestled, and the woman who had created works of art for his pleasure, Phillip was not sure how he'd react. It might be his own humiliation that would rise in his heart. To see Shimon shamed might lead Phillip to violence against the person of his king. This was the softness in his heart that he was now beating back. This was the impulse to weakness that he loathed in his soul.

"This is the *pancratium*," said Phillip to his men. "No one must touch the Jew while he yet lives."

"Not even if I kill your master," said Saul.

"That is correct," said Phillip, smiling at the man's impudence. He was a clumsy wrestler, this Saul, and had beaten the graceful Shimon at that art only because the handsome brother-in-law had been afraid of hurting his sister's husband. When Saul wrestled with Phillip, each had his turn as victor. But the Jew was not a trained athlete. And whatever strength he had in his fists and his shoulders and his belly would not be a match for Phillip's years as a soldier, a boxer, a killer of men.

"In the event of a miracle, no one touches this man. He is as free as when he came in here, an athlete among athletes in the sanctuary of the gymnasium."

"If you're not a coward," said Saul, "even though you are a liar and your mouth is filled with dirt, you will tell your men that if I win, I may leave, and take with me my brother-in-law, and that they will witness the fact that we are both of us free and blameless under the eyes of your law."

"You are crazy, my friend," said Phillip.

"I am not crazy, and I am certainly not your friend," said Saul. Phillip nodded at the truth of this: he could see that Saul believed he had a chance to take him down and grind his skull into the dust. Saul would fight; he would not surrender. The general ordered his men to swear to the safety of Saul and Shimon in the event that

Saul won at the *pancratium*. "And I hope that you will not be such a coward that you will want to lift your index finger at me," added Saul, going into a low crouch, refusing to lift up his hands in the boxer's stance. Let Phillip try to hit him: he would throw himself at the boxer's knees.

And then Saul whispered a single phrase, familiar in Aramaic and Hebrew to every child in Judea: "Lead me to the rock that is higher than I," he said, sure that the words of the psalm had first been spoken by King David, praying for strength from his God.

Saul did not notice the effect his words had on the general. Phillip had begun to throw off the oppressively conflicting thoughts that threatened his concentration: he was ready to move in quickly, land hard short blows to the belly and breast of this crouching, angry man, and have done with him by driving the point of Saul's chin to his knee. But the image of the old man who had suffered so needlessly was brought back to him clearly by the Hebrew psalm. He had been stripped to the waist and flogged in the windy square, a soldier counting out the blows of the scourge as if he had no connection to this dishonor. But still the old man would not consent to pay homage to the altar of Zeus, would not agree to taste of the meat of the pig, and insisted to the king's face on the supremacy of the Jewish God.

And so they flogged him until the white skin was flayed from his back, until the sight of his pain was too much for men to look at. Never once did he ask for mercy of the king; more amazingly still, his God did not grant him a quick descent to death, or even senselessness. The old man remained alive, in pain, and defiant.

Until at the very end, when the weight of his broken body pulled heavily at the yoke holding him up for the whip, when men who had routinely murdered in the service of kings felt shamed, the psalm had come to his lips, a peaceful cry, a lone entreaty: "Lead me to the rock that is higher than I," the old man said, and in that instant his God gave him death.

So when Saul dropped to one knee before Phillip, reaching up and grabbing at the back of the general's knees, he was successful in throwing the strong man flat on the hard ground. Phillip had the wind knocked out of him, but instead of reacting in the spirit of the *pancratium*—raising his foot to Saul's groin or reaching out for a grip on his head of hair—he hesitated, seeing the old man's lips close around the prayer, swallowing his last breath of earthly air.

Saul had no such hesitation.

Shimon was half dead, Rachel had been called a whore, his people had been disgraced, and rage filled his body with strength and certainty. With one wild motion he landed on the supine general, driving his elbow into the man's uplifted neck, his knee into the man's groin. He didn't hear the officers shout as he continued to punish the head, and to absolutely no point:

The blow to Phillip's throat had instantly killed him.

Chapter
6

Rachel was busy at her work when the slave brought Saul to the studio. A clay die of the pagan goddess Athena had been prepared by Cilissa, and now Rachel was tapping a very thin sheet of gold over the die's raised pattern. Her father, Mordecai, had asked for the work for a Cyprian wine merchant who had been useful in bringing messages to and from Mattathias in Modein. The latest messages had pained her father. All about the country, Jews were learning to pray to the false gods, learning to mimic the culture of license and idolatry. Added to the inducements of athletic glory and wanton celebration, was an earthly fear. Mordecai was incensed at the depths to which this fear ran. The pagan conquerors had assumed awesome proportions in the hearts of too many Jews; their fear had led them to look to Antiochus and his men as correct, because they were strong. There were those men of Judea who had learned to sacrifice to Zeus not only to placate the conqueror but to emulate him in asking the false god for favor.

Rachel's movements were light and precise as she tapped the skin of gold, bringing Athena's face to life. Rachel thought her beautiful, and wondered what love Cilissa had put into the die's creation. The legends told about the goddess were childish: how she was born—fully armed and grown from the head of Zeus; how she was valorous—as helpmate of Herakles and Odysseus, and of Perseus, when he killed Medusa; how she was wise—as the tutor of

Argus and Danaus, as the patroness of Athens and the liberal arts. But what had these heroic attributes to do with the ineffable, with the Name, with what was truly divine?

"Madam!" said the slave, not taking care to avoid breaking the goldsmith's vaunted concentration. Rachel stopped her hammer in midflight, but kept her left hand firmly in place at the edge of the golden sheet. She put down the hammer slowly, not wanting to shake apart the equilibrium that she needed when at work; there would be an explanation for this interruption, but she would not let it destroy her creation.

But as she turned to the slave, she saw her husband stagger forward, his tunic torn and filthy, his lips twisted in pain and caked with dried blood. Her left hand dropped the sheet of gold, and so swiftly did she get to her feet and turn about that she swept off the table tools, and dies, and the delicate goldwork.

"I am all right," said Saul.

"Blessed be the Name," said Rachel. She held him in her arms, feeling the pain and the defiance rise through the layers of dirty clothing. "Shimon?" she said, and he told her through swollen lips that her brother was all right, but badly hurt, and awaited the physician in his own soft bed. "But you," said Rachel. "You must see the physician yourself."

"No, my darling," he said. "I must bathe, and be with my wife."

"Whatever my husband desires," said Rachel, feeling the terror start up within her. This desire to be with her so urgently, with her brother hurt in the adjacent house, could only mean that Saul was preparing to leave her, and at once. She not only feared for her husband, but for her unborn child. Rachel was shamed by self-concern as well, facing her wounded husband; but the vision of the mad king and his musicians who had three times visited her could not be held back.

Phillip's men had not forgotten their master's orders. When they had pulled Saul off the general's corpse, they had beaten him; this had not dishonored Phillip in the first moments of their rage. But they had let Saul go, letting him carry the half-dead Shimon out of the gymnasium into the crooked, hilly streets. The dead weight after the beating was nearly impossible to support, but once out of sight of the gymnasium grounds, a carter stopped his oblivious donkey and helped Shimon and Saul find room among the casks of oil in his cart. Saul wanted to negotiate a price to take them to the merchants' quarter, but the carter was a Pietist, and would not think of profiting from another's misfortune.

Rachel hurried Saul into the main house, and shouted instructions at the scurrying, solicitous slaves: water was to be heated and poured into the bath; the bathroom's charcoal braziers were to be lit; the cook was to prepare a thick vegetable porridge; incense was to be burned in the room where Rachel and Saul slept.

"I am going away," said Saul.

"Yes, my husband," said Rachel, helping him remove his blood-stained clothes. She would not question him, she would not contradict him, nor would she ask him to take her with him. If it was safer for her to be with him than in Jerusalem, safer for herself and her unborn child, Saul would say so. He knew her heart was with him, would be with him wherever he went as she knew the strength and certainty of his love for her. A slave handed her a warm, wet cloth, and she dabbed at his lips and eyes and nose, loosening the dried blood and the dirt.

"You must stay here," he said, the words ringing in her ears like the direst of judgments.

"I will miss you," said Rachel, sitting on a footstool as she wiped the dirt from his legs and feet. She helped him into the bath, redolent of olive oil, and supervised the slave as she poured in additional hot water. "Now leave us," she told the slave, and she took a sea sponge to her husband's neck and curly hair, and gently pulled at his tense fingers, slowly massaged the pain from his shoulders and forehead and scalp.

"I will join the rebels of Modein," said Saul.

"But there is no rebellion," said Rachel.

"Not in Modein," said Saul. "But there are Jews who live half a day south of our village, in the caves where the priests of my father's time used to hide. There they celebrate the Sabbath without fear, and bring the joy of circumcision to the parents of a newborn boy." Saul hesitated, then added:

"It won't be safe to visit me, not until after the baby is born." Rachel still had not asked him what had happened at the gymnasium. He would tell her when and if he desired; it was enough to know that what had happened was dreadful and dangerous, and that Saul feared for his life.

"Do you feel all right, my darling?" said Saul.

"Yes, my husband."

"I was worried about the shock to you," he said. Saul waited a moment longer, and then he told her of the *pancratium*, that he had killed Antiochus's favorite general, and that regardless of the Greeks' sense of honor, a mad king was capable of doing anything.

"You will be all right," said Rachel, breathless with fear. She could already hear the musicians heralding the king's approach to her workshop; she could already see his leering smile as he insisted on talking with Saul; she could already imagine his rage at finding him gone from the city, gone into hiding.

"But you know where to find me?" he said.

"I know the caves, my husband," she said. "After four years in Modein, I know half that countryside better than the Holy City."

"I am not asking you to come to me, my darling," he said. "I wanted to know in my mind that you could find me, you would know where I was and how I could be reached if it was ever urgently necessary."

"Quiet, my lord and master," said Rachel. "You are talking far too much for one about to run away." She brought her lips to his, shutting her eyes against the pain in his face. Her own pain was waiting for his departure. Now she wanted to reassure him: she could feel his sadness rising momently, as if the certainty of his death was blowing up before his eyes, the reality that he would never again have his wife in his arms was twisting a knife in his heart. "It will be well," she said. "You will go away and hide, and then very soon all will be well, and we will be together."

But words couldn't change the sense that she was lying in her heart. Rachel felt that this was the last time she would see Saul alive. A feeling was not a fact. Even a holy prophet could make a false prediction; even a seer could misread the sadness within his soul. But Rachel was lying. The truth was to tell what she saw, and she saw this hour as their last together. She cleaned her husband's wounds; she dressed him in fresh clothing; she fed him a sustaining porridge; she led him into the high-ceilinged bedchamber and let down her long red hair. He wanted to make love, but this was not all. He wanted to touch her fingers, bring them to his eyes; he wanted to hear the sound of her voice; the way her lips moved around the sensuous Hebrew vowels; he wanted to examine the breadth of her shoulders, the softness of her breasts, the gentle swelling of her belly. Saul wanted to have her by heart, memorized, as if he would take her essence with him to the place of hiding, to the place she would never see, as she would never again see him.

And so their lovemaking was built not only around endearments, but around the delicate fabric of a mutual lie. She told him that all would be well, and he told her that he would come back to her, and she told him that their son would be born into a free Judea, and that both sides of their priestly families would celebrate the rite at a rededicated Temple.

But the lie was like a bubble, kept afloat by urgent words. Soon the words ceased. They were quiet in the high-ceilinged room, built that way to keep out the heat of the Jerusalem summer. Now they clung together against the wintry drafts. With each kiss, the bubble's skin stretched further out of shape, threatening to burst into truth. As she stroked his broad chest, her hand trembled, remembering the death of Phillip, understanding how simple it was for the Lord to remove the living from the earth. Saul felt weak at the touch of her hand, as if the rush of love he was experiencing for her and his unborn child was leaving him bereft of any strength or will. He understood then how a tyrant works: by threatening one's family, by taking the responsibility of life and death from the Lord of Heaven, a tyrant could make the strongest of men despair. To let this woman live, Saul could be weak. He could pray to the false gods if Antiochus would let him remain in Rachel's arms.

Then he said her name, as if he were calling to her from some distant place. He pressed the full weight of his body against her small-boned frame, he pulled wide her lips as if to pour his entire essence into her being, but his voice seemed to be drifting toward her through some ethereal cloud. When he entered her, she cried out, not from any physical pain, but from the effort of imagining that all would be well. Bright with life, his phallus warm and thick and urgent inside her, she could taste death on his lips, she could taste the sharpness of a widow's tears from her own shut eyes.

"Rachel," he said, and the lie was broken, because the name had twisted from a passionate exhalation to a valediction. She couldn't bring herself to contradict him. He was saying good-bye, and she loved him too much to disallow this.

"I won't betray you," she said.

"Don't speak," he said, moving slowly inside her, wanting once again to obliterate thought but unable to forget that this sweetness all around him was soon to end, that he would end his life on the run, that the most he could look forward to was rebellion, riot, fighting back before he himself would be killed. But then his wife spoke again, repeating her words of assurance, so that it was as if she were praying to be faithful to his memory, strong in her resolve and in her faith.

"I won't betray you," she said, whispering the words as if they were endearments, as if they were as much a part of their lovemaking as kisses and caresses.

All at once she had understood the impulse to promise Saul what every woman owed her husband. To betray was unnatural, to be faithful was in accord with God's plan. But Rachel was afraid. Her fear was vaguely realized, a terror at the appearance of the king. Saul had killed Phillip, had struck at the heart of what was oppressing her people. If she told the truth, she wanted Phillip dead, as she wanted Antiochus dead, as she wanted the enemies of her people gone from the Holy City, as she wanted the altars to Zeus and Aphrodite torn down and burned, as she wanted the pigs driven from the Temple Mount, and the priests brought back to rededicate the Temple to the One God.

This was the truth, and she must be true to this, in spite of the baby in her womb, in spite of her fear. They would come for her, they would ask her to pay homage to the false gods, they would demand that she taste of the sacrificial meat of the unclean pig. But she held tight to her husband, she felt the power of his love, and she battened on this like a glutton at a final feast. "I won't betray you," she said again and again, as his slow thrusting grew quick and savage, as their desire rose up to overwhelm all fears.

"I won't betray you," said Rachel, and long after he had gone, leaving the city for the safety of the caves near Modein, it seemed that all that she had left of her husband was the unborn child in her womb, and the unbreakable promise of these words.

King Antiochus waited for seven days before calling for the wife of Saul. He had mourned his general Phillip after his own fashion, eating and drinking to abandon every night for a week. It was said that he had taken no women in this period, neither hetaeras, nor common whores, nor concubines, nor mistresses from Antioch. He had wanted nothing that reminded him of love or sexual excess.

But as soon as Rachel was brought before the king, she could sense his sexual hunger, a dark and heavy force that clouded the meaning of his words. "Your husband murdered my friend, madam," he said, by way of greeting.

Rachel had looked up at him when entering the great hall of the governor's house. Quickly she looked away from the bloodshot eyes, the familiar leer, half desiring, half loathing. Phillip had lived here before the king had arrived in Jerusalem, and remained even after Antiochus had usurped most of the rooms for himself and his attendants. The lion's-head knocker on the front door had been replaced with the imperial symbols; the porter had been supplemented with a heavily armed troop of Syrian Greeks. Heavy rugs from Persia had been thrown over the cold mosaic floors for the greater comfort of the sybaritic king. But even the household slaves from Antioch, the philosophers from Athens, the purple robes of the king, couldn't completely remove the sense of austerity and purpose from this place. From here Jerusalem was ruled, and ruled despotically.

"Your husband has done a great disservice to your people," said the king, getting up from his chair on its raised platform. The winter sun penetrated the tiny windows at the highest point of the room, framing the tall king on his dais with a magisterial aura. "He has inspired rebellion."

Rachel didn't know whether to speak, whether to look up at the man or down at the floor. She had dressed simply, her red hair covered with a matronly cloth. Shimon was convalescing at home in his bed; their father waited in a covered litter outside the governor's house for the end of Rachel's interview. "He will ask you to pay homage to Zeus," her father had said. "Or eat the meat of the pig."

Mordecai had not counseled her on how to answer these commands. Three days before a holy man had been tortured before the Temple gates. He had been scourged, burned with hot irons, his fingers broken one by one before a horrified crowd. But he had continued to refuse to violate the Holy Laws. Mordecai could not tell his pregnant daughter to choose death over life. He himself didn't know what he preferred for her: a life lived with shame, or a death to no purpose.

While the king mourned his general, his officers had zealously carried out the anti-Jewish proclamations. Men had been boiled alive, women had been raped before they were strangled, babies had had their heads dashed against stone walls; all had shared the crimes of following the Holy Law, or of refusing to abandon it. But still, with the exception of a few fugitives hiding in the Judean wildlands, and some pockets of resistance in Samaria, there was no revolution. The martial spirit that had been the glory of the Jews of Joshua's time, of Deborah and Samson and David, the fierce temper that had been as characteristic of the Jews as their adherence to a single, invisible God, had vanished. There were martyrs, drawn from every level of the population, random souls picked by fate for a terrible trial and death. But alongside these martyrs were too many who had given in to the dictator.

And who could blame them? thought Rachel. All around was the evidence of what defiance led to, and what compliance meant as well. Alongside every tale of woe were ten examples of Jews who had profited from the conqueror; profited in lands, in gold, in prestige if not in their souls.

"Members of your class do not ordinarily rise up with the rabble," the king was saying, remaining on his feet. She had tried to keep her eyes from him, but could not do it. It seemed disrespectful, and so she continued to be open to the power of his baleful leer, the sense of destruction heading her way. She wanted to scream, right then, to get on her knees and ask them to kill her and have done with it. There was no need for an inquisition, for an hour of asking her to do something that she must needs refuse. Already she could taste the fear rising from the back of her throat. "When the others see the rich turn against the imperial power, it leads inevitably to desperate measures."

"My husband didn't rebel, sir," said Rachel.

"What?" said the king, cutting short his peroration. He pointed a finger at the young woman before him. Rachel realized that she had spoken in Hebrew, and stupidly. This was not a man to whom one could appeal with reason. She spoke in Greek.

"I'm sorry, sir," said Rachel. "I am appealing to you as a defenseless woman, carrying a child, and loyal to your kingly powers—"

"Remove your head covering," said the king.

"My head covering," repeated Rachel wonderingly. She was not fast enough for Antiochus, and he barked a command at a slave girl. The slave hurried to the confused young woman and ripped off the cloth with amusement. "I am sorry, sir, to have angered you," said Rachel. "I don't know why I am treated this way."

"A king needs no reason, no more than a god needs a reason," said Antiochus. "Shake out your hair, let me see the waves and the thickness of your Jewish hair."

He stepped down from the platform and came toward her, and as if it would stop him, she hurried to do as he had bid her: her hands found the heavy hairpin that Cilissa had fashioned from the large chunk of ivory brought by the king the first time he had visited her. The memory made her tremble. Antiochus came closer as she fumbled unsuccessfully with the clasp.

"What a pretty pin," said the king, coming up behind her. Taking hold of her chin from behind, his other hand released the clasp and pulled it gently away from the thick strands of red. "I want you," he said.

"I am sorry, sir."

"There is no need to be sorry," said the king. "You will obey me in all things, in any thing I desire, for that is the way of kingship, do you not agree?"

"I am a married woman with child, and my ways are not the same as yours, my lord," said Rachel.

"Did you hear that?" said Antiochus, addressing slaves, soldiers, and sycophants in the great hall. "She admits that she follows the forbidden ways. Therefore her punishment is death. Death by stoning? Death by molten metal poured down your throat? Death by exposure? Death by suffocation in a deep grave beneath the damp winter ground?" The king had turned her around, and looking at her terrified face, he took hold of her cheeks between his soft palms and brought tight lips to hers. He kissed his prisoner, chastely and quickly, and then he pulled away from her and laughed. He laughed so hard that he had to sit down, laughed until there were tears in his wasted eyes.

"Please, sir," said Rachel. "I am sorry. I want to go." She was aware that she was making no sense, that nothing terrible had yet transpired, but she was afraid of the unknown things he could do to her, afraid to show him what a coward she could be. Already, she could sense the fear spreading to her bowels, to her womb, to the unborn child. A palpable pain, like a gripping of the muscles about her womb by an unseen hand, forced her to push out a sharp breath of air. She turned to where the king's laughter was no longer coming.

"Please, I will eat pig," she said. "I will pay homage to Zeus. My family is very well known, and of priestly descent. It will show good faith. It will show that the right way is obedience. Only let me and my child live."

"Am I so disgusting to you, Jewess?" said the handsome young king, getting back on his feet. "Would there be anything you could do to stop me from sending you to Antioch, from letting your baby be thrown into the sea and keeping you for myself, for my pleasure?" Once again, he had taken hold of her chin, but this time he was gentle, and he looked into her green eyes with something very much like love.

"Please, sir," said Rachel. "I am not a martyr. I am not one of those who wants to prove something by my death. I want to live. Let me live."

He moved the fingers of his right hand along the edge of her jaw. It struck her that only a king could be this personal before a small crowd, such as that assembled in the great hall. Next to him, they were insignificant. He could eat, sleep, battle, or make love before them. They had no more substance to him than a pet dog, chained to the wall.

But Rachel felt not only the humiliation of being handled by a man who was not her husband, but by the crowd that was invisible to the king. They were all too real for her. She seemed to feel them smiling and smirking all about her. It was as if her lack of courage had excited in them a loathing stronger than any fear. She felt loathsome. It was true that she had just offered to pay homage to a false god, offered to eat what was unclean; and now she was allowing far worse. A man other than her husband was touching his soft hand to her face, speaking to her in the tones of a lover. Music played, so that against her shut eyes, it was as if she had been transported body and soul into a nightmare.

"If you want to live, Jewess, open your eyes," said the king. But Rachel could not do this. The nightmare was already tangible enough. She wanted to live, but she felt the words of the king's question falling on her like hailstones. There was no way she could open her eyes while there was the shadow of a doubt that she had it in her to betray the man she loved. "If you want to live," the king said, "you will tell us where your husband, the murderer Saul, has gone to hide."

She felt the king draw close again, taking her by the shoulders with the force one applies to a recalcitrant child. He shook her, but not with anger. His tone was sweet, his voice, even in Greek, strangely pleasant, a temptation: "There is no need to kill your baby, there is no need to die. You have knowledge of a criminal and you must tell me what you know."

"I will eat of the pig," she said.

"I don't care about that," said the king. "Look at me, girl."

"I will pay homage to Zeus. I will sacrifice in the profaned Temple," she said. Her words grew smaller and sharper, as if her throat was twisting about them, throttling the blasphemies by its own desire. She could barely breathe, so powerful was the cramping in her abdomen. Suddenly, she felt the urge to urinate, felt the pressure of her bladder grow as one more reminder of her pregnancy and her shame.

"Open your eyes and tell us where your husband has gone. Then I won't have you torn limb from limb by my favorite horses. Open your eyes, girl," he said.

The pain within her womb started so violently that she felt the tears come from behind her shut eyes. It was as if her unborn baby was trying to speak. She could imagine him, red-faced with fury, curled up with his knees to his chest, his little fists pounding inside the frail walls of her body. He was in pain, inside her, and all she gave him was the sense of her own fear, and all he gave her was this fear transposed to fury and indignation, and doubled and redoubled in intensity, until Antiochus's words, Antiochus's men, were but a small part of her horror, the least part. There was no help for her from the king, no help for her from giving in to cowardice. She remembered finally the only source of ultimate solace, the solace everyone in the world remembers in their last moments: the Name.

Rachel took hold of this, seeing the Name, hearing its soundless echoes deep within her pain-wracked body. She felt her eyes, mouth, and hands all open at once, as if eager to let in the world.

The king was looking at her, and smiling; this angered her. She knew that the others in the room joined in his mockery, that their crooked smiles were at the expense of herself and her people.

"You are unworthy," she said, blurting out the words, reverting to Hebrew without thinking. The pain was yet within her. But it was reaching out to her now, not clouding her judgment but urging her to action. The words of the Holy Books, forbidden by the king's laws, came to her, and she spoke them out, suddenly defiant: " 'The heart of kings is unsearchable,' " she said, and there was a silence in the room, beginning with the king, and rolling backward to the others, who seemed to be so intent on this reversal of terror that they had stopped breathing. " 'The king that faithfully judges, only his throne shall be established.' "

"What are you saying, you harlot?" said the king, not understanding the Hebrew that many of his servants spoke perfectly well.

"I am saying that you sin against the One God," said Rachel, and she felt the pain in her womb let go of her, slowly, rapturously loosening the cramp, so that she smiled in spite of herself, so that Antiochus saw her suddenly defiant and unafraid. But this no longer mattered to her. Antiochus had no more significance. There was no fear greater than self-fear. She had felt her body turn against her, felt her womb rise up in anger as if it would strangle and spew forth her own child. Rachel remembered that she had strength. She had promised her husband not to betray him, never to betray him; and she possessed the knowledge of the Name.

"I am saying that God breaks evil the way He breaks a tree. I am saying that even in the shadow of death, I will fear no evil. Do you hear what I am saying? I read the Holy Book, I honor the Sabbath, I spit on your false gods, and I shall never betray my husband, who is a righteous and loving man."

There had been martyrs before her, and there were many more in the years of Antiochus's reign after she had gone. Whether she met death under the whip, or in the fires with which they burned her, was soon forgotten; legends sprang up which had her killed by a great spear, or hurled from the city wall in chains, or trampled by the Indian elephant of the tyrant. What mattered was that she had died without betraying her husband.

Mordecai, her father, escaped with his son Shimon to Modein, where the story of Rachel became well known. The respected elder Mattathias must have been affected by this story as well. Perhaps his anger and his courage would have been as great without her martyr's example. Still, it is certain that the story of her defiance had preceded a delegation of pagan priests and officers of the king to Modein, who had come to enforce the rules of apostasy. Mattathias was offered gifts and high rank in exchange for leading the people of his town to sacrifice before the pagan altar. He not only refused, but killed the first of his people who was induced by cowardice and greed to submit to the demands of the king's men. A moment later Mattathias, followed by his sons, attacked the officers sent by Antiochus and began the revolution in Judea.

Mattathias never lived to see the culmination of his dream, when

three years later, his son Judah, known as the Maccabee, conquered Jerusalem, ousted the pagan priests and soldiers, and rededicated the Temple of the Jews. Even in those days, few believed
the legend that the cruse of oil Judah lit in the Temple burned for
eight days; but it gave rise to the celebration of Hanukkah, the
Festival of Lights. Even freethinking Jews like Shimon, son of Mordecai the *Cohen*, observed the candlelighting rite, and passed the
tradition on to their children.

The Family of
Mordecai the Cohen
of Jerusalem
167 B.C.—64 B.C.

Six years after the death of his sister, Shimon's wife gave birth to a girl, and they named her Rachel. Saul, Shimon's brother-in-law, the fugitive rebel against Antiochus's power, had died two years after his wife; he had taken a spear at Emmaus, during Judah the Maccabee's defeat of the Syrian-Greek forces. Mordecai, Shimon's father, had died two years after that, in the same year as the frustrated King Antiochus. But even without a grandfather and an uncle who'd shared the life of her namesake, the little girl grew up under her spell. Rachel wanted to be brave, as brave as her father's sister; she wanted to be an artist in gold and gems; she wanted to be bright-haired, the focus of men's desire.

She met her husband Shlomo during the last year of the terrible war between Rome and Carthage. North Africa was not so far from Judea that she couldn't imagine the cries of the widows, the misery of the enslaved, the glory of the warriors. Shlomo was a young man of the priestly caste, pale and handsome. Before their marriage he seemed courtly, a young man possessed of an elder's diplomacy. But once living under his roof, sharing his bed, she discovered Shlomo to be what she most despised: a coward. He supported first one, then another of the priestly factions. He was alternately a

Pietist, a freethinker, a lover of Rome, a partisan of Egypt, a believer in the Messiah, a follower of the godless patriots of Judea. When Jonathan, the youngest brother of the dead Judah the Maccabee was murdered, another brother, Simon, took his place. Rachel's husband's position in the Temple remained secure during this upheaval; when Simon was murdered by his son-in-law Ptolemy and succeeded by John Hyrcanus, even when John's rule was usurped by Antiochus VII Sidetes, Shlomo's little power remained secure.

Rachel tried to invent reasons for her husband's wavering beliefs and lack of will. They had four children, all of them boys, and Shlomo wanted them to have the respect and comforts that had been denied him under the persecution of his class. He wanted to live so that no one would persecute him, or his children. When Tiberius Gracchus was murdered in a Roman riot, Shlomo thought the tragic death indicative of the reforming tribune's lack of wisdom; Rachel thought it as noble a death as any in Homer. As she grew older, she turned more and more from her husband, whose attitudes toward life had infected their sons. All of them used the priesthood and the secular powers to further their fortunes, and whatever courage they possessed was turned to crossing distant lands and seas in search of more gold.

Rachel found solace in her youngest brother's son Saul. She was thirty-nine at his birth, an old and venerable age in those years, but even when Saul had grown to young manhood, she was still capable of the closest kind of goldwork, of striding up the hilly streets of Jerusalem, of talking through the night, retelling her father's stories of the Maccabees. Unfit for politics or the priesthood, Saul learned from his aunt the intricacies of jewelry design. He had a talent for goldwork, but he was more inclined to listen to Rachel's stories than to labor at his art.

His brothers, cousins, and uncles were men of business and politics, men who used religion and philosophy to conceal greed and ambition. He was an impractical man, like his aunt. Izak, Rachel's eldest son, sent Saul to Parthia during the warlike reign of Mithridates, with a fortune in gems. Brigands attacked his caravan on his first day across the Parthian border; they were pleased enough with his fortune to let him keep his life. Saul learned that he had been carrying a bribe, arranged by his uncle for a Roman general. The loss of the gems would result in an unnecessary battle between

Parthians and Romans, and Izak was warned that his life was in danger on either side of the Mediterranean. Saul traveled to Mesopotamia and Armenia, then sailed to Thracia where he was taken in by the small Jewish community and was once again able to practice his family's goldsmithing trade. When the series of skirmishes that would later lead to war between Rome and Parthia had temporarily quieted, he went to Macedonia, now a Roman province. Here the Jewish community, made up of many political exiles from Judea, had some news of his family.

Saul didn't marry until he was forty years old, an old man by any standard, but his wealth in gold was substantial, and his dreamy ways and long stories of distant places fascinated many of the young daughters of his friends. His bride was a native of Creta, born to a Jewish exile who pined for the high ground of the Temple. Saul took both wife and father-in-law to Judea, sailing first to Tyre, and joining a coastal caravan in the year 80 B.C. He had not been in Jerusalem for two decades, and expected to find little of the family he remembered still alive. Rachel's son Izak, who had entrusted him with the gems whose loss had prompted his years of exile, had been dead for ten years. Also dead were Saul's father and mother, Rachel's sons and husband, and many of the children of Rachel's long-dead brothers.

But Rachel herself was still alive.

She was old, but still vigorous, and men and women revered her for her age, as if it were a mark of God's favor. Babies were brought to her thin hands for blessing; her pale eyes were beseeched for wisdom of the future, for contact with the past's departed.

"I have lived to see you," she told Saul, bringing his hands to her dry lips, looking over his young wife's belly for the swelling of pregnancy. "I was waiting for a hero to come to me," she said. Saul protested. He was not a hero but a simple man, a dreamer whose fortune and skill with gold had enabled him to earn a living and marry and return to his city. But Rachel shook away his protestations. She had the peremptory power of old age. Saul had brought her a hero, even if she would never live to see him. A hero who would be as great in his time as her own aunt Rachel had been in hers. Saul rejoiced at these words. It could only mean that his wife was pregnant, and that she would soon bring a boy into the world.

A week later the old woman died, and soon afterward Saul's wife was assured of her pregnancy by two respected midwives. But

Rachel's prediction was inaccurate. A child was born, healthy and loud with indignation; but it was a girl, black-haired and black-eyed like her mother. Though the parents were disappointed that their firstborn was not a male, they were pleased with the baby's beauty and intelligence. They named her Rachel, and prayed that the name would confer on her the attributes of her great-aunt, and her great-great-aunt: they wondered if she would be brave, and if she would enjoy a life long in years.

But the year of her birth was the beginning of a time of trouble in Judea. The end of Sulla's dictatorship in Rome was felt all about the Mediterranean. Salome Alexandra reigned in Judea, but the threat of civil war hung over the successors to the dynasty founded by Judah the Maccabee eight decades before. Shortly after Rachel's twelfth birthday, Salome died, and her sons declared war on each other, dishonoring their mother's memory. The Romans sent a legate into the internecine struggle. When his power was defied by Salome's son Aristobulus, Pompey, famous throughout the civilized world for clearing the Mediterranean of pirates four years before, was called upon. The great general was asserting the power of Rome throughout Bithynia, Pontus, Cappadocia, and Syria. From Damascus, his all-conquering legions turned toward an already weak Judea. Pompey put Jerusalem under siege and, within three months, overran the Holy City's walls. There was a massacre, but it produced only a few thousand corpses; this was a small sum in an age that required a minimum of five thousand dead enemies for a general to receive a "triumph" from the Senate and people of Rome.

But Pompey had long since surpassed this paltry requirement in his path of conquest. From little Judea he took few lives, and only a thousand random captives to add to the tens of thousands to be sold into Roman slavery. Among these thousand citizens were the goldsmith Saul, his wife Mira, their fifteen-year-old son David, and their sixteen-year-old daughter Rachel. As they were driven along the wharf at Joppa, loud with lamentation, Rachel's parents wondered what manner of heroine spent a life in chains, separated from her people by an endless sea.

THE FAMILY OF MORDECAI THE COHEN OF JERUSALEM
167 BC–64 BC

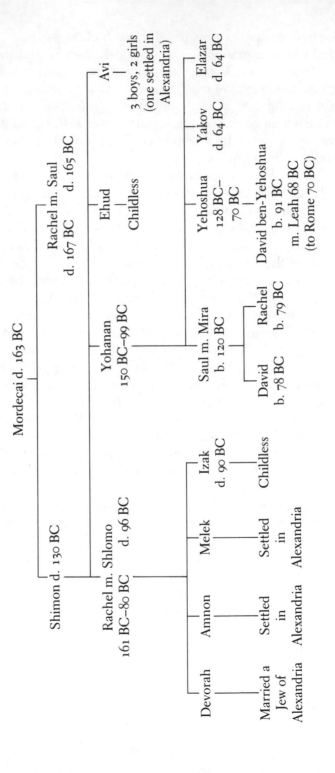

Part Two

Rome, 63 B.C.

Chapter
7

They sailed in an enormous ship with blue sails and gilded masts. Once the ship had belonged to pirates; it was they who had gilded the masts, who had built dens of pleasure above the holds heavy with plunder. But Pompey had smashed the pirates, had sunk their ships or converted them to Roman use, had slaughtered their seamen or sentenced them to the silver mines in Spain. Rachel knew that no savior would come for her from out of the sea—no Jewish fleet, no pirate boat, no Angel of Death sent by the Lord. The endless sea was Roman. Even a storm wouldn't dare raise its head against this Roman ship and its Roman sailors and their cargo of slaves.

Half the complement of Jewish captives was on board, along with papyrus and linen, glass and alabaster, and gold. The rest of Pompey's slaves were sent to Rome on smaller ships, galleys that hugged the coasts and were propelled by double banks of oarsmen. Rachel never learned of their fate, but in the first days of her voyage, her brother comforted her with suppositions about their probable route.

"First northward to Tiberias and Tyre, and certainly they'll stop at Laodicea," he said, his eyes looking across the expanse of chained slaves all about them on the vast deck and out to the pale blue horizon. "They'll want Syrian wine, of course, and dates and figs, but mostly the wine. It's very popular with the aristocracy."

"Oh yes," said Rachel, smiling in spite of herself. "The aristocracy." The word was bitter on her lips, and not simply because overnight she had become a slave. Among her own class in Judea, in Jerusalem, the Holy City, there had been those who had supported the coming of the Romans; even among the *Cohanim* there had been traitors who had agitated for the welcoming of Pompey the Great as the bringer of order. Some priests had discovered hints of Pompey's conquest of Jerusalem in the Torah, and accepted him as part of God's plan for His people.

Rachel found a certain justice in that along with families like her own, who gave of their fortunes and their lives in defending Jerusalem and its Holy Temple against the pagans, were families who had supported the Romans, aping their customs, language, and rituals, worshiping the power that had given them the rule of the civilized world. Among the enslaved Jews were rich and poor, observers of the Sabbath and freethinkers, men whose hearts had broken at the news that the pagan Pompey had entered the sacred Temple, and others whose dream of glory was not to ascend to heaven in Elijah's chariot of fire but to become a citizen of Rome. But to Pompey's legions, there had been no need to make distinctions. A thousand slaves were to be taken, and so a section of the city had been surrounded, the population rooted out of their homes, chained one-to-one, and set in a slow-moving march to the sea. The forced march had already killed two dozen captives, among them the mother of five young boys, and a scribe who was said to have known the languages of eighty peoples. The very rich, if they survived the voyage, could be ransomed by their relatives; the rest would share the lot of any slave among the Romans. Only one's master would determine whether life would be a gentle burden or a series of horrors. "We shall learn all about the aristocracy," Rachel said to her brother, her smile twisting into a miserable grimace.

David, younger than her by almost a year, began to preach in his superior way: "Father says that there are no Jewish slaves in Rome, or weren't you listening? It's the obligation of the Jewish community to pay a price for each of us and then set us free. At the very worst, we will be technically enslaved for a few days or weeks. But in the name of all that is holy, Rachel, we shall have nothing to fear, nothing."

"Where will the other slave ships stop?" she asked, to shut him up. "After Laodicea?"

David hesitated. He was stuffed with knowledge, and knew very well that so much learning at fifteen years of age often made him appear ridiculous. Rachel, who believed in demons and angels, who could recite by heart only the smallest part of the Torah, was still quick to find him foolish, without maturity or common sense. It was obvious that she thought his reassurances silly, that what she wanted from him was not logic, but words to bury her fear of their destination. But if words were what she wanted, he would give them to her gladly, as he would give her anything of which she had need.

"After Laodicea," he said, "they will certainly stop at Seleucia, if only for its linen. Then Tarsus, for figs, and westward along the Cilician coast to Aspendus. I confess that I know of no specialty of that city."

"Slaves," said Rachel. "The slaves of Aspendus are very docile." She pulled up her back sharply from where she sat on the sunbaked deck, rolling gently in the endless sea, so that the chain connecting her left ankle to her brother's right ankle—the same chain that connected brother and father and mother and two score other individuals clustered together in that part of the deck—clattered. It was not a very loud noise, not loud enough to wake her old father or startle her brother out of his lecture. But the sound struck deep into Rachel's heart, exaggerating the chafing about her skin, screaming aloud her slave status. "I want to go, David," she said. "I want to get off this boat, right now."

"I never heard about the slaves of Aspendus," said David.

"She was joking," said their mother, Mira, turning to her children with bloodshot eyes. "Be still, Rachel."

"No, I can't help it, Mother," said Rachel. "It's the spirit of evil in me. It wants to be let loose. It wants to be in charge, and I have no strength to fight it."

"You have no wisdom to fight it," said David. "There is no such thing as an evil spirit, certainly not one that lives in your soul, always fighting your good spirit—which doesn't exist either."

"If there are no evil spirits, why are we all in chains?" said Rachel. Mira placed her large hands on her daughter's wild black curls. There were many answers to that question, perhaps as many answers as there were captives in chains. The religious believed that God had punished the Jews for following the ways of the heathen, for becoming slack and lazy in obeying the commands of

God's Law. The superstitious blamed Satan, or the configuration of the stars in the spring sky. The freethinkers spoke of politics, of strong men looking for easy conquests, of weak princes looking for foreign lords to strengthen their hold on their people. But there were some of the religious who felt they were being sent into exile as a signal of the coming of the Messiah; others felt that God meant them to mingle with the Gentile to exhibit the ways of the God-fearing to the world; many simply felt that their punishment was an end in itself, that they must needs die in slavery before a new generation of the free could inherit the Holy Land. Among the superstitious there was even more dissent: some blamed foreign gods, while others refused to countenance their power; some claimed that the spirits of good had sent them into slavery, like scapegoats into the wilderness, so that the demons assaulting Judea would follow them to Rome, liberating the Holy Land. The free-thinkers argued knowledgeably about the relative merits of Pompey and Caesar, whether there were vestiges of power in Egypt and Syria; some predicted a further clash between religious Jews and Jews who were nonbelievers, while others insisted that Jewish history would be decided by one thing: whether Rome would be content to rule Judea through a puppet, or would insist on direct tyranny.

"Do not think of the chains. Think of yourself in God's hands," said Mira. But Rachel wasn't comforted by this. She could feel the spirit of evil within her, a large and willful force, swelling up in her heart, rising in her throat; terrible words blew up against the back of her tongue, and she clamped shut her mouth to keep back the unutterable phrases: "God is nothing, *Adonai* is without power, Jupiter and Mars and Venus are the true gods, the Jewish God is the god of slaves."

"Father is sick!" said Rachel, the words twisting through the labyrinth of evil phrases. "I want to go home!"

"Darling," said Mira, taking hold of her daughter's hand. "You must be quiet. This is a bad time, but it will pass. Let the Lord be your refuge. Close your eyes, and think of the Lord."

But Rachel could think of nothing but the willful force within her. She wanted to break away from the chain about her ankle, she wanted to dive off the miserably crowded open deck even if she had to drag a hundred people with her to do it. Defying her mother, she got to her knees, even though the slaves had been ordered to stay seated, their hands and backsides on the deck. "Sit down, you idiot," said her mother, suddenly angry with her daughter's lack of sense. In a moment any one of two hundred savage sailors could be upon them, ripping into their backs with a rod or a whip.

"It's all right, Mother," said David, forced to get to his knees to accommodate his sister as she moved violently about in her little square of space. "It's the heat and the sea."

"Please, David, tell me more," said Rachel. "Tell me where they stop. Tell me, please." She held on to her brother as if he alone could prevent her from getting to her feet. David smiled now, the younger brother in command.

"Of course I'll tell you," he said. "After Aspendus, to Xanthus and Rhodes," he said.

"Xanthus and Rhodes," said Rachel, repeating the famous names as if they were magical incantations. Carefully, she swallowed the unspoken blasphemies, forcing them with her thoughts back down her throat, into her belly. She heard her brother speak of the Greek islands, and the emeralds, gold, and marble they'd bring to the Roman ships. "And what about Pergamum?" she asked, remembering the city as one with a great library, where men had begun to write on "parchment," a material made from dried and scraped and stretched sheepskin and far more durable than papyrus.

"No, we won't go to Pergamum," said David sadly. "But they might touch at Athens, where certainly there are fine libraries—"

"Slaves," said Rachel, feeling the evil spirit take hold once again. She could see the once-proud Athenians chained one-to-one, defeated by the great Sulla in 86 B.C., their temples ravaged, their artworks looted, their false stone gods rattling in ox carts next to statues of philosophers, athletes, and kings. "Athenian slaves," she said. David hadn't stopped talking. She could see his handsome face alive with intelligence, calling forth the names of a dozen slaves of the Greek city-states who had gone on to win their freedom from Roman masters, and with this freedom fame and fortune and slaves of their own. Aristotle's name was invoked, and with it his ancient opinion of the value of slavery: some men were higher than others; some peoples lacked the stronger character needed for freedom.

"And then from Greece to Italy," said David sweetly, trying to bring his sister back to a comfortable position on the deck by the force of his will. "In Rome where the representatives of the Jewish community will be waiting, ready to fulfill their duties by buying freedom for every captive on board."

"In Rome where the Jews are slaves, where the Greeks are slaves," said Rachel. The deck had just been washed with seawater, but the fetid smells of five hundred chained captives could not be so easily banished. "On the sea, where the Chosen People sit in their own shit and piss," said the evil spirit within her. Her sunburned face turned white with the effort to hold back these words from speech. She heard clearly the names of Mavet and Resheph and Dever, pagan gods of death and plague and pestilence; but these were foreign gods, and had no hold on any daughter of Israel, if only she was strong in her faith.

"Rachel," said Mira, "think of your great-aunt whose name you bear, think of the Rachel before her who defied Antiochus."

"There is no plan," said the evil spirit within her. "There is nothing that happens that God has willed. All is willed by men, and the strongest of men are Romans, and they are strong because their gods are strong and numerous and share their glories here on this earth."

"There is only one God," said Rachel, shouting the words in Hebrew, so that everyone around her on the deck turned about in their heat-induced torpor and stared.

"What is it?" said her old father, Saul, the son of Yohanan, too sick to raise his head from the deck where he had been dreaming of old wars, different seas, lost fortunes.

"Rachel has had too much sun," said David, turning to his father with respect and consideration.

"She feels the Evil Inclination in her," said Mira. "The Evil Wind must blow far to reach us here."

Saul closed his eyes, trying to understand the superstitious words. Of course there was such a thing as evil spirits. He himself had been felled by them in his youth, when he had flirted with various foreign gods, and the power of the One God had left him open to the *shedim*—the gods of the Gentile. But Rachel was a believer. The only demons that could attach themselves to her pure soul dwelled in the Judean desert, their strength drawn from the wreckage of dead cities, half buried in the dust. Usually these spirits were sent by the Lord, carriers of doubt and disease to test the fiber of His people. But there was no need for further testing of his daughter. Was not the loss of liberty as complete a test of one's faith as the Lord required?

"There is only one God," repeated Rachel in Hebrew, and then she voiced these words in the Greek common to Judea and Syria, speaking softly at first, and then shouting the name of *Adonai*, the Hebrew God, as if it were a challenge flung in the faces of the Roman sea-god, Neptune, and his brother the sky-god, Jupiter.

Somehow this defiance of the spirits worshiped by her captors quieted her soul. The terrible blasphemies that threatened to erupt from her lips retreated once more down her throat to her rumbling belly. She was light-headed, not from lack of water or want of food, but from a sudden strength. The iron ring felt lighter about her ankle. She smiled at her brother. He was very handsome, very brave, very bright; surely, he was right about what awaited them at Rome. There were fifty thousand Jews there, some said, and even if there were but ten thousand, that would be ten thousand with an obligation to ransom their coreligionists from among the quarter million slaves that served the city of Rome.

"Rachel, sit down at once," said her mother, speaking with an urgency that penetrated her fear. One of the sailors was coming over to them, surefooted and erect on the gently swaying deck, a metal-studded scourge in his hand; this was not an instrument of punishment, but a killing tool.

Rachel sat, her weak knees collapsing jerkily, so that the chain pulled at her brother's ankle, bringing his face close to hers. But all the confidence had drained from David's eyes. There was a fear that she couldn't comprehend, until she felt the hand of the sailor on her shoulder.

"Up," he said.

Rachel looked at him with her wide black eyes. This was what had frightened her brother, she understood, but she couldn't share this fear, having just vanquished one much greater. This was no spirit of the dead, no hairy demon, no agent of Satan or Belial, but a man.

"I say up, slave," he said, and he brought the handle of the scourge under her chin, and forced her head back, so that the sun blinded her eyes, and he could stare at her beautiful face. David quickly got to his feet and extended his hand to his sister, to whom he was chained; he wanted to get her to stand before the sailor would turn the scourge about and whip into her innocent flesh.

But David's help hadn't been called for.

The sailor, without thinking, drove the whip handle with force across the boy's head; if he had used the same force with the metal-studded end of the whip, he would have killed him with the single blow. As it was, David was knocked off his feet, blood gushed from his nose, and the half-dead Saul rose for the first time in three days to defend his family.

Mira, much younger than her husband, was filled with rage. She ignored the scourge in the sailor's hand and threw herself at his back as if she were the only thing between Saul and murder. David, very much dazed by the blow, looked up at the sun-bright figures of his father and mother, their thin frames shaking with violence. But the Roman sailor—actually a half-Italian son of a Cisalpine Gallic peasant woman—was under no threat. He seemed to turn in slow motion, as if swimming through a lake's tranquil waters. David tried to shout a warning, but there was blood in his mouth, and fear in his throat, and the scourge moved inexorably, like a wave coming to shore, but moving side to side, first caressing his mother, then his father, the leather straps flashing their studs like baleful signals from some demonic rite.

Suddenly, the sun seemed to be raining blood. David and Rachel's parents were felled like dead trees; he could hear the bones cracking. For days afterward the sound lingered in the wind-filled sails, in the creaking of the gilded mast.

Rachel stood, and turned her eyes to the sea.

She begged the sailor to stop, but understood that he wouldn't. He was as much a part of her fate as the winds that drove their ship across the Mediterranean, as the civil war that brought Pompey to Judea, as the love that had brought her parents together and that was even now together releasing them from slavery. She could hear the scourge, even after her parents had fallen, even after their earthly lives were through; she could hear the terrible, easy rhythm of the sailor's hatred.

Rachel stood very still, hoping that he wouldn't turn the murderous weapon on her brother, praying that the particular destiny that had driven him to the unforgivable sin of murder had completed its course. She had tried not to hear the screams of her parents, but now that they were gone, they filled the air about her, sharper than the cries of the slaves to whom they were chained, deeper than the sobbing of her brother. Screams seemed to come from every corner of the deck, from the sea itself, as if the water spirits were repelled by the crime on deck.

"Rachel, don't leave me," said David, speaking the Hebrew of their ancestors, the language of despair and hope, of trial and triumph. Already a black slave had been brought to her and was beginning to hammer at the bronze fasteners of the iron ring about her ankle.

"No, my brother," she said, trying to imagine him with his first beard, trying to imagine a meeting, a reunion, with both of them alive and well.

"Don't forget me," he said.

"Never," said Rachel.

She wanted to kneel down and wipe the blood from his dear face, but she was unable to move from her upright position lest anything she did would bring more death and destruction in their wake. Her father's body lay on its belly, the tufts of white hair along the nape of his neck streaked with blood, the thin legs under the ragged tunic already as inanimate as the chain that bound him to his wife. Mira lay faceup, regrettably, her black eyes wide, her fists clenched in immortal rage. Rachel would never forget the cast of her broken face, nose, and right eye mangled by the studded whip: her mother had not simply forgotten that she was a slave; she had remembered that she was free, and responsible only to God.

"Come," said the sailor, and though her ankle was free of its chain, the man had taken hold of her wrist in his rough hand. She allowed him to pull her half a step before resisting. "I want to kiss my brother," she said, praying that the words would lead to nothing ill for David.

The sailor hesitated, looking from the young girl's beautiful face to the corpses of her parents and the young brother sitting in a pool of blood, his dazed eyes memorizing the scene for a lifetime of nightmares. David's chain was now brought noisily across the deck to another captive, a woman just released from her connection to Mira. As much as this woman seemed to recoil from the contact with the dead, she seemed now to recoil from being chained to David; he and his were bad luck.

"Come, slave," said the sailor, and he pulled violently at Rachel's wrist so that she stumbled across the deck on shaky legs. She had no need to look back at her parents. There were images enough of them in her memory, happier images. But she owed them a prayer, and she mumbled this through steady lips, loud enough for her brother to join her, in voicing the refrain: *"Blessed be His Holy Name, forever and ever."*

The sailor pushed her again, seeming to enjoy the power he had over her frail frame. All about them were the slaves sharing the sea voyage; Jews of her city, of her neighborhood, all of whom were reduced by slavery and physical abuse to a sameness. Chained, half starved, half clothed, half asleep, they were half men. All were waiting, like half men always waited, either to be returned to full human status, or reduced to nothing at all.

But Rachel was no longer waiting. She didn't feel herself to be half human. There was no longer a fear of what awaited her in Rome, or on this ship, or in this life. Already she had lost her parents, the company of her brother, her liberty.

There was little more they could take from her. She felt herself a dark, powerful force, an instrument of a fate that was momently unfolding. She might be burned on a pyre or torn limb from limb, but not without some divine reason. The sailor's grip was strong, but his life could be crushed, his dreams shattered just like any man's. Somehow, she would be connected with this. Not to take revenge on a single sailor, but to be one link in a chain that would wrap itself around the throat of Rome itself.

There was a powerful plan in the universe, God's plan, and she was a part of this. Whether she lived or died this day or in fifty years was out of her hands. Whether the sailor had turned on her parents because she herself had refused to rise with speed was a worthless question; God had wanted the deaths, as he now wanted the sailor's grip on her wrist. This was not, as the rabbis explained, and as her brother loved to expound, an excuse for immoral living. There was always a choice between good and evil, cowardice and courage. It was simply that when an event was done, a step taken, a day and night passed, it was clear that God had knowledge beforehand of what would take place; and because He had control of everything in the world, if He had allowed something to pass, there was a reason for that event, even if that reason was outside the understanding of man.

The sailor pushed her. "Faster," he said, as if he was irritated with her presence. Toward the front of the ship the slaves were being fed, and their clamorous attention to the sailors doling out their scraps pained her. She wanted their silence. She would have liked to feel their hatred directed at these men of Rome, their contempt. Slaves must be fed in order to live, and they must live in order to fetch a price. Beyond those who died of exposure and those who were murdered to maintain order, each man, woman, and child had a price. Her father, old as he was, might have been worth three times the average able-bodied man, if the slave masters had known of his skills with jewelry and gems. Perhaps when the sailors delivered their cargo to Pompey's representative in Rome, her father's name and approximate worth would be found on a scroll; and this murdering sailor would be disciplined for so readily destroying the general's property.

"There's a nice ass on this one," said a voice behind her, and a moment later, she was being touched from behind. A hand was on her buttocks, on her neck, on the backs of her legs, accompanied by laughter. She recoiled, blinded with anger, but the hand followed her, and the sailor who was leading her only grew angrier at the attention.

"This is for Manilius, you idiot," said the sailor, turning Rachel about the front of the boat toward the general's "house," an elaborate superstructure affixed to the forward center section of the vast deck. A soldier, wearing light armor and a heavily ornamented helmet, stood at the foot of the ladder to this "house." The sun had nearly put him to sleep, but he grew sharply alert at the sight of Rachel.

"Who goes there?" he joked, touching his callused hand to Rachel's face. Without thinking, Rachel slapped the hand away.

"I'm taking her to Manilius," said the sailor.

"You're taking her to Manilius, if I say you're taking her to Manilius," said the soldier contemptuously. He had ignored the slap, and now brought his hand to her shoulder, pulling at her tunic to bare the skin.

"Come on, slave," said the sailor, pushing Rachel to the ladder and away from the soldier's hands. He didn't brandish his heavy whip, but it was clear that he held it in greater readiness than a moment before.

"All right, fish-face," said the soldier, raising his sword. "Working on a slave ship in the service of the Republic of Rome doesn't give you the right to even look at a Roman citizen and soldier. Put your stupid whip down."

"I am bringing this slave to your general," insisted the sailor.

"And if you want me to drop this whip, you'll have to cut my hands off first."

"You're such a brave sailor," said the soldier. "You think you can hurt me with that little thing, don't you?"

"Just let me pass."

Both men were aware of the group of sailors who had come up to them, all of them without swords but armed with cudgels or whips. Two hundred sailors were on board the enormous cargo ship, none of whom were pleased with the daily contempt hurled their way by the dozen soldiers attached to Manilius, a highborn general in Pompey's legions, notable for his arrogance and his brutality.

"I told you to put that whip down," said the soldier, showing not the least trace of fear. The sailor smiled at this, as if the soldier had exhibited a weakness in not killing him at once. He pushed Rachel forward.

"Go up the ladder, slave," he said. Rachel put one foot on the first rung and then felt the soldier's hand pull her back with great force.

"You don't move, slave," said the soldier. "The sailors aren't your masters here. You'll do as I say, won't you?" He had managed to put two paces between himself and the sailor, with Rachel at his side. The sailor squared his shoulders and jerked the scourge with which he had killed Mira and Saul into the air.

"This isn't your boat," said the sailor, unnecessarily. If he had been seriously rebellious, he would have whipped metal-studded straps across the soldier's face. But instead he retreated a half step, speaking more loudly, waiting for the nearby sailors to join with him. But on a ship where the punishment for breaking discipline was being flogged to death, or worse, being dragged behind the boat with chained ankles until drowned, no one was quick to join their mate's little insurrection.

"She's a pretty one," said the soldier, bringing Rachel closer with his free hand. "I haven't had a girl since Joppa."

"Not one of us has had a girl or a boy," said the sailor.

"Every girl on this boat's been fucked five times a day by you and your friends," said the soldier smilingly. "Don't lie to me, sailor. I know you don't like blood on your hands, but you never say no to cunt juice."

Rachel didn't understand every word of the Latin dialect they spoke, but she could see the tension between soldier and sailor had eased. Somehow, they had turned about their animosity, concentrating it on her. The soldier's grip had grown rougher. Now he pulled at the tunic as he had done before and tore it at the shoulder. When she began to protest, he laughed in her face.

"She doesn't know she's a cunt," said the sailor, relaxing his grip on the whip.

"Maybe you'd like to teach her," said the soldier. He replaced his sword in its scabbard and pushed Rachel toward the sailor with great violence.

"Thanks, but I think Manilius wants her in one piece, and I'd probably break this bitch in half."

"Let's see," said the soldier, taking hold of Rachel one more time. He pulled her into his arms and brought his mouth over hers as if he would devour her. Eyes wide, pushing at his embrace with all her strength, she thought she must be going mad. The soldier was forcing his tongue into her mouth, tearing at her lips with his teeth, driving his thumb into her underneck, raising his hairy knee into her groin. The more she pushed back at this attack, the more he seemed to enjoy it. She felt his heart race, felt the blood beating into her throat, felt his breaths grow hoarse and rapid, even as all her senses rioted at the mockery of love.

"She needs it bad," said the sailor, and Rachel heard these words without comprehension. She wanted to shout now, remembering what her mother had told her to say if they were separated at the auction block: "*I am not a brothel girl, I am a jeweler, trained in gold and gems, and of very good family. I am a jeweler and worth more to you than any mistress or whore.*"

But she couldn't speak, not with her mouth filled with his teeth and tongue, and she couldn't move, not with his thick arm around her and his knee forcing her against the ladder. Rachel had never been betrothed, though marriage at her age of sixteen was common in Rome and Judea. But she had felt the attraction of infatuation with young men, felt the difference between love of family and an imagined romantic passion. She had read the Song of Songs, had imagined the beauty that her mother possessed when her father had taken her into his arms and declared his love.

But this was violation, not passion; she was being beaten down, not lifted up. The soldier's joy was like a dog's, and coupled with the lowest form of man's desire: the urge to dominate. Rachel felt the man's hand move under her tunic, tear at her underclothes, already ragged from the long march and the days at sea. He had long fingernails, and her soft inner thighs pulled back at their touch. But there was no room to move. It was not a question of meeting someone's desire with revulsion, and thereby repulsing it. It was being a slave. She had no choice. There were men about her, and none of them recognized in her anything sacred, anything inviolable. She was property. The soldier was laughing and the sailor who had moments before been his enemy was now laughing too, joining in his pleasure. It seemed that everyone on board was gathering about to watch the soldier humble the slave girl who had not yet learned her station.

So it was necessary to pin her back against the ladder; it was essential to hold her at the throat with one hand; it was useful to keep the pressure of his helmeted head against her screaming face as he drove his filthy hands up along her inner thighs and thrust the sides of his fingers against her vaginal opening. It was a moment that seemed without end. She would never feel the end of this pain in her throat, in her lips, in her chest; she would never rid her body of the humiliation done to her private parts. And yet she didn't want this to end. She could feel his rising anticipation, understood that this horror was only the beginning. When he would remove his tongue from her mouth, when she would no longer hear the laughing of the sailors all around them, it would be because she had been thrown to the deck; she would be mounted like an animal, dishonored, and removed for all time from the possibility of love.

But then suddenly she felt his fingers pull back from her private parts. She heard herself scream, felt the taste of her own blood in her mouth, could see that the huge metal-cased head was no longer overwhelming her field of vision. Rachel couldn't hear anything, so wild was her fear, so strong was the pounding in her chest, so certain was she of being raped.

"What do you mean touching what is not yours?" said a gentle voice speaking Greek with a rhythmic cadence. He repeated himself, and Rachel wondered wildly if someone was speaking to her. All she could do was reach her hands across her chest, pulling up her tunic, straightening it about her shoulders, moving away from the ladder, her eyes afraid to lift to the source of speech.

For there was suddenly a much greater fear all about her, a fear that didn't come from herself, but from the men who had been enjoying her humiliation, and the soldier who had been the cause of it.

"I meant nothing, sir," said the soldier.

"You are a thief when you take what is not yours. And when you take what is mine, you are worse than a thief. You are a thief who is disloyal."

"I was trying to get her up the ladder—"

"Silence. Give me your sword."

"I beg your forgiveness—"

"Are you a soldier, man? What are you begging, and to whom do you think you speak? I have given you an order."

Rachel felt her heart slow. She raised her eyes and saw the soldier extend his sword to his general, a man in a simple white tunic, with three gold rings on his fingers. He was without armor, but his posture, his shaved cheeks, his heavily muscled forearms, the deep scar across the bridge of his broad nose, all suggested a military man. He took the heavy sword as if it weighed no more than a chicken's feather.

"Place your right hand forward, soldier," said the general.

The soldier looked at his leader with wonder now. There was nothing more to be done at this point than follow his commands; if he must die, he would die with honor. And honor meant obedience to one's superior. He put forward his right hand and waited.

Manilius looked directly into the man's eyes. "You will never again touch what is mine, soldier," he said, but he didn't hurry to move the weapon in his hand. Instead he waited for the man's hand to shake in fear, or for a plea to come from his mouth. But the soldier's hand remained steady, and Manilius smiled. "Good," he said, and then his eyes moved to the hand, and he tried to drive the sword in one motion across the man's knuckles, but because the sword was unfamiliar to him, he miscalculated. The blow struck cleanly into the man's wrist.

"By all the gods," said Manilius softly, over the man's uncontrollable screams. The soldier fell to his knees, clutching his wrist, and the hand that dangled from it. Blood pumped rhythmically from the severed blood vessels; but the hand itself hadn't been cut away from the wrist. Manilius was astonished at his own clumsiness. He supposed the man had moved before the sword cut into his skin, but even so—his blow should have been swifter. He cared nothing that the man would die; he was simply vexed at his swordmanship. Manilius had wanted to chop off the fingers of both hands, at the knuckles, and then toss him into the sea. But because he had hit high, and without enough speed, there was this awful mess of blood and pain.

He turned with annoyance to an aide. "Well, go on, cut his throat," he said, throwing the bloody sword, hilt first, to him.

Rachel remained near the ladder, her eyes staring straight over everyone's heads, toward the place where the sky met the sea. Manilius took a step closer to her and looked at her sunburned face and wild hair.

"You. What's your name, slave?" he said.

Rachel tried to answer, but she couldn't make sense of his question, though he had spoken in perfectly clear Greek. All she could feel was the dead man's half-severed hand clawing at her genitals, pumping blood over her body, trying to drag her down to a region worse than death; a region where the only emotion was terror, the only sensations were of redness filling one's vision and an endless pounding overwhelming one's brain. As if dissociated from her body, she saw the general smile at her through the sun and the sky and the sea and the blood; she felt his hand on her cheek; she noticed coolly that he was stripping away her tunic and underclothes until she stood naked on the deck, her sunburned skin much darker than her breast and belly and loins.

Only because her parents had been murdered that day did she think once more of trying to speak. Rachel felt she owed it to their honor to obey their wishes. Like a corpse unearthed to utter the words of some immaterial spirit, she spoke the words they had given her. "I am a jeweler," she said very softly in Greek, looking at the gold clasps in the general's toeless military shoes. "Not a brothel girl. I am very much more valuable as a jeweler, sir, because I know the ways of pearls and emeralds and gold in all its forms. I can make rings and talismans and I speak five languages and am honest and of good family. I am a jeweler, sir, and I know nothing of the ways of men."

Manilius listened to her entire soft speech, and smiled a very little smile. "Turn around, slave," he said, and when she was slow to move, he gently moved her himself, touching her only at the shoulders. When her back was turned to him, she heard him laugh, and then he slapped her backside, dismissing her.

"Wash her well," he said. "Then bring her to me. She will be my woman for the rest of this voyage."

Chapter
8

Buying a Jewish slave was a problematic investment. Able-bodied men without skills were cheap in those years of Pompey's conquests. Slaves poured in from Parthia, Syria, and Greece. Yellow-haired barbarians from Germany and Gaul, big-muscled men with painted bodies, were brought into the republic in endless lines, chained at the neck, and sold to the owners of Italian plantations and Spanish silver mines. Worked from first to last light, kept in chains throughout the night, these men had little reason to live. Spartacus's slave rebellion had been crushed a decade before; the memory of his rebels dying the slow death of crucifixion on six thousand crosses lingered among slave and free alike. With rebellion beaten out of them, these slaves lived short, nasty lives, and were replaced with cheap flesh from the next slave ship. As many as ten thousand lives were bought in a single auction after a conquest; as many as one hundred thousand captive slaves might pour into Italy in a month filled with triumphs.

Skilled slaves were more expensive. Greek tutors, trained in language and philosophy, always commanded a good price. Syrian actors, Egyptian courtesans, Macedonian leather workers were always in demand. One didn't want to sell a literate man, capable of the rigors of letter writing, or a physician capable of healing, to a marble quarry, or a mill, whose owners bought and used human flesh because it was cheaper than that of animals. So every shipment of slaves was sifted through by the secretaries or bailiffs of the businessmen who had paid to bring them to auction. Usually these subordinates were themselves slaves, and knew what to look for: physical beauty, grace, charm; an eagerness to please, to be subservient; a special skill; the knowledge of languages. An educated boy who played the flute would never end up in Lusitania, digging stones out of the earth in a line of chained slaves; a blond-haired beauty without a word of Greek or Latin would still never end up carrying water pails on her back to half-dead plantation workers.

So a young boy like David, son of Saul, fluent in seven languages, as familiar with Plato and Aristotle as with the Torah, capable of singing, able to copy and correct writing in Greek and Latin, must certainly bring a decent price at auction.

If only he hadn't been Jewish.

In that year, there were still few established Jewish families in Rome. David's notion that ten thousand or fifty thousand Jews lived in the great capital was an exaggeration built up by their commercial successes, disproportionate to their numbers, and by their great differences from the rest of the population. Since the days of Judah the Maccabee, nearly one hundred years ago, Jews had been coming to Rome; as representatives of the Judean state, as businessmen, and in the last dozen months, as slaves. The small Jewish community already resident in the city, foreigners eager to please its haughty rulers, were slow to proselytize among the pagans. That most upper-class Romans had only a ritualistic interest in their temple services, a duty to sacrifice and pay homage to the state and to the unity of the republic rather than to any sense of piety made little difference to the Jews of Rome. To them all religions outside their own were pagan; they defined the world as made up of Jew and Gentile, Our Nation and Strangers. Whether upper-class Romans were looking for inspiration outside their pagan rituals was of no interest to most Jews; to instruct the new masters of the world in the esoteric details of Jewish living seemed as pointless as teaching dogs to dance or birds to utter philosophical phrases.

Even when half the aristocracy seemed to be visiting Chaldean astrologers, or sitting at the feet of priests newly enslaved from Cappadocia or Mesopotamia, or haunting the booksellers for the latest scrolls to explain where one went after death, and where the soul lived before birth, the Jews didn't urge them into their small houses of worship, the synagogues they'd built on the right bank of the Tiber, where many of the poor and the newly freed classes lived.

But it was different with the Jewish slaves.

A slave had no privacy. The mystery of the Sabbath was quickly explained to the masters of Rome; the religious Jew would do no work every seventh day—and this in a time when the Romans followed an inaccurate calendar with ever-changing monthly units of time. Gentiles had no concept of the week. They broke up the month into smaller units based on when farmers came to market, either every eighth day or every tenth day. There was no notion of taking a rest on a day that was not a festival day, taken from the month in honor of a particular god. The notion of a seven-day cycle running throughout the year was just one more oddity of the Jewish slaves.

The mystery of Kashrut was quickly explained in similar fashion: no religious Jew would eat the meat of the pig, or taste oysters or crabs or clams. Their religious books forbade it. Some of their wise men believed that devils tempted one to break the Sabbath, to eat foods called unclean by the Torah. A reckoning would come in the life-to-come. Their wise books were circulated all around the world, in Greek as well as in Hebrew. Many Jewish slaves had these writings by heart, and if their masters asked, they would tell them the ways of their Law.

And so to buy a Jewish slave was risky.

He might very well prefer death to working on the Sabbath—and who heard of giving a slave freedom every seventh day? He might prefer starvation to eating foods good enough for a consul. He might infect the other slaves with his religious ardor, giving him something to live for other than the whims of his masters. Brotherhood was preached, and equality before God regardless of class. These were dangerous doctrines for free Romans to partake of; in a household where the slaves outnumbered the masters, they were inflammatory.

And so a handsome young Jew who might make a fine tutor often ended up on his knees in a copper mine; a man skilled in musical composition might be set to chopping vegetables, the tongue cut out of his mouth to ensure silence. Jewish doctors, philosophers, lawyers, and priests were bought and sold in the markets of Rome. But many were afraid to buy them, lest they disrupt the homes of their masters.

"I am part of a family," said David, son of Saul, to the elegant young man who had boarded the slave ship at Puteoli, one hundred and fifty miles south of Rome. From here, slaves would be sent overland to the capital, and in smaller ships to dozens of designations along Italy's western coastline.

"Your age, slave?" said the young man, listening to the cultured syllables of David's Greek.

"Fifteen, sir. But I am not alone on this ship, and in my studies of history, if I may be permitted to say so, it is not unheard of for whole families to be sold together, particularly when there is the chance of an eventual ransoming."

"Your name?" said the secretary, who had been free in Athens and was now a slave in Manilius's great suburban villa at Actium. But he was a slave who slept on soft linen, who ate the same food as his masters, and whose name, Eumenes, was uttered with respect by the scholars and philosophers who visited the general's learned wife Marcia.

"My name is David, son of Saul, who was murdered on this voyage, as was my mother, Mira, murdered without cause before five hundred witnesses."

"David," said Eumenes, with great kindness, for tears had started up in the young boy's eyes, tears that would have been laughed at or beaten down in a Roman household as unmanly. But Eumenes was Greek, and sentimental. He had been allowed to cry as a young boy, and to find beauty in poetry and the flowers of the fields. Carefully, he put down the wax tablets in which he had been etching notes on each of the slaves; later he would copy these notes onto papyrus in his artist's hand.

"There are laws concerning captives, are there not?" continued David through his tears. "I don't pretend to know the Roman law, but every civilized nation has a standard of behavior—"

"Silence, slave," said Eumenes. "Listen, if you want to live, and one day see your kinsmen. Do not criticize your masters and lecture them on their laws. They have the power of life and death over their property, and all that you must think of now is how to make yourself as good a piece of property as possible, so that you don't end up as a galley slave."

"My sister is still alive—"

"You will tell me this later, boy," said Eumenes. "What I want to know now is what I ask you. Do you know what this is in my hand?"

"The tablet? Do you think me an idiot, because Pompey conquered my city? I don't know a Jew who can't read and write."

"Have you ever heard the name Plato?"

David laughed, in spite of his misery, in spite of the iron ring about his ankle and the cacophony from the slaves on the deck. "Plato the Athenian?" said David. "What shall I tell you about him? About how he learned from Socrates or how he taught Aristotle? Would you like to hear of the mystical dialogues or the political dialogues—"

"You're very proud, slave." said Eumenes.

"Not so proud, sir," said David. "But if you ask me a question that is so simple—"

"What about one more difficult: Aristotle had a great library. What became of it?"

"It went to Theophrastus, his heir," said David easily. Then he screwed up his young face, remembering: "Apellicon of Teos had it later, but then it was lost to Greece when Sulla conquered Athens. I suppose it's in Rome now."

"I was there as a child," said Eumenes.

"In Aristotle's library?"

"Aristotle's been dead for nearly three hundred years."

"For two hundred and fifty-nine years, sir," said David. "If I may be allowed to speak. He died in Chalcis, at the age of sixty-two."

Eumenes said: "Are you some sort of Hebrew sage? A priest? A holy man?"

"I can remember," said David. "Words come to me from the scrolls I have read. It is not holy, but it is a gift from God."

Eumenes started at the mention of the Hebrew deity. Used to the invocation of a hundred gods on the slightest occasion—the god of ships for a crossing by ferry, the god of the phallus for a night of license, the god of thieves for a purloined apple—the secretary was daunted by the simple piety with which the word was uttered. He felt the uncomfortable sense of being in the presence of a knowledge thus far denied him. It was as if the boy had used the word "world" or "universe" and endowed it with meaning. Eumenes had looked into the Jewish Holy Books in their Greek translations. Often he had been confused by their labyrinthine logic, the twists and turns of arguments based on scrolls he had never read. Once he had abandoned all religion: there was nature, there were men; and the myriad gods were but testaments to man's imaginations. But now this credo had paled.

"A gift from which god?" said Eumenes. "From Athena, goddess of wisdom, or from Mnemosyne, mother of the Muses and goddess of memory? Or perhaps it was a gift from the god of words, or the god of books—"

David looked up at the young man's face. Beyond the mockery was a question and a fear. He remembered the words of Hosea: "Thou shalt know no god but me: for there is no savior besides me." But David didn't voice the words of the Torah. For the moment this man was his only friend in the world. "Athens was conquered twenty years ago. Were you at the library as an infant?"

"Not to read, boy," said Eumenes, who was himself only twenty-five. "My father showed me the library from the outside and the inside. I can still remember the way the light poured in at midday, with dozens of scholars hunched over their scrolls, ignorant of everything about them. I thought it was the most wonderful thing in the world. To read, I mean." Eumenes stopped himself. This was not the time for conversation with a Jewish slave. He picked up his tablet. "You speak Latin, of course?"

"Of course," said David.

Eumenes wondered if he would be suitable as a secretary. Marcia, the general's wife, would be glad of another Jewish scribe about whose religion she could question at length. Besides, he might be useful in copying her mediocre poetry into the scrolls she sent to her numerous literary friends. "Is your handwriting legible?"

"Not terribly so," said David easily, as if he had no idea how he was being judged, and for what purpose. "My sister has a lovely handwriting, but unfortunately only in Greek and Hebrew. I would imagine she could improve her Latin, but at the present time it's not her strong point."

"Do you know anything of medical value?"

"Only what I've read in books, sir."

"I am looking for your special skills, David," he said, with an exasperation that penetrated. "You will have to tell me why we should give you a place in a patrician's home."

"Why?" said David. "Well, sir. I am under the impression that the Jewish community will ransom me in any case. I don't suppose I would make a very good slave at all, as I am what the Torah calls a stiff-necked person, of a stiff-necked people."

"No one will ransom you, boy," said Eumenes.

"Sir, I am sorry, but the ways of my religion will force every Jew in Rome to come forth and ransom all of us here on this ship."

"This ship isn't going to Rome. And there's no big Jewish community that's going to ransom you. Listen, you are a slave, and will remain a slave. But I would like to help a young scholar get a position that will not kill him."

"I have family in Rome. Also a David. David ben-Yehoshua, perhaps you know him? He is the son of my father's brother—my first cousin and much older than me. He will surely ransom me—"

"No one will ransom you, you idiot, as no one ransomed me," said Eumenes. "You are brought here a slave, and you must make the best of it, do you understand?"

"But *you* are not a slave?" said David.

"Of course I am a slave," said Eumenes. "Taken with what was left of my family and sold with my brother and sister whom I have never again seen."

"But that's not possible, you're a great gentleman."

"I have not seen them since I was five, and they were younger. I don't know what names they go by, or whether they're dead, or in chains, or on some foreign throne. Now please, give me a reason to put in my book why the general Manilius should keep you for his own household staff at Actium. It is right by the sea, and our mistress is very pleasant."

David shook his head at Eumenes, trying to maintain his composure: "No, sir. I am sorry. I won't leave this place, I can't leave this ship, without my sister. My parents are dead, and she is my responsibility." He could feel the sense of loss building up in his heart, and with it a weakness in his body that led to tears. David tried to keep his eyes on Eumenes, to fix them with his intelligence, to make point after point, as if this were an argument in a study room. "We were in chains together," he insisted, ignoring Eumenes' pitying look. "On the road from Jerusalem to Joppa, and on this ship, and when she was taken away they say she was given to the men like a whore, but that is not possible, the Romans are famous for their laws. They will avenge the murder of my parents, and allow me to see my sister alive and well. We must be in the same household. We are both very useful. She knows a great many things. She's beautiful and sings very well, and she has a handwriting that's beyond compare. Perhaps your mistress has need of a maid. I would be happy to teach young children. Even though I am young, I have tutored before in Judea and not just Jews, but the children of Syrians, and also my family, all of us, we are great jewelers. We are skilled in gold and gems of all kinds, my sister

Rachel especially. She is a wonderful jeweler, and that is what she is best suited for. If we can leave this ship together, may God pour blessings on you forever and ever."

"There is no need for you to cry," said Eumenes. "The Romans do not like to see tears coming from a man."

He had almost put his hand on the young boy's head when he felt his master's presence coming up from behind him. The rush of quiet in the murmuring of the slaves, the tramp of booted feet on deck unaccompanied by voices, the sense of fear reaching toward him like a quickening current were all Manilius's doing. Though Eumenes was a valued slave, he knew himself to be despised by the general; he knew Manilius could whimsically dispose of him regardless of years of service. An ordinary master might have already freed him; under Manilius's rule he might be sold, he might be beaten, he might be killed in a drunken rage.

"You must be careful with these," said Manilius to Eumenes, not bothering to greet him or inquire after his own wife after a year of travel. "Some of these Jews have skills. It would be a pity to get less than their price."

"Of course, General," said Eumenes. "It's very good to see you again, sir. The gods have been good to you—"

"I've been good to the gods," said Manilius.

"Will you be wanting more scribes for the library, sir?"

"I want more girls for fucking," said Manilius. "As for the library, if it makes my wife happy, you may keep one or two, but only if they are pleasant to look at."

"Yes, sir," said Eumenes.

"And no more blondes. I fancy dark girls. After all those brothels filled with Gauls, it's been a pleasure to taste some of these Jewish cunts. There's one I'm keeping that I've already found. You can get me a few more candidates and bring them around for an inspection."

David couldn't hear Eumenes' respectful answer to the general's abruptly turning back. As the secretary of the great man's house smiled at him and expressed his satisfaction that David, son of Saul, could indeed join Manilius's slaves at Actium, David could only hear the general's filthy words echoing in his memory. Somehow the Lord God, God of Abraham, Isaac, and Jacob, God of Elijah, God of Job too, had not only allowed the taking of Jerusalem, the humiliation of Judea, the enslavement of one thousand of

His Chosen People, the murder of David's God-fearing parents, but He had insisted, in His infinite wisdom, to make David's sister Rachel a whore.

The young boy felt his faith, hard and pure and tempered in the flames of experience, crumble from the inside; it could no longer live in his loveless heart. All he felt was rage, all he longed for was violence, a chance to be free of his chains with a knife in his hand.

"Did you hear what I said, you ungrateful boy?" said Eumenes. "You will go to Actium, and I shall look and see if your sister can be given a position there as well."

"Thank you, sir," said David. But he knew that Rachel had already been granted a position, and for this, and for his parents, he would break the Lord's commandments, he would lie and steal and commit murder. "I shall be an obedient slave, and make you glad in your choice."

"But you must do me one favor in return," said Eumenes softly. "You must teach me of your Holy Books, you must tell me the story of the One God, and how He is different from all others. You must teach me what it means to be a Jew."

"I will teach you," said David, but he could barely talk, so full was his passion, so strong his desire to be one with his murderous fate.

Chapter
9

This was how Rachel, daughter of Saul the *Cohen* of Jerusalem was prepared for lovemaking:

A barefoot Gaul, Latin-speaking and loyal to Manilius for a decade, took hold of her at the right wrist, bent low, and pulled her onto his broad back. When he stood straight, the young girl was still and limp, like a fresh-killed deer. When the Gaul moved, his shoulders arched with pleasure, feeling the soft skin of her belly along the nape of his neck. He pulled on the wrist and brought his free arm through her hanging legs, so that the crook of his elbow rubbed against her sparse, dark pubic hair.

"I can feel your bones," said the Gaul. "You will soon fatten up, I can tell you that. There's not a better master than Manilius if you do what he demands."

Rachel heard the words, but her attention focused on the deck as it swayed and bounced beneath the Gaul's easy stride. She felt her nakedness, felt her inability to move, felt her shame; but these were felt from a distance. This moment was a piece of her fate, and she watched herself, a figure in a dream, ghostlike and ethereal, dead, or nearly so.

"Easy now, girl," said the Gaul, and she felt herself begin to slide off his back, feet first, and when her feet hit the deck, she realized that she had been taken out of the sun, into shade. "Why so pale, girl?" said the blond-haired man raising her chin with his thick-fingered hand. His eyes were blue, shot through with green, and

Rachel remembered that there were demons with eyes that changed color, from blue to red and from orange to yellow. He came closer, very gently bringing his comfortably bearded face to her.

"Why do you have a beard?" she said. She spoke in Aramaic, the common language of the simple Jews who had never mastered Greek, and with so little emphasis that her words might as well have been a collective sigh. It was not a strange question for that moment. All the Romans aboard shaved their cheeks religiously. Most Jews were bearded, and those men who shaved daily when in Jerusalem had grown beards during the march to the sea, and the days on the water. So complete was her state of shock that she could no longer see the complex world, made up of a myriad of men and events, with any understanding; she could not bear to look at it whole. One moment, one man, one piece of the world at a time was all she could absorb. It was enough to dwell on the scent of the sea or the shadow of the mast on the deck or the fact of a friendly beard on the face of the oppressor.

Now the beard moved to envelop her, and thin lips smiled as they placed themselves about the dry listless lines of her mouth. He was kissing her, but what she felt was the taste of unfamiliar herbs; she wondered which of the Romans' vast array of spices had been used in the man's last meal. His tongue tasted the inside of her mouth, and she felt the violation of this briefly; soon it was enough to imagine what he must recognize in her mouth: barley, leeks, lentils.

"Come on, my beauty, your smell is good enough for me, but we must prepare you for a nobleman." Her foot had been placed into cold water, and as she turned to look at the tub into which the Gaul was pushing her, she saw her other foot lift and step in. This second foot had worn the chain, and as the water had been drawn from the sea, the salt shocked the chafed and bruised skin. The pain startled her, brought tears to her eyes, and it was at that moment that she realized that the Gaul had his hands on her breasts and was forcing her into the tub before a small crowd of admiring sailors.

"Where is David?" she said, the shame reminding her of the last person in the world who could share it. But the Gaul didn't respond to her words, spoken in a language indecipherable to him, and continued to push her into the cold bath. She could hear the pleasured laughter of the sailors as he leaned on her shoulders, forcing her into the water up to her neck. Now he kissed her again, and she felt his hand touch her neck, move gently to her breasts, and then less gently his fingers closed about first right then left nipple, and he spoke more words, and these were no longer in Latin, but in his own outlandish tongue.

"Please, you must tell me: where is David?" she said, but the beard came close, and the tongue drove into her mouth, and all at once she felt her head forced under the stinging water and held there. The Gaul pulled her head up for air and surprised her with another kiss; now his blue eyes were brighter and narrowed, the laughter of the others mingled with shouts and cheers.

"Come on, whore," he said in Latin, and he pulled at her under-arms so that she was half out of the water. "On your knees, you slut." The Gaul scrubbed at her thick curls with both hands, forcing her first to kneel, then to squat on her toes, then turning her about, he rubbed at her smooth skin with a rough cloth. "You are a delicious baby, you are as sleek as an infant, you are made for men's pleasure, there is no doubt about that, you are made for us to enjoy."

Rachel was pulled completely out of the tub, pushed into a patch of sun, feeling the gentle breeze chill her to the bone. She looked away from the Gaul, who was now anointing her body with oil; not content with fondling her breasts, he rubbed the oil along her inner thighs, then touched her where the soldier had touched her only minutes before. But she allowed all this, ignored all the sensations God had given to her body to recognize love, and looked instead at the quieted sailors. Whatever the Gaul was doing to her excited them, brought them nearly to what Rachel knew as a state of worship and reverence.

"This cunt's no bigger than the eye of a needle," said the Gaul, shaking his head. "She's so dry, the general's going to have to break into her with a spear point."

"I want my brother," said Rachel softly, her gaze resting on one of the sailors, smaller than the rest, his eyes both voracious and ashamed. The Gaul scraped at her oiled body with a strigil, pulling away the days of grime, but the girl felt nothing of the purification that had always accompanied the use of this tool. Of course, the last time she had been cleansed, a slave had pulled at the strigil, and she had been free; now it was she who was the slave, and the soldier who cleaned her did so only to prepare her for an act of degradation.

"You should give her your head of whore's hair," said one of the braver sailors. The women of Gaul supplied the Romans with their blond hair, bought up in mass by the guild of brothel keepers. Blond wigs were used almost exclusively by prostitutes. Some cities under Roman jurisdiction insisted on the wig as an identifying mark for those women who plied their trade outside the brothel walls.

"It is only because the Romans admire our hair so much that they give it to their whores," said the soldier, not at all riled by the sailor. "Their wives are brunettes, and are given nothing but contempt. Their whores are the women they want. That is why they get jewels and fine clothing and the beautiful hair of my country. You cannot insult me by calling my hair the hair of a whore, when whores are what your masters desire, when whores are the only women loved by Rome."

Rachel wasn't sure how much of this speech she heard, and how much she spun out of the terrible memories of that day. But she remembered that she was not taken naked into the general's presence. She was given a silk mantle, woven by the women of Cos; even in her dazed state, Rachel could see that the transparent fabric served to exaggerate the shape of her breasts and thighs. Her wet hair had fallen into extravagant curls, and the scent of the olive oil hung over her not like a tawdry perfume but like a bride's innocent odor; fresh, and young, and clean.

She was taken up to the "house" built up on the deck. Whether she walked or was carried on the Gaul's broad back she didn't remember; but what lingered in her memory was the face of her master when he saw her enter his room.

Manilius's brutal face lit up with a joy that nearly transformed it. He was so pleased by the vision of this sixteen-year-old girl that for half a moment, he had the air of a suitor, about to trip up on some witty remark.

"Leave the slave," he said to the man who had brought her, and his voice was gentle, caressing. He got up from his couch and walked the three steps to where Rachel stood in her transparent silk. "I must be careful with you," he said. "You are a little too beautiful." He pulled her into his arms and kissed her softly, more softly and sweetly than the Gaul. Against all reason, she could feel his heart go out to hers, his murderer's heart. "I bought this gown for one of my women. I have many women, all slaves. They are all beautiful, and none of them rule me. I make certain that they remember that they are not wives, or concubines, or mistresses. Slaves. I have beautiful slaves, and do with them what I please, and none of them can get me into their power, no matter how strong their beauty, now matter how much they claim to love me."

Manilius stepped away from her now, stripping off his tunic with one easy movement. He placed himself on the edge of the couch and motioned for her to approach. Rachel did so. Her eyes were wide open, and saw quite clearly the demon beneath the surface of his smooth skin, the evil spirit who had without hesitation hacked away a man's hand. "Go on," said Manilius sharply. "You know what you must do. You must please me, girl."

Rachel slowly moved her hands to where the gown was fastened at her neck. But she was not quick enough for the general. He pulled her close to him painfully, twisting her wrist, and tore at the silk so that it fell off her back in a liquid instant.

Rachel, still standing, closed her eyes.

There had been a boy, of the family of Malachi, who used to speak with her brother in the streets of Jerusalem, but only so that he could catch Rachel's eye. David had told her of the boy's infatuation, and Mira, their mother, had said that his family was of the best stock, and wealthy and pious. Because he was a handsome boy, and witty with her brother, she had spoken of him to her girl friends, many of whom were betrothed. Friends of hers who had already married never spoke to her about the marriage bed; neither to express pleasure nor pain. But she knew there was a bed, knew there was a lying down, knew there was a penetration, and that all of it was part of God's commandment to His Chosen People to be fruitful and multiply.

"Bitch!" said Manilius, his voice still without harshness. Rachel was flat on her back, and she could feel the powerful man's knees resting on her wide-open thighs; she could feel his wet phallus, but could not imagine its size or shape.

She tried to hold on to her images of Jerusalem, the light golden in the clear mountain air. The boy of the family of Malachi was tall, and with an auburn beard, still patchy with youth. When he looked at her, there had been love in his eyes, and now she tried to imagine love was weighing down on her thighs, that passion and desire, not lust and loathing, was forcing itself into her vagina.

124

"I should break you with a stick," said Manilius. "You might move, girl. You might pretend to be alive."

She didn't know if the hurt he was causing her was deliberate, or the natural accompaniment of this act. Her body felt assaulted along its entire length. His toenails were long, and scratched her shins; his hands pulled at the roots of her hair; his muscular chest and belly were as heavy as boulders on her frail frame; and as he moved more and more violently into her vagina, the pain seemed to centralize itself into a single intense region, red and enraged and trying to push back the invader. There was nothing of love here. In place of endearments, Manilius spoke out complaints in his silky voice: she was dry, she was still, she was pushing him back, she was small, she was hurting him.

But few of these words penetrated.

His penis felt like an instrument of torture, his breath stank of garlic, and the weight of his body seemed to increase with each passing moment. It was impossible to keep Jerusalem in her mind. She opened her eyes and saw the scar along his broad nose, saw the rawness of his shaved cheeks, and hated him. She tried to harness the hate, to draw strength from it so she could repulse him, turn back his body, expel him from her private parts. But the more she fought, the more he seemed to grow strong; and with his strength came greater pain.

"Oh yes," he said, as if he knew she was struggling, knew she was crumbling, knew his mastery would take her wherever he wanted to go. He kept at her, driving his penis further into her vagina until he was as close to her as he would ever be. He was joined to her. She felt his heartbeat against her own; she felt him begin to twist and move inside her, slowly, easily, as if now that he had conquered the space, he wanted to make it completely his.

And then, as if belabored by a devil, beset by a fire too great to repulse, Rachel allowed her body to rest. No longer actively pushing against him, her pain lessened with speed. She felt the muscles along her thighs loosen, the tension along her forehead fade against the force of fatigue. All this shamed her: to give in to a rapist, to a demon, to evil; to allow her body freedom from pain she had acceded to sin.

"By the gods," said Manilius. "By all the gods."

Once more she was fighting him, and the pain returned, larger than before.

His breath came faster, more urgently, and she felt the unknown

125

mass that was the man's penis push back, grow large, thrust slowly and painfully, and than all at once, with violence, as if all his desire was to break apart the walls of her body.

"By the gods," said Manilius. "You tight little bitch. Great Jupiter's balls! You miserable, murdering, beautiful little bitch!"

As the man moved, faster and faster, driving his penis through her, she felt the pain begin to lift her away. Soon she had no more sensation of his long toenails, his heavy bodily weight, his pulling at her hair and shoulders and neck.

Finally Manilius slowed his own rhythm.

"You're very nice," he said. "I fixed you good, and now you're very nice."

He was inside her, pressing her shoulders to the couch, smiling into her black eyes, as if they were lovers, instead of rapist and victim. Rachel watched the man's lips twist out of control: the smile was gone, and in its place was a kind of happiness she had never seen on a man's face.

The general was moving inside her again.

His phallus felt like the trunk of a tree, like a metallic instrument, like an inanimate object dipped into the center of procreation. He was breathing wildly, and his penis seemed to be growing in strength and size with each new breath. He moved faster, slamming his pelvis into hers, expelling his breaths with such force and rapidity that she thought his heart must burst.

But then he exploded, inside her, unexpectedly. A hot stream burst into her, broken by stabs and thrusts. Manilius was for a moment not the master. He shivered uncontrollably. He held on to her shoulders and rattled her body, and then all at once, pulled back, pulled out of her, and laughed out loud.

"By every god who's fucked! By every cunt, by every cock that's ever fucked. You—" He couldn't go on, so funny did he find the spectacle of her blood on the couch, the tears running down her cheeks.

He got to his feet, threw on his tunic, and rang the bell. "Get dressed, slave," he said to her, still laughing and shaking his head at the excess of pleasure she had given him. When a moment later his aide entered, Rachel was still naked, still unable to move. Worse than the throbbing pain was her unending humiliation. Only someone possessed of the demons could have allowed this to happen and still want to live.

126

"Feed her," said Manilius. "I'll want her again."

It was the closest thing to a compliment he paid her throughout the voyage.

When Eumenes came to collect her two weeks later, she was chained to three other young women of Judea, all of whom had been raped by their new master during the trip across the sea. Two of them were widows, but the third, Michal, had been a virgin like Rachel. For days, Michal would say nothing, not even cry out loud, even though tears would run steadily down her cheeks. She was fair-haired, fifteen, and shapely, but so miserable and broken that even a monster would find it unpleasant to force his way with her. Rachel's shame grew under Michal's shadow. Manilius sampled each of the women and took one of the widows twice to his bed. But it was Rachel that he wanted, day after day. Rachel pleased him. She knew that his lust was wild with her, that great shouts and cries came to his lips, regardless of whether he offered her praise or thanks or a facsimile of tenderness. She was a slave who was also a whore, and it was her great sin that her body didn't reject the abomination of its master. It was her great sin that her body pleased him; she knew that the *shedim*, the thousand devils of foreign lands, would repay this sin with an eternity of torment in the world-to-come.

"Which of you is the daughter of Saul, the *Cohen?*" said the secretary Eumenes. He was accompanied by the black slave who had first freed her from the chain that had linked her to her family.

"I am Rachel, daughter of Saul, the *Cohen*," she said in the Greek that Eumenes had spoken. For half a moment, she thought she felt Michal's sad eyes turn to her, at the mention of "*Cohen*," the priestly designation. But perhaps it was only her imagination that the miserable girl would turn to a daughter of the priestly caste, horrified by her debasement. Later Rachel would hear that the three of them, Michal and the two widows, would be sold to a plantation owner in the south: not even worthy of a city brothel, they'd end their lives servicing the pathetic lusts of farm slaves, field whores for filthy barbarians.

"Unchain her," he said peremptorily to the black slave.

"Daughter of Saul, murdered by the Romans. Daughter of Mira, murdered by the Romans," she said quietly, in Hebrew, to the women from whom she was being released. But none of them responded. They seemed to know that she was being selected for some greater station, befitting her beauty and her ability to sin. Before she was taken from the ship, a metal collar was closely fitted to her slender neck. On it was her master's name and the name of his villa at Actium. Other slaves were being fitted with these collars, men and women, perhaps a dozen all told; these were bakers, barbers, cooks, house servants of all kinds. Rachel wondered if she would be listed on the secretary's roll as Manilius's whore.

There were scores of wagons and carriages waiting for the ship to empty its cargo, and as Rachel followed her fellow slaves to Manilius's train of vehicles, she craned her head for one last chance to glimpse her brother. Only the endless sorrow over her parents had stopped up her misery over David. Even if she would not see him for years, there was always the possibility of meeting. But her mother and father were simply gone. "David," she said softly to the mass of faceless slaves left behind. "Be healthy and well till we meet again."

But then his voice, his touch, his familiar scent blew up at her, as if in a dream, or in a conjuring. Rachel turned about violently, and David had come up to her, red-faced with exertion or embarrassment, breaking up the orderly line of slaves.

"Rachel," he said, touching her elbow, and then quickly withdrawing the contact of his hand. It was as if he had touched fire.

"David, darling," she said. "How in the world—?"

"We are bought by the same master," he said. The line continued to move, and he stepped in front of her, so that she would follow. When she brought her fingers to the nape of his neck, she felt him recoil.

"Thank God you're here," said Rachel, scarcely able to believe that it was really David who preceded her in line and not some wished-for phantom of her fevered brain. "At least we will have each other."

"Yes," said David, and when the line of slaves stopped for a moment, he turned to look at his sister, as if to examine her, judge her. But it wasn't this that Rachel saw, but something deeper, some terrible wound.

"David," she said. "What have they done to you?"

Like the other slaves selected by Manilius, David had been given a fresh tunic and a bath in seawater. The metal collar was as ugly and humiliating about his neck as it was about any of theirs. But the change Rachel saw in her brother had nothing to do with this. The intelligence that had always gleamed in his eyes now burned there; what had been youthful and whimsical had been replaced by something old and steady. He had always been young for his fifteen years, in spite of all his learning. Now he seemed old, like a teenage soldier who had suffered through carnage; like an orphan; like a man who had lost faith.

"It will be all right, my sister," he said, pulling her close as they tramped in bare feet to an open wagon. Soldiers hovered about them, though Eumenes and Manilius were nowhere to be seen. "We will live for vengeance," he said, speaking the Hebrew words with force.

"It is to God that we turn for vengeance, my brother."

" 'I will make my arrows drunk with blood,' " said David, quoting the Holy Book of Deuteronomy. "I will make my own revenge, my sister."

"But what have they done to you?" she insisted, wanting to offer comfort where none was desired. "I asked for you, and no one would tell me where you were. I didn't know if you were dead or alive. You could be as dead as mother and father. We have so much to be thankful for, praise the Lord. I felt that you were alive, but I didn't know if this was a feeling sent by a demon to confuse me and thwart my soul. Even if you were alive—and not to be able to see you—not to know it! David, we should offer a prayer of thanksgiving. We have survived while others have died around us, others who were more pious and worthy. David, give us a prayer to say, something in praise of the Lord for letting us see each other again."

Her brother's eyes widened, as if searching a thousand scrolls of Hebrew verse locked in his memory; then they narrowed, and his lips lifted slightly at the corners of his mouth.

" 'I was at ease, but He has broken me asunder,' " said David, quoting Job.

"That is not a prayer of thanksgiving," said Rachel.

" 'Whoso offers prayers, glorifies me,' " quoted David from the Book of Psalms. "I will not offer prayers while the general Manilius lives. When he is murdered, I will offer prayers. I will offer prayers of thanksgiving for having spilled his blood."

They were crowded in the wagon, and the ride on the famous

Roman roads was rough. Over the sound of the wheels there was little chance for talk. A soldier sat up front with the driver, and the slaves could look out at the colors of spring. They passed lakes, an oak forest, and orchards, rising in the foothills of some great mountain. There was little traffic on the road, but many conveniences along the way. Benches seemed to appear around every bend; every half hour would be another way station to change horses or buy refreshment. There were inns at frequent intervals, and the soldier pointed to one and announced that it was the place where he had had his first woman. In Rome every inn was a brothel, thought Rachel, as the object of every man's desire was a whore. The slaves of Judea recognized olive and carob trees, but strange varieties of oak and fir and chestnut accentuated their own foreignness; they were aliens in a rich and forbidding land.

"I have heard," said a slave who had been a baker in Jerusalem and would now be a baker in Manilius's villa, "that fugitive slaves are branded on their foreheads."

"They chop off your toes if you try and run away," said one of the women.

"And where would you run?" said another woman, pale and gray, and therefore unsuited for whoring. Rachel watched her admiringly. She must be possessed of some special skill discovered by Eumenes for his master's pleasure. "Would you run across the sea? Would you run to the refuge of a synagogue? Would you ask the nearest kindhearted Roman to please take off your inconvenient collar? Assuming, of course, that he even speaks Greek!"

They all fell silent after that, listening to the clattering wheels on the roadbed built by slaves. It grew dark, and the scent of the land was strange after all the days at sea. They were hungry, and no one came to feed them. Even sleep was denied the slaves. With their destination so near, and their fate so unknown, none could still their hearts enough to give in to fatigue.

Her brother broke the silence of many minutes.

"It is good that they chop off your toes if you try and run," said David. "And good that they brand your forehead if you try and run. And good that they have put metal collars on our necks and removed our shoes and left soldiers to guard us, because it tells us that in great Rome, slaves do not always remain so. There would be no laws, no terrible penalties if the offenses didn't occur. Do not forget that Spartacus's slaves could have toppled Rome. And do not forget that our own country is great and ancient. Only ten years ago Judea and its queen ruled Samaria and Edom, Moab and Transjordan. Gadara, Pell, Gerasa, Raphia, and Gaza were ours. No Roman walked through Galilee, and the Temple in Jerusalem wasn't profaned by the pagans. We had the greatest Jewish kingdom since King Solomon ruled nine hundred years ago. The strongest."

"Babylon too was strong," said the baker.

"And it is strong again," said David. "There is always a Babylon, even when its name is Greece, when its name is Rome."

Another slave spoke up, a young man with a rough-hewn face. But like most of the captives, he was learned in the Torah, and the words of Isaiah came easily to his lips: " 'Babylon, Babylon is fallen. And all the graven images of her gods He has broken unto the ground.' "

Rachel could feel her brother move away from the slaves around him, move closer into himself. He was tired of the words of the prophets, tired of the after-the-fact rationalizations for why God had abandoned His Chosen People. " 'The Lord has raised us up prophets in Babylon,' " said David with the easy arrogance of youth. "Shall we quote the Torah at each other as they pull on our chains, while they murder our parents and rape our sisters?"

He didn't look at her as he spoke, but Rachel felt his fury as if it were directed at her. It was as if he had slapped her, as if he had been there, looking over her shoulder when Manilius had driven his sex into her body, possessing her, and was now calling her to task.

The baker spoke again, and his words had the authority of experience, as if he had witnessed the toppling of cities, the crushing of empires under the weight of God's displeasure. " 'Babylon, the glory of kingdoms, the beauty of the Chaldees' excellency, shall be as when God overthrew Sodom and Gomorrah,' " he said, quoting the words of Isaiah.

"Isaiah," said David. "If only Isaiah could have seen the glory of Judea while it was still strong."

Rachel spoke tentatively, wanting the words to come from her love for David and not from her anger. "Judea wasn't strong in faith," she said.

"Do not lecture us, my sister. Faith is for the faithful. I have no reason for great faith in anything except my hand," he said. "That is the faith of the Romans, and it has given them the world."

The wagon's horses were drawn suddenly to a halt. Ahead of

131

them the first of the wagons had found the dark roadway leading to Manilius's villa. Rachel's knowledge of the Torah wasn't extensive, but she and all the others knew the great words of the Psalmist, and its lugubrious Hebrew melody.

" 'By the rivers of Babylon,' " she began, and her metal-collared head swung into the rhythm of the song. " 'There we sat down, yea, we wept, when we remembered Zion.' "

Soon the whole wagon, even as it entered the villa's grounds, rocked with the chanting of the Jewish slaves, singing the ancient words of longing and defiance.

Chapter
10

A week after her arrival at the villa of Manilius, Rachel was called from the slave quarters to the main house. The slave who had been sent to bring her was very small, with fine bones and gray eyes. She wore no metal collar, because she worked for Manilius's wife, Marcia, and the great lady trusted her slaves or sold them at a loss.

"May I ask where you're taking me?" said Rachel pleasantly, speaking in Greek. The slave looked at her briefly, without contempt or interest. It was as if a stone or a bit of deadwood had suddenly burst forth in talk, and she was far too sophisticated to believe that such a thing could be. "I am not trying to be impertinent," continued Rachel as mildly as she could, wondering if perhaps Greek was the wrong language to use with the imperious slave. "But I would take it as a great kindness if you would tell me some news of my brother, David, son of Saul, the Judean? He came at the same time I did, and I've not heard a word about his whereabouts."

They walked along a path of crushed marble, bordered by flowering trees, encompassing a series of man-made ponds. The slave didn't turn to look at her this time, but simply dragged at her elbow, pulling her away from a huge sundial and along a smooth-paved way past a swimming pool and athletic court. Overshadowing these was a great slender tower, perhaps for looking at the stars, or looking down on the mere mortals who worked the vast estate in bond-

133

age. Rachel assumed that she was being taken to Manilius. That would explain the silence of the slave, the hatred beneath the hauteur. She tried to steel herself for his touch, for the terrible things he would say to her in his sexual pride.

"Is it the master who's wanting me?" she said, against her will, trying to hold back her fear with speech. Manilius hadn't sent for her since she'd come to the villa. Every girl in her tiny slave quarters had been working since the first day they'd arrived, except for Rachel. It had become clear to them that the nature of her work would be occasional, that she would be otherwise pampered. When they returned to their pallets long after nightfall, exhausted with drudgery and the abuse of the older slaves, they turned their resentment on her. Rachel had no response to their insults. She was a whore, and worthy of contempt; she could always take her life, though her God forbade it.

The slave walked more quickly, taking her through a back porch, hung with vines, and into a wing of the house that smelled of perfume. Incense burned from sconces and in bowls set up before the proud bellies of fat stone gods. They walked on mosaics of tile and marble, under high ceilings, gilded and intricate with stories told in pictures. Carpets hung from the walls, silk brocades ruffled in the breeze coming off the sea. Frescoes adorned walls that caught the best light, with colors more brilliant than those of nature. Statues of gods and heroes lined a wide corridor, with windows letting in the sun from west and east; this led into a simple atrium, with a view of the Mediterranean far below. Crossing this atrium, the wind whipped at them, and Rachel felt suddenly cold in her silk mantle. Only she of all the slaves was dressed in so expensive, and so revealing, a fabric, and it accentuated her disgraceful position in the great house.

They entered a small drawing room, with what seemed like mother-of-pearl inlaid into parts of the ceiling and walls. A brilliantly colored representation of the signs of the Zodiac took up both walls of the long corridor that led to a spacious room, brilliant with sunshine. Rachel had to squint to see the woman sitting under the south windows, reading a papyrus scroll.

"Madam," said the slave. "I bring you Rachel, daughter of Saul, the Judean."

"Thank you," said the woman, remaining at her desk. She was dressed in white linen, with gold rings on every finger, her hair as dark as Rachel's but long and straight, and twisted into a fashion-able knot at the back of her head. "Please, come closer, girl," she said to Rachel, and as Rachel did so, she noticed the thin lines of gold embroidered into the woman's dress: this could be no one but Manilius's wife, Marcia. She had dark green eyes, and wore rouge on her cheeks and paint on her lips. A wax tablet and stylus lay to one side of her opened scroll, and in the back of the room two scribes were copying texts with patient care. "How old are you, Rachel?" said the great lady.

Carefully, in her best Greek accent, Rachel told her that she was sixteen.

"Why are you wearing that awful collar about your pretty neck?" said Marcia. Rachel didn't know an answer to this question. All the new slaves wore Manilius's dread name about their necks, and Marcia's imperious slave quickly told her this in her sharp-toned way: almost as if to say that it was clearly the fault of the slaves that they had this burden to bear.

"You will have them removed, today," said Marcia.

"Yes, madam," said the slave.

"Are you hungry, girl?" said Marcia, getting up from her bench and coming around the desk to look more closely at Rachel.

"No, madam," said Rachel.

"You're very beautiful," said Marcia. "I can see why my husband has bought you." She paused, and when there was no response from the girl, she continued: "Do you love my husband?"

"I am a captive and a slave," said Rachel.

"You are still allowed to answer the question," insisted Marcia. "Do you love Manilius?"

"No, madam."

"Do you hate him then?"

Rachel found her eyes drifting over the great lady's face to a wall of cases, stuffed with scrolls. Her brother would know the answers to these questions, as he knew the answers to most questions. In a moment, he would understand what Marcia wanted to hear from her husband's whore, twenty years younger than herself; but Rachel was perplexed.

"Do you hate him? I won't punish you for telling me what you feel," said Marcia. "Just answer me with the truth."

"I hate him," said Rachel.

"Good," said Marcia, walking about the girl, looking up and

down her shapely body in its meretricious silk wrapping. "Now please tell me why you hate my husband, the great general, this asset to mighty Pompey and therefore to the Senate and people of Rome."

"I hate him," said Rachel. She hated him for the deaths of her parents, for the murder of her brother's soul. "I hate him," she said again, not realizing that she had repeated the words, and she felt a sharp stab of discomfort in her heart, as if a spirit had raised a tiny fist against the center of her being.

" 'You that love the Lord, hate evil,' " said Marcia, her Greek words mimicking the Psalmist's Hebrew in a frail approximation of the original's power. But Rachel recognized the words: no Roman spoke of the Lord unless it was a borrowed speech of her own people. "You agree that he is evil?"

"Yes, madam," said Rachel.

" 'There is a time to love and a time to hate,' " said Marcia. From Psalms she had turned to her latest Hebrew Holy Book, and pride showed clearly in her handsome face. "Your brother is correcting my translation. I have the Septuagint, but it is not the same as the Hebrew. And Ecclesiastes is too profound to learn in an incorrect translation."

Rachel wondered if the woman might be crazy, to speak so directly and earnestly about hate in a manner that brought mistress and slave on the same side, and that side was against her husband. And if this weren't bad enough, to violate the laws of wifely loyalty and obedience, but to do so while pedantically—and flippantly—discussing the merits of literature seemed the mark of one who was crazed. But how else could one married to Manilius be?

"Elais," said Marcia sharply to the slave who had brought Rachel. "Bring Eumenes."

"You wish to be alone with the new slave?" said Elais, the imperious slave, her tone once again making a statement that was clearer than her words.

"Bring Eumenes at once," said Marcia. Elais bowed and left them quickly. "Do you know the Holy Books?" said Marcia.

"Yes," said Rachel. "Not perfectly well, but well enough—"

"Come, sit," said Marcia, drawing her around the desk in the brilliant sunshine and urging her down on the hard bench. She clapped her hands sharply, and one of the scribes hurried up from where he sat with bowed head and brought her a tightly rolled scroll. "Open it," said Marcia, and when Rachel did so, she saw that it was Hebrew, written in a fine hand. "It's the Book of Daniel," said Marcia excitedly. "You will read me the first and second verses. Where it talks about the Lord of the Jews, the One God."

Rachel swallowed her nervousness, understanding that this was an opportunity, that this woman was a source of power and protection: already she had countermanded an order of her husband's. Perhaps she would really soon be free of her metal collar. Rachel read the Hebrew phrases, and translated them as quickly as she could into Greek.

"Jehoiakim, King of Judah, was in the third year of his rule when Nebuchadnezzar, King of Babylon, attacked Jerusalem, and put it under siege. The Lord, the One God, delivered Jehoiakim, King of Judah, into the power of the King of Babylon."

"Now stop," said Marcia excitedly. "That's the point. The Lord, your Lord, delivered your king into the hands of the enemy king."

"Yes, madam."

"Good," said Marcia. "Now, tell me. Do you know the story of the fox and the grapes?"

"No, madam."

"Excellent. I shall tell it to you. It is the story of an ancient storyteller, a slave from Phrygia. His name was Aesop. He lived five hundred years ago, and he understood the speech of animals. Every animal has a special language, and he alone of all men knew every one: how the fox threatened, how the deer talked of love, how the sheep whispered with fear. Well, anyway, this is one of his stories. A fox, a little fox was trying to get at some grapes. They were very sweet. He could see that quite clearly, and naturally he was excited about the possibility of stealing a great bunch for himself to eat. But they were up high on the vine and he was a pretty small fox. So he jumped for them. He jumped once, twice, three times, each time higher, but never high enough. And he couldn't reach the sweet grapes. It was impossible for him because he was too small and weak. And so do you know what he did?"

"Madam," said Eumenes, walking into the library with the air of a free man, of an equal. But his words were courtly. "You do me honor to ask for me. How may I be of service?"

"One moment, Eumenes, I am telling the child a story," said Marcia. "You do want to hear how it ends, do you not?"

"Yes, madam," said Rachel. This was perfectly true. In spite of everything that had happened to her, she had been reduced to childhood by Marcia's storytelling. This could have been a tale told by Mira, her mother, while she sat at her side, lost in a contemplation of innocence.

"Well, it's quite simple. The little fox looked up at the grapes, shook his little head, and said to himself: 'Those grapes aren't sweet. I should have noticed that right away. They're obviously of the sour variety, and I wouldn't want them in my mouth, not even if they fell there all by themselves.' "

Rachel started at these words, mostly because of the ironic way in which Marcia stated them. Now she looked at the Jewish slave and asked her: "How did you like the story?"

"It was very interesting," said Rachel. "But we are taught in Judea not to draw lessons from legends, but only from the Holy Books themselves."

"But this is the point," said Marcia heatedly. "This is what I must know from a Jewess, do you understand?" She smiled at Eumenes suddenly, with a warmth that surprised Rachel. "You will please pardon us for one moment more. Feel free to listen and be enlightened."

"Thank you, madam," said Eumenes. "I shall indeed."

"Your Holy Book, this one, this Book of Daniel. It says quite clearly that you were vanquished, you Jews, locked in Jerusalem, under siege. The great king of Babylon raises his ugly head and comes in and takes over. Is that correct? Nebuchadnezzar conquers Jerusalem and takes away your king and your nobles into exile?"

"Yes, madam," said Rachel, feeling for a moment that here and now was a second exile for her people, sentenced not to exile in Babylon, but in Rome.

"But what does your Holy Book say? It says that it was not the king of Babylon who conquered you, not the gods of the Babylonians, and certainly not the weaknesses of your own God. No." Marcia brought her hands together as if she were fashioning a delicate piece of clay. Softly, she continued: "Your Holy Book says that it was your own God, the One God, your Lord Most High, He was the one who delivered your king to the foreigner. Do you understand? This is true what I am saying. Your people were beaten in warfare, and they write their books in the spirit of the Holy God, and they say that they lost because it was the will of their God. Do you believe this to be true?"

"Well, yes," said Rachel, not fully understanding the question.

"And do you see how it is all like the little fox who said that the sweet grapes were sour after all?" said Marcia, even more softly than before.

"What?" said Rachel. "I'm sorry, madam, I don't see how the very lovely story you told—"

"Eumenes, you know the story of the little fox and the grapes. Tell her what I mean."

"The Lady Marcia is asking you if you are a daughter of faith, I believe," said Eumenes, speaking with great dignity. "There are those who say that the Holy Books of the Jews are written after the fact, and are not prophetic. . . . Therefore any great disaster that has happened to them, they can simply ascribe to their God's divine will. Just the way that the fox can say, after he can't reach the grapes, that he doesn't want them, because they're not good anyway. There are those who want to see in the defeat of the Jews not the workings of their God but the proof of his nonexistence."

"Yes, that's precisely it," said Marcia. "You are very good, Eumenes. Now you will answer us once again, my dear."

"I believe that the Lord exists, that He made the world and knows all past and future events. All my people believe this. Therefore if He has made the world, and He has given us His Torah, is it not foolish not to believe in His power? If we are sent into captivity in Babylon, it is part of what He has seen and allowed and desired. It is, according to the Holy Books, simply His Will. If Jerusalem is conquered, it is always the Lord who delivers it to the conqueror. That is what I believe."

"You will see that she is removed of that collar this hour," said Marcia. "Elais is to see to the removal of all these barbaric restraints from the Jewish slaves. And my husband must be informed that I want this girl for my own. If he wants her in his bed, it will cost him this estate, and he'll never sit in the Senate, no matter what he does for Pompey. You tell him, Eumenes."

"Yes, madam."

"And get her decent clothes," said Marcia. "She's only a child, by the gods." She smiled, as if she'd fallen into an offensive joke. "By the One God, I mean." Then she smiled at the two slaves as if they were all part of one big happy family, all equal before the sight of God.

"Have you seen my brother?" said Rachel to Eumenes as soon as they were out of the library, walking on the mosaic tiles that led to an interior garden, with great marble columns supporting a ceiling that was open to the sky.

"I see your brother every day," said Eumenes. "It is because of your brother that you are here."

"How is he?"

"Let us attend to your collar first, shall we?" said Eumenes. "It will be good to see you out of it, even if only for a short while."

"Why a short while, sir?" But he was hurrying her out of the interior garden, through a short passageway to the rear of the house, and didn't take time to answer her. Eumenes took her past the swimming pool and toward the stables.

"Your brother is well," he said. "He is teaching us the mysteries."

"What mysteries?" said Rachel, but Eumenes spotted a wagoner and stopped him with an upraised palm. He told the man to take them the short distance to the smith's workshop, and helped Rachel climb onto the bench. "Please, sir. You were telling me about my brother."

"Silence," said Eumenes curtly. She wasn't hurt by this abrupt order. How could words hurt after all she had suffered? But Eumenes apologized to her when they left the wagon nonetheless. "It is unwise to discuss your religion before anyone but the Lady Marcia."

Rachel hadn't realized that they had been discussing religion at all. Soon the deafening noise of the smith's hammer blows shut up her thinking until her neck was free. When she was given water to wash and then oil to soothe the chafed skin, she was so happy with this ordinary bit of freedom that tears started up in her eyes. A slave brought her fresh clothing, of ordinary linen, and when she had wrapped herself in these, so that her body was no longer available to everyone's eyes, so that her shame was no longer evident to the world, she looked at Eumenes as if for the first time. He had not given the order to remove her collar or to clothe her decently, but in place of the great lady who had, her heart rushed out to him in gratitude.

"You are very kind, sir," she said.

Eumenes stopped short at her look. He had observed her beauty from the first time he had seen her; but this beauty had always been obscured by rage and self-loathing, the concomitant of slavery.

Suddenly, she was a young girl, grateful for a kindness, and her innocence shone through the veneer of pain.

"I am only doing what the Lady Marcia commanded," he said. "Besides, didn't your prophet Ezra proclaim that the One God would not forsake you in your bondage?"

"Yes, sir," she said, noticing that the corners of his eyes seemed to lift slightly as he spoke, furrowing his brow. It was as if any words that he spoke were well thought out, any small thought required a dipping into deep waters of intelligence. When the secretary hesitated before speech, she had the feeling that he was running through a wealth of scrolls, neatly tied and ready for his use. Philosophy, business, methods of war and love were there, behind the handsome, cultured facade. "But I don't understand how you know of Ezra. And what do you mean when you speak of my brother teaching you mysteries?" They had walked far from the smith now, and were in a little copse, overlooking the sea. It looked like nothing she had ever seen from the shores of Judea—the hilly region and orchards were farther inland from the seashore, and the color of the Mediterranean was darker here, more forbidding—but there was something absurdly familiar about the moment anyway. She had envisioned herself this way many times: a handsome young man, a vista of blue water, the shelter of fruit trees.

"Mysteries of the holy men, Rachel," said Eumenes carefully. "There are many of us here, slave and free alike, who are studying the ways of the Jews. More than one senator has a wife who studies your impossible language, and goes with her slave to a synagogue to hear the reading of the Law. But your Law is not simple. The words of your Torah are not always clear. There is frequent contradiction and obfuscation. Your brother has studied the Holy Books, and has great stores of knowledge. Madam thinks the world of him. There are many of us who believe that this world we inhabit, so full of inequities and misery, is but a place of trial for the world-to-come. You can't know what it means to those without faith to see someone like yourself, the victim of unspeakable tragedy, so completely secure in your knowledge of the One God. It is a gift to be able to believe like that. It is what we want to learn from you, and all the Jews who are come here. We too want a Messiah, the descendant of the House of David who will bring peace on earth to all men."

"But I do not believe in any such thing," said Rachel. "You must be careful what you learn from the mouth of my brother. He studies with wise men, it is true, but they are not the only wise men of my country. Nowhere does the Torah say that a descendant of King David will bring peace to all men. We are a very particular people, inward-seeking, isolated—"

"Yes, yes," said Eumenes with excitement. "David has explained that there is much disagreement, argument. In the words of Zechariah, predicting the coming of a king, riding on an ass, bringing salvation, there is much that is worthy of debate. But we must learn. Here in Rome, where all our gods are but the silliest phantoms of childish dreams. Where the priests are without training, and more corrupt even than the people. We must learn the mysteries and pass them on, so that our lives may not vanish before the coming storm. I want to be one who welcomes the bringer of peace, I want to learn so that I may sit at his feet, so that I may recognize him when he makes himself known to us. Regardless of the danger, I must learn. It is fitting that there are those who fear us, those who want to forbid the passing of this knowledge, when before all cults and creeds were tolerated in the republic. Because we are dangerous. If there is but one god, and He is the Lord of the Hebrews, the One God, the Lord of Hosts, He that speaks through the Torah, then all power of Rome is ephemeral. Alexander ruled the world and died before he was thirty-four: what good was all his earthly power if he had not learned the way of the Eternal, if he did not make his peace with the One God? What good is thirty-three years of glory and an eternity of torment? Manilius and his kind will surely try and break the backs of those who want to change the old order, but he cannot possibly succeed. He will try and kill faith, but he will choke on his own blood."

Rachel recognized in the man the zeal of the fanatic. Many truth seekers came to Jerusalem in search of religion, but most left without faith. The laws of Kashrut and Sabbath, the intricacies of the Torah and its myriad injunctions were not instant revelations of the spirit world; neither did they heal wounded hearts or terrible disappointments with the rapidity of pagan rituals. Eumenes seemed to have drunk recently, and without appropriate caution, from the murkiest of Jewish philosophical waters. Rachel didn't think of her religion as a matter of life and death, but as a way of life; not as a means to discover the world-to-come, but as a way to live in the world-that-is-now. Surely she believed in spirits, demons, heaven and hell, angels of light and angels of darkness. But it was her brother, while laughing at her "superstitions," who derived from the Torah clues, secrets, riddles that allowed him to discover the exact lineaments of future kingdoms, future saviors. Still, if he was teaching Eumenes of a Messiah from the House of David, it might mean that his faith was not dead. Perhaps the hate he had absorbed in the crossing from Judea had evaporated, unable to live in his pure soul.

"I'd better take you down, my dear," said Eumenes. He took her hand and led her through the thick trees, lost in calculation. Below them they could see the windowless jail where unruly slaves were kept chained to the floor, starved, whipped, and branded with the letters of their crime: Runaway, Pilferer, Man of Insolence. There were workers like that on many of Manilius's properties. There were slaves who were never removed from chains, neither working nor sleeping, and whose only gifts from their master were a pair of wooden shoes and a rough tunic once every three years.

"When can I see David?"

"I'm taking you to him, my dear," said Eumenes.

"What did you mean when you said that about my collar?" said Rachel suddenly. "That it would be good to have it off, if only for a little while? Why only for a little while? Is it possible that—"

"Yes," said Eumenes.

"The master?" said Rachel, momentarily so dazed by the prospect of a return to the heavy metal about her neck that the imminent meeting with her brother flew out of her mind. "Is he going to chain me again? There's no place for me to run, sir. Where am I to go? Couldn't you or madam speak for me? The metal is so hard on my skin. I don't know how to sit. I can't sleep with it on. Why would madam let me take it off, if her own husband would just—"

Eumenes put his arm about her shoulders. Rachel's head was bowed as if already bearing the indignity of the collar, and her entire frame was shaking. "Look, my dear. All things are possible in Rome. Even a consul can end up in chains. Perhaps you will be all right. You don't understand the relationship of a man and his wife in this country. Manilius and Marcia hate each other, and this is normal for a husband and wife. Both have been divorced, Manilius four times to Marcia's twice. Marriages are not love matches. Fidelity doesn't exist. What remains for the nobility is the virtue of alliances. Manilius has an official power over his wife, a power of life and death. But Marcia is of an ancient family—of the Julian *gens*. An ancestor was consul more than four centuries ago. If Manilius wants to be a senator, he has to give in to his wife's will, and more than occasionally."

"But she has asked you to free me of the collar—that is her will," said Rachel. "If he wants to be consul, you just said that if he wants to be consul—" Once again, she was making no sense, reaching for a block of logic that would release her from fear.

"Please, Rachel, we're almost there," said Eumenes. "Your brother will want to see you looking well, don't you think?"

"Yes, of course," said Rachel. "David. We're going to see David. But just explain to me. I'm sure David will want to know. Where is the master? Do you think he will undo what the mistress has done? Is he not here at Actium? Please tell me what I can expect, what my rights are, what will happen to me, because surely David will want to know. He's younger than me, but he is always looking after me, or trying to—"

"Manilius is in Rome," said Eumenes.

"Is that far away, sir?"

"You needn't call me 'sir,' " said Eumenes. "You may use my name, my dear, as I use yours." He seemed to be reaching deep inside himself for some reserve of strength. His face reddened, as if from sudden laboring, and he turned his eyes to the ground. "My dear," he said. "Your brother is in there."

"David?" she said, turning to what the secretary had before pointed out as the villa's jailhouse. "I don't understand."

"Your brother is being kept there, Rachel," said Eumenes. "Only the will of the Lady Marcia has prevented Manilius from crucifying him. He is kept there in chains, and when Manilius returns from Rome, his fate will be decided, as will that of all the Jewish slaves. Manilius holds them all; you and the others too, as equally responsible."

"Responsible for what?" said Rachel, afraid to descend the last few steps to the guarded jailhouse, afraid to see what they had done to her brother in the name of justice. "Do you mean that he could be executed for preaching the ways of the Jewish religion? Simply because he has helped Marcia with reading the Holy Books, the master can have him killed?"

"The master needs no reason to kill any of us," said Eumenes. "He could kill me, and say that I had raised my voice to him or left

144

the room without the proper deference. He could kill you and say that you didn't perform your duties, that you defied him."

"But what then?" said Rachel. "Let us go to him. Is he all right? Is he well? What did he do?"

"Please," said Eumenes. "Remember that he is the one who is in chains, and in the dark. We go to give him courage, and learn from his strength and will the power of the Torah." Eumenes took her up to the guard, and as the man nodded briskly to the secretary and unbolted the heavy gate, Eumenes explained to Rachel why her brother was in this terrible place.

David had waited four days, apparently not allowing his temper to ruin his chance of success. Manilius had more than once been in his presence, when David had sat quietly at Marcia's side in the sun-dazzled library. And David had kept his eyes averted, his fingers in place along the line of Greek or Hebrew script. But on the fourth day, Manilius and Marcia broke into violent argument, and Manilius had struck his wife across the face.

"It wasn't because Marcia was in danger," said Eumenes. "He admitted this freely. He didn't try to intervene in a dispute that could have led to his mistress's death. It was simply because of the opportunity. Manilius's back was turned, his hands were raised, his eyes were completely on his furious wife."

"He tried to kill him," said Rachel.

"Yes," said Eumenes.

"Because of me," said Rachel.

"Yes," he said again, and then he took the young girl into the jailhouse, where hope withered under the dark and fetid air.

Chapter
11

A candle sputtered in a dish on the dirt floor, illuminating David against the dozen odd prisoners about him, none of whom had been gifted with this source of light. He was chained at the neck to the wall, and when they drew closer, she could see that his ankles and wrists were manacled, and that all about his tiny square of space were papyrus scrolls and sheets. Rachel saw his bloodshot eyes grow brighter as they focused on her form. When she entered the outer edge of his light, he blinked against her sudden brilliance.

"Sister," he said, speaking Hebrew, and she could sense that the anger in his heart had not quieted, not against Manilius, or against the God of her people. "Come closer, sister."

There was a rumbling all about them from the other prisoners. None were distinct in the darkness save David, and when Eumenes had entered the candle's circle, the chained men began to call to them, some in anguish and supplication, some in hatred and violence. The close air was noisome with sweat and human waste, and the darkness, instead of covering the misery of men chained in their own filth, exaggerated what was awful: the rasp of metal on stone, the sharp moment of a self-pitying cry.

That David had been allowed a candle by the direct intervention of Lady Marcia had not cheered the hearts of the others. Seeing the young man sit in the luxurious light, poring over the scrolls, brought no solace to them. If it relieved their boredom, it also served to remind them of what they were denied. After a month in the jail room, it had been possible to forget the precise lineaments of study, friendship, contemplation. Watching Eumenes in his fine clothes take instructions from David accentuated their self-protective apathy. They had learned to accept their chains, the lack of light and air, the silence imposed by hunger and thirst and depression. All had rebelled, either in word or deed, and now eagerly absorbed the strictures of their master: obedience, servility, an inhuman attempt to lower themselves through the dark to a point where Manilius would finally raise them for another chance at life. Watching David read by the cheap candle raised their hopes and dashed them all at once. It made more vivid their desperation, their longing to return to the world of light, among men and women, where the air moved and water ran clear and strong from the mountains to the sea.

"David," she said to him in Hebrew, taking his badly bruised face in her hands. "Praise the Lord that He has allowed you to live."

"Yes," said David. "Praise the Lord, certainly." He could see that she was examining him, attempting to keep the pain from her eyes. "I am well, in spite of how I look, in spite of having missed my chance of killing the man who ruined you." He shook his head, as if to hold her back from speech. "I am not become a pagan, sister," he said. "I pray to God, the prayers of morning when I wake in the dark, and the prayers of the evening before I sleep in my chains. My anger is for Manilius and for Rome, not for the Lord Most High, the Master of the Universe. I understand that I am His instrument, one of many perhaps, but His instrument nonetheless. I was meant to try and kill Manilius, and to fail in that attempt, and to be sent to this hole so that Eumenes could take instruction from me, and learn the ways of the Jews."

Eumenes had only a little comprehension of spoken Hebrew, and in David's rapid Jerusalem-accented speech, he could barely make out the contours of his own name. In Greek, the secretary interjected: "Please, David, do not tire yourself. You have promised to be tranquil and allow yourself the rest your body craves once Rachel—"

"He is like a grandmother to me," said David brightly in Greek, so that Eumenes would understand. "He brought you here to help me heal, so that I can come in triumph to the great synagogues— pardon me, the great *temples*—that the new followers of the Jewish

God will build in the capital. That is, of course, if my Jewish God plans to give me a few more months or years of life in this world, or if His plan is to sacrifice me to Manilius, so that my followers in the years to come will grow strong in the memory of my crucifixion, like Spartacus before me—like all the slaves the Romans love to destroy."

His beautiful voice had changed during his short captivity. What before was mellifluous, seducing, was now caustic, dry. Nothing he said rang true, for it was always suffused with bitterness. He could pretend to harbor no anger against the Lord Most High, but the anger was there in the contour of every syllable, in the soft broken whispers wherein he mechanically praised the Name. Eumenes understood the bitterness, but saw beyond this the unshakable faith that he wanted to see. Rachel couldn't share Eumenes' vision. She was not a sudden convert, eager to absorb mysteries made all important by the chance of doom. She knew her brother, remembered his faith, and could see in his eyes not love of Torah, but a wild and powerful intelligence, rooted in the ways of earth. Heaven had lost its pull on his soul. He was sick with a desire for vengeance, and if teaching Eumenes the Holy Books was one way to achieve this, it didn't mean that the words of the scribes would be able to recapture his faith.

"David," said Eumenes in Greek, his voice conspiringly low, as if the other prisoners might be listening, spies for the man who imprisoned them. "Your situation is not hopeless. I have explained to you that the general might accede to the Lady Marcia's wishes in this matter, if she will agree to support him in his quest for a place in the Senate."

"I should have killed him," said David.

"Do not speak like that," said Rachel. "You are not a murderer, and the Lord wanted you to remain free of sin."

"Not a murderer because I was weak," said David, and for a moment his voice had all its old, graceful power. "If I had been strong, and unhesitating, and wild, he would be dead, and we would all of us be free." He looked around himself wildly, at the prisoners along the walls, at Eumenes, at his lovely sister. "Free," he said.

"Lady Marcia is going to make all that possible, David. You must not despair. She will prevent Manilius from taking your life, and she will remove Rachel from among her husband's slaves."

"What do you mean?" said David. For a brief moment he had been remembering his attempted murder in the library: there had been a great deal of sun that day, sun through the windows, sun in the gold and gems worn by Marcia, sun in the squinting eyes of the scribes, sun in the wood and marble and papyrus and parchment all about him. He had been deeply absorbed, comparing a Greek translation of the Song of Songs with the original Hebrew, meditating on the wonders of language, on its varied forms in a thousand lands.

No language was perfect. There was a beauty in the Greek version of the Songs that was peculiar to that language; it was wrong and inexact, but it conveyed a sense of passion that complemented the Hebrew version. In the Hebrew the passion had been visceral and intellectual, directed at God and at what was godly in man. The love was written large, in bold strokes that could only come from the desire of a man for a woman. But the Hebrew subsumed this passion under the all-encompassing love of the Lord for His Chosen People, or at least, made this interpretation possible for those who wished to find it there.

In the Greek, this was not possible. The allegory fell apart under the secular words. What passion was added to the original was the passion of flesh and blood, a flesh and blood that had no links to the divine: flesh and blood were but part of the body of the universe; all words were holy, having derived from the Name.

And then in the midst of this large room filled with light, with the heightened tension brought on by silent people thinking separate thoughts, came Manilius, dark and angry and loud. David kept his eyes on the scroll, but he could feel the impulse to murder rise up uncontrollably from his belly to the tips of his fingers where they touched the holy ink of scripture.

He was light, and he left the bench silently, feeling as if dark angels, spirits of the netherworld believed in by his defiled sister, were pulling at his wrists and elbows and knees and feet. Manilius struck Marcia across the face, and his broad back was turned to David in the sunshine, his broad neck, bronzed from the Mediterranean sun, and one image after another assaulted David: his sister dragged along the deck, his parents unchained and thrown into the sea, Marcia's face recoiling from the blow of the general's hand.

There was no need to cry out then, if murder had been all that was on his mind. But David did scream, even as he threw himself about the man's neck, still holding on to the small scroll in which the one hundred and seventeen verses of the Song of Songs were contained. This became a weapon, for David used the scroll to press against his master's neck. What he wanted was suddenly very simple. Even as the other slaves screamed out alarms, as Lady Marcia opened her bloodied mouth to howl in pain and confusion, David had been concentrated on one act: to bring the bit of olive wood, on which the carefully sewn papyrus sheets were wound, directly through Manilius's Adam's apple and out the other side of his hateful neck.

But the general had been alerted by the boy's scream.

David was able to throw himself upon Manilius's neck, to pull at the scroll with all his force, but the general had been able to tuck his chin against his chest and turn the powerful muscles of his shoulders slightly askew. Half a moment after David had attacked, Manilius had dropped to one knee, and thrown the fifteen-year-old boy flat on his back onto the floor.

"He didn't know what he was doing, he was only trying to protect me, he didn't realize who you were, he only saw you from the back, he is a scholar and not responsible for his actions—" David could hear Marcia run on as they took him away, and later on, when Manilius's men had beaten him, even after he had freely confessed to wanting their master's death, even after saying before witnesses that he had not tried to save Marcia but only to murder the man who raped his sister, David knew that a part of Marcia's defense was correct: he hadn't known what he was doing. There had been no need to shout. He could have softly crept up behind him and driven the scroll hard into the throat; or better, he could have secreted a knife from another slave and stabbed the general in the back. A part of him had wanted to fail. A piece of his fate had decreed that he would make a mess of things, that he would end up in this hole facing his sister's innocent face and Eumenes' adulation.

"What do you mean?" said David. "How can Marcia take Rachel from the man who owns her? As my sister, as the woman I was seeking to revenge, surely Manilius will want her under lock and key, under his own power."

"You don't understand politics, least of all family politics," said Eumenes quietly. "Marcia has the power that he needs, and the money that will help him wield it. For that he will do almost anything."

But David didn't hear the last of Eumenes' words. He was thinking far too quickly to keep the slow pace of another's speech. There were laws he'd been reading, Roman laws, labyrinthine in their complexity, ludicrous in much of their reasoning, but laws by which the Romans ran their ever-growing world.

David felt himself straining against his chain.

"Rachel, you must not allow yourself to leave Manilius," he said. "No matter what you think, what you believe, listen to me if you only listen to me once in your life. Do not leave Manilius."

"What is he saying?" asked Eumenes, because David had spoken in Hebrew.

"He is a good man, my sister, but does not know everything. If you ever loved our parents, ever believed in our Lord, listen to me: do not let Manilius send you away."

David was shouting at her now, trying to force her skeptical mind to accept the illogic of his words. "Tell me that you will do this, tell me that you will not let Manilius send you from him, tell me."

Rachel didn't understand, but she could feel the good spirits that dwelt within her alongside all that was evil, all the weak and bad spirits that had grown so powerful in her weak soul, suddenly warm with promise. She felt compelled to take the path urged by her brother. It made no sense, but if David wanted it, she would do it; she would make certain that no amount of Marcia's goodness would turn her from her master. And nothing that Manilius wanted, no money or power, would force him to give her away. Rachel would see to this. He would want her more than Solomon wanted the Shulamite, more than Solomon's father, King David, had wanted Bathsheba; he would want her even at the cost of his own destruction.

"I will not let Manilius send me away," said Rachel. "I will do as you say, my brother, I swear it."

Chapter

12

Nearly a month passed before Manilius returned to the villa.

Rachel learned of his arrival from Marcia, who seemed to be studying her face for a signal of what this homecoming meant to her. But if she had been looking for a flush of anger or the wide eyes of fear, she was not satisfied. The young girl's sober expression faded for a half moment, as if twisting further away from display; Rachel seemed to be putting a second mask in place over the one that already shielded her from Lady Marcia's good intentions.

"He thinks I am crazy, of course," she continued, following the news of his arrival with a litany of Manilius's complaints. "That today is the Sabbath should be known to him, by now, with thousands of Jews already in the capital, many of them emancipated, a few of them with fortunes—and all of them observant of this day! And so naturally he forces pen into my hand, demands laborious work of me—demands, not asks—insisting on a complete list of my financial resources, insists on a letter of credit for some Syrian, insists on knowing whether or not I will support his candidacy—" Marcia stopped herself short and looked even more directly at Rachel. "You have not changed your mind?"

"No, madam."

"I do not pretend to understand all the ways of your religion, but it seems quite clear that if you allow my husband to possess you, you are breaking the laws of your God."

"If I may, madam," said Rachel. "It would be more correct for you to simply refer to Him as 'God.' 'Your God' makes little sense, unless you are implying that there are many."

"If you are trying to behave like your brother, girl," said Marcia sharply, "it would be better to put a chain back around your pretty neck, and give you a more dramatic way to spout nonsense."

"My brother doesn't say anything other than what is true and sensible, madam."

"Your brother tried to murder my husband, though he had no chance of succeeding. Failing in this, he has attempted to ruin any chance we might have of freeing him from the jail room, and now, at the very moment when we might give you the chance of freedom from the man who has raped you, he has convinced you that it would be more sensible to stay his whore." Marcia paused and walked briskly across the sunny parlor where she and Rachel had been reading from the Book of Genesis to a large silver mirror, another salvaged bit of wreckage from the conquest of Athens. It was impossible to tell whether Marcia was staring at her reflected image or at that of the unfashionable terra-cotta gargoyle looming behind her. This had once adorned the outside of her grandparents' seaside home and now rested on a marble column, as if in homage to the bad taste of her ancestors.

"No, madam," said Rachel. "He has convinced me that the ways of the Lord will be best served by following his impulse."

"I do not understand this."

"This instinct," said Rachel. She tried to explain, but it was useless. David had tried to describe the fast-flying vision in his head, a mix of remembered laws and learning, and a glimpse of death and danger. He couldn't be clear. He shied away from calling what he saw prophecy, but Rachel understood that to a Roman matron trying to turn from the excesses of paganism to a rational search for the One God, David's instincts were either holy and prophetic, or they were pagan and superstitious. "It happens sometimes in my family. My father spoke of it, though he himself never experienced it. But a vision, a notion that grows fast and overwhelming in the mind, so that one must give in to it. When David told me not to leave Manilius, I could see what he was experiencing. It was obvious. He is not given to omens and superstitions. But he had a vision. I am certain that it is God's will that I return to your husband whenever he wants me."

"Well then," said Marcia, so sharply that for the first and only

153

time, Rachel thought it possible that this God-seeking woman could harbor jealous feelings toward her husband's mistresses. "I shall have to hope that my husband doesn't want you."

But Marcia's hope was not to be realized. Manilius sent for Rachel that same evening. A slave girl came for her, carrying a lamp, and escorted her silently along the high path that looked out to the sea. Beyond the lamplight no sea was visible, no shore, no rolling hilltops covered with trees. The moon was covered with an uncharacteristic cover of clouds, and the bells and pipes that hung from silver chains clanged and whistled in the rising wind.

Manilius's chambers were in the opposite wing of the house from where Rachel gave his wife instruction in the ways of the Jewish religion. There was little furniture. Lamps burned in profusion, the flames dancing in the drafts from open windows and doors. One vast wall was covered with a shockingly sexual painting. Winged women whom Rachel supposed to be goddesses bent lasciviously over leering mortals in martial dress. The vividness of the flesh tones and the scale of the frescoes seemed like a deliberate affront to the Mosaic prohibition against the creation of pictorial and graven images. Manilius watched her gawk at the painting from where he reclined on a low couch. He ate little pastries and drank wine. Rachel saw that the wineglass sat in a bed of snow, contained by a golden bowl, and wondered what toil, what misery it had cost to bring the cold from the top of a mountain to chill the general's drink at the edge of the sea.

"Leave us," said Manilius to the slave girl who had brought her. Another girl, Rachel's age or younger, squatted silently before where her master lay on the couch. She held a silver tray in her hands, and Manilius turned to this tray and spoke to Rachel, no longer looking at her: "There are oyster pastries, peacock livers, sows' udders," he said. "You may eat."

"No, thank you, sir," said Rachel.

Manilius gestured for her to come to him.

Merely the mention of the unclean foods made her stomach roil. As she grew closer to the general, the smell of the delicacies was more distasteful to her than the fetid odor of her brother's jail room.

"Here," said Manilius, his eyes turning from the tray to Rachel. She had not come quickly enough, and already his temper was rising. Rachel hurried about the couch in the large room, and was

154

astonished to see that the squatting girl—whom she had taken to be bare-armed, dressed in some harem girl's costume—was in fact completely naked. "Kneel," said Manilius to Rachel.

Rachel did so at once, feeling the room begin to swirl about her head. She told herself that she was kneeling in homage, not to a god or to a representative of some foreign spirit; she was simply bending her knees to a madman, in order that she might remain alive and fulfill her brother's demands.

"Where is your collar, slave?" said Manilius.

"The collar was removed, sir," said Rachel.

"Why do you not eat the food that I offer?"

"I am sorry, sir, but I am forbidden—"

"You are forbidden what your master forbids you," interrupted Manilius. "I am still your master, slave. You do remember that?"

"Yes, sir," said Rachel, but she shut her lips as he seemed about to strike her; she closed her eyes so that she would not have to see the blow. But then she felt his hand softly grip her chin, felt herself pulled forward, so that she opened her eyes and held out her hands to avoid falling off her knees. Manilius was moving her face to his open mouth, his eyes wide and unfriendly, perhaps deliberately so; it was as if he wanted to devour her, and was afraid that his wild lips would twist into a kiss.

"I am giving the Jewish slaves to my wife," said Manilius.

"Yes, sir," said Rachel.

"Your brother will be released, and given to her as well. She can use him for a scribe, or she can fuck him till his cock falls off—it's all the same to me, slave," he said. "All the Jews, they go to my wife, you understand?"

"Yes, sir," said Rachel. "But not me."

"Not you," said Manilius. "You don't want to leave my service?" But of course he already knew this from Marcia.

"No, sir," she said, but she couldn't quite finish her words, because Manilius had pulled her mouth to his and now kissed her quite gently, as if exploring the perimeter of her lips for a sign of faithlessness. Then abruptly, he drew back, staring into her black eyes.

"Remove your clothes, slave," he said to her, his silky voice as hard-edged as he could manage. Before, on the voyage to Italy, he had often called her Rachel, had tempered his arrogance with a leavening of love talk. But now he wanted to hurt her pride. As

Rachel carefully regained her feet, he shouted at her. "I want you on your knees, slave. Do not rise unless I tell you to rise. Did I tell you to rise?"

"No, sir," said Rachel.

"Take off your clothes, slave," he said. "Take off the hideous clothes given you by my wife. Since the silk gowns I gave you were not good enough, you may take off this modest gown, fit for a rich man's daughter—but very inappropriate for a slave-girl whore."

Rachel felt the tears coming to her cheeks, and was surprised by them. She would have thought it impossible to be stung by humiliation after what she had already suffered. After all, she had been this man's whore, she had decided to entice him to let her remain so at her brother's request: why should the truth, voiced by the man she loathed, have the power to twist her heart?

She began to pull at her tunic, and as she bared her breasts, the general barked something at the naked girl next to her in the harsh language of the Gauls. The girl, blond and long-limbed and fearful, put down the silver tray of delicacies and turned to Rachel. Very gingerly, she put her hands to the hem of Rachel's garment and pulled at it, remaining in her squatting position. It was clear that the general had ordered her to help the Jewess undress, and that the order had frightened her; but perhaps, thought Rachel, everything frightened her.

"Whores are not to wear undergarments," said Manilius. "And you will wear what clothes I give you, even if it means showing off your cunt to the field hands. You do understand what it means to be a whore and a slave, since it is that position you are so anxious to retain?"

"Yes, sir," said Rachel mechanically.

"And how will you like to wear my metal collar around your pretty neck?" he said, moving his lounging body to a more upright position on the couch. "How will you like it if I tell you to break your precious commandments and eat of the pig and break the Holy Sabbath?"

"I am your slave," said Rachel. "You will do with me what you please."

And she was naked, and on her knees as she spoke, the blond slave girl squatting next to her with her eyes to the marble floor. Rachel remembered the defiance of her ancestors, of her namesake, and tried to draw on this memory as a source of strength.

Defiance was easier now, she told herself. To stand and drive her fingernails across his face, to throw over the tray of unclean food, to call him a pagan and challenge him to find the courage to murder her: this was far easier than allowing his eyes the slow transit of her body, far easier than mouthing words of shame, far easier than swallowing the stuff of slavery and pretending it to be sweet.

"Now stand, slave," he said, and then he said the same thing to the blond girl in her language, for she stood a half moment after Rachel, and she was taller than the Jewess by the breadth of two hands. "Turn, slave," said Manilius in Greek, so that Rachel knew the words were for her. "Turn and look at what beautiful whores we import from Gaul." Rachel turned to the girl, and looked at her shapely body in profile, at the blond hair that fell past her shoulders in thick waves, at the gentle swell of breasts and belly, at the pale skin, unmarked by the sun. She smelled of musk, and a dampness clung to her thick hair, as if she had been freshly washed; a pale blue shadow rimmed her full lips. She seemed like nothing so much as a young girl trying to hold back her shivering so that her mother wouldn't order her out of the cold stream where she swam on a summer's day. There was no sign of the whip on her back, or the collar about her neck. What Rachel had taken for a practiced submission—the girl on her knees with the tray on her hand, used to her nakedness and her shame—was in fact the shock of the new captive. Manilius must have bought her in Rome, and brought her back to Actium this very day.

"Slaves from Gaul do not bother us with any ridiculous religions. There are no wives of senators trying to force the customs of barbarians down the throats of free Romans. There is no Lady Marcia trying to free every blond-haired lovely and make her into a priestess of a new cult that mocks all the old gods."

Manilius once again barked a command in the girl's guttural tongue. Quickly the girl turned from facing Manilius on the couch to Rachel. "Look at the whore," said Manilius in Greek. "Is she not much prettier than you? Why should I keep you, why should I keep any of the Jewish slaves with all their talk of the soul and the Lord Most High and the world-to-come? Look at my blond whore and tell me why shouldn't I give you away to my wife and her endless scheming plans?"

Rachel couldn't formulate an answer to this question. It was within her power to drop once more to her knees and bury her curly head in his lap, to feign tears of passion for the Roman who had raped her. Perhaps his arrogance would allow him to believe that a slave could love her master, could even love the fact of her chains. But in spite of the need to imagine the words and the actions that the general wanted from her, Rachel was too swept up in the contemplation of the barbarian girl to speak. Looking at her slender form, the high cheekbones in the too-thin face, the blue eyes wide with shock, Rachel found an image of herself—lighter and taller and younger—but an image of a girl who had suddenly learned of rape, and mastery, and powerlessness. She wanted to speak to her in her own language, to urge her to drift back from the present, to remember the lands and the skies of her home before the Romans came. She wanted to tell her to leave her body for the brutes, but let her soul loose, let her inner eyes wander to distant regions, where innocence reigned.

"Did you know that they are mutilating the statues of the gods?" said Manilius. "Zeus and Apollo and Mars have all had their shrines desecrated. Noses and ears of stone have been smashed, marble foreheads have been dabbed with the blood of animals. The sons of Roman warriors are dressing like women, painting their faces and fingernails, while the barbarians grow strong—in Hispania and Gallia and Germania. It is religion that makes us weak. The loss of our gods, and the acceptance of new ones. Gods from the East. Fire-gods, sex-gods, fish-gods, mystic gods in the shape of men; but no gods are so bad as your God. No god is as bad for Rome as the One God. That is what I am telling the Senate. That is why I shall join their body, I shall live to be consul, I shall return Rome to its proper course. Do you understand me, slave? I shall destroy your people because they follow the scroll and not the sword; I shall rid this country of Jews before they destroy our taste for blood forever."

The speech had brought him to his feet, and he towered over both of them, strong in his clothing, in his anger. He pushed Rachel aside and took the blond girl into his arms.

Rachel watched as he kissed the Gaul, bringing his hand along her thighs and waist and then to her backside. She made no sound that Rachel could hear, and her body seemed as resistant as a corpse. For a moment, it seemed that she must have fainted from hunger or terror, or that some spirit had taken pity on her and placed her in the arms of an unnatural sleep. But when Manilius let go of her, his mouth pulling back from hers, Rachel heard the girl's moan: it sounded distant, as if she had gotten herself into another room.

Then Manilius turned to Rachel, so quickly that she could barely check the revulsion that started up at his touch. But soon she allowed her taut body to relax in his embrace. She let his tongue explore her mouth, and moved her breasts against his belly as he raised his knee into her groin. Then Manilius pulled back from the kiss peremptorily and smiled.

"On your knees," he said to her in Greek. And then he turned to the Gaul and spoke in turn in her language.

Rachel did as she was told, letting the palms of her hands rest on the marble floor, her lovely face turned to the sight of the Gaul disrobing the general with clumsy, frightened speed. Manilius spoke to the Gaul again, and she joined Rachel on the marble floor, on her knees, and then Manilius looked down at them, the dark one and the light one, and he laughed, and Rachel averted her eyes, feeling the quickened breathing of the girl at her side, sharing her humiliation.

"Now you'll show her what to do, slave," said Manilius in Greek, so that Rachel knew the words were addressed for her. He lowered himself slightly, resting a knee on the edge of the couch. Rachel knew what he wanted: for her to place her mouth around his penis, already rising in the anticipation of pleasure. For a moment the thought crossed her mind that her brother's instinct was wrong, that it was madness not to accept Marcia's offer, folly to insist on remaining with the general; but then a rush of terror reminded her what lay behind the urge to refuse David's wishes. Evil spirits were there, eager to turn her astray. A true message had been filtered through David's soul, a message of import to their God. She must fulfill her place in the divine plan, even as David did. Whatever urged her to flee, or to tempt martyrdom with an attack on the Roman, was wrong. Only submission was right, a submission based on artifice. Somehow what was carnal and base and humiliating would lead to faith and righteousness.

Manilius pulled at the blond girl's head, bringing it close to Rachel's as she placed her mouth around his penis. Rachel shut her eyes and felt his flesh stiffen and throb between her teeth. Manilius held Rachel's black curly hair in one hand and pulled at the roots. He moved her head backward and forward in this fashion, as if she were an inanimate object, an open mouth created by a sculptor of flesh for the pleasures of sophisticated Rome. She tried not to gag, and to hold back the tears of pain as his penis grew and he thrust more deeply and moved more widely in her too-small mouth. Somehow she remembered that he must believe he was pleasuring her. There must be a reason why she would want to stay with him. If she were as miserable under his attentions as the girl from Gaul, her profound desire would be seen as a lie. Perhaps Manilius would give her to Marcia then, particularly if he was about to begin his campaign for the Senate on a program of ridding Rome of its Jews.

She used her tongue, the way he had taught her. Carefully, she grazed his skin with her teeth, then brought the lips over her teeth to caress where she had bitten. And she pulled at him, she sucked his shaft, and soon she felt his hand on her scalp weaken and let go. He was allowing her to move on her own.

"You like that, don't you, slave?" he said, but his words were full of breath, and he was soon taking in more pleasure than he wanted, and so he pulled roughly away and out of her mouth.

Rachel fell off her knees and half onto her back.

"Get on your knees, I said," said the general. He was proud of his erect penis, turning it now to the other girl and raising her close-mouthed face. He shouted at her in her language, and once again she didn't hesitate, but opened her mouth, without joy or fear or loathing. It was the opening of a door in the house of the dead, of an actor's hinged-mouth mask. Manilius drove his penis into her mouth, and he held her head the same rough way he had used with Rachel. But he was obviously displeased.

"Prepare her for me," he said suddenly in Greek, and he withdrew his penis from her mouth and pushed her heavily to the hard marble floor.

"Sir?" said Rachel, not understanding.

Manilius hit the Jewess across the face. "Prepare her. I'm going to fuck her. You're going to open her up for me."

Rachel still didn't understand, but carefully she bent over the young girl and smoothed the blond hair from her face and tried to calm her. But the Gaul was long past being calmed. She was able to follow a simple command, to accept a push or a shout. But a caress meant nothing to her. Rachel's hand on her brow offered no solace. What she saw in the Roman's rich chambers had nothing

160

to do with kindness or love; ever since she had been taken in chains from her homeland, life itself had dwindled to a dull flame. She was indifferent to Rachel's touch. It might have been a blow as easily as a caress.

Manilius shouted at Rachel: "Open her legs."

Rachel placed her hands on the girl's thin shoulders, feeling the bones shake against the smooth young skin. She had come around behind her and, on her knees, eased the girl's head to the floor. "It's all right, dear," she said, speaking Hebrew without thought. She ran her hands along the Gaul's upper arms, along her neck, trying to absorb the tension and make it her own.

"Just open her legs," repeated Manilius softly. He had knelt down suddenly before the blond girl on her back, and faced Rachel, who held the girl's still shoulders. Rachel didn't answer him, but kept her eyes on the man and bent low so that she could run her hands along the girl's sides to her knees.

"Yes, darling," she said in Hebrew. "It will be all right, darling." Then gently, she pulled at the girl's knees, separating the soft thighs, and she held her like that as Manilius drew closer, his mouth twisted into a leer.

"Don't cry," he said. "You'll get your turn."

"Yes, sir," said Rachel. Then she was blinking back the tears, for she knew that the half-dead girl beneath her was a virgin, a creature of the Lord, the recipient of pain from a hundred sources. Who knew how many of her people had died in the wake of the Romans? As Rachel's parents had been murdered, so surely had been this girl's. Perhaps she had lost brothers and sisters, perhaps her betrothed, taut-muscled and tattooed, had been struck down in her defense and then nailed up on a makeshift cross like a thief or a murderer.

"Please, sir," said Rachel. "Come to me, sir."

Manilius seemed genuinely pleased. The beautiful Jewess had finally made him believe that she wanted him. She cried for him now, she lusted for him, and was jealous of the beautiful blond captive. The general smiled.

"Open her wide, slave. Wide," he said, and then he lowered himself over the young Gaul, and for the first time, Rachel felt the tension in the girl's still frame rise into resistance. This was slight at first. She could hear a sharp cry, muffled by the girl's quickly closed mouth. But she could feel the muscles of her thighs pull

161

inward. And looking over her from the back, Rachel could see the blue eyes open, not close, against the looming neck and chest and belly of the rapist.

"Master," said Rachel, running up her breathing as if in a state of near ecstasy. "Please, master, come to me."

"Open her wide," said Manilius. "Caress her breasts. Relax her. Prepare her. Do what I tell you!"

But Rachel was already letting go of the girl. Her thighs wanted to close, and no power on earth could urge her to act as an accomplice in the Gaul's rape. David's fiery insistence on keeping her with Manilius was forgotten, or thrust aside. What was important now was beyond any memory of duty or promise. This girl had become her responsibility. They shared the same fate of the captured. They were open, naked, women without defenses, and Rachel wanted to protect her, to force her body between the general and her no matter what the consequences.

But Manilius was immensely strong.

And he was already there, ignorant of any threat from Rachel, only pleasantly aware of what he took for her passion for him. But he shouted at her anyway. Rachel had let go of the Gaul's knees, and the pretty blond girl had moved them back together, so that the general himself had to open her with rough force.

"Do not fight me, bitch," he said in Greek, and then repeated the words in the girl's language, and he turned up to Rachel to demand her aid, but Rachel was coming close to him, her mouth open, her eyes half shut.

"I will give you your turn," said Manilius, his eyes returning to the Gaul, his knees pressing against her inner thighs, his erect penis pressing into the sparse blond pubic hair. He had become very excited, as he always did with two girls; but now, with one resisting, and one imploring him for his favors at the same time, with the good wines of Syria running through his blood, with the pact made with his wife for her money—coupled with her ignorance of his treachery—he was in shut-eyed bliss.

"I want you first," said Rachel, her face and breasts coming up over the supine girl so that she had almost usurped Manilius's position. But the general had become oblivious of Rachel, so strong was his passion. He forced the Gaul's thighs wider with his knees, he held her neck in his left hand, he guided his penis with his right, and he prepared to drive into her dry and closed vagina when the blond girl let out a shriek.

162

"By all the gods," said Manilius, battening on this evidence of pain, for the shriek wouldn't end, and the girl, so long passive, was now fighting, her weak muscles trying to slam together her thighs, her shoulders and neck trying to rise against the weight of his body and his hand, her half-dead spirit growing wild for one final breath of rage.

And then Rachel threw herself on the general.

There was no design, no careful plan; but a kind of artifice had taken place automatically. She had not hit at him with her young girl's fists, but opened her arms to embrace him, her mouth wide to swallow his insults and anger. Because at that same moment the Gaul had been pushing back at him with all her force, the two girls had gathered enough strength to topple him backward. Rachel was suddenly on top of him, her mouth not kissing him, but drawing his tongue into her mouth, her hand not loving him, but pulling on his penis as if to take control of the center of his strength.

"Rachel," he said. Instead of being angry he had grown absurdly fond. It was as if a well-trained dog would not let up licking his hand, demanding his attention because of an excess of love. "You go too far."

But she could not hear him. Only the Gaul's shriek ran in her ears, and as she placed herself over his erect penis, she took in nothing of his ecstasy, nothing of the release he had been seeking. All she wanted was his strength, so she could crush it; she wanted his life, so she could destroy it utterly.

He was inside her, moving quickly, then more slowly, feeling the response within her body that shamed her, but was beyond her control. And though a smile crossed his face, though his eyes rolled up in unbridled pleasure, it was not enough for him. He called to the Gaul, whimpering now behind them, terrified at the fact of her rebellion. But she couldn't hear him, or if she did, she couldn't respond, her knees pulled up to her chest in a memory of the womb.

"Not yet, Rachel," he said, using her name again, stroking her teary cheek, and then he pushed her back, not yet ejaculating, wanting more than one girl could offer.

She watched in amazement as he pushed her gently off him, regaining his power. He was smiling, proud of his manhood, as he turned over the other girl now and roughly tore apart her clenched knees, forcing her once more on her back.

"She'll learn," said Manilius, as if Rachel was his accomplice, his practiced partner in matters of rape. She wanted to shout at him, to get him to understand that she hated him more than any devil, that what she had done she had performed out of compassion for a fellow woman, not out of lust for a rapist and monster.

But there was no room for words.

Manilius wanted the blond girl, and the blond girl was resisting, and so he hit her now, slapping her face, then slapping her breasts, then driving his knee into her groin to keep her legs apart, and then he was shouting at Rachel.

"Come, slave, open her," he said, and then Rachel came back to him. Ignoring his order, she placed her hands on his shoulders gently as if enamored of him, insistent in her desire. He shrugged her away, and when she persisted, he spared a hand to push her away with violence.

"Leave me," he said. "Attend to the girl."

"No, master," said Rachel. "You can't leave me."

She could feel the Gaul's spirit begin to give in beneath the man. It was a greater call for help than any shriek could be. It was as if she was witness to the life spirit, the flame that burned inside the heart, the soul that was God-given riding in a crescent of earthly fire: and she could see the glow begin to quietly dim as he tried to enter her.

And so Rachel came at him again, and he was angry now, because no matter how much she wanted him, she must needs learn her place. He turned his head about ferociously, but Rachel had grabbed his penis now and forced her naked breasts against his chest and once more they were together, the general and his Jewish slave girl, and in spite of his anger, he was weak in her hands, and in spite of his weakness, Rachel's hatred remained constant and violent.

"You killed my parents," she said in Hebrew, holding him responsible for the events on the ship. "You want to murder my people," she continued, the words so quiet and smooth in her Jerusalem accent that they sounded like endearments to Manilius. Then she pulled him into her vagina, letting him come on top of her, and she arched her back and stretched her body like a luxuriating cat.

Carefully, she used her extended hands to pick up the silver tray laden with the unclean delicacies.

"All right, yes," said Manilius. "You will be my slave. I will keep you, you will be my slave and you will be safe." He said all this in spurts, as he moved, as he relaxed more and more, forgetting his anger at the Gaul, at Rachel's interruption, forgetting everything but these moments of ecstasy.

And then all at once his head exploded.

Manilius fell back, his penis diminishing in size as he clutched his head in his hands and saw the glittering silver tray in Rachel's hands that had just struck his forehead with force.

She had struck with every bit of strength she possessed, but flat on her back, with a man inside her, moving the tray from behind her head across to his face, the force had not been enough. Manilius was dazed, and blood ran down his face, but he was not dead, not nearly dead, and he was a fighter.

"You tried to kill me, slave," he said, wiping the blood from his eyes, as if the very motion cleared his head, renewed his strength. The silver tray shook in Rachel's hand. She had defied her brother's wishes. Manilius would not be murdered, and she would not live under his care, and all the plans that David saw for her with the certitude of intuition were dashed.

"Now I will kill you," said Manilius.

And he began to get up, only a bit shaky, and Rachel knew that he would tower over her, that he would wrest the silly weapon from her hand, and that he would then kill her, he would kill her brother, and he would kill every one of her people.

But then the defeated Gaul got up on her knees.

Rachel had never seen anyone transformed so quickly.

The Gaul had been defeated, she had been nearly dead, the life-force so diminished that she could no longer voice a cry of pain. But now there was voice, there was strength, there was the violence of a barbaric people.

The young blond girl steadied herself on her knees and placed her hands about Manilius's neck, and then she went nearly berserk. She shouted, trying to strangle him. She held him with her legs about his waist, waiting for the tray, and Rachel was moving with her now, the two victims becoming one in their purpose.

The tray was no longer a puny weapon, for Rachel was on her feet, and though the general struggled, the Gaul held him, whether because of the wine in him or because of the first blow struck by the Jewess, or simply because the spirit of the Gaul's defeated people was beating wildly in her veins.

Rachel brought down the tray once, twice, and then again, each time with greater force, and soon Manilius no longer screamed, and still the Gaul held him with force, still Rachel continued to hit the man's head again and again, crushing the skull, beating down the top part of his head until no trace of life or thought could ever come from that place again.

Only when the Gaul had dropped the man's body, only when Rachel could barely hold the tray in her hands, only when the blond girl came softly to her and took away the tray, and put her arm about her shoulders and quieted her with the softly uttered guttural sounds of her language, did Rachel understand what she had done.

She had murdered, she had broken a commandment of her people, she had contravened her brother's plan and in so doing had taken the life of one of God's own creatures.

But she had no regrets. The spirits in her were warm and full of praise. These were not evil spirits. She had no cause for shame. The Gaul glowed with gratitude and the spirit of vengeance fulfilled. Rachel's lips moved in prayer to her God, thanking Him for allowing her deed. The Gaul's lips moved too, whether in prayer or in thanks to her fellow slave, Rachel would never know. All that she was certain of at that moment was that she had broken no desire of the Lord Most High. Whatever instinct her brother had, had been less strong than her own. She had known, in the suffering of the Gaul, that she could no longer submit to evil.

She allowed herself to grow calm in the embrace of the Gaul, knowing that she had fulfilled the will of her God, knowing that in the murder of an oppressor she had become worthy of her ancestors and her name.

Chapter
13

Manilius owned many hundreds of slaves throughout Italy. Some were educated men like Eumenes, but most were field hands, laborers, and whores. There were girls in brothels outside Rome who were his property; there were philosophers and businessmen and government functionaries whose lives had been his to dispose of. All of these, every man, woman, and child owned by the murdered general, were threatened with execution in the wake of his murder.

The law was clear: in the case of a master's murder, all his slaves were considered to be accessories to the crime. This was logical, to some minds, as the chief function of the slave was to see to the welfare of his master; if the master was murdered, he could not have been successfully performing his duty, and therefore deserved to die.

The execution of a murdered master's slaves was not always carried out. A murder committed by pirates on the long sea route of Africa could not be blamed on the murdered man's household slaves in Rome. Occasionally, there would be a humanitarian cry for the exoneration of slaves who could not possibly have wished harm to befall their master. But in general the law was upheld, particularly if the man died in his own house. It created a very good reason for slaves to worry about the safety of their master.

In Manilius's case a compromise was reached by the courts. Only those slaves who were part of his household at Actium were sentenced to death. Slaves owned by his wife were not included in the sentencing. Because Manilius had transferred ownership of his recently acquired Jewish slaves, including David, to Marcia, none of them was considered an accomplice in his murder. The only Jewish proselyte to be executed was Eumenes, who, along with the other slaves owned by the general, was tortured during the questioning by the civil authorities looking into the circumstances of the crime. Eumenes revealed no conspiracy that supported the actual murderers, the two girl prostitutes, and under torture he was heard to utter praises to the Hebrew God. This further prejudiced those anti-Jewish elements in Rome who were determined to see in the death of Manilius an attempt to secure the monotheistic proselytizing that the general had abhorred.

But in the torturing of Manilius's other slaves—a routine followed whenever slaves under suspicion testified—a different sort of conspiracy emerged. The general, without the knowledge of Eumenes, had been planning the murder of Marcia. No less than five of his most trusted slaves were privy to this secret; indeed, two of them were to have committed the actual murder. Manilius's transfer of the Jewish slaves to his wife's name would have killed them as surely as their new mistress would have been murdered. It was David's knowledge of the law that sentenced slaves to die with their masters, coupled with an instinct that Manilius would murder his rich wife, that led him to urge his sister to remain with the general, at any cost. David had a vision of Rachel surviving all of them, all the slaves from Judea; he imagined that she would be ransomed one day, and set free in the Jewish community growing in Rome. She would never marry, of course, but she would tell the next generation of Jews, those born in exile, of the glories of Jerusalem, and of how one day they would return to their Holy City.

But this vision was never realized.

Of the slaves of Manilius, Rachel and the Gaul were the first to die. They were tortured, but had nothing to reveal other than their loathing for the man who had tormented them. Their execution was painless, for they had lost consciousness on the rack and probably never felt the flames that consumed their earthly frames.

Ironically, it was David who had survived, David who was eventually ransomed by a kinsman, David who was free to tell the next generation of Jews of the Holy City and of how they would one day return to their country and their people.

*

168

But of all David's stories of past glories and present calamities, of the valiant warrior kings of ancient Israel and the martyred captives of Rome, no stories so fired the imaginations of the young as those he told of his sister.

This was not simply because the circumstances surrounding her killing of Manilius were greatly exaggerated over time. Nor was it because Manilius's anti-Jewish campaign for the Roman Senate came to be remembered as a plot to exterminate all the Jews of Italy. Mostly it was because of the tradition of the name Rachel.

It began to achieve mythic proportions in the consciousness of David's family. When one Rachel died, the next girl born into the family was given that name; and this name giving was an honor. No other girl would be called Rachel within that family circle until the present Rachel would pass on to the world-to-come. Not every girl so named would be called upon to achieve the heroic; but every Rachel that stemmed from David's family in Rome would know of the Rachels who preceded her. She would hear of Rachel of Modein, and Rachel of Jerusalem, and Rachel of Rome; she would hear of the Legend of the Brave Rachel who had refused to betray her husband, a fighter with the Maccabees, and of her descendant, who had killed a mighty general of Rome without a knife or a sword.

And if the stories were changed in the mouths of the tellers and in the passing of the years, a certain part of them remained constant, and this part was the most important: that the latest Rachel was one of a line of namesakes, all of whom were capable of courage and faith, all of whom took their strength from the bottomless well of tradition.

The Family of David,
The Scribe of Rome
64 B.C. –488 A.D.

Tradition places eight distinct ancestors bearing the name Rachel between the Rachel who died in Actium in 64 B.C. and the Rachel born to Miriam and Ezra ben-Ahiav outside of London in 461 A.D. There were family charts that this last Rachel's father had copied from a crumbling scroll brought to Britain by his grandfather Shimon a hundred years before. That was a time when taxes were still paid to Rome, and when Rome repaid its citizens with security from the barbarians.

Shimon had come from Cologne, in Germany, where descendants of David, the freed Jewish slave of the murdered Manilius, had settled early in the second century. Before Cologne, members of the family had left Rome for Alexandria, where distant cousins had lived for centuries. Before Alexandria, other descendants of David had emigrated to Judea, to Persia, to Gaul, looking for riches or love or God. No one could accurately chronicle the births and deaths of such a numerous family. David the Scribe had nine children after Rachel, with three different wives; some of these stayed in Rome, some followed the armies pushing back the imperial frontiers, some went overseas for gold and spices. All married, were blessed with children, male and female, long-lived and short-lived, destined to travel the world or remain rooted to the growing Jewish community along the right bank of the Tiber.

Like every family, they lost touch with second and third cousins, and soon, in the blink of time that a century is in the eyes of the Lord, descendants of David in Syria had forgotten about their Italian cousins, or those rumored to have gone to Germany or Greece. Occasionally, when a *Cohen* family would achieve some measure of distinction, or when the Jewish people as a whole would suffer some terrible fate, a familial relationship would be claimed, or wondered about.

Judah the *Cohen* of Rome, whose brother Hayim had emigrated to Egypt in 38 A.D., during the mad reign of Caligula, heard forty years later that a child of Hayim's had died in the fall of Jerusalem and the destruction of the Holy Temple by Titus. Judah's grandson, Jason ben-Shmul, an uneducated and proud businessman of Rome, somehow confused the rebellion that led to the fall of the Temple in 70 A.D. with Bar-Kochba's famous insurrection in 135. Jason's great-grandson Abraham ben-Samuel, who was the first of the family to move to Cologne, ingenuously told his daughter Rachel (born in 244) that the great Bar-Kochba was a descendant of David the Scribe of Rome.

But if the larger picture of the family of David the Scribe became unclear, legendary in quality to its members, the smaller picture of that part of the family that passed on the name of Rachel remained sharp. If a Rachel in Germany had wandered away from the rituals of her people to those of a handsome Roman soldier, the next generation might remember her less well than the Rachel who returned to Judea in the wake of the destruction of the temple, or the Rachel who defied the short-lived imperial ban against circumcision, or the Rachel who defended with her life her scholarly husband against the charge of necromancy. But all the Rachels were remembered, their names written into the bloodlines, the dates of their births and deaths recorded, the honor of which son would be allowed to give the first girl born after Rachel's death her name carefully ruled by tradition.

Because the Rachel who died in 244 had only one brother, Samuel ben-Melekh, and that Samuel had only one son, Abraham, news of the death of Rachel in Rome at the age of forty-four was sent by messenger to Cologne, where Abraham had moved. His chance at honor was quickly fulfilled when a girl was born to him a year later. The first Rachel of Cologne lived a long time, nearly eighty years, and it is unclear as to how Isaac, son of Mordecai, son of Eli, son of Abraham, was able to achieve the honor of naming his daughter Rachel; by then the community peopled legitimately and illegitimately by Abraham's grandsons was prodigious in number.

But once this second Rachel of Cologne was ensconced as the authentic inheritor of the name, the line was clarified. Her brother Benjamin had a single son, Shimon, and when the various prohibitions in Cologne against Jewish ownership of slaves and land had given him the impetus to try a further outpost of empire, he took with him the right to name the next Rachel. Britain was at the end of the world, surely, but its richest Roman citizens consoled themselves by indulging in fine silverware, exquisitely designed swords, and delicate ironwork that protected their windows and hearths. All this work in silver, in gold-and-gem-encrusted hilts, in iron delicate to the eye and powerful to the touch, was said to be traditional in the family for centuries. Shimon in turn handed this skill to his sons and to his grandsons. In 409, after hearing of the death of his aunt in Cologne, he named his granddaughter Rachel.

This Rachel was especially skilled with ironwork, with twisting the ethereal shapes that guarded the windows of the rich in the terrible times in which she lived. Her much younger brother Ezra, named for the fierce biblical scribe, was more talented yet than she; and when she died, one of hundreds murdered in a Saxon raid on the defenseless city of London, he dedicated his life to vengeance against the barbarians who had killed her.

His own daughter Rachel was gentle, an enemy of violence and bloodshed. She married a pious man and walked in the restricted way of the Torah, refusing to let hate fill her heart. No outrage of the Saxons could let her forget their humanity, and the God-given sanctity of their lives.

But then, after a hundred stories of mutilation and murder, after nights of terror and prayer, after memorial services for aunts and uncles and cousins—captured, killed, or tortured for sport by the barbarian—Rachel's devotion to peace ended abruptly. Her husband, Ambash, returning unarmed to their villa, hurrying home in the near-dark on the eve of Sabbath to be with his beloved wife, was waylaid and murdered. The barbarians had not been content with his gold coins or his blood. They broke his dead bones, they tore out his eyes, they left face and torso so disfigured that even a woman of strength and love found it hard to hold the mortal remains in her arms.

Rachel was left childless, at twenty-seven, in a villa whose shabby grandeur reflected the state of the world, civilization acquiescing to barbarity. But Rachel had so twisted her gentle heart that she longed for nothing so much as violence.

She had always been subject to dreams, nightmares of apocalypse that had left her weak with helpless rage; in the wake of Ambash's death, these nightmares became increasingly violent, and visionary. She had met with the Britannic general Ambrosius on two occasions before the death of her husband; Ambrosius, who was famous for his visions, recognized in Rachel a kindred soul. Dreams she related to him in the city of London, he later interpreted as predictions of Saxon massacres in the northwest.

But she resolved to do more than just wait for the barbarians to complete the destruction that was all around her. She would use her skill, her knowledge, and her faith, and she would strike at them. They were mindless, they were godless, and with the right ally, she would rid them from the land.

THE FAMILY OF DAVID, THE SCRIBE OF ROME
d. 10 BC

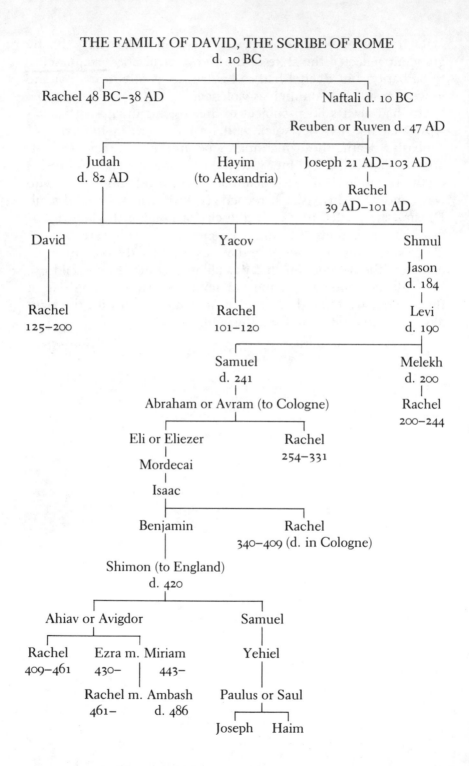

Rachel 48 BC–38 AD

Naftali d. 10 BC

Reuben or Ruven d. 47 AD

Judah
d. 82 AD

Hayim
(to Alexandria)

Joseph 21 AD–103 AD

Rachel
39 AD–101 AD

David

Yacov

Shmul

Jason
d. 184

Rachel
125–200

Rachel
101–120

Levi
d. 190

Samuel
d. 241

Melekh
d. 200

Abraham or Avram (to Cologne)

Rachel
200–244

Eli or Eliezer

Rachel
254–331

Mordecai

Isaac

Benjamin

Rachel
340–409 (d. in Cologne)

Shimon (to England)
d. 420

Ahiav or Avigdor

Samuel

Rachel
409–461

Ezra m. Miriam
430–   443–

Yehiel

Rachel m. Ambash
461–   d. 486

Paulus or Saul

Joseph   Haim

Part Three

London, 488 A.D.

Chapter
14

That night he dreamed of Julia, a dream without light or shade or substance. She was colorless, like a lowering cloud, and when her lips opened, she had no voice, and when he brought his mouth to hers, he tasted earth and dust and ashes.

"The sun is rising," said a voice from beyond the dream, soft and insistent, repeating the strangely accented phrase with a steady rhythm, so that the words grew slowly louder, emerging from silence the way dawn breaks moment by moment from the dark.

Joseph opened his eyes, fully awake, his hand flatly extended over the horn grip of his crude double-edged sword. A hairy face looked down at him from a great height; in the near dark, Joseph could see yellow teeth frame a smile.

"The sun is rising, master," said the old peasant, lowering his handless arm so that for a moment Joseph imagined that he was offering the stump to help him rise. But the arm whose hand had been severed by Roman justice nearly a half century before prodded the still figure next to Joseph, that of his younger brother Haim.

But Haim wouldn't wake.

"He is tired, master," said the hulking old man, the Latin syllables made harsh by a guttural mixture of Saxon and Celtic vowels. "The God will not miss him if he needs the sustenance of sleep."

It pained Joseph to watch the way the boy flinched from the

touch of the stump, the way he turned his shoulder into his body, twisting away from consciousness, from light, from the way of the world.

"Haim," said Joseph, speaking in Hebrew so as to spare his brother shame. "It's all right, Haim, it's me, Joseph, you are safe and no one will hurt you."

"Rachel," said Haim, his blue eyes opened and shut again so quickly that they could have seen nothing but the muted colors of soggy thatch, the dusty woolens that blocked the low entrance. But the near dark didn't frighten him further. His shoulders relaxed, his form stretched slightly lengthwise. "Rachel," he said again, "you said we would get to Rachel."

"We will," said Joseph, speaking softly, aware of their host's curiosity at the unfamiliar language. But the peasant had a natural courtesy, and bowing slightly, he hurried away toward the growing light from the hole cut in the wall of wattle and daub.

"I am going to the prayers," said the peasant, and as he vanished, Joseph grew suddenly impatient.

"I must go too, Haim," he said. "Will you come to pray with us?"

"What if the Villa of Gold is burned?" said Haim. "What if Rachel is as dead as Mother and Father and Julia?"

"We must have faith," said Joseph, pushing his brother back onto the dirt floor on which he'd slept.

"Julia is dead," said Haim, ignoring the threat of Joseph's hand on his chest. "Mother, father, Julia—all dead. All the Christians, dead."

"They are with our Lord," said Joseph, remembering to check his anger, to save his fury for the Saxon hordes.

"Your Lord was a false Messiah," said Haim, the blue eyes filling with tears. "Your Lord led a hundred astray, and the hundred led a thousand, and the thousand led an empire—and when the empire led Father—"

"I am going to pray," said Joseph. "Then we will continue our journey to Rachel, daughter of Ezra."

"Where was your Lord?" said Haim clearly, standing up to his brother as Joseph brought his sword carefully into its cracked leather sheath. "Where was your great Lord when they came for His new converts and your good Christian wife?"

"You are a boy and you are an idiot, and if you were a man, I'd slap you down, but seeing as you are a boy—"

Joseph stopped himself from continuing and hurried outside, where the old man waited to take him to the sacred grove.

"Your brother, master? Will he be coming?"

"No," said Joseph, suddenly very hungry in the misty dawn air. "He is not a Christian."

"Well, perhaps he will learn to look for the Lord in the sky," said the peasant. "And now we must hurry to join the others."

He had wanted to ask Joseph if he and his brother had been speaking Greek, but felt the question would be unseemly from a host, and held back his curiosity as he had learned to hold back so many other things: his lust for women, his passion for the secret signs in the night sky and in the entrails of freshly killed beasts, his adoration of the gods of water and earth and fire. There was one God, and He was a jealous God, and the peasant had learned to pay homage only to Him.

"I am sorry if I was short with you, old man," said Joseph as they approached the copse of young oak trees. He took a bronze coin from his purse and pressed it into the peasant's lone hand. It was nearly worthless, a London imitation of a Roman silver coin of Theodosius's reign. But the peasant was overcome with gratitude.

"Oh, master," he said, kissing the coin and then bringing his lips to Joseph's hand.

"Stop it," said Joseph. "The sun will be up."

"Yes, master. We must greet the God. We must greet our Lord Jesus and thank him for sending us this foreign-speaking stranger who shares the One Faith, like all true Romans everywhere."

They were within a day's walk of the walled city of London, still called Londinium by the many Britannic lovers of the crumbling Roman empire. In the four centuries of Roman rule, London had been a great city, its place at the periphery of the civilized world compensated for by its fortunate position on the Thames. Both at the center of the island's land routes, where wheat and hides, lead and gold, and especially, slaves, were driven in great wagon trains, it also fed into the estuary that faced the Continent and the hungry legions of Gaul. Once great ships, not only from Gaul but from Spain and Africa, had braved the stormy channel, carrying oil and fine pottery, marble and silk and silverplate for Roman citizens of the imperial province of Britain. Soldiers of every rank, from every part of the world, had settled in the city and in the fertile farms where they built villas every bit as splendid as those of Italy. No more than half of the city's vast population of one hundred thousand was native-born, and among those "natives" were the children of generations of traders and soldiers and invaders—Celts and Teutons and Gauls and Greeks. In the great days of the fourth century, when barbarians who plagued most of the empire ignored distant Britain, peaceful London grew fat from trade; ships from as far as Persia landed their exotic cargo and dark-eyed men. But now it was not Greeks who arrived in London, but Britannic refugees from the north and east, where the Saxons invaded with clumsy spears and axes, murdering and pillaging in the wake of the country's desertion by Rome.

Joseph followed the peasant through heavy brush and coarse ferns. There was a path, but it was covered with moss and branches, and at every step thorny arms reached out to block his way. But the light was growing, and the peasant eased his pace so as not to lose the richly dressed stranger.

"Roman," he said, pointing to a ruined stone column, dragged into the brush from some deserted villa. A cross had been cut crudely into its surface, and Joseph wondered if this was a pointer to the place of congregation. "Have you been to the great city of Rome, master?" said the peasant suddenly.

"No," said Joseph, looking past the man to the ring of planted young oak trees, set in a circle. There a group of men, women, and children faced the east, kneeling on the damp ground,

"But you are a Roman, master?"

"Yes," said Joseph.

"And do you believe that they will come back and save us, the Romans?"

"We must be Romans," said Joseph. "We must save ourselves."

The old man clutched at Joseph's arm to share a confidence. "A monk came to us, in the winter, two years past, and he was of Rome," said the peasant. "He came from Rome and he left us a powder from St. Peter's bones. It cured my son of the chills, but only when he came to have faith. It cured others too, of pains and fevers, and we have some left. If ever there is a terrible plague, we shall be saved, we who have faith."

There was no priest, no monk, no leader at all for this congregation; and as Joseph took his place among them, he could see that there were no real Christians either. They were sun worshipers, who had been converted with miracles and fiery words and the promise of salvation. Whatever traveling man of God had taught them of Jesus and Bible and Church had done so long ago. What they chanted had once been a psalm, but was long since mangled into something pagan.

Still the chant was in Latin, and the voices full of conviction. Joseph felt something familiar and warm as the whole assemblage, nearly a score of them, bowed to the east and intoned: "The Lord is the sun, and so we bow to the east, the Lord is God-that-shields, and so we bow to his sky home. The Lord comes from the place-most-high, the Lord is the sun."

Joseph watched, and imitated the congregants as they now rose, turned their backs to the east, and then bowed low from the waist three times.

"I pray the mighty Lord," they shouted. "I pray the mighty Prince! I pray the mighty Spirit!"

Then once more they faced the east, dropped to their knees, and shouted "Hallelujah! Hallelujah! Hallelujah!" Joseph could see that the woman next to him, flaxen-haired and high-browed, with the nose of a bird of prey, had tears in her eyes. All the congregation seemed to be gathering their breaths for a collective final shout; complete silence reigned as the devout heads slowly raised their eyes to the "sky home." But instead of speech, there was a final burst of reverence, as everyone prostrated themselves fully, their foreheads resting in the wet morning earth.

"Is it right, master?" said the old peasant, the first to raise himself from the ground. "It is a long time since we have met with a Roman Christian."

Joseph didn't know what to say. In the church outside Verulamium where he and his murdered wife had once prayed, there was a daily mass, morning and evening prayers, responsive choral singing. Everything was regulated by Church edict. Men and women were separated by an aisle, congregants rose and sat and knelt according to the signals of the priests. The psalms were sung in harmony by professional singers, whose only task in life was to perfect their sound for the glorification of God. To compare the gorgeous vestments, the cool basilica, the literate and pious community of the Christians of Verulamium with this paganized twisting of a psalm in a copse reminiscent of dead Druidic ritual, was useless.

"We read the psalm differently," said Joseph.

"What is a psalm?" said the peasant. Joseph was aware that the other congregants were watching now, neither with love nor loathing, but greedily. They wanted to know what he knew.

"A psalm is a hymn of praise to God. The psalms I speak of were written in ancient times by David the king."

"David the king," said the old peasant, very loud and clear, turning to the others. Some of the congregants repeated this phrase, as if it were itself a form of prayer.

"What king, master?" said the old peasant then. "A Roman king?"

"David was before any Romans, before even great Alexander. He was an ancestor of Jesus. Surely you have heard of how Jesus the Messiah is of the House of David?"

"Perhaps, master," said the old peasant. "But it is so long since we have heard from a man of God."

"I am not a man of God. Just a simple Christian—"

"Of good family, master," insisted the old peasant. "Roman by birth, Roman by ancestry—your clothes, your speech—you are not what we are used to. If you would tell us the psalm, the way you read it, among the Romans, perhaps we will try and learn it."

" 'For the Lord God is a sun and a shield,' " said Joseph swiftly, remembering how he had learned this psalm and all the psalms of David at his mother's knee. " 'The Lord gives grace and glory. No good thing will He uphold from them that walk uprightly.' " Somehow they had twisted this ancient imagery into an identification of David's fierce Old Testament God with the Celtic sun deity.

"Master, we do not understand the language of the prayer," said the old peasant. "It is not Latin, not any Latin we understand."

Joseph shook his head at the rising sun. He had been reciting the psalm in the original Hebrew. Carefully, and with unfortunate clumsiness, he translated the psalm into Latin. It was not one of the psalms used frequently in Christian prayer, so the words didn't fall into place from memory. Even so, their authenticity thrilled the peasants. Some of them dropped to their knees before him, until Joseph shouted at them to stop; this was an outright desecration, he told them, not a sign of respect.

"Will you bless my son, master?" said a young woman, sallow and bright-eyed. "I will bring him to you for your blessing, for he cannot walk—"

Others crowded near him, men and women, imploring him for

182

a word or a touch of his smooth hands. The young woman with the sick son seemed to be waddling unsteadily as she hurried from the group, and as she turned into the path past the ruined Roman column, he noticed that her left arm had been severed at the shoulder, creating the imbalance in her gait. He wondered if the mutilation was the result of disease or war or justice. If Julia had lived, she would have been disfigured too, he remembered, feeling the rage run through his blood. He prayed that Rachel, the kinswoman he'd never met, still lived, that the desperate journey from the ruins of their home would not lead to another ruin, another mass of rubble and ashes.

"Will someone show me the way to the Villa of Gold?" he said, thrusting away all possibility of blessings and kindnesses.

"That is not a Christian place, master," said the old peasant. The men and women who had been pressing against him were now stepping back, as if they had become unexpectedly afraid.

"I must go there. Will you show me the way?"

"It is off the highway to London, master," said the old peasant. "But that villa is a place of evil and magic and visions. Sorcerers live there, prophets and seers, followers of the black arts."

"I must go there," said Joseph. "It is where I must go to find arms and armor, and where I will learn to join those men who fight the Saxons."

"But, master," insisted the old man. "It is no such place as you describe. It is a place of bats and vermin, where men walk on all fours and beasts breathe fire and dragons guard the gates. It is the home of nonbelievers. Even the holy man of Rome who visited us with the powder of St. Peter's bones was afraid to go there. It is said that the killers of our Lord live on its grounds, the murderers of Jesus recline on its couches, sipping on the blood of innocents."

"Look, old man," said Joseph sharply, impatient with this distorted vision of the Jewish race. "You don't know what you are saying. I am going to the Villa of Gold, for there I will find my salvation."

The old peasant took Joseph and Haim as far as the first Roman milestone on the highway from Verulamium. It would be safe for an hour's walk, he told them, for the local peasants gave a goodly share of their crops to Lord Cerdic, a full-blooded Saxon who fancied himself a Roman warlord. Cerdic had men of many races under his command, speakers of Latin as well as his own ugly-voiced compatriots from across the North Sea. But Cerdic himself spoke Latin, insisted on being addressed by the title *Comes*, the Roman designation for a general which hadn't been heard in Britain in half a century.

"Thank you for giving us shelter, old man," said Joseph.

"You did me great honor, master," said the old man. "We will remember the day a Roman Christian instructed us in the psalm of the great king."

Haim fixed his childish eyes on the old peasant's handless arm. "Was it a Roman Christian who cut off your hand, old man," said Haim. "Or just a plain ordinary Jupiter-and-Apollo-loving Roman?"

"My brother," apologized Joseph, "is a young fool, and speaks without thinking or respect for anyone."

"Or was it Lord Cerdic, the great *Comes*, who found you stealing—"

"Haim!" said Joseph, and though the insult was directed at a peasant, he would have struck his brother nonetheless, if the old man hadn't gotten in his way.

"It's all right, master. The boy is full of hate, and is not of our faith. I forgive him. That is what we are taught to do." The peasant cleared his throat. "I was a thief before I was a Christian. I was caught, on market day, in London, near the old slave market. I had grabbed two little bronze statues. Not gods, just little statues— for decorating some great house. They were heavy, and I was very young, as young as you," he said to Haim. "Fourteen."

"I am not fourteen," said Haim. "I am nearly sixteen."

"No matter," said the peasant. "I was young then, and I'm old now, and when they caught me, there was no magistrate, no law. There was a terrible fear in those days that Hengist's Saxons would overrun the city itself, and the big officials and the Roman legions had left years before. All the young men were busy with fixing and building up the city wall, and when I was caught, it was the merchants who sentenced me, an old executioner who cut off my hand, and a Christian doctor who stopped the blood. I was a thief, and I was sentenced, and I was made to suffer. But what did it matter, since I had found the God-Most-High? Through my suffering I learned to know Jesus on the cross, who took our sins and made it possible for us to enter Up-Heaven, where the sun rests!"

"It was the doctor who converted you?" said Joseph, moved by the old man's words. Once again he realized that it mattered little how much one knew of rites and customs and Gospels. This peasant, with his half-Christian prayers to the sun and his inarticulate forgiveness of the brutes who mutilated him in the name of justice, was as good a Christian as any. He had faith and forgiveness, while Joseph knew that his own faith rested on a memory of love, and in place of forgiveness, his heart lived only for vengeance.

"Yes, master. He saved my life, and then he put me to work at the villa of his family. I lived there for years, in a Christian place, with a Christian master and a Christian wife. But they were murdered. It was to the east, where Saxons have been for many years. I have heard that they too will be converted to the love of Jesus, but I don't want to think of it. I don't want to remember the hate I have fought to conquer most of my life."

The old man left them with a humble bow, and Haim looked reluctantly at his departing figure. He would have liked to apologize for his coarseness. But soon the desolation of the once-proud highway, the endless tramping toward the famous city of London, returned his heart to fear. The highway, once thick with traffic, trains of groaning wagons, carriages filled with families, hard-marching troops imitating the rhythmic steps of their Roman leaders, was now without a human soul. Off the road, beyond the heavy forest, were ruined villas, clusters of huts put to the torch, isolated cottages open to the wind and the rain. The Saxons not only murdered, raped, and plundered, they destroyed whatever they had no use for. They smashed statues, polluted baths, slaughtered sheep and dogs and men. Only the road was left in peace; when every monument built by Roman power would sink into the debris left by war, the imperial highways would remain, linking cities that would rise from the dust for a thousand years to come.

"All the peasants are dead," said Haim.

"Stop talking nonsense," said Joseph sharply.

"Is it nonsense to talk about what is right in front of your eyes? I curse the day I was kept alive."

"You and I were kept alive for a purpose."

"What purpose? To die a month later? To scrounge around like beggars, begging for crusts from peasants, just so we can get to the famous Villa of Gold? You heard the old man—this land is already Saxon-ruled."

"Remember who we are, Haim, and what we must avenge. If there is justice in the world, we have nothing to fear—"

"If there is justice in the world, why is our family dead?"

"They are only dead to this world, not the one to come."

"Are you speaking now as a Jew or as a Christian?"

"If you weren't such a fool, you would see that there is very little difference, except for the Jewish arrogance of being different from all the other people in the world. There is a world-to-come, there is a God, there is goodness and there is evil, and there is a right way and wrong way—we are talking about the same religion. Except that you refuse to accept the fact that the Messiah promised by our own Bible has come and died for our sins!"

"I had a Frisian pony when I was a boy," said Haim. "She was big and black and she loved me. Do you remember how we used to race past the brook—"

"Haim," said Joseph, who knew at once what his brother was trying to do. "There is no point—"

But Haim insisted on continuing. "I was studying Greek, and so naturally, like you had, and father before you, there was a tutor, not simply Greek, but a Jewish Greek, who taught me Plato as well as Philo, who brought me up sharply every time I imagined that philosophy could somehow disprove a word of the Torah—"

"Please, Haim, that world is dead."

"And what was so wonderful about us Jews—Christians, if you prefer—at least we weren't sacrificing humans like the Druids—what was so wonderful about our life, was that there was all this learning, and then all this cleanliness. The baths. The tepid bath, the hot bath, the cold bath. Can you imagine the two of us on big black Frisian horses, dressed in the finest Welsh woolens, boots of soft Spanish leather, galloping up this road, the peasants and the slaves coming out from behind the walled villas to salute and shout greetings all the way to London?"

"This world is not the only world," said Joseph.

"This world killed my father and mother and your wife. Don't tell me a Messiah came into this world and gave us Saxons and murder and rape and barbarians. If a Messiah had come, this world would be a heaven, not a hell-on-earth. And if this isn't hell-on-earth, without law, without civilization, without books, without family, without any way to even stay alive—"

"Haim," said Joseph. "Listen to me, once and for all. We are brothers. We have been left alive by the will of God, and we are here to avenge the deaths of our loved ones. Anything else you tell me is wasted on my ears. Any complaints, any philosophy, any crying about what was once and is no longer. I hear nothing but the cry of revenge."

Suddenly, Joseph saw his brother tense. Haim's hand reached for the ornate Roman dagger in his belt, as his eyes lifted wildly heavenward; for a moment Joseph thought his brother had decided to take his own life.

"They're coming," Haim said. "Draw your sword."

And Haim began to run up the road, his mouth open for a soundless scream. Joseph went after him, his hand holding his sword steady in the makeshift scabbard, the weapon a disgraceful legacy of the night of horror in the villa of his parents—the night Saxons murdered his wife, his family, their servants and cattle. When Haim and Joseph had returned to the villa after carrying a message to the sorely beset Roman community at Camulodunum to the northeast, they had gone blindly from smashed room to room, averting their eyes from the bodies, in search of weapons. The armory had been pillaged, of course, the strongbox had been pulled out of its flint-lined hole and taken away to some ghastly new home. All that they had been able to salvage was this Saxon sword, abandoned by one of the savages in his joy at finding the jewel-hilted swords of Rome, that and his own mother's dagger, lying on the scallop-shell mosaic floor next to her broken body.

"Haim, wait!" said Joseph, because he too could finally hear what his brother had heard a moment earlier: the muffled clatter of ox carts, the clinking of iron chains. Saxons were coming their way, from beyond the next rise. In a moment they would see the bright coarse woolen costumes, the enormous ashwood spears, the crowd of women and children sitting amid the stolen treasures on wagons and carts. Clumsily, Joseph drew his sword, wondering what madness had taken hold of his brother, so terrified of the enemy that he couldn't sleep through the night, and now so eager to meet them that he dared fight them without armor, without shield, with nothing more than a lady's elegant jeweled knife.

But as Joseph ran up the road, turning his eyes up into the sun-bright path where his brother ran, he saw no blond-haired giants with hide-covered forearms, no immense and clumsy wood shields with primitive bosses, no line of captives chained neck to neck, no train of pillage winding along the imperial road. For a moment, so bright was the sun reflecting against polished metal, that he could barely see his brother, a tiny figure raising its arm against a lone horseman, horse and rider both encased in silvery, coruscating mail.

"Haim!" shouted Joseph, knowing that his brother could no longer hear him, so wild was his anger, so eager was he to meet his death. The horseman had already begun his charge, his lance raised, his body inclined slightly forward as the powerful black horse bore down on the dagger-waving boy.

"No! Roman! Friend!" shouted Joseph, as if somehow the warrior could hear through the clatter of hooves, the wild raging of the blood, the sun beating in his temples through the mirror-smooth finish of his helmet.

Everything seemed to slow down as Joseph watched. It was as if God had allowed the terrible moment to be studied and contemplated for a lifetime to come. The warrior's horse had ceased its gallop, each muscled leg stepped daintily and carefully as it bore down, slowly but relentlessly closer; the lance in the man's hand was not yet flung, but it moved slowly about, a circle in the sun, catching and enjoying the light; Haim himself had ceased to run, his feet striding eagerly, but with infinite patience, a long-striding cadence to death.

Then the two figures, horseman and boy, met in a flashing of reflected light. The lance, twisting like a winged snake in the air, struck at him. But there was no blood. As Joseph drew closer, he could see the boy holding his hands to his lips, looking in astonishment at the horseman as he reined in his horse and turned about, returning to where he had knocked the silly weapon from Haim's fist into the dust.

Joseph held the sword in his hand, but kept the blade lowered as the horseman dismounted in his noisy suit of mail. He wore a sword and battle-ax attached to his belt, and in his hand was the lance, long and deadly.

"Forgive my brother," said Joseph. "He wants only the blood of the Saxons."

"You won't kill a Saxon with a dagger, boy," said the warrior.

Haim looked at the man evenly, still speechless after his manic charge into the unknown.

"We will kill them, sir," said Joseph. "With daggers if need be, and with stones and bare fists if that is all we have." He hesitated, because what this man possessed—courage, skill, armor, and weapons—were precisely those things after which he lusted. The warrior had knowledge: he knew where to find equipment for killing, and how to master the equipment through practice and a brave heart. It was all Joseph could do to restrain himself from getting to his knees before the man and begging him to take them to his war camp, to his commander. He had never seen a man wearing so much protective armor. There was nothing this man could be but one of the Roman-British mercenaries who guarded the last villas and towns of the dying remnants of empire against the barbarians. It was to meet one of these men, to be able to join one of their companies, that Joseph had begun the voyage to the Villa of Gold. But in the wake of the man's disarming of his brother, looking up at the man's powerful, invulnerable facade, Joseph could not bring himself to speak out his desire.

"You speak a Roman Latin," said the warrior. "Who was your father?"

"Paulus of Verulamium. Son of Yehiel, son of Samuel."

"Only Paulus is a Roman name," said the warrior.

"My great-grandfather was a Roman citizen, of Cologne," said Joseph. The warrior nodded at this. Every freeman who wanted to be a Roman citizen was a Roman citizen in the last days of the empire. What did it matter to an illiterate, unwashed Saxon if one claimed lineage from a slave or a Caesar? The Vandals sacked Rome more than thirty years before; five years later they sank the great Roman fleet at Cartagena. In 476 Odoacer, the German barbarian, deposed the last emperor of the Western Roman Empire. Twelve years later the warrior in his Roman suit of mail, the Latin-speaking Joseph standing in the crumbling Britannic province of imperial Rome, could not fully believe that their world was shattered forever.

"My family has been in Britain for four generations," said Joseph, "but we've been Roman citizens for hundreds of years."

"You came from Verulamium?"

"Yes, sir."

"Verulamium is dying," said the warrior, not asking a question but stating a fact of nature. "You lived outside the walls?"

"Yes."

"Your family is dead?"

"Yes, sir," said Joseph. There was no piety in the man's voice, but this was natural in this year of destruction. Who knew what horrors the warrior had seen that day, that week, riding the length and breadth of the ravaged countryside.

"There is nothing this way but death," said the warrior, indicating the road to London. "Except for London itself, though the city has little food, and no work and no houses of charity."

"We want no charity," said Haim, speaking for the first time.

"I offer none, except for not killing you when you raised your hand to me, boy."

"We are looking for the Villa of Gold," said Haim sharply.

The warrior looked at him with sudden curiosity. "The Villa of Gold offers no refuge, boy. It would be better for you to go back to one of the villages along the road, until the country is safer."

"No, we must go," said Joseph.

"It is a dangerous road to the Villa of Gold," said the warrior. "And the villa itself is guarded, closely guarded so that no intruders are allowed."

"We are looking for the daughter of Ezra," said Haim finally. "She is the reason we are going to the Villa of Gold."

"The daughter of Ezra," said the warrior. He took off his helmet, revealing closely cropped black hair, the head of a hundred Roman battle leaders on statues and wall paintings. "If you want the daughter of Ezra, you had better tell me, why." He took a step closer to Haim and lifted the lance an inch off the ground.

"We want to ask for her help," said Joseph.

"Aren't you afraid to ask the help of a witch?" said the warrior.

"I don't believe her to be a witch, but a woman of vision," said Joseph, speaking carefully, so as not to anger the man. In an age where religion and superstition walked the same tortuous path, offense was given easily, and without intent.

"Vision," said the warrior. "I am glad to see the fame of Rachel's dreaming has spread so far as Verulamium. Are you hoping to hear the future from her lips?"

"No, sir," said Joseph. "We are looking for a different sort of help." For a moment he was reluctant to voice his desire to dress himself in the sort of mail that the warrior wore, and that protected his horse as well. The warrior might laugh at him, or worse, find him impudent.

"Everyone wants her help," said the warrior. "Why should she give it to you?" The warrior was unaccountably agitated now, his hand tightly clenched on the slender lance, his eyes wide with urgency. "Why should the daughter of Ezra give anything to you?"

"Because we are the kinsmen of Ezra," said Joseph finally. "And Rachel the daughter of Ezra is our cousin, and when we ask her for arms and armor to avenge our murdered family, she will be unable to refuse us."

"You are Rachel's kinsmen," said the warrior, relaxing his hold on the lance. "The sons of Paulus, son of Yehiel, son of Samuel. Of Verulamium." He had been looking at the cross around Joseph's too-thin neck, but now looked up at his naive and innocent eyes. "I beg your pardon, young sirs," said the warrior, without any trace of irony. "It will be my privilege to escort you in safety to the Villa of Gold."

He replaced the helmet on his handsome head, and Joseph was prepared to follow the man anywhere, with no questions asked. But Haim could not but wonder aloud at the change in the man's attitude. "Why are you taking us, sir?" he said. The warrior looked at him briefly, but with renewed respect in his eyes.

"You are Jews, are you not?" he said.

"Yes," said Haim, answering before Joseph could complicate the issue with the history of his conversion to the new religion.

"We men of Ambrosius honor those who help us to survive the Saxon," said the warrior. "No matter what sorcery, what black arts they practice. No matter if Rachel the daughter of Ezra is a witch, a demon, or a goddess, I owe her my life, and I will protect herself and her kinsmen with my own."

The warrior's name was Artorius. He was a battle leader in the great and growing army of Ambrosius Aurelianus. Much later, long after dark, as they neared the gates of the Villa of Gold, they learned that Rachel had not only fashioned the armor that he wore, and which indeed protected him every time he went to battle, but that she had also had a vision that had saved his life. She had begged him to refrain from taking the road north of her villa, to the high country, after she'd met him for the first time. Rachel had dreamed of a conflagration on that road, of walls of fire collapsing amid the screams of valiant men. Because he was not superstitious, Artorius had laughed at the dream, but Rachel had become insistent, urging him to stay at the villa for another day. She went so far as to suggest that her family would make no more armor for him if he dared not grant her wish. Artorius had agreed, finally, flattering himself that the Jewess had taken a fancy to his handsome face. Later that day he learned what her apprehension had meant: a Saxon war party had ambushed two of Ambrosius's men, and burned them alive, in their coats of mail.

But it was not simply her visions, and her artistry with iron and steel that had earned the warrior's devotion. The daughter of Ezra was a widow, and beautiful, and the pagan warrior Artorius was so much in love with her that his passion had become an obsession, his every waking moment suffused with desire.

Chapter
15

Rachel was tall, broad-shouldered, and unsmiling. She wore a heavy black woolen cloak over a tunic, and thick-soled boots. The footware was an affront to the tessellated floor. Her hair was unfettered by net or kerchief, and it hung in long black waves over her shoulders and down her back. She was blue-eyed. After she had greeted Artorius in Latin, she spoke to her kinsmen in Hebrew, excluding the warrior from the conversation. Yet the battle leader seemed to follow the shape and pitch of her every syllable.

"Who was your father?" she said, the blue eyes resting on the cross about Joseph's neck.

"Paulus," said Joseph. "Of Verulamium. The Son of Yehiel."

"I know no Paulus," said Rachel.

"The son of Yehiel," interjected Haim. "He was known as Saul until he was converted to the new faith."

"And who was the father of Yehiel?"

Joseph was sure that she knew the answer to this question, as she knew the answer to every question she had asked and would ask. Her eyes ran so deep and wide that it seemed to him that she must have known of their coming before they had even set foot from the ruined villa. It was clear why some men could fear her as a witch, clearer still how others could find themselves spellbound with desire. "Samuel," he said. "Samuel who was the son of Shimon, who first came to Britain from Cologne."

"You are telling me that we share an ancestor," said Rachel. "Shimon who was my great-grandfather, you claim as your great-great-grandfather."

"Yes, madam," said Joseph.

"You are both circumcised according to the covenant between Abraham and God?"

Joseph, wary of the rising anger in his cousin's voice, hesitated before answering, and in that moment, his brother spoke again: "We were born as Jews, into an ancient Jewish family, and were circumcised according to the Law."

"According to what law?" said Rachel.

Anger was bringing her face to life. Something childish appeared in the stern facade, a violence of spirit that was immature and insistent. Yet the power beneath the pale skin wasn't puerile. There was grave experience in the beautiful face. Joseph could see thin lines of gray in her thick hair, and the hollows under her eyes weren't from age. He could understand how Artorius would want to calm the restless fear in her haunted eyes.

"The Law of Moses," said Haim, as if she were his tutor, and this was an exhibition for his parents. "Specifically Genesis, Chapter Seventeen. 'You shall be circumcised in the flesh of your foreskin; and it shall be a token of the Covenant between Me and you.' "

"Yes," said Rachel, her lips silently following the words of the scripture, trying to quiet the sense of anger against the memory of her scholarly husband, whose knowledge of the Holy Books was without peer throughout the diocese of Britain. But she couldn't quell her hostility, even in the face of the boy's youth. The cross that hung about Joseph's neck was like a red-hot metal pressed against her flesh. Here, in her own house, surrounded by the ghosts of the empire, was yet another convert to the new religion. It was not enough that the Christians had broken the fiber of Rome, bringing knights and slaves and barbarians to the same level, all awaiting redemption and the false promise of heaven; they now claimed the souls of Jews as well. In the confusion of her widow's mind, she was as angry at Christian preachers as she was at Saxon murderers, as furious at the collapse of her world as she was at the promise of a new one.

"My father," said Joseph, jumping into the silence, "often spoke of your father, Ezra, and of his sister, after whom you are named. He told us that you were the finest creator of swords and—"

But Rachel interrupted his words of kinship and conciliation. She felt her hands move for Joseph's throat, urged by a madness to tear away the symbol of disaffiliation from his people.

The move was so fast that he had almost no time to react; he had anticipated no threat from her quarter, and as he sucked in his breath and threw up his hands, he felt his shoulders grabbed from behind with incredible strength. In that same half moment, Rachel ripped the cross from about his neck, breaking the slender gold chain as if it were made of flowers.

"Give me the cross," said Joseph, speaking Latin.

Artorius gripped his shoulders more tightly; Joseph felt a flash of pain run from the base of his neck to the small of his back. But the cross had been Julia's, and it was a symbol of belief not just in his God, but in the everlasting quality of his love. He was seventeen, and when his bride was taken away from him forever, he had sworn a vow of celibacy. There had been no women before Julia and there would be no woman after her. He felt the pain in his shoulders like a confirmation of his vow; there would be no woman, and there would be no rest until he had avenged the murder of his wife.

"Give me the cross," he said again, not realizing that the pain was making him shout. He saw Haim's face pass before his eyes, speaking Hebrew phrases, first to him, then to their cousin. He felt the battle leader force him down to his knees, he saw his cousin move close to him again, this time not to tear away an ornament but to slap his face. She was shouting, her pale face reddening, but as she swung back her hand to gather strength for her blow, some force held her from behind, and the savage and beautiful face burst into tears.

"I'm sorry," she said, unless he heard this in his dreams, for Rachel's tears were hot and full on his own cheeks, he could taste them drifting along his parched and lonely lips. "I'm sorry, forgive me, my cousin," said Rachel, but her image was confused with that of a long-haired man in antique clothing, helping him to his feet, apologizing for the excesses of his daughter. A very pretty old woman, her neck and arms circled with exquisite gold jewelry, touched her fingers to his shut eyes, but somehow he saw her clearly: soft and ageless, her sophisticated smile urging him to sleep. He felt himself falling, yielding to exhaustion. "Give me the cross," he said again, and another woman drifted through his memory, tall and angular, the bones of her face as rough as a peasant's carving. Joseph steeled himself at this vision of his mother. Not until the cross was finally placed in his hands did he allow sleep to sweep through his body, eager and overwhelming as a lover's caress.

When Artorius had first led Joseph and Haim to the Villa of Gold, they had looked past the walls, past the guard at the gate, past the porter's lodge where four men in crude leather armor had leaped to their feet. They were not looking for the relics of imperial glory, but for Rachel, the source of arms and armor. The entrance hall, where every wealthy Roman family stored its extensive records of births and death, of marriage and alliances, of bloodlines and property, had been stripped of statuary and wall hangings, but neither Haim nor Joseph had noticed details of stripped walls, cracked mosaics, or broken bits of terra-cotta tubing used in the villa's heating system. This was not a time to be startled by ruin or impressed with possessions; Joseph had learned that one owned what one was able to retain.

Rachel had entered the entrance hall from the adjacent library, and their first interview had taken place within its bare, unfriendly space. Once great processions of high-ranking visitors had been greeted there, but then the hall was wild with Mediterranean colors, antidote to the perennial cold and misty weather of this far outpost of Empire.

As Joseph woke, he caught flashes of color, bits of memory: there was a smell of spikenard, which his mother had used to perfume their own villa's family rooms; there was a tinkling of bells, like the sound of the tiny bronze circles hung in the drafty air in the sleeping quarters he shared with Julia. They were pretty little things, blessed by a pagan priest, meant to bring luck to newlyweds. Born a Jew and now a Christian, Joseph had little use for superstition. But the "old gods" of the people couldn't very well hurt them with a charmed amulet, an ancient incantation, or a lucky set of bells. He wondered if they rang on the night of Julia's murder, if the onrushing Saxons beat the air into a frenzy that sent the circles dancing into macabre song. He wondered if the bronze circles rang out their powerless blessing as they ravaged her defenseless body.

Joseph opened his eyes and saw no Saxons, no Julia, but a pagan scene: Dionysus, or more properly, as the Greeks called the great god of wine, Bacchus, joined with his immortal spouse, Ariadne.

Incredibly, against the wall, lit by bright sunlight, was a perfect mosaic, surely of marble, depicting the gods in an amorous embrace, surrounded by a brood of naked children.

"Drink this," said the pretty old woman, who hovered over where he reclined on a bed of wondrous softness. She held a Samian beaker in her hands; its red glazed surface was precisely like those that had graced his parents' household. They were imported from Gaul, and were nearly two hundred years old.

"Where did you get that beaker?" said Joseph. He spoke in Latin, for the woman was so unmistakably a Roman matron.

"Drink," she said again, and he took the beaker from her with two hands and sipped. It was a bitter brew, herbs steeped in boiling water, but not really unpleasant to get down, for drinking it was reminiscent of life before the Saxons, when every trouble had a cure; a headache with a compress of warm mint, a bee sting with a crushed-up clove of garlic. Now he was exhausted, and he drank the herbal drink greedily, knowing that strength would return to him, and with it clarity of mind.

"I am Miriam, wife of Ezra and mother of Rachel." She was watching with the closeness of a physician looking for signs. "You must forgive our daughter. Ever since the murder of her husband, she has lost her tolerance. She has forgotten that to be a Roman is to be tolerant. The Romans always respected the religious beliefs of their people."

Joseph sat up, looking about at the crimson cushions, the locked cupboards of a guest's bedroom. He drank more of the brew as the woman's prattle continued: "No nonsense you can tell me about feeding Christians to the lions or chopping off the heads of the Jews. That has nothing to do with tolerance. The emperors were tolerant, always tolerant, but the times were not always tolerant. The people are bloodthirsty, the freed slaves screaming in the amphitheaters. Politics is not to be equated with justice, or are you too young to understand these concepts? Justice is luxury that we can only sometimes afford." She smiled brightly as he finished the drink she had prepared for him. "This beaker is from Gaul, of course. Samian ware. It used to be cheap, it used to be everywhere, with thousands of slaves working in the factories, day and night, sending it out to every outpost of the empire. But then what? The Franks came and tore down the factories, massacred the slaves, destroyed the pottery, the kilns, the wheels. Barbarians have no need for tableware, whether they're Franks or Saxons. Their fingers are good enough, and they can drink from pails like the animals they live with."

"I am surprised to hear you defending the tolerance of the emperors—"

"Surprised?" said Miriam. "I am surprised that you show so little reverence for your emperors. When will we see them again? I can remember Flavius Julius Valerius Majorianus, dead before you were born, no doubt. And before him, Avitus, and before Avitus, Maximus. We still have the coins of the realm of Valentinian the Third, dead two years before the Saxons slaughtered us at the River Cray. I will not desecrate the memories of any of our rulers who were forced to succumb to the pressures of the mob."

"But surely," said Joseph, feeling with surprise the clean tunic he was wearing, wondering how he had been washed and dressed and prepared for sleep. "Surely you feel angry at the decrees of Constantine for prohibiting marriage between Christians and Jews—"

"Constantine was a great hero of Rome," said Miriam.

"And what of Theodosius, in the century after Constantine, when he denied Jews all civic offices and positions, forbade the building of synagogues—"

"What do I care about that?" said Miriam.

"But you're a Jew."

"I am a Roman, you idiot," she said. "As you are, and my husband is, and my Rachel too, and the pagans who fight for the memory of Rome—what difference does it make—Who cares about dead decrees?"

There was a slight hissing behind his head, and in the growing silence, Joseph marveled at sounds of the hypocaust, which was releasing heat through tubing embedded in the mosaic walls. Even before the Saxons ravaged his parents' villa, their hypocaust system had languished in disrepair, with only half a dozen small rooms still properly heated throughout the winter. Charcoal had become scarce, and gathering the quantities of brushwood necessary to heat the furnaces was difficult in a time of fewer slaves.

"Are you all right?" said a voice over Miriam's shoulder, and as she stepped closer, he could see Rachel, her face composed into intelligent and peaceable lines.

"Yes," said Joseph. "Where is my brother?"

"He is with Artorius," said Rachel. "I am here to offer my apologies, cousin." She knew her apology must seem as strange as her attack, her steady gaze as frightening as the tearing away of his cross; she wished there was a way to explain mad actions with logical words. Trying to be kind, she sounded brusque; trying to be accepting, she sounded fanatical. "I have apologized for striking you, but I shall not quit trying to reclaim your soul," said Rachel. "The cross is back around your neck, but I shall fight you with words and thoughts and deed. You shall see. Now get up, if you are well enough."

"I am well."

"You were not so well if a few pats from a woman's hands put you to bed for three days."

"That is enough, Rachel," said Miriam. "Has not his brother told you how they have suffered? As you have lost a husband, he has lost a wife. Imagine the miles they have walked, without weapons or escort or knowledge of the land."

"Little Haim hasn't taken to his bed," said Rachel. "He trains with Artorius and grows strong."

Joseph stood up quickly, barefoot in his tunic, feeling the warmth of the furnace rise through the concrete and mosaic tiles. The entire floor was raised on thick pillars to create an underfloor space for heat to pass through, released into terra-cotta tubing that rose through the floor and emerged, hidden in an intricate design, from the walls. But heat generated through the floor itself was the most pleasant aspect of the hypocaust system. Joseph had long felt the collapse of his world in the mornings of cold stone and marble floors in a once-grand villa.

"You are correct in shaming me, cousin," said Joseph simply. "I had no idea how long I had slept. You have every reason to think me weak and cowardly. But I swear to you that I am here not to be a burden but to be a source of strength. I want only the chance to fight against our common enemy."

"You want arms and armor," said Rachel.

"Yes."

"You shall have them, cousin," she said, leaving the guest room quickly, before the sight of her young cousin's grateful face could weaken the show of her coldness. He was a boy, for all his claims to manhood—marriage, the death of a wife, the uprooting of his home. Soon her anger at his apostasy would turn to pity. She would allow him everything—her armor, her confidence, her heart. And Rachel revolted from this. She wanted to give no more of her heart; her heart was reserved for her husband, and her love for him must remind her of the need to avenge his memory.

She hurried along the colonnaded walk that flanked the guest and family rooms, and looked out into the courtyard. The flower beds had long since been trampled by the men sent by Ambrosius to guard her. Soldiers in motley dress, few of them in mail shirts, lounged about in the sun, taking advantage of the unseasonal brightness. It was symptomatic of the times that the very men sent to guard the chief armorer of Ambrosius's forces were mostly protected by thick leather overshirts, and carried swords little better than those of the Saxon invader.

She passed the extensive bath suite, three enormous rooms that had been devoted to cold, tepid, and hot bathing. Now only the hot bath was functional. There was enough cold in this climate without looking for it in a plunge bath, no matter how ornate the mosaics or how traditional the custom. Across the courtyard stood the slave quarters, in worse repair than the rest of the house. Soldiers took refuge here, taking their pleasure with some of the ironworkers' daughters. Ezra, her father, had made it clear to Artorius that no girl was to be forced, no matter how low her station. Any soldier accused of rape would not only be sent from the villa, but would run the risk of cutting off Ambrosius's supply of armor. Two years ago, one of the heavily muscled blade grinders choked a soldier to death with his own hands. His daughter, a Christian like himself, had been dishonored by the man, and his Lord had told him to seek vengeance. Only Rachel's threat to quit work saved the man's life. That was in the days when Rachel's husband was still alive, of course; it was doubtful that Artorius would ever believe her capable of quitting work now, when she drove herself harder than anyone would dare ask.

The villa was shaped like a great letter U, with the gate and porter's lodge at the letter's opening. The courtyard was thus nearly rectangular, capped by the gate at one end, the entrance to the great reception area at the other, and by the long colonnaded walks of the house's two long wings. The house was single-storied, on a stone foundation said to be two centuries old; the slate roof was waterproofed with lime native to the region and essential in the

damp climate. No such niceties of foundation material were practiced in constructing the dozens of outbuildings beyond the slave
quarters. Artorius was always afraid one of the cottages, once used
to house animals or farm workers, and now used to produce arms
and armor, would collapse under the incessant rain. The battle
leader thought little of the slaves, many of them Saxon or half-
Saxons, who labored through every hour of daylight, in the clamorous, close conditions. They were warm, which was more than
could be said for most barbarians, and he had no sympathy for any
of their race. His fears of collapsing walls, thatched roofs catching
the flames of the iron furnaces, were only for Rachel, and not her
trained slaves. Artorius cared nothing if a barbarian had given up
Frig, the Saxons' Great Mother of gods and men, and now worshiped Jove and Juno, or even Jesus. Sun worshipers, Christians,
idolaters, sacrificers to Thunor or Woden or Tiw—these things
meant nothing to the battle leader. There was the memory of great
Rome, and all else was barbaric, worthless. But Rachel had more
than simple worth; she was priceless.

"Not simply because I love you," he would say. "But because
you are indispensable to Ambrosius."

She was afraid of his love talk, and tried to undermine it with
unkind thoughts. He was a pagan, literate only in Latin, barely
cognizant of any religious teachings, even that of the Christians,
so common to his class. Even the widespread controversies of the
day, famous throughout the world in Christian and Jewish communities, were unplumbed mysteries to the battle leader. When
she had told him how Ambash, her scholarly husband, had traveled to Verulamium and Eburacum to meet with Jewish rabbis and
Christian monks in an attempt to decipher the mysteries of free
will and predestination by close examination of the Book of Ezek-
iel, Artorius had simply nodded his head.

"If a Saxon kills you, what difference if it is predicted by some
god in the sky, or if you fall into it by your own bad luck? If you're
dead, you're dead. That's all the religion I need. Anything else is
just talk to me, words and words, when the people coming to kill
us can't even read or write."

Worse than his refusal to look for God or find solace in books or
religion, Rachel told herself, was his impossible strength. He could
say nothing that could reduce his stature, render him ridiculous.
When he expressed love for her, she could string a hundred nega-

tives together in her mind to put him in an unattractive light, but Artorius remained inviolate, shining in his ignorance like a beacon.

"And you will love me," he would say, with no less conviction than anything else he said or did. He was exasperating because he was surefooted, he was maddening because she needed him so desperately; if not for a husband, then for a friend. Even to be angry at him for his talk of love had become a solace to her; even to shout at his intolerance and arrogance. It had been a long time since she had realized that she was shouting not at him, but at herself.

He was married to a chieftain's daughter from the far west who was famous for her beauty; their children had the blood of Rome, Ireland, Frisia, and Wales in their veins, and Artorius swore that they would live in a land ruled by Ambrosius and not by Teutons. He was himself from a more "Roman" family; his father's father had been an officer in Gaul. His mother's family was related to the last Praetorian prefect of Gaul, to whom the vicar of Britain reported in the days of imperial rule. He was without religion, yet allowed the legends of his invulnerability to grow among his men, who claimed him to have been born under a lucky star. Artorius and his black horse inspired a thousand superstitions—visions and dreams and visitations by witches were food for the sorry Britannic troops in those days when the Saxons continued to pour into their island and, once there, multiply at a dizzying rate. Christian officers asked for his blessing, knowing it was a sin; Ambrosius's closest advisers would rather follow Artorius into combat than their own general, because they believed that he could never lose a battle, so strong was the armor fashioned for him by the magic at the Villa of Gold.

All these legends and exaggerations he equated with Rachel's religion, and with Christianity; and these kindred religions he put on a plane with sun worship and the soothsayers' study of the entrails of beasts. If he had any reservations about the power of an unseen god, it was related to Rachel's own visionary gifts. There was no way he could justify a belief in them, any more than he could in those of Ambrosius, his general. But there was no doubt that her vision had saved his life; and when she told him with simplicity and gravity of a tradition in her family, going back for countless generations, of women sharing her name, and with it a gift of premonition—a confusing gift, often mixing foresight with glimpses of the past and flashes of lives never lived at all—Artorius wondered if he could leaven his disbelief with an element of the preternatural. Still, he steeled himself against this. There were too many predictions, too many visions, not only from Rachel and Ambrosius, but from half the soldiers' wives, from every fisherman selling his wares off the docks on the Thames. Too many were quick to imagine him something that he had no wish to be.

As she walked past the houses' slave quarters toward the first of the outbuildings, she found her pace quickening and did her best to slow down. She remembered gentle Ambash, and her reason for remaining alive. Work was to be done, and that was her reason for going to the armory, that and nothing else.

She was coming up to the large outhouse where corn was dried in the kiln whose double-floor construction was first brought to the island by Roman soldiers hundreds of years before. Beyond this was a small granary, where the seed corn was stored, and next to this were the ruins of a barn and a stable. Here Artorius was working with Joseph's brother Haim, the fourteen-year-old boy swinging the sword—a good Roman short sword—at a thick stick that Artorius repeatedly flashed before him. She was about to call out to him when she remembered that this was unseemly. She had business with the slaves five hundred paces from where they stood; they were preparing a new mail coat for Ambrosius himself, and she wanted to see how the work was progressing.

"Rachel!" said Artorius, and she looked up, feigning surprise, as if she had only just noticed him. He began to run toward her, his stick in hand, clad only in breeches and a linen undershirt, when she heard the hoofbeats coming up fast behind her.

A horseman on a piebald was coming at her, waving not a sword but a leather-wrapped roll. He was dressed in mail, like one of Ambrosius's warriors, wearing that leader's red-dragon insignia over the metal.

Artorius could not possibly reach Rachel before the horseman, but so wild were his shouts that the horseman reigned in the piebald to look at where the man with the stick seemed to be attacking him.

For half a moment, he seemed to debate whether to draw his lance or his sword; and then for another half moment, he simply sat and stared at the crazed image of his own battle leader out of his armor.

"Sir," said the horseman. "Artorius. It is I, Velius—" But the charging man gave no sign of recognition. As the horseman placed both hands on his helmet, Artorius struck at the horse with the stick, so that the animal reared up, nearly throwing its rider.

"Sir!" shouted the horseman. "It is I! Velius!" He brought his horse under control as Artorius stood firmly in front of Rachel. Now he shouted at the horseman. "Remove your helmet then," he said.

Velius did as he was told, revealing a beardless face, pink with embarrassment.

"How did you get past the soldiers at the gate?"

"I know the soldiers, sir. They know me."

"You are to dismount before entering these premises," said Artorius.

"Yes, sir."

"Well?" said the battle leader, waiting for the horseman to do so.

"Yes, sir," he said swinging lithely off the skittish horse.

"I'm sorry," said Artorius to Rachel. "I'm sure I frightened you."

"Oh, no," said Rachel. "It takes more than the sight of a lunatic swinging his club at a poor horse to frighten me."

"I was afraid the man might mean you harm."

"With a scroll in his hand?"

"A man can draw his sword in an instant. A man in mail could throw himself on you from horseback and crush the life out of you. From a charging horse that scroll could break a skull. I know that all that might seem unreasonable to you, but then it is I who makes himself responsible for your safety." More quietly, he said: "And not simply because I love you."

"Yes, I know," said Rachel, as Haim came up to them, sword in hand. "Because I am indispensable to Ambrosius."

"Let us see this scroll then, Velius," said Artorius sharply. The young officer handed it over to his battle leader with as much crisp ceremony as he could muster. As Artorius removed the scroll from its container and tore off the string that bound it tight, he continued his criticism. "The purpose of every order is not always understood by everyone. Can you imagine a Roman legion where every soldier decided to modify the orders of his general according to the mood he was in?"

"Sir," said Velius. "Ambrosius said that it was urgent—"

Artorius stopped the young man with a glance. "Do you believe in the glory of the empire?"

"Yes, sir."

"Do you believe in our struggle to free first the five provinces of the diocese of Britain and then go on to Gaul, and Italy, and Rome itself? Do you believe in this, or are you simply a young hothead who wants to dress up like a man in mail coat, so he can parade about before the pretty whores of London?"

"I believe," said Velius simply.

"You do not interrupt your commanding officer when he is speaking. And you do not disobey any other order until that order is expressly revoked." Artorius stopped speaking while he read the communication, his lips moving silently about the words, as if he were tasting the syllables.

"Your brother is better," said Rachel, speaking in Hebrew to Haim.

"Praise the Lord," said Haim.

"Rachel," said Artorius. "Is the mail coat ready?"

"I don't know. I was going just now to check on its progress. Is there a problem? I thought there was no special hurry."

"I'm afraid there is. A special hurry. Hengist means to bring his Saxons to the gates of London. A great force has landed to the northeast, and they are five days' march from the city."

"I shall go to it at once," said Rachel. "There is no reason why the mail coat can't be finished before nightfall, if it is not finished yet."

Artorius was shaking his head. "I am sorry, Rachel, but our general demands more of you than that." The battle leader looked down at the scroll, as if to check once more its contents. "Ambrosius believes in many things, as you know, many things that I cannot share. But he is our general, and I shall follow him, even as he follows the kings of the Britons. A monk has brought him three gemstones of great value that have each touched the shrines of Peter and Paul in Rome, and are said to have been discovered in the holy earth of Jerusalem. He wants you to place them into the hilt of a great sword, the greatest sword ever made, not only in Britain, but even in Rome. He wants you to place these gems with their power into his sword, so that it shall be a cross that he can use to beat back the enemy for now and for all time."

Artorius rolled up the scroll, placed it in its leather pouch, and returned it to Velius. "And he has asked you to come to London, though it is a dangerous place. He has asked you, in the name of the kings of the Britons, to come at once, and to bring his armor, and make him his great sword."

"Then I must go," said Rachel, looking from Artorius to Velius. "Since it is an order from your general."

"No," said Artorius. "You don't have to go. London is terribly dangerous, and the roads are unsafe all about the city. And the Saxons under Hengist—"

"Now, brave battle leader," said Rachel. "You know that I must go, since I am needed." She smiled at Velius. "I always try to follow orders, even when I am offered encouragement to disregard them."

"Yes, madam," he said, but relaxed his incipient smile under the glare of his battle leader. But Rachel prevented any further unpleasantness. She hurried Haim off to tell her parents of the trip, for Ezra would have to accompany her to the city, as his skill at blade making was without equal in the country. Miriam would surely refuse to remain alone in the villa and would throw the slaves into a frenzied search for ancient, once-elegant clothes. As she hurried to look over the progress of the general's mail coat, Artorius caught up with her.

"I only meant that as you are not a soldier, if you wanted to avoid this trip, I would be happy to explain your refusal to the general and to arrange for the gems to be brought to you here."

"Thank you, Artorius. But if the Saxons are within five days' march of the city, it is clear that we are in a very great hurry. I must make this trip today, and begin work on the sword at once. You may laugh, but I have often dreamed of making a jewel-hilted sword, one that flashes fire and screams at the wind." Rachel smiled, and shrugged, as if accepting the warrior's ridicule of her dreaming as a matter of course. "I shall do exactly as Ambrosius has demanded. I shall make him a sword that will last a thousand years, and that will be remembered forever."

Chapter
16

"We used to travel in trains of litters," said Miriam. "No matter how rough the road. The slaves would run like the wind, and we would be so comfortable we could drink wine from full beakers without spilling a drop. Not a drop."

Rachel's mother talked clearly but quietly, her words not addressed to anyone in the old carriage but to some nebulous shades of the past. Ezra and Rachel chatted perfunctorily, in Hebrew, over the noise of the fast-turning wheels on the bad road. They wondered about the quality of the iron ingots awaiting their inspection in London and hoped that Ambrosius had not paid dearly for gems made of colored glass. Miriam spoke in Latin, of course, the language of reminiscence.

"This is not a Roman carriage," she continued. "A Roman wagon has an undercarriage, and is separated from the jolting of the road; and this is not a Roman road. A Roman road is maintained. Every soldier works on the road. The Roman legions built their strength out of working with shovel and spade. No soldier works with shovel and spade anymore. That is why they flee when the barbarian comes. That is why the Roman legions have left us."

"We're going to London, Mother," said Rachel, breaking her mother's self-absorption. "We will be safe behind its wall, no matter what danger arises."

"I care nothing about danger," said Miriam sharply.

"I know."

"It is not for myself that I grieve, but for the end of all that was wonderful. London! Do you think I care to see that ruin! Once it was called Augusta, great and powerful London Augusta, an honorific name given to the people of the city by the great and noble Theodosius after he broke the siege of the city. Does anyone even remember the emperor who sent him? Valentinanus, who sent us a true *Comes* of Rome, not like the little chieftains from Wales who dare call themselves *Comes* and *Dux* and *Praefectus*. Valentinanus, who ruled for ten years, until the great drought in Britain, that ruined so many farms, so many lives."

Rachel turned her attention more fully to her mother, for the woman was beginning to cry at the memory of something that had happened more than a hundred years before, something that she might have heard at her grandmother's knee.

"Mother, there is no drought today. You think of the days of Valentinanus the First."

"And Maximus," insisted her mother tearfully. "The terrible drought in the land."

"After Maximus, Count of Britain, defeated the Picts and became the emperor of Rome," said Rachel with flat emphasis, "he was himself killed by Theodosius. That death was one hundred years ago. It is one thing to give glory to Rome. It is another to cry for what is long dead as if it were yesterday. The Bible tells us that there is a time to mourn and a time to dance."

"Do not tell me about the Bible, please. Your husband Ambash was a great scholar of the Holy Books, and he is as dead as any Roman emperor. And are you mourning for him, or dancing?" She looked with sudden sharpness at her daughter: "Or is it eperhaps time to get a new man altogether?"

"Miriam!" said Ezra, injecting his dour presence between mother and daughter. "I will not tolerate sacrilegious talk."

"Naturally. You don't tolerate sacrilegious talk, and your visionary daughter doesn't tolerate her Christian cousin or her handsome pagan suitor—because you have both forgotten what it means to be Roman."

"We are not Roman, Mother," said Rachel. "We are Jewish. Rome is no longer an empire, and we are residents of Britain, which is fighting to repel a barbaric invader. If you had any faith at all, you would realize that all your talk of slaves and litters and imperial roadways is empty and ephemeral." Her angry tone was a connection to Ambash, to his defense of their people, to an intolerant rage against fellow Jews who looked for other ways of life than the Way of the Law. But more than that it was to shut up her mother's insinuations. That Artorius loved the beautiful widow was known, even accepted as a mark of the disintegration of their society; but Rachel had never admitted the possibility that she could return the pagan's love. "Before Rome was born, we Jews were praying to the One God, and now that Rome has fallen we will continue to pray to Him, and from this day forth and forever."

"Amen," said Ezra.

"Superstitious rubbish. Unworthy of a Roman," muttered Miriam. But she had kept her voice down, so that Ezra would not grow angry enough to strike her, and resolved to stare out at the countryside, beautiful and green, in spite of all the ravages of the barbarians and the neglect of the country by Rome.

She was not crazy, Miriam reminded herself, no matter how they treated her. It was simply a question of sensitivity and values. There was a period among the Roman upper classes when religion was all the vogue. There were subscribers to the rigors of Judaism even before the Christians made their great conversions in the fourth century. And certainly among her own class, in Britain, most of the women she knew were Christian, and had read Augustine, and could talk endlessly about a dozen fine points of the life-to-come. But Miriam preferred her Lucretius to her friends' Christian theology and her own family's Jewish Bible. She had loved to quote the Roman poet to Ambash over her daughter's nervous complaints: "So powerful was religion in persuading us to do evil deeds."

The carriage was accompanied by two horsemen in mail coats, Artorius and Velius, both of them wearing the red dragon of Ambrosius's troops across their chests on linen bands. Joseph rode on Artorius's right. In place of mail, he wore a hard leather vest that was covered with iron rings, each sewn individually in a random pattern across his chest and back. Haim, riding next to Velius, wore a leather vest without any iron at all; but even this armor seemed to him a great solace against the arrows and lances that might be flung at them at any moment. Half a dozen soldiers rode behind the carriage, and these men were dressed in the same leather armor as Haim, except that their armor was marked with the scars of battle and the stains of blood and sweat.

"Vortigern was killed in such a vest," said Artorius to Joseph. "Welsh leather, but of many colors, and the iron rings were bigger and fewer, and when he ran from the enemy, they rang together in shame."

"Did you ever see Vortigern?" said Joseph.

"Do you doubt my story, boy?" said Artorius, speaking with a gruffness that Joseph took for show.

"It is only that I have heard the same story, of the ringing of shame, from the peasants around Verulamium. That, and his great fear of Ambrosius, even when he was just a boy." He paused for a moment, looking at the road ahead in imitation of Artorius's watchfulness, and to gauge whether he had irritated the battle leader. "I would have thought you to be the last one to believe in what has already become legend."

"Vortigern wore leather armor," said Artorius, "because he had little use for the ways of Rome. That much is a fact. In Wales, they have made such armor forever—thick-cut cowhide, boiled in oil until it's soft enough to shape into the figure of a man. Some wore the armor over shoulders and arms and legs, and some, the leaders, painted the leather, in imitation of the Picts, whom they have fought for centuries."

"Only the Picts paint their bodies, not their armor," said Joseph.

"If you know so much, Joseph, son of Paulus, why don't you tell me the rest? How Vortigern learned to fear Ambrosius, how the country has learned to praise our general as their salvation, and the king who came before him as their traitor?"

Joseph took this as a challenge. Knowledge was a rare commodity in those days of chaos. The alliances of fierce enemies led to frequent retelling of stories of the kings and warriors who ruled in little bursts of power in the absence of the majesty of the Roman legions.

Vortigern was a Welsh king, and not yet a Christian. Unlike much of the aristocracy, he didn't turn his heart to Rome for advice or dreams of glory. He carried a Celtic sword, swearing that the manufacture was superior to any steel invented in Greece or Rome; he prayed to the gods who had lived in Wales for a thousand years before the coming of Christ, and when he had to defend his mountainous countryside from Scots and Picts and Saxons, he was further besieged by Britannic forces still loyal to the ways of Rome. Maddened by the harassment of Britons who he felt should have rallied to his banner, the king's hatred of the leftover remnants of Empire was great: former soldiers and sons and grandsons of soldiers of the last legions to leave Rome in 440 were rooted out of his army. While other British kings wore Roman armor, the heavy ornamental bronze breastplate and throat piece, the highly valued helmet imported from Italy that cost more than a good Frisian horse, Vortigern wore the leather armor of his humblest soldiers— though marked, according to the legends, with the colors and symbols of kingship.

"I have been told that the story is greatly complicated," said Joseph, "but in its simplest form has to do with faith."

"Faith?" said Artorius. "There is no faith in the story. Only superstition and blood." He held up his hand to slow down the riders, and then motioned for Velius to come up to him.

"Sir?" said Velius, and Artorius asked him to ride ahead. The road ahead had been blocked by ambushers two weeks before, and he wanted Velius to scout for any sign of skirmishers.

"Yes, sir!" shouted Velius, and raising his lance, he galloped off, leaving their party behind like slow-moving figures in a dream.

"Yes," said Artorius to Joseph. "Faith, you were saying. You mean because Ambrosius, like you, is Christian, he has won the hearts of the people?"

"I believe that the Lord wants our leadership to be Christian," said Joseph. "Yes. And moreover, that it is Ambrosius's belief in the Lord that lets him have his great victories. Even as Germanus had his victory—"

"We are going too fast," said Artorius. "My faithless heart is worried about the lay of the land. Let us go slowly and wait for Velius."

Joseph knew the legend of Ambrosius being brought to King Vortigern as a small boy. Like his cousin Rachel, Ambrosius was said to have visions, and not only at night, like hers, but during the day; great thundering visions of wild horses, rushing water, swords piercing stone, and blood raining from the sky. Vortigern was nothing if not superstitious. The boy was said to have predicted a drought and a storm and an invasion of Jutes; each event was preceded by a vision. Brought to Vortigern, he stood very straight before the towering king. When asked to give prophecy, Ambrosius was said to have fallen to the ground in a fit, writhing about entranced, uttering gibberish. The frightened king helped the boy to his feet, personally brought a cup of wine to his lips, helped him to a chair. And when he was finally at rest, Ambrosius predicted two things: that the Saxons would conquer Britain, and that the Romans would return to conquer the Saxons, and Britain, and the entire world.

"Is it true, sir," said Joseph, "that Ambrosius killed Vortigern?"

"Is that what the peasants say?"

"Yes."

Artorius thought for a moment. Then he nodded his head. "Of course it is true. Vortigern deserved to die, and so Ambrosius set fire to his castle and burned him and all his retinue alive."

"Were you there?"

"No." Artorius smiled, because Joseph seemed to be curious about his every word, his every action. "I was still a boy, untrained in the ways of war."

Vortigern's memory was hated by the common people because it was said that he brought the Saxons down on their heads. Joseph accepted the truth of this; Vortigern had invited the terrible Hengist and Horsa, wild Saxon chieftains, to come with their savage warriors to help him fight the Picts and Scots. Hengist and Horsa fought these barbarians very well, and were paid for it in tribute and lands, but when Vortigern had no more need for their mercenaries, the unfettered soldiers began to run wild in the land. They remained the vanguard of the further invasion of the island, not only by Saxons, but by Jutes and Angles—those fair-haired warriors sometimes called "English."

"But, sir," said Joseph. "Why did Ambrosius let the son of Vortigern live, and go on to rule? Wasn't he fearful of the consequences? Didn't he have the chance to rule the land himself?"

"The chance, but not the desire," said Artorius. "Ambrosius is not a king, but a soldier. Some soldiers have dreams of kingship, but not the best soldiers. The best soldiers stay with what they know, and what their mission is. Ambrosius's mission is clear. To beat the Saxons back from our shores. Even your saint Germanus didn't want to become our king—and with the people as superstitious then as now, he could have easily accomplished it."

"Germanus was a holy man more than a soldier," said Joseph.

"It seems that you are always correcting me, boy," said Artorius.

"Naturally, where it concerns my religion, I should have spent more time in study and contemplation than a nonbeliever—"

"You're quite right," said Artorius. "I know very little about fighting Picts and Scots, as I am a fighter of Saxons and not a student of history. I was simply trying to educate you in the ways of Ambrosius, a Christian whom you hope to serve."

"Even a soldier and a nonbeliever must agree that Germanus's victory can teach us something—"

"Miracles teach us nothing. They are like earthquakes and avalanches. You can't rely on them," said Artorius. Once again, he raised his hand to slow down their party, and then he stopped horsemen and carriage altogether and motioned for silence.

Joseph was struck for a moment by a sense of having seen this image before: a warrior, his hand raised, the sun flashing in his mail, the sounds of man and beast and nature quieting at his command. Perhaps it was only the mention of Germanus, the great bishop of Auxerre, sent by the bishop of Rome to Britain in 429. He had been given command of local troops fighting the barbarian, and positioned them in a ravine that led from a shallow river. When the invaders had forded the river, Germanus had raised his hand for silence, and had come out alone to face them, his sword raised high over his head, the jeweled hilt on top, so that his weapon was not a blade but a cross. And he shouted, "Hallelujah! Praise the Lord!" Like a man possessed, he stood there in the sun, in his Roman armor, with his Christian cross, and shouted before the invaders, and all about him, hidden in the ravine, the local troops he commanded shouted "Hallejujah" as well, so that the Picts and Scots thought the ravine ran riot with demons. They fled, stumbling in the river, with the Britannic troops following them now with swords, not crosses, and cutting down all those who didn't drown in the tricky current.

There was no cross in Artorius's hand now, and no victory looming before him on this road. But as he held up his hand for silence, Joseph recognized the fabric of dreams. A preternatural film seemed to envelop the battle leader, his horse, and the little bit of roadway on which they waited, so tense with strength and power that horse and man both seemed to be creatures of a simpler, more heroic world.

"Someday, you'll hold a cross," said Joseph, forgetting to maintain the silence called for by the battle leader. But it no longer mattered, because his words were not uttered into silence, but into a sudden rush of frenzied sound. Velius was returning, galloping toward them, his mouth screaming words that at first no one could hear.

"Them," he was saying. He had drawn his lance, and his small iron-studded leather shield held a Saxon ashwood arrow almost at its center.

"Them," he said, again and again, galloping past Artorius almost to where the carriage waited for the battle leader's command. Joseph could see the fear in Velius's bright blue eyes, but overwhelming this was anger. He seemed to want nothing more than to throw himself at the enemy, as if this were the only way to hide the substance of his fear.

Joseph drew his sword, raised his shield, and looked to where Artorius was slowly and articulately calling out orders; the soldiers behind the carriage were to group themselves in a phalanx in front of it, Haim and Joseph were to take positions behind it, and he and Velius would scatter the enemy at once.

And now the sword was in his hand, and Joseph's eyes were riveted on it as the blade caught the sun. Holding it at the hilt, the cross was inverted, unlike the victorious image of Germanus, but with the same sense of ineluctable power. Joseph felt no fear, felt no possible chance of defeat, even as Artorius had described his men's superstitious feelings about following him into combat. Ready to turn about his horse, he heard his brother scream out a single curse in Hebrew and rush not toward the carriage but straight ahead, up the road where the enemy, as yet uncounted, approached. He had disobeyed Artorius, but the battle leader seemed to take no notice of this. With perfect grace, he inclined slightly forward in his saddle and, holding sword and shield, began his charge, with Velius screaming at his horse to try and keep apace.

Both of them passed Haim almost at once.

Joseph realized at once that he could do no less. He followed his brother up the road. In the distance he could see a small group of archers, perhaps a half dozen, at the side of the road. Coming up behind them were warriors on foot, dressed in bright colors, brandishing the great spear that was the weapon of their chief god, Woden. Such spears could be thrown with great accuracy, or used for wholesale slaughter at close range, as had been done at the villa of his parents.

Because Artorius's charge avoided the archers and the spearmen, Joseph's eyes were drawn to the third group of skirmishers, half a dozen helmeted men with shields and swords, dressed in red-and-blue-leather breastplates. Their helmets were of metal and horn, with enormous birdlike ornaments; with metal nose guards and great beaks rising from the tops of the helmets, these Saxons looked like two-legged birds of prey, as dangerous as malevolent gods.

But they were not dangerous.

In the distance, Joseph could see these men raise their swords, shout their battle cries, shield their bodies as Artorius and Velius charged into them. These proud Saxons, leaders of the group that had lain in wait for them on the road, turned their beaked helmets, their brightly colored armor, their double-edged swords to the horsemen in mail. They tried to hack and slash at the onrushing men, because their swords were round-pointed, not suitable for stabbing; but even if they had use of sharply pointed blades, it was unlikely that they could have stopped Artorius and Velius. The Saxons' primitive weapons glanced off the heavy mail coats, while the forward momentum of the riders lent enormous power to their own sweeping blows. Artorius slashed through the horn plates of a helmet as if it were butter, crushing a Saxon skull; leaning over to his left, he drove his bloody sword into the exposed neck of another barbarian as the man raised his puny weapon in vain against the wall of charging metal. Velius's lance tore through a Saxon's round leather shield and continued into his chest; he had to pause to tear it free from the dead man's broken corpse. In their mail, they were like two gods sporting with weaklings. It was not a battle, but a slaughter.

The other barbarian spearmen and archers at first joined their leaders in attacking the two mail-clad warriors. But as arrows and spearheads glanced harmlessly off the sinuous metal that covered both riders and horses, more than one began to flee. Joseph found himself caught up with his brother as Haim leaned over his horse and struck at a spearman from behind.

"Haim," said Joseph. "Let them run!"

He wanted to stop his brother from committing murder, even if this was the vengeance to which they had both sworn themselves. Velius, much farther up the road, was swinging a battle-ax as if it weighed no more than a feather, crushing heads from horseback, shouting like a man possessed. Artorius was no less bloodthirsty.

His sword rested in a corpse trampled by his horse, his lance pinned another Saxon to the hard ground off the road, and now his battle-ax was swinging wildly as he urged his powerful horse after and into the fleeing men.

Haim rushed past Joseph, as the man he had slashed fell to the ground. Though the brothers' armor was little more formidable than that of the Saxons', they had the great advantage of being on horseback and part of the tiny force that included Artorius and Velius; the seeming invulnerability of those two mail-clad warriors extended a fearsome aura to these inexperienced boys. As Joseph followed Haim into what was left of the battle, they chased men too terrified to see them for the callow soldiers they were.

But if Joseph was reluctant at first, the closeness of the barbarians, the sight and smell of them in their garishly colored and coarse clothes, brought back his mindless hate for the murderers of his wife and parents. He struck not at a single person, but into a thicket of fleeing bodies, archers and spearmen; like Haim, he bent at the waist and swung low and hard as his horse charged into the scattering bodies. There was blood, and there were the harsh guttural cries of the alien tongue, but there was no repugnance at bloodshed. Again and again, he swung his sword, crying out in a confusion of hatred and pain. These men were the murderers of Julia, whom he had worshiped; these men were the destroyers of his life in Verulamium; these men had placed him on a path of vengeance, violence, and death. Amid the screams of the victims, the frenzy of the horses, the clash of steel, it was simple to distance oneself from the act of murder. There was no thought to severed muscles, crippled lives, of widows and orphans, of ruin and waste and destruction; there was only a blind anger, that fed on itself, that lent greater ferocity to each mad blow.

But suddenly, the slaughter all about Joseph stopped. Artorius had turned his horse about and was riding fast back toward where the carriage was now advancing. Haim had pulled back from pursuit and brought his horse back to the main road. Velius was, as always, at Artorius's heels. For a moment, Joseph could actually see what he had done. Turning his horse about, he saw a barbarian clutch at his blood-filled eyes and stumble after the few men still capable of flight.

"Come on," said Haim. "Artorius has called us."

But Joseph couldn't take his eyes off the stumbling man. None of the others waited for him, and every few steps he sank to his knees. As pity began to rise up in his chest, he remembered Julia, not the desecrated corpse that they had left for him, but in life, his bride, wild with youth. He raised his bloody sword and turned his horse back, slowly at first, walking after the oblivious barbarian. Then more quickly, he charged, screaming, and, bending low, drove the edge of his sword against the back of the man's skull.

"Hurry," said Haim, who had ridden after him. "Artorius will be mad enough that we didn't stay with the carriage to begin with."

But Haim was wrong about this. Artorius was pleased with their zest for the blood of battle, even if this was a battle where the barbarians offered no threat; the battle leader had met many men who had no taste for blood at all, even when it was the raised-up throats of murderers, ready to be slit for their crimes.

Besides, his anger had been reserved for the carriage driver, who had listened to Rachel's order to advance, and to his own soldiers, who had not been able to prevent the carriage from leaving its defensive position.

"I told them that it was your wish, Artorius," said Rachel. "They believed me." He looked at her closely as if to see if there was relief in her eyes for his coming through the battle without harm. "Are you all right?"

"Because of your great skill, yes," said Artorius.

"And your own," said Rachel. "You are the battle leader all men praise."

"I am looking for a woman's praise," said Artorius. "Rachel. Only you could have gotten the carriage past my soldiers. Maybe because you're a witch," he said. He took off his helmet, searching its surface briefly for the scars of battle. "Or perhaps simply because of your beauty," he said, joking with her, at least in part. "The beauty of a siren, a sorceress. Seeing as you make it difficult for me to think of anything but you, even in the heart of battle."

"That is only because you wear my armor and wield my sword," she said.

"That still gives you no license to advance in the middle of the fight—"

"There was no point in killing all of them," she said. "It is always best if some survive. They will live to teach the others fear of men in armor. Such stories can have greater results than a hundred warriors."

"Yes, great and clever witch," said Artorius. She had left the carriage, and the warrior walked with her where golden wild flowers pushed through the furze at the roadside.

"We had best not linger," said Rachel.

"We are not afraid of the barbarian," said Artorius. "Not in our coats of mail."

"Ambrosius awaits us," said Rachel.

"I will leave my wife and children," he said. "I will swear to follow your god or any other god you want me to follow. I will do it, Rachel, though you can barely stand the sight of me."

"No," she said. He pressed his sweaty face to hers, his helmet in his hands, and Rachel felt the simple urgings of desire through a chaos of guilt and fear. But Artorius ignored her, and insisted on the kiss, and when their lips met, she felt a rush, like wind starting up on an open plane; but this wasn't air, but spirit, not a change in weather, but an opening of her heart.

"You don't understand," she said. "I don't love you. I can't love you. My husband was a wise and holy man, a man of my people—"

"Your husband is dead, Rachel," said Artorius. "I am alive, and I will have you, no matter what you say or do. I will have you, no matter if your husband comes back from the dead, or my wife becomes empress of Rome, I will have you."

"No!" she said, and this time the word was a shout, because what Artorius had declared had penetrated. Given to premonitions, glimmers of chance futures that penetrated her consciousness, she was terrified of a fleeting vision of her own death—the death of a widow, sudden and alone. But worse than this was the shame that accompanied it, as if the very earth screamed at her corpse as it was lowered into her grave. He had sworn to possess her, and she shouted back at this, as if the power of her voice could swallow up what was inevitable, written into the fabric of fate. She would die a widow, but she would not follow her husband to the grave without any other man between them; she would not join her husband in the world-to-come without having loved another man, a warrior, a leader of immortal fame.

Chapter
17

For all her bravado after the battle, the moments of actual fighting had terrified Rachel. There had been first the possibility of Artorius's death, then a moment later, a contemplation of what would succeed such a horror: A mourning, a loss of friend and protector, a rekindling of every other loss that had befallen herself and her family in the terrible years of invasion. Fear for her own person was last, as it was for her mother and father in the carriage. Death was a release, a return to a careless world; even if the exact contours of that ghostly country were unknown, it was clear to all three of them that somehow justice would prevail there, an exchange for the unjust anarchy that the Ruler of the Heavens allowed on His earth. There were no Saxons in the world-to-come. There Ambash studied his Holy Books, Ezra would be reunited with the sister whose name Rachel had inherited, Miriam would sip contentedly at the cup of Roman civilization.

After the battle, after the procession was once more underway, everyone was silent in the carriage. There had been a victory, of course, but as the miles of countryside began to wind slowly uphill, approaching the high ground where elaborate suburban villas had once stood, proudly looking down to the Thames, all tasted the ashes of futility. The little roads that led off the highway had once led to the greatest villas in the province; here visiting dignitaries of the empire had spent weeks hunting for wild boar, fishing the teeming Thames or simply reading and writing, away from the intense activity of the metropolis. Now the little roads led to ruins, as these homes were among the first to fall to bands of barbarians too intimidated to try the walls of London itself. And all of them knew what London had become; all knew that half the cause of its present decrepitude lay not from the barbarians—still unable to breach its walls—but from their fellow Britons, rushing to the crumbling city for protection.

When they had reached the highest part of the road, a little island in the river below them became visible. Here the dull red of rooftops, partly hidden by the tops of the trees, seemed strangely protected by its walls of water; the inhabitants of those old houses in the river may have felt little of the changes that had so torn apart the lives of their neighbors in the great city.

"I wish we hadn't come," said Ezra.

"It is better to see the river, and close our eyes and remember what was, not what is," said Miriam. For a moment, she broke out of her private, continuing grief. "You are thinking of your sister, Ezra," she said.

"Yes."

"Her murderers will pay for their crimes," said Miriam.

"How can you say that if you profess no belief in the One God?" said Ezra. Almost at once, he stopped his angry retort. "I'm sorry," he said. "You were right, of course. I was thinking of my sister Rachel, and the men who murdered her. We spent many good times together in the city, learning the ways of iron. Our family once dealt mostly in gold, you know, and she was the best there was, better even than our daughter with goldwork, and we would come here to learn from the smiths, and to teach them, for the annealing of gold and the annealing of iron is not so very different."

"She is going to marry a Gentile, Ezra," said Miriam.

"Who is? What on earth are you talking about?" he said angrily, torn once again from thinking about his sister to worrying about his mad wife. But Miriam was looking to Rachel, whose eyes were filled with tears. "She is not crying for London or for your sisters, Ezra. She is in love with the battle leader."

"You speak nonsense," said Ezra. But he touched his daughter's arm softly and asked her if she was all right.

"Yes, of course, I am," said Rachel, but she wouldn't turn her head toward her father, because the tears wouldn't stop coming. Ambash had been murdered on this very road, two years before, hurrying from London to be home with his beloved wife for the Sabbath. As they neared the city, isolated gravestones appeared at the roadside in ever-increasing numbers. Soon nearly every step of the way was lined with these markers of where men's mortal remains had been buried. The highway had become a macabre road through the past lives of thousands. They were hurrying through a cemetery to a city facing death. Uncannily, her mother had known she was thinking of Artorius, even if she couldn't understand Rachel's tears. She cried not for Ambash's memory, but for her own treachery to that memory. Try as she might, she could conjure up nothing more than respect and a longing for his great friendship; and worse, the growing strength of her desire of the battle leader eclipsed even these dim memories of her husband. "I was thinking of Ambash," she said. "Whom they murdered, and whose death I have sworn to avenge with my art, all the days of my life."

"It's all right," said Ezra. "Your mother doesn't know what she's saying."

But then Miriam interrupted once more. "London," she said.

A fine mist had been slowly rising from the river, and because the afternoon light had begun to dim, the huge western walls of the city loomed unblemished, the long wooden bridge that led across the water and up to the famous gateway seemed every bit as magical as its place in Miriam's memories.

"I don't remember this," said Ezra, breaking the spell. His voice, heavy with despair, was of a piece with the landscape. At the approach to the famous bridge, a little collection of huts that for many generations had housed bridge workers, dissidents, and prostitutes banned from the city, had been burned down. It had not been a pretty place, but the motley assortment of races and occupations, the sudden cacophony of petty merchants and peddlers trying to lure visitors to their stalls before the greater enticements of the shops within the city walls, had been a welcome introduction to the metropolitan jumble of the city itself.

"It was burned years and years ago," said Rachel.

"But they had come back, I thought," said Ezra. "They were living in tents and guarded by soldiers, and one or two houses had been put up and painted—"

"You don't remember, Father," said Rachel. She had last been to the city with her husband, half a year before his murder. It was she who had been summoned by Ambrosius, but her husband always accompanied her, not only out of fear for her safety, but so as to preserve the appearance of wifely purity. "Three years ago some merchants put out tents," she said, "but only for the daytime. At night, there are soldiers at the gatehouse to the bridge, and that is all. This is not a happy sign, that there are no merchants sitting here, even among the ruins."

The carriage slowed to a halt as they approached the brightly painted barbican at the south end of the bridge. A depressing silence hung over the roadway, extending to the water below, where every variety of ship used to be exhibited, their sails catching the sun in a shifting wave of color. Noise had floated up from the decks of the great grain ships, destined for Gaul, the endless flotilla of skiffs and wherries, which pulled fish from the Thames in such profusion that the richer inhabitants of London shunned it as poor man's fare.

"I remember a war galley," said Miriam, "rowed by black slaves, singing a song." As she looked from the carriage to the water, it didn't matter to Rachel or Ezra whether Miriam's memory was of an incident in her childhood or simply a twisting about of someone else's memory, someone who had been old enough to have enjoyed the glory of imperial London, when all the country was bright with Roman peace. Every passing day brought Rome farther into the past, and into legend. Everyone could remember better days, if not before the coming of the Saxon leaders Hengist and Horsa, then at least before those leaders turned from mercenaries in the war against the Picts to marauders against the Britons who had hired them. And it was not just great events that marked the declining of happy days. When Rachel had been a child, every member of her household, including slaves, bathed daily, and often more than that. Gradually, there was less fuel, fewer slaves to maintain the heating system. Many Britons who still bathed daily were doing so in cold water, and were considered eccentric. This was not so terrible as a loss of liberty, or worse, the constant threat of annihilation; but it was one step away from civilization as it had been practiced by Roman Britons for two hundred years and more.

"There is nothing in the river," said Miriam, as they got down from the carriage at Artorius's request. The great bridge was in such bad repair that they had to walk across and let the carriage enter the city without passengers. "When the *Magister Militum* came from Rome, there were so many war galleys in the water that you couldn't see the quays, and all the fishermen had to bring their rickety little ships downriver, so as not to clog the way."

There were quays now, quite visible along the city wall, but their paint was nearly gone, and their wood seemed bloated with neglect. Miriam stumbled toward the barbican, where bowmen stood guard in the tower. There were tears in her eyes as she remembered what had been.

"We used to have to wait here for the customs, Rachel," she said to her daughter, and Artorius dismounted and led them past the soldiers who stood at the foot of the barbican and onto the rotting timbers of the bridge itself. "If you didn't know someone, you could wait here for hours, especially on festival days, or market days—do you remember? Do you remember the crowds?"

"I remember the crowds," said Rachel. Her cousins, Joseph and Haim, joined them, and she could see in their eyes the wonder of the looming walls, as tall as five men standing one on top of the other, as thick as a man and boy are long, circling the vast city so that no estimate of its three-mile length could be made at first glance.

"It looks so safe," said Haim, his voice eager and beseeching. He was not so young that he didn't know that the terror of the barbarians extended to the great city itself. But he was young enough to believe the fears unfounded. Along the western wall, the setting sun illuminated tiny figures, barely moving; it seemed to be men walking a distant parapet on top of the wall itself.

"No place is safe unless it rests on a bedrock of faith," said Joseph. He had heard so many conflicting stories about the Christian community within the walls that he didn't know whether to run across the timbers of the bridge or slink back, behind the others, delaying the moment of disappointment. But Joseph reminded himself that Ambrosius himself was a Christian. They were his men who guarded the barbican to the bridge, and beyond that, on the other side, the great twin towers that flanked the enormous main gateway from the bridge, through the wall, into the city.

On foot, Artorius and Velius flanked Rachel, and Joseph and Haim flanked a trailing Miriam and Ezra as they slowly wandered onto the bridge. Even Artorius was subdued by the quiet of the waterway. "Not even a fisherman," he said to Velius, who needed no reminder of the pall of fear that was descending with the coming of dark. Artorius warned Rachel of a crack in the timber and took her arm as he did so. His hands were cold and dry, and as he walked, the battle-ax and sheathed sword in his heavy belt beat rhythmically against the ends of his mail coat.

"Maybe this will be the great battle," said Rachel suddenly.

"Do not fill me with superstition, please," said Artorius. "You will have Ambrosius himself soon enough, and you can talk to him of your dreams and your gods and your great visions."

"I am not the only one who has dreamed of a great battle," said Rachel.

"Yes," said Artorius. "Nor the only one who speaks of gods invisible, who believes in ultimate justice, in a day of final reckoning. Welcome to London, city of delusion. You will find Ambrosius a ready accomplice."

"I thought you said you would follow any god of mine, great battle leader," said Rachel.

"Yes," said Artorius, suddenly more serious. "I said that and meant that, but all that can only be if you allow me to love you." The rotting timbers groaned under their feet, and the tiny sound took flight in the spacious silence over the deserted water.

"I've never seen such a bridge," said Haim, marveling at the complexity of the framework of the supporting piers. Its elaborate bronze work had survived the peeling paint, and the fading light now exaggerated the one and obscured the other. Miriam tried to fill him with what his eyes could not see: the crowds of visitors, coming and going in two lanes of ceaseless traffic; wheels and feet mingling with the shouts of the boatmen below; soldiers, priests, slaves, peddlers, magistrates, whores, lamplighters, bathhouse attendants, seers who had all hurried to and from the wide gateway through the walls.

"It is named for Lud," said Miriam to Joseph and Haim, for Ezra wasn't listening to her but to his own thoughts of half a lifetime ago. "A great god of the Britons before the Romans brought us Neptune and Jupiter and Mars. There were those who wanted to name the gate in honor of Jupiter, but the Romans always respected the gods of the countryside. Even when Jews and Christians came to the city, they were welcomed, and allowed to pray in their own way. Even then."

The gateway was thirty-five feet wide, flanked by towers that stood fifteen feet higher than the wall itself. A tight group of disciplined soldiers in mail saluted Artorius as they approached. One of the soldiers quickly stripped away his mail and ran off to tell Ambrosius of their arrival.

"Stay close," said Artorius, retaining his hold on Rachel's arm but speaking to the others as well. As they hurried past the soldiers, off the timbers of the bridge and onto the elegant stone paving of the city, they were met almost at once by a beggar woman, pathetic in her rags. Her young face was toothless, marred by sores.

Velius threatened her away with a rude curse, even as Haim reached into his purse for a small bronze coin and tossed it to the incredulous woman.

"You mustn't encourage them," said Artorius sharply, almost as if he were afraid of the fragile creature.

"Our Bible commands us to follow the ways of charity," said Rachel. She turned to her cousins, and smiled at Haim. "Do you know where it says in Proverbs, 'He that has a bountiful eye shall be blessed—' "

Joseph interrupted her to finish the phrase, his Hebrew sharp and precise: " 'For he gives his bread to the poor.' "

"I'm surprised our Christian cousin knows the Jewish Bible so well," she said.

"It is the Bible of Christians and Jews," said Joseph. "Even the bishop of Rome has declared that the Jews shall always serve a great function for the Church in keeping alive the Old Testament."

"I suppose," said Haim, "that is why the great sport in Italy has become the sacking of synagogues."

"That is not the work of the Church," said Joseph, "but of pagans. Jews are protected by the Church, even if only to preserve the prophetic words of scripture, which indicated the coming of the Christ long before He appeared to mankind."

"I said to stay close," said Artorius, and he pulled Rachel closer to his side and drew his sword, all in the same motion.

The main street was very wide, perhaps sixteen feet across, the paving blocks in perfect condition, the buildings standing one next to the other in a contiguous line of red brick, four stories high. But the shops that filled the ground floors were all boarded up with rough planks, and the lamps that should have been nearly ready to light were without wicks or oil. Stranger still, raucous people that would have ordinarily filled the taverns near the gate and eagerly

225

pointed visitors to the obligatory first stop in the city—the labyrinthine complex of bathhouses—were nowhere to be seen.

"There is no word in my Torah that says anything about Christianity," said Haim heatedly, ready to quote chapter and verse at his equally disputatious brother; but as Artorius drew his sword, they turned to face what the battle leader had dreaded.

From behind the facade of main-street buildings, a small army was descending upon them. They were wild-eyed, and would not be stopped.

They were children.

Artorius didn't bother to shout. He swung his sword in a great arc, easily, from side to side. If someone stepped into the path of the blade, it wouldn't be his fault. "Draw your weapons," he said softly, and Velius unsheathed his sword with a great shout, leaping athletically forward, as if to scatter the mob with his eagerness to kill. Joseph and Haim drew their swords less readily, holding the weapons as if not sure what to do with them.

"Keep walking," said Artorius. "Do not let them close, or they will tear you to pieces for your clothes." The children continued to come closer, their hands extended, their eyes wide on the dazzling movement of the blades.

"Alms," they said, in a dozen dialects of Latin, in scores of tongues native to Britain and Ireland and Wales. "Bread. Give us our due." They were fair-haired and dark, rawboned and delicate, the children of Italians, Greeks, Saxons, and Picts and every possible crossbreed between north and west, south and east. They were fatherless, and their mothers begged for food, and stole, and gave their bodies for a crust of bread. They lived where once the grandest shops of the city stood, but not safe behind brick walls, under wool blankets, well fed and warm. All about the twelve gates to London were camps of stragglers, living amid the rubble of burned out houses or against the outside walls of mansions. Children huddled together like kittens or rats, warming each other with yellow, malnourished skin. Rachel could still vividly recall an enormously fat bull, a festive garland about its neck, being led up a wide street, filled with cheery, drunken pagans, urging their priests forward with this great fleshy sacrifice to the gods. She had been a child herself then, and her parents had pointed out the pagans' great temples to Jupiter the Preserver, and Neptune, the sea king, but which of these gods was left the ashes of the bull that day she couldn't remember. Only the sense of a mob lingered, happy in its shared purpose, eager for the animal's blood in the name of their god.

Velius killed the first one, a large boy with a stone in his hand who lunged toward where Ezra gripped Miriam. The warrior swung his sword into the boy's side, and the boy arched his back and screamed, and the scream died before it could grow to full size. In that moment, a half-dozen others came at them, clutching at Rachel's tunic, reaching ravenously for Miriam's golden armlets.

Haim struck with his fist and with the flat of his sword. Artorius and Joseph swung indiscriminately, eager to strike terror, to keep the wave of bodies back. The soldiers behind them drew their swords too, and they kept a part of the mob away, forming a line of six men with dancing double-edged blades. But there were too many of them about Artorius and Velius, trying to protect Rachel, and as the dark street grew thick with screaming children, it seemed that a thousand of them might have been tossed up suddenly from the bowels of the earth, and that not even their mailed might could stop hungry, murderous children.

But of course, they were not a thousand children, but fifty, and they were not in a desert, but in the midst of a city that still was ruled by force of arms. There was a sudden mutual cry, as if the children had all heard the same dire note, and all at once they began to fall back from the circle of swords. Rachel felt her arm being grabbed once again, by Artorius, and at the same instant she heard the horses and saw the flashing of lances as a dozen of Ambrosius's men came to their rescue.

"No," she screamed, in spite of herself. She wanted to tell them that the children would fall back, they would run away, leave them alone not only today but for all time. Rachel wanted to explain that these children were not the enemy, but simply the refuse of war and poverty and the disintegration of plenty, the logical end product of the collapse of great Rome. But the warriors of Ambrosius wouldn't have listened. Their battle leader was under attack on the way to the general in their own capital city. These were not children, but demons, and quickly they drove their lances through their starved bodies, crushed their heads with battle-axes, trampled their childish bodies into the perfectly cut pavement stones laid by slaves centuries before.

"Come," said Artorius, and he pulled Rachel away from the

slaughter, and Velius and the other soldiers knew the way, and they were soon off the main street and into one of the narrow byways, where lights burned from every house, and soldiers guarded every other door.

"They're only children," said Rachel, but Artorius couldn't hear her, and if he had he wouldn't have bothered to answer. This was not a time when one had the luxury of such facile distinctions. There were Ambrosius's warriors, who lived to create order, and there were the breakers of that order—be they Saxons from without or the homeless children of dead men from within.

They paused for a moment, to let Ezra and Miriam catch their breaths.

"Where are we?" asked Miriam, surprised to find herself in a quarter of modest houses with graveled streets. "This seems to be the quarter of the slave market."

"It was," said Ezra. "Thirty years ago."

It had become safer for many of the rich to live here, in this low-rise section, separated from the vagrants' camps by narrow archways, guarded by soldiers. During the day, the streets near the gates were still safe, and merchants continued to offer their meager wares. But by late afternoon, the population hurried to be behind barricaded doors, close to their weapons, and reliant on Ambrosius for maintaining the curfew that began a half hour before darkness.

"Then where are we going? Surely Ambrosius isn't quartered in a slave pen?" said Miriam. Crossly, she adjusted the jewels about her throat and looked sharply into the rim of darkness at the top of the street, as if it were peopled with barbarians whom she would defy.

"We will be there shortly, madam," said Artorius. He led them through another narrow alley, paved with rammed flint; by then the soldiers had to carry torches to light their way.

There were streets with lights burning in every house, and there were streets of empty shells, with the rubble of collapsed colonnades and statuary so thick in the street that it seemed as if an entire fortress had been felled only the day before. Later they would learn that much of the destruction—of houses, monuments, household articles, entire blocks of the city's slums—had come about in the last few days, and at the express orders of Ambrosius. The great three-mile wall about the city had to be repaired, built up, and buttressed, and there was no stone within the city except what was wasted in deserted houses and monuments to dead gods and forgotten heroes. Just as the wall had been built up to nearly twice its previous height a century earlier—also at the threat of invasion—as the threat of the Saxons march on London within the next few days had led to a frenzied destruction and carting of stone to the base of the wall. The parapets that had so thrilled Haim and Joseph in the waning light, were sagging; the stone face that beat back the sun was irregular, a disgrace to Roman construction; the buttressing ignored the lessons taught by Rome for four centuries and reverted to the most primitive forms of engineering.

But the Britons had added fifty bastions, fortified every gateway, and prepared boulders to drop at any boatload of barbarians daring to row up to the wall for a closer look. Save for their own hostile thieves and beggars, the city's population had more to worry from siege and starvation than from being run over by a force powerful enough to break through the walls. Even an army of twenty thousand men couldn't break through, Ambrosius had sworn. Even a legion of Romans couldn't breach their defenses.

The streets grew gradually wider again as they approached the center of the city. As Miriam remembered, the streets were steeper here, taking one up the high plateau where the temple of Jupiter stood; from a high point on the bridge to the city, the roof line of the temple had once been visible. It had been glorious to approach London, looking down to the busy river, up over the wall to the colonnade and bright rooftop of the distant temple. Today, she had been too distracted to search out its shape through the mist. Perhaps the wall had grown too high, or the bridgework sunk too low. But before they could approach the way to the temple, the party once more turned, skirting the forum, and leading north to the basilica, where she had once seen a Roman legate address two thousand people.

"Joseph, look," said Haim. It was incredible to the others that he could be impressed with the magnificence of buildings, when their lives had so nearly been forfeit. But they had lived outside Verulamium, and that city's basilica, though large and imposing, was like a toy next to this gargantuan structure of brick and ashlar. "It must be a mile long."

Not a mile long, but one-twelfth that length at four hundred and forty feet. It was one hundred and ten feet wide, held up by columns towering at forty feet. The exterior was lit by crude torches, but because the darkness was not yet complete, and the basilica was on an open unshaded plain, it seemed to glow with radiance, as if the warmth of the sun had not yet left it for the night. They followed Artorius inside, and all of them were asked to sit near the entrance while Artorius brought Rachel forward to greet Ambrosius Aurelianus.

"You will insult my family, if my father, a great artist in gold as well as iron, does not accompany me," she said.

"I am terribly sorry, madam," said Ambrosius's chamberlain, an old man with a beard of yellow and white. "I meant no disrespect, but only wished not to tire him."

"Ezra is not so easily tired," said Rachel. "A walk through town cannot exhaust a man who beats out plates of armor from solid ingots."

"It is not of Ezra that I speak, but of Ambrosius," said the chamberlain. Rachel's father took her arm and joined Artorius and the chamberlain in a slow, stately walk down the wide central aisle of the basilica. Once used as places of assembly, these huge halls had taken their places beside the forum and the great temples as marks of every city in the empire. Now, as temples collapsed and forums disappeared under peddlers' stalls, basilicas had taken on new functions: sometimes as churches, sometimes as leaky shelters from the rain for the homeless. In London, the great central basilica had become a temporary military quarters. The large apse at the eastern end, where the pagan mosaic floor had been ripped up fifty years earlier and replaced with floriated Christian crosses, was now a depository for arms and armor. Scores of soldiers, in motley uniforms and odd pieces of leather padding, leaned against the marble-covered walls, a striking contrast not only of peace and war, but of civilization and its decline.

Much of the flooring along the central aisle had been ripped up. Mosaics both pagan and Christian were incomplete, like pieces of badly remembered dreams. Torches burned along the walls, so that the light sputtered and reflected, lending a wavelike quality to Rachel's growing image of Ambrosius, surrounded by his officers, sitting on cushions where crumbling maps were laid out on the tessellated floor. Near the maps were oil lamps, which burned brighter and with less variation, so that as Rachel neared the great general and entered his private sphere of illumination, he was like something sharp and clear in a world that was otherwise dim and imprecise.

230

"Sir, it gives me joy to see you," said Artorius. Rachel found herself staring at the emaciated man, whose skeletal face she could barely recognize as the vigorous general she had last seen two and a half years before. She knew he had been unwell, but hadn't realized that the fate of Britain was being entrusted to a man who looked like a corpse waiting for its winding sheet.

"Come closer," said Ambrosius. He looked at none of them, not Artorius, Rachel, Ezra, or the chamberlain as he spoke, but each understood that the sick man was addressing the young woman. He was clutching something bright in his right hand, and as Rachel stepped closer, she saw the dull green gleaming of an emerald in his fist. Ambrosius never took his eyes from the stone as he spoke.

"They say it is from the Holy Land. It is one of three. A ruby and a diamond. Only the diamond and the ruby flash. Show her the stones."

One of the officers handed Rachel a leather pouch. Carefully, she extracted the larger stone, a diamond, a gem that she had never seen. It was crudely cut and tinged with blue, but was still so amazingly brilliant, reflecting back the paltry light of the oil lamp more than any other gem that she had ever seen, that for a moment she was sure it must be glass. Working with emeralds had taught her to beware of great brilliance, for they seldom occurred naturally with those bright green stones; rubies were quite reflective if well cut, and then usually not as brilliant as their glass imitations.

"Is it glass, the diamond?" said Ambrosius's weak voice.

Rachel felt the warmth of her hand extend to the diamond, whose name was derived from the Greek *adamas*, and was put into Latin by the poet Manilius nearly five hundred years ago. She didn't know that this sudden warming of the stone was a property unique to diamonds, and one of several ways of authenticating it. But as she felt the stone warm in her hand, she was certain not only that this was a real diamond, but that the nature of this stone was not at all foreign to her. Somehow her life was connected, if not to this particular stone, then to another, of the same unique variety. In her hand, the warmth was one of relationship, familiarity. Never before in her life had she touched a strange object and received such a powerful impression.

"No, sir," said Rachel. "The stone is authentic."

"And the ruby? Is it real or glass?"

Reluctantly, she let go of the diamond and returned it to the pouch. She knew already that she would make it the center stone of the general's sword. She took hold of the smaller ruby, a stone some rabbis thought had been one of the twelve gems in the high priests' breastplate, but which Ambash had proven to be unknown in ancient times in the Holy Land. Rachel had enough familiarity with this jewel to know that it was almost impossible for it to have been unearthed in the Holy Land, since the only ruby mines known to her were from lands east of Persia and India, from where the stones were brought, at great expense, to the aristocrats of ancient Rome.

"I asked you if the ruby is made of glass," said Ambrosius.

"I believe not, sir," said Rachel.

"You are less sure than you were with the diamond, it appears," said the general. It suddenly struck Rachel that Ambrosius was holding on to the emerald for its medicinal purposes. To stare at the stone was supposed to calm one's nerves, soothe a fevered brain, and restore one's eyesight. Other superstitions were associated with the stone: it was supposed to keep away demons, and all the trouble ascribed to them. Therefore the stone was worn as a preventative for anything from a bad stomach to a weak heart.

Rachel held the ruby closer to the light. Squinting, she could see no telltale bubbles in the surface, which frequently were visible in faked glass or paste gems. If she had time, there were certain ancient tests to determine whether the stone was true or not; but she doubted that Ambrosius wanted to hear that the stone was false, or that he had the time to let her heat it until it would turn green—as a true ruby will at sufficient temperature—then wait for it to cool and return to its natural color. The man was dying, and wanted his sword to take to the last battle before the grave.

"I am quite certain, sir," said Rachel. "The stone is authentic."

"Well, good," said Ambrosius. "I know that the emerald is true, for it has calmed my nerves, and relaxed my every muscle. I believe that the room is even brighter." He paused for a moment and finally looked at her with his dull, filmy eyes. "You have come to make a great sword, the most excellent sword ever devised."

"Yes, sir."

"Have you dreamed of such a task?"

Rachel could feel Artorius's eyes on the back of her head as she answered. "Yes, sir. I have not asked for such a task, but I believed that such a task would find me."

"And the great battle? Have you dreamed of the great battle?" said Ambrosius, more eagerly than before.

Rachel hesitated, not because she was reluctant to give an answer to this question, but because an eerie sense of warning, as if the ground on which she had stood had become suddenly unfirm, like shifting sand, had precluded thought. Ambrosius, a bit crossly, repeated his question.

Rachel wanted to answer, but was suddenly so dizzy that she had to reach out for support. The hands that grabbed her were Artorius's. "I believe that she is overtired from the journey, sir," said the battle leader.

"No," said Ambrosius. For a moment, it seemed as if the general would rise, to look more closely at the young woman's wide-eyed face. "She needs wine." He was certain that what was overcoming her in the great hall, so full of men's fears and aspirations, was prophecy, revelation. Rachel turned to face Artorius, and for half a moment the handsome face was changed: drawn, saddened, wise, and infinitely experienced—as if he had lived a thousand years. The chamberlain brought a silver goblet to Rachel's lips, but Ezra interceded sharply.

"I beg your pardon, Ambrosius," he said. "But the laws of our religion prohibit drinking the wine of the Gentile."

"No, Father," said Rachel. "It is all right to drink this wine of the general." She remembered Ambash discussing the fine points of Kashrut, the many controversies of the pious over what may be eaten and drunk by the followers of the Law. But she knew she needed this liquid, this connection to Ambrosius, to the feelings that were sweeping through her, and that were connected to Ambrosius, to Ambash, to Artorius, to the diamond she had touched, to the people of this island. She spoke again, and the words would have angered Ambrosius if he himself were not given to visions and foresight. "The diamond will be the central stone," she said.

"Yes," said Ambrosius. He watched as the young woman drank the wine in the goblet, a huge single intoxicating draft. "And the battle?"

But she smiled now, holding out the goblet for more wine. As the chamberlain took it from her hands, she was overcome with another whim, and she voiced it at once: "Please give me the diamond."

Exasperated at her words, the chamberlain blurted out: "Ambrosius has asked you a question, woman!"

"Silence, fool," said Ambrosius. "And give her the wine. Give her the diamond. Don't you recognize the gift of prophecy after all the years you've served me?"

Artorius, afraid of the proceedings, unsure of the violence that might be unleashed by desperate men looking for a sign from an uncaring heaven, urged restraint. "Surely, sir, the woman is tired, and unused to wine—"

"You look afraid, brave warrior," said Ambrosius. "Do you fear the words this woman will speak?"

Artorius paused to measure his words, and in those few moments realized with amazement that he was indeed afraid. Rachel drank and clutched the diamond, and some of Ambrosius's men made the sign of the cross, and others mumbled secret phrases to older gods. "Yes, sir," said Artorius. "I fear the words that might confuse us all, when what we all must do is study maps, listen to the reports of our scouts, plan our battle—"

"You have no faith, great battle leader," said Ambrosius. "That is why the kings of the Five Britains have given me their trust, and worry about who will live to replace me. All the soldiers know and love you, and they are full of faith; but the people, and the kings and the men of the Church and the priests of the false gods—they fear a leader who has no belief, not in gods, not in fate, not in prophecy."

"More wine, sir," said Rachel, extending the goblet to the chamberlain. Her hands shook, and her eyes were focused at nothing within her path. The chamberlain took the goblet and filled it with speed. "I have dreamed of the battle," she said. "The last battle."

"Yes," said Ambrosius. "The last." He watched as she drank the wine. His own herbalist, a Christian convert, had steeped the drink with a dozen kinds of mint. He had needed to combat his lethargy, his sense of sliding into a pit from which there would be no release. The drink hadn't returned his physical strength, but it had sharpened his waking and sleeping mind. His dreams were vivid, his thinking acute. He could see the change wrought in the young woman: she was not drunk, but alive, not out of control with the world around her, but more alive to that world that few men could see.

"It will be a great battle," she said, turning her eyes slowly from Ambrosius to Artorius. "A great battle, where the men will rally behind the sword I shall make."

"Yes," said Ambrosius.

"It will be a Christian sword," said Rachel. "The men will rally behind the sword of the leader, and that leader will be Christian, and that sword will spill blood, and when turned around, the blade held in the leader's hands, its three-jeweled hilt will be a great cross, an inspiration." Tears had begun to form in her fixedly staring eyes. "An inspiration," she repeated.

"It is the wine talking," said Artorius.

"Yes," said Ezra. "And my daughter is exhausted. If you have had us come to you for the making of this sword, you had best take us to our quarters and let us sleep."

Ambrosius, usually quick to take offense at interruptions, hardly heard Artorius and Ezra. He was so close in spirit to the words coming from the young woman that he felt nearly capable of mouthing them a half instant before she gave them voice.

"Ambrosius," said Rachel. "The sword is not to be made for you, and the Christian leader of the great battle will not bear your name."

"That is enough!" said the chamberlain. "Sir, this woman is—"

"I am dying," said Ambrosius, his words not a question, but a statement of agreement, as if Rachel's unstoppable vision was simply the report his own spirits had been reluctant to tell out.

"Yes, sir," said Rachel.

"And the leader, the Christian leader?" he asked.

"Artorius," said Rachel.

And then she could say no more. The wine, the vision, the sense of ineluctable doom that hung over the prediction of a great, final, victorious battle overcame her. Before she could fall to the hard tiled floor, the battle leader had swept forward, catching her in his powerful arms. No one else, not even Ezra, noticed the fainting young woman. A moment after she had uttered Artorius's name, Ambrosius Aurelianus slumped forward, his hand expelling the cool emerald onto the sharply defined mosaic floor. The gem didn't crack, but Ambrosius Aurelianus was dead.

Chapter
18

Rachel didn't wake until the middle of the following day. She was in a high-ceilinged room with shuttered windows, which beat back the cold incessant rain through which she had slept. Rachel sat up slowly. She was very low to the floor on silk cushions, with her mother mixing a potent-smelling brew at her feet.

"Where am I?" said Rachel. "Where is Artorius?"

"Drink this," said Miriam, "and then we'll talk."

It was a Welsh drink, made from honey-stuffed lemon baked in a slow oven, laced with water in which licorice root had been steeped for ten days. Rachel drank it tentatively, then more quickly as she realized how tight and dry her throat was. The sweet brew shocked her palate. She grew sharper, and understood that she had slept for a very long time.

"What happened? Where is father? Where is Artorius? He caught me. Wasn't it he who—"

"Finish the drink," said Miriam. As Rachel did so, Miriam told her what everyone else in London already knew. Ambrosius was dead, almost at the instant of Rachel's prediction. Only Artorius's fierce gravity had prevented the general's soldiers from tearing her apart in the wake of his death.

"I don't remember," said Rachel.

"You fainted," said Miriam. "Artorius took charge almost at once. If you had been right about the general, it seemed logical that you were right about the battle leader as his logical successor. But then your own cousin threw your life—all our lives—into jeopardy."

"What cousin?"

"Joseph," said Miriam. "The Christian. Finish the drink, or you will not be strong enough for the day ahead. Your father has been laboring since before first light on the sword blade."

"What did Joseph do?" said Rachel. But then, even as her mother answered her, she remembered her prophecy and knew what the boy had done. She had called for a Christian leader, a warrior who would carry the great sword as a weapon and as a cross, and Joseph had surely insisted that Artorius must fulfill the words of the prophecy. If he wished to lead the warriors of the Five Britains, he must be what Ambrosius was, and what Rachel had seen him to be: a Christian.

"He did what any true Roman would have done," said Miriam grandly. "Artorius is nobler than any local religion. He understands what is needed for leadership, and in this instance, it was but a small sacrifice to make—"

"What are you saying? Artorius has become a Christian?" She told herself that there must be no reason why this should have troubled her, but Rachel was moment by moment more agitated. Her head pounded, and she knew this was not from any residue of sleep or the quantity of wine she had drunk the night before. "Where is he?"

"He is with the priests," said Miriam. "He has been with them since dawn."

"His wife," said Rachel. "She is a Christian."

"So much the better," said Miriam.

"He will never leave her then," said Rachel. "Not his wife and his two children, not his Christian family."

"What in the world are you talking about, girl?" Rachel's mother smiled at her, as if she were a child of ten instead of an adult, long since widowed. "What does his marriage have to do with love? Have we grown so far from the ways of Rome that you can only imagine loving Artorius if he sheds his mail, and rids himself of his wife, and becomes like Ambash, cloistered in a Jewish study, growing a holy man's beard—"

"Mother, stop it," said Rachel. "You are not a pagan, you are a Jew, though you forget it, though you mock it and me and Ambash and all the ways of our people. You are a Jew, just as I am, and bound by the laws of Torah."

"I see that the drink is taking effect," said Miriam dryly. "You have ceased the clearing of your throat that troubled your sleep, and you are clearheaded enough to join your father at his work."

"I want to see Artorius."

"He will come to you later. After the priests."

"I must see him," said Rachel. "I must explain to him what I have seen."

"Listen," said her mother. "Artorius is a Roman. He believes in no superstitions, neither pagan, Jewish, nor Christian. He needs no explanation of visions or omens or any of your nonsense—"

"No, Mother," said Rachel. "You don't understand. I must see Artorius. I don't want him to die." She could have said that she loved him at that moment, for all about the sense of fear, the images of a wondrous sword and the bleeding warrior who held it high about his pain-wracked body, was a passion, an insistence on life. More wondrous still was the notion that this life was desired not only for Artorius, but for herself as well; for the first time since the death of Ambash, she wanted to live, to face long nights and dreary winters, to stir the fires of the hearth and dream of the return home of her man, her warrior.

"If you don't want him to die, you must go to your father and see to the new general's sword," said Miriam. "And no silly decoration on the blade. We are not Celts, and neither is Artorius. Make him a Roman sword, suitable for the leader of the Romans of Britain."

Ezra, red-eyed and sweating, met his daughter's somber gaze as she entered Ambrosius's armory. Though the iron ingot from which Artorius's blade was being made had been reheated between massive layers of charcoal half a dozen times before Ezra's arrival, he had insisted on further reheating. Steel developed on the surface of the iron in this process of reheating; the more times this was done—and the greater the care—the greater the eventual quality of the steel.

Ezra had seen iron blades that bent and broke in the heat of combat; he had seen Roman blades made one hundred years before that were of superior strength to those imported from Gaul

238

twenty years ago. His blades were as good as those of old Rome, perhaps even as good as those of Seric steel that the Romans imported from distant Asian lands. Ezra's blades were used as far west as Isca Dumnonorum, as far north as Luguvallium. Kings and battle leaders bought his swords, both of the classic *spatha* design, for thrusting, and the more common blunt-pointed cutting variety; his swordsmith's mark—a tiny lion, symbol of his tribe of Judah— could even be found punched into the smooth surface where the blade joined the hilt on swords in Gaul and Italy, gifts from the periphery of the dead empire to the warlords of its former capitals. Every blade he made was unique, special in the number of hours it was heated, in the number of blows it received in being flattened, shaped, drawn into deadly force. There was an intimacy that developed between forger and blade. After a time, the hammer beating the blade against the anvil, the firing in the charcoal furnace, the hissing in the cold murky tank of water all contributed to a kind of music, a song of vast effort, of divine intent. It was magical to the religious Ezra how what were once ugly clumps of ore could be metamorphosed into balls of iron, collecting like bits of refuse amid the ashes of the furnace; these "blooms" could be hammered by strong men, with good tools, into ingots; and ingots could be transformed with heat and skill and hammer blows into armor plate, chain mail, door knockers, helmets, arm guards, greaves, daggers, swords. Any shape that his daughter could make with gold, he could approximate with iron. Indeed, the very process of annealing, refined by family tradition over the centuries, was similar in both metals.

Swords could be beaten into ploughshares, and spears into pruning hooks, but this wasn't the magic of the blacksmith's art. It was the fact that the Lord had allowed iron ore to exist in nature and then had given man the intelligence to discover what wonders lay within the unprepossessing lumps of stone. Micah speaks of the time when "nation will not lift up swords against nation," but to Ezra, this vision of peace was less stirring than the fact that man had risen so far above the beasts of the field that he had discovered tools, fire, gems, craft. When Ezra made a sword, he didn't stop to think that swords or some other metal weapon had slain his beloved sister. Swordmaking was too ennobling an action to sully with thoughts of the Saxons. With each step of the swordmaking process, the blade in his mind came closer to being drawn out of the

239

tortured metal on his anvil; when the sword was finally fashioned, Ezra was released of a spirit, the way a woman is delivered of her newborn. But the bond that began with his first blows into the ingot, strengthened with the shaping of the blade. Letting go of the creation did not mean breaking that bond. Ezra could remember a hundred swords, each unique in heft and weight and size, each a child.

But of all his special swords, this must be yet more special. While Ezra was not given to visions, he had no need of them now to fire his strength of purpose. The Saxons, who had murdered his sister, who had slaughtered the happiness of his island, were coming, and the man who would repulse them would be bearing his sword.

"Are you ready to work?" he said to Rachel.

"I am afraid for Artorius," she said, but in spite of her fear, her eyes found the blade, perfectly formed, as an armorer drew it from the water tank and placed it flat on the anvil. "Beautiful," she said in Hebrew. "Powerful."

"Are you ready to work?" repeated her father. It was galling to him, a man of considerable vanity, to see how the workers, freemen and slaves, had quieted at the entrance of his daughter. This was not because of her beauty, nor was it even because of the awe inspired by her pronouncement in the moments before Ambrosius's death. These men were workers in iron, and they knew of Rachel, the maker of mail, the artist in iron and gold. When the sword for the new general of the Britons would be finished, it would be Rachel, the fashioner of its ornamental hilt, who would be remembered as the sword's creator. In the flashing of the great sword's jewels would lie its fame, though the quality of its blade would be what gave it its true power.

"He will die with this blade in his hand, Father," she said, still speaking in Hebrew to exclude the others from her fears. "I must see him. Why is he becoming a Christian? He has no belief. He said he would follow my God, if only I would allow him to love me."

"He is a Gentile," said Ezra. "What difference does it make if he is a Christian or pagan? If I had thought there was any truth to the nonsense your mother talked about in the carriage—"

"I love him, Father," said Rachel.

Ezra held his massive frame suddenly still, as if afraid that the slightest movement would lead him to strike a blow at Rachel's unhappy face. His face, already red from his exertions, grew darker, as if in growing still, he had ceased breathing. "Father, please," said Rachel. "I will not marry a Gentile. I will not marry anyone, but the truth is in my heart. I fear for the warrior, because I love him."

Ezra finally moved. He turned about and shouted at one of the armorers: "The blade is tempered. See that my daughter is satisfied with its tang. Give her whatever she requires, for the general must have his sword by nightfall." He turned once more to look at his daughter. "I shall try and forget your words, daughter, as you sinned by forgetting who you are, and what your husband was." He left her then, and Rachel slowly lowered her eyes, to lose herself in a contemplation of the blade.

The tang, the upper portion of the sword's blade, had been made long and narrow. Even an oversize hilt could easily be slipped over this securely, and Rachel had no wish to make a hilt too big for Artorius to hold easily. This sword was not for display before a crowd of admirers in the basilica, but for use in battle.

"Where are the sheets of gold?" she said softly, and two slaves rushed to bring her to the goldworker's bench. Rachel needed to work, to concentrate on nothing but the gold and the gems in her care. She would not dwell on Ezra's anger or on her confused feelings for Artorius. When she had spoken of love, she had no notion of what to do with such an emotion. It was impossible to imagine the warrior in her arms. All her imaginings placed him at the head of his soldiers, raising the sword that she would complete. She was fearful, because her love had an incipient growing quality, as if it had been long held in check and was now desperate to make way. It was of a piece with her fears for the battle. She wanted to express her love for a man whom her own prophecies might be sending to his death at the head of the last great Roman-British army.

The hilt was in three parts: guard, grip, and pommel. The guard had already been fashioned at the Villa of Gold. Weeks before, she had decided to carve a new guard for Artorius's sword, an intricate crisscrossing of flowers that Ambash had once told her would en-sure survival in battle. (Though Ambash had qualified this, in his usual legalistic way, by pointing out that what the rabbis spoke of as "survival" did not necessarily mean earthly survival.) At the time, the idea of spending the long days of work on the man's guard

241

hadn't been a mark of love or even infatuation. She had felt for Artorius's safety, had been flattered by his many attentions and love talk, and thought it only proper to give him a token of her gratitude. Now, looking at the loving detail she had lavished on the metal, she understood that she had made love to the guard as a substitute for the flesh-and-blood warrior.

She decided to lace the iron grip with gold, so that the jewels of the pommel, set in thick cells of gold, would seem to be the flowers on a golden vine, extending upward. Rachel had no great mystical belief in the healing properties of gems, but at the same time, she knew there could be no harm in having a sword whose great jewels would rest securely against Artorius's wrist, feeling the beating of his strong pulse, infusing it with the strength of diamond.

Rachel began to work the sheets of gold. At the goldsmith's table, her concentration was total. She lost the sense of urgency, the necessity to finish the work before the sword would be needed in battle. But she was quick, her hands moving tirelessly, taking sustenance from the beauty they wrought. Periodically, food and drink were brought her, and when she continued to be oblivious of these, one of the workers swallowed his awe and wondered aloud whether she wouldn't grow sick if she didn't eat.

"What?" she said. Then she touched the tang of the blade and ran her slender fingers along the blade's flat surface. "There is wonderful work in this. The annealing has left it without a trace of brittleness."

"Is it that you're not permitted to eat while you're working on the holy sword?"

Rachel, who had not heard the first worker's worries about her not eating, now looked at the slave who had questioned her. "You call this a holy sword?" she asked, and the slave bowed to acknowledge her question, and she continued: "But what makes this holy?"

"Madam," said the slave with great humility. "Your touch makes it holy."

There was no cross about his neck, and she could see by the badly executed tattoos on both his forearms that he was no member of the Church, but was an adherent of an ancient cult. Perhaps he made no difference between Jews and Christians, could find no conflict in a Jewess's prediction of a Christian leader; perhaps "holy" for him was not a religious concept, but a preternatural one. Rachel wondered how many of the pagans in Artorius's great army would have learned to believe in their general, in this sword, in the legends about him that grew faster than ever in the wake of Ambrosius's sudden death. She knew the thought would have scandalized her father, and her dead husband, but she would not have been indifferent to a great conversion within the army of pagans to Christianity. In spite of the gulf between them, Judaism and Christianity were sibling religions, sharing a belief in a single, omniscient God, and she would rather Artorius lead an army of Christians than an army of idolators.

Eventually, she ate a bit, and the gold in her capable hands seemed yet more malleable, the gems that she placed in the pommel glowed with greater power. Her father returned to the armory, long after nightfall, discovering many of the workers asleep near the still-burning charcoal furnace.

"I beg your forgiveness," said Ezra.

"No need," said Rachel.

"It is because of your name," he said. "You share my sister's name, and she shared it with all the others of her name, all the heroines of our family. We are apart, you understand. I don't know why, but we are apart, and what has happened to Joseph in joining the converts to Christianity will happen to others of our people, but it cannot happen to you. Not to Rachel. Now let me look at the work of your hands."

"But, Father," said Rachel. "Surely you understand that I would never desert our people. I loved Ambash the more because of his wisdom, but even if he had attempted to divert me to the ways of the new religion, I would have abandoned him."

"Joseph fell in love with a Christian girl—"

"His whole family became Christian," said Rachel. "And I am not a young boy, but a mature woman, though I have no children. Father, you really do misjudge me—"

"It is only that I am afraid of what love can do," he said. But then he looked at the delicately worked cells of gold that held Ambrosius's gems to the pommel. "Rachel," he said. "It's magnificent."

"It had to be, to be worthy of your blade."

She watched as he fitted the three pieces of the hilt, guard, grip, and pommel to the tang. When the guard was secure, he punched his swordsmith's mark just below it. All the pieces of the hilt were holed, so that the tang fit at their exact centers. When Ezra had

243

finished securing the pieces, the sword had become a single piece of steel and iron and gems. It rested on the worktable, deadly and rich with power.

"You first, Father," she said.

"I don't think so," said Ezra. "It is your gift to him, more than it is mine. Though it is forbidden, I understand something of what you feel."

They were arguing over which of them should have the honor of first raising the completed sword. Finally, Rachel smiled, and placed both hands about the grip, and tried to raise the long-bladed lovely weapon.

But it wouldn't budge from the surface of the worktable.

"Go on," said Ezra. "You haven't grown so fragile that you can't lift a Roman sword." But he watched her face closely in the lamp-light. There was not exertion there, but wonder. Tears started up in her eyes, and she felt the coming of death as surely as the love that had incapacitated her.

"No one can lift it but him," she said, the words strangely dull, automatic.

"What nonsense," said Ezra, reaching for the grip that was in her hands.

"No one but him," insisted Rachel, and though she couldn't pull the sword out of her father's reach, she hissed the words so sharply that for a moment he resisted the impulse to slap her hands away and raise the weapon high over his head.

"Rachel," said Ezra. "I think you had better get some sleep."

"He will come," she said. "He will be here to see his sword. I want to see him raise it high. You will see. Now that it is one piece, no one else can raise it at all." They had been speaking in Latin, and though the workers had no wish to intrude on their privacy, they could not help but hear the quarrel, and the young woman's extravagant claims. Rachel lifted her hand suddenly from the grip of the sword. "Go ahead, Father," she said. "You will see for yourself."

Though he had been nearly ready to slap her hands away from the weapon a moment before, Ezra hesitated. He was suddenly conscious of the workers, slaves and freemen both, who were watching, and he felt the strength of his daughter's certainty: no one but the battle leader would be able to lift the sword.

But this was folly, and it irritated him, and so with one lunge he grasped the sword he himself had lifted only minutes before as he had fitted its elaborate hilt; he grasped it firmly, with all his strength, and he tried to lift it from the table.

But it wouldn't move.

"It's a spell," he heard one of the workers whisper.

Ezra tried again, closing his eyes to shut out the intense gaze of his daughter's blue eyes. It made no sense. Even with five swords, he could lift them all, and the worktable on which they would rest; even ten swords. He tried to laugh, to make it seem as if this were all some sort of joke or dream. But he knew that men and women believed in the power of his daughter's sight; he knew too that such things were possible. Even his own sister had predicted births and deaths, good times and catastrophes. For the third time, he tried to lift the sword, and then he felt strong hands, the hands of a warrior, firmly take hold of his.

"All right, Ezra," said Artorius, and Ezra opened his eyes, and the warrior stood there, as handsome as a god in a simple white tunic, an empty scabbard hanging from his belt, a wood cross about his neck on a leather string.

"It is very strange," said Ezra. "There is no reason why—"

"Only you can lift it," said Rachel to Artorius.

Though they held the new general in greater awe even than Rachel, the workers were all on their feet, stepping closer to the worktable, eyes wide as if witnessing a birth. Ezra let go of the great sword and stepped back, his hand reaching out to his daughter as Artorius placed both his hands on the bejeweled hilt.

"Thank you," said the warrior to father and daughter. His eyes rested on first Ezra, then Rachel, and when they lingered on her, she could sense a change in the man. What was once simple, a desire that had followed a straight line, had become complex. There had always been impediments in the way of their love, but his need had shone through these obstacles, had been unstoppable. Now something had stopped within him, or at least had been rechanneled. His desire was strong, but it was not directed at her. There was a purpose about him, inchoate, self-contained, assured. "Thank you for making me this sword."

Artorius turned his head and looked at the sword resting on the table, the hilt in his hands. The jewels flashed in the lamplight, and the steel itself seemed suddenly radiant, as if the strength of metal and gems were flowing into the warrior's veins.

"Victory for the Five Britains," said Artorius softly.

He raised the sword from the table in one motion, effortlessly, as if the point of the blade was pulling up toward the ceiling of its own volition. Artorius held the blade straight up in the silent room, and slowly turned about, letting the lamplight reflect off steel and gems as he kept the sword steady, reaching for the heavens.

Then all at once he smiled, and he dropped one of his hands from the hilt, so that only one hand held the sword. Then, with incredible speed, a warrior's speed, he flashed the sword in a wide arc, high and low, thrusting and pulling back, slashing and twisting it through the astonished air.

But then the smile vanished.

Artorius grew suddenly somber. Gently and carefully, he turned the sword about in his hands. He held it just above the point of the blade, so that the jeweled hilt had become the top of a magnificent cross. With steady hands he held this cross upright to the workers in the armory, and once more, very softly, he said: "Victory for the Five Britains."

With one voice they answered him, Rachel and Ezra and all the workers of the room echoing his words: "Victory for the Five Britains," they said, and then, with lightning speed, he turned the sword about, letting it sail out of his hands for half a moment, so that he could catch the jeweled hilt in the air.

"Victory," he said again. "With God's help, it will be ours."

And then the warrior sheathed the sword with another burst of blind, sure speed, and turned from the others to Rachel and softly spoke her name.

"Artorius," she said, and would have said much more, would have spoken out the terrible images that were assaulting her now, the images of glory and destruction, of victory and sacrifice, of death and immortal life for the warrior with the great sword. But there was no way to speak. Artorius was no more in charge of his fate than she was of hers; certain things were predetermined. Choices were made by men, but God knew what those choices would be. She had chosen, Artorius had chosen. She wouldn't wonder anymore whether her choices had been made with free will. Such arguments were for the rabbis, for Ambash. In her mind, in her dreams and premonitions, she had found shame lying in wait, betrayal preordained. Quite clearly she had seen herself lying with Artorius, becoming his woman, forgetting her dead husband in the warrior's embrace.

246

But now she understood that this premonition had been false, or, at least, only partly true. She would never lie with the warrior, never allow him to possess her in defiance of the laws of matrimony.

But she had already betrayed Ambash. If she had not become Artorius's woman in the flesh, she had learned to love his spirit, had pushed her soul up against his, had joined with him in the creation of his sword, in the sharing of his destiny. Rachel had never felt as close to Ambash, not lying in his bed, as she did to the warrior, standing aloof and all powerful in the crowded armory.

"Rachel," he said again. "Come to me."

Ezra had let go his hold on his daughter. As Rachel moved forward, she felt as if her father and every man in the room were accomplices to the act of her union with the warrior.

"I am going," he said softly as she came to him, and though everyone could hear the words, their meaning was clear only to Rachel.

He was going. He had chosen. He would never possess her. There would be a battle, there would be a great victory, there would never be a time when he and she would share their love.

Except for this time, these brief moments.

"Yes," she said, and only he understood what her choice had been, what her word meant: Go, Artorius, find the glory awaiting you.

And more than this: Go, leave me, let me stay on my path.

"Yes," she said, and he understood that she had chosen to remain. He understood that she could not leave behind her people, her Law, her sense of history. She was the follower of a God, a way outside his ken, beyond his sympathy; she had chosen to follow this path without a new adherent, clinging to the rules of a people that were not his, to a conversion based not on principle but on the love of a woman. And as he had chosen to turn from their love to a different destiny, so had she chosen.

"I love you," he said, and these words were even quieter than those he had spoken before, but they rang off every table, every wall, every bit of metal and wood and tile and plaster in the room. He was saying good-bye. He drew the magnificent sword, and there were those in the armory, not understanding what was transpiring, who sucked in their breaths with fear.

"And I love you," she said.

He held the sword at the hilt, and then sank to his knees, so that the point of the upraised blade was above Rachel's waist. He waited a half moment, and then Rachel, without thought, drew her artist's hand across the sharp point, bloodying her palm.

Artorius looked at her, searching her eyes for pain. But Rachel felt nothing of the sharpness of the blade. She was in suspense, waiting for the warrior to join her. Slowly he rose, and when he was fully erect, he passed his hand across the blade and then sheathed the sword. Slowly, they brought their bloody palms together, mingling their blood as they kissed, their lips meeting for the first and only time.

"Thank you," said Artorius, when they had finally pulled away from each other, letting their lovers' arms fall awkwardly to their sides. "Thank you for the gift of the sword."

A moment later he was gone.

A thousand and more legends stemmed from the battle that raged between Artorius's Roman-British troops and those of the Saxon barbarian Hengist, three days' march from the walls of London. Some say that Artorius slew ten thousand men by his own hand, that his horse ran across the surface of the water in the pursuit of the invader, that from defeating the Saxon, Artorius turned at once to Gaul and Italy, not stopping until he had been crowned emperor of Rome.

Rachel, living out her days in the Villa of Gold, never imagined the extent to which her lover's fame would grow. All she knew was that he had fought bravely, leading his men for three days and nights without sleep, holding his sword both as a weapon and as a jeweled cross. Ultimately, it was his refusal to rest, to relinquish the symbol of the sword, that urged his men on. He held the cross aloft when their energy flagged, he held it high overhead when the waves of Saxons seemed unending, unstoppable. But his troops did stop them, and more than that, they pushed them so far to the north and east that for the rest of Rachel's life, there was no sign of the invader within two hundred miles of London.

Artorius never returned from that great battle. Rachel didn't see the corpse that his men buried near the river where they had fought. Some said it had no wound, no blemish, and that in death, his lips had relaxed into a smile more serene than any they had framed in life. Warriors buried the sword alongside their leader's body, though some men swore they had seen it rise from the grave and fly heavenward, a beacon of light and power.

Rachel never knew what men would call Artorius in later years —Arthur—or that they would remember his sword as something magically pulled from a stone, a sword named Excalibur. She didn't know the legend would put him on a throne, would place him at the head of a round table of knights in shining armor, for such armor and such knights never existed in her lifetime.

But she did know that he would be remembered. Rachel understood that his life would somehow become a symbol, a source of strength and inspiration. Nothing less than this could make sense, for she and Artorius had both given up too much not to be recompensed by fate. In choosing to turn from their earthly love, something magnificent, something grander than simple glory must needs survive in its place.

She hoped his legend would be great, that it would fire passion in the hearts of men for an eternity. Rachel missed him all the days of her life. Even on the day of her death she fancied she could feel his blood beating in her veins. Even in her final moments, she could feel the dead weight of loss, the endless sorrow of love left unfulfilled.

The Family of Haim
Ben-Saul of Verulamium
488–756

Little is known of the journey of Haim, son of Saul of Verulamium, from the land of the Britons to the city of Sura in southern Babylonia, on the other side of the known world. His descendants knew well only the reasons for his trip. Sura was a center of Jewish learning, and it drew pilgrims from every corner of the earth. Haim's brother Joseph had become a Christian; Haim's cousin Rachel and her aged parents remained immured in their armory, and in their dreams of the past. He had need of a wife, and his people.

Some legends tell of his perilous crossing of the North Sea, where Frisian pirates took the gems given him by Rachel to support his pilgrimage. Ransomed in Cologne by coreligionists, he made his way along the Rhine to Mainz, where Jewish merchants, active traders in the incense then becoming common in Christian ceremony, allowed him to join an overland caravan to the distant Black Sea. That route at the end of the fifth century could not have been more dangerous: scores of barbaric tribes continued to pour down from the north, tearing apart shaky alliances left in the wake of the destruction of the Western Roman Empire. Though an emperor still sat in splendor in Constantinople, nominal ruler of a vastness of lands and races, the Eastern Roman Empire offered little security for a man who would be a citizen of the world.

Universal peace was no longer even a memory, but a legend. The very notion that a single source of power, emanating from Rome, could have ruled the world's myriad savage peoples, forcing upon them a common language, law, and religion, suggested a messianic dream. Great Rome was five times captured in the sixth century; its Senate decimated, its wealth dispersed, its population of a million souls reduced to forty thousand starving paupers. When men now thought of imperial Rome, they thought of Constantinople: and from this great city emanated not justice and absolute power, but treachery, bribery, compromise.

A man who wished to travel the world needed friends, and gold, and cunning. If Jewish merchants were successful in those dark years, it was because they shared a language with far-flung coreligionists, and were welcomed in their remote communities with trust. Links were established from one corner of the world to the other based not only on the bonds of commerce, but of family.

Still, Haim could not have covered the miles from Mainz to the northeastern shores of the Black Sea sleeping only in Jewish villages. These tiny communities would have been blissful and rare breaks in a routine of desperate caution. And even had he survived Thuringians, Bavarians, Lombards, Bulgarians, Avars, and Goths, he would have had to find passage across the Black Sea itself during a time of retaliatory warfare between Zoroastrian Persia and Christian East Rome.

More likely, Haim never made it to Sura at all. Family records list his marriage as having taken place in Ratisbon, on the Danube. Not until his son Joseph was sent to study medicine in Sura, sometime in the mid-sixth century, is there any proof that a member of the family reached that city, then under the rule of the Persians, at all.

Haim named his first daughter Rachel in 531; as he himself was nearing fifty, he thought it safe to assume that Rachel of London and the Villa of Gold was dead. Though Haim had heard nothing of his family, Christian or Jewish, since he had left Britain as a young man, the naming of his daughter with his cousin's name, linked his heirs not only with whatever remnants of the family survived in Britain, but with the family's ancient history: Rachel, daughter of Haim learned not only of Verulamium, but of Rome, and Judea, and the glory and responsibility associated with her name.

Though Haim's son studied medicine in Sura, he never took his physician's oath. The city's fortunate location in the fertile region where the Euphrates splits into two famous rivers, induced Haim's descendants to follow first agriculture and then the making of wine and beer instead of the less lucrative healing profession. Joseph's grandson Akiba, named for the famous scholar, was scorned by the Jewish communities through which he passed for his lack of knowledge of Talmud and Torah; yet he gave away half of his substantial income to support aged scholars in Pumpeditha and Sura, and to revive the academies of Jerusalem during the glorious years from 614 to 617, when the conquering Persians allowed the Jews to rule their ancient city.

If Akiba knew little Torah, he knew something of the legends of his family. After his grandfather's sister Rachel died, Akiba named his newborn daughter after her, and presented her with three precious stones: an emerald, a ruby, and a diamond. Along with the ancient stories of the Maccabees, and the Legend of the Brave Rachel, this Rachel learned of her ancestors' artistry with gold and gems. When she was old enough to hold the stones in her fist, she felt the kinship of distant generations. Rachel fancied there was a power within them, a power through which she could draw the strength and succor of all her namesakes, a power open to her alone. When she was sick, she slept with the stones next to the skin of her breast. She claimed she could feel the pulsing of a hundred hearts, sending courage and health into her bloodstream.

Rachel, daughter of Akiba, lived a long life in those years of pestilence and destruction. It was well known that her namesake had lived nearly nine decades; when Rachel, daughter of Akiba, lived to be seventy-nine, there was much competition among the many descendants of Akiba for the honor of passing on her name. Hananiah, oldest son of Anan, son of Dan, son of Akiba, received the honor, and with it the three gemstones. Like his father, Hananiah was a religious man, poorly educated but pious. Trade had carried his father from Babylonia to Armenia, and from there to the flourishing city of Nicomedia on the Black Sea. But war had broken the trade route from Persia; with the Arab conquests sweeping as far as Armenia, Rachel's father and grandfather, living in Christian East Rome, were cut off from their extensive family in Amida, Antioch, Sura, and distant Ispahan. No longer could they count on transports from Alexandria, once ruled from Constantinople, now part of the Baghdad Caliphate, suddenly become the largest empire in the world.

Turning their backs to the east, they traded within the remnants of the Eastern Roman Empire: water wheels to power the mills of Europe, bed frames for the aristocrats among the Franks and Lombards, glass windows for stone churches rising on the ashes of barbaric temples.

It was not a flourishing trade. Every other year was a new persecution, an expulsion or a forced conversion of the Jews somewhere within the Christian world. Jews were faced not only with murder, but with the slow deaths of poverty and humiliation. From international traders, Hananiah and his son Elimelek became carpenters in a tiny cluster of Jewish homes outside the city of Nicomedia; it had become dangerous for the unbaptized to live within the city's walls.

In this nameless Jewish village, Rachel, daughter of Hananiah, achieved a certain renown. Forbidden to own land, forbidden to buy and sell slaves, forbidden tapestry weaving, blacksmithing, and a hundred other minor trades, the Jews who clustered together on the outskirts of Nicomedia were carpenters and artisans. Christians bought their wares because they were cheap, meanwhile stigmatizing the community as a source of well-poisoning and pestilence. In 716, the year that the Arabs conquered Lisbon, a fever inflicted itself on the city of Nicomedia. Half the children in the city were dead or dying when the Christian women began to take their children to the Jewish village, in search of Rachel and her unholy blessing.

She was only seventeen then, and frail, but she had green eyes, eerily shot with yellow, and she believed in the power of her gems. As they had allowed her namesakes to live long, they had cured her own illnesses. She was convinced that their power could, with God's blessing, extend to others. Though the Bishop of Nicomedia had strictly forbidden the use of Jewish physicians to his flock, this ban couldn't possibly extend to an uneducated girl, unmarried and without any desire to proselytize her accursed religion. Rachel's success as a healer of her own people was known to the Christians of Nicomedia. They saw her power in the absence of fever among the Jewish babies of her village and, clutching their own children, arrived at her door.

Humbly she asked the One God for his blessing, silently she

placed the gems against the fevered foreheads of infants; some died, some lived—but the people of Nicomedia were convinced that those who had survived the fever had done so because of Rachel the Healer.

A hundred superstitions sprang up around her and her stones. Her brother Elimelek believed completely in her black powers. When she died at the age of thirty-seven, he swore to the village rabbi that he saw black-faced angels carry her heavenward, where her presence was wanted by He Whose Name Cannot Be Uttered.

It was not only Rachel's immediate family that was superstitious. The Jews of Asia Minor, beleaguered by oppression and sequestered from the outside world, retreated from a close examination of what was real to a scrutiny of what was not. In this they were not so different from other peoples of their time: reasons were needed to explain why evil triumphed, why good men died horrible deaths, why innocent babies expired in their mothers' arms. If religion provided a framework for solace, superstition laced through the framework provided the promise of controlling the forces outside man's ken.

While the Talmud, the vast body of Jewish Oral Law, finally codified in Babylonia around the year 500, condemned the "ways of the Amorite," specifying numerous superstitious practices forbidden to Jews, few ordinary Jews followed every precept in its nearly two and one-half million words. The common people who made up the village into which Rachel, daughter of Hillel, son of Elimelek, was born in 736, were certainly pious, eager to follow the word of their rabbi. But along with his rulings on jurisprudence, ethical conduct, marriage, and ritual, was a belief in the unseen world, in demons, angels, in the powers within graveclothes, roots twisted in the shape of genitals, in stars and stillborns and madmen. Rachel received the gift of the three gems from her father at birth, and when she was old enough to know of their power and of what was expected of her—to use them to heal the sick—she never questioned the possibility that such things weren't possible. Already she had heard the whispering of past Rachels in the moments before sleep; already she had felt the urge to lay her jewel-dazzled hands on the heads of the sick.

Though her father was poor and without much education, it surprised no one that the rabbi's son was betrothed to Rachel when she was three and he was seven. In a community that valued spiritual over material worth, what better bride could there be than the namesake of Rachel the Healer, the possessor of the Healing Gems, the inheritor of what could only be a gift from the One Most High?

Ordinarily, Rachel and Moshe, the red-haired son of Rabbi Amnon, would have been married when he had finished his studies at eighteen years of age and was ready to begin a family. But Moshe had finished his studies in the village when he was eight, not eighteen; at an expense that the village could ill afford, he was sent to a higher academy of learning outside of Smyrna, where he astonished his teachers with his arrogance as much as with his knowledge of the Talmud. There were those of his teachers who wanted to wash their hands of him, thinking his disrespectful attitude a mark of God's displeasure, but the majority understood that his temper was an indication of Moshe's own frustrations—his mind and his will were too strong for the little academies of Asia Minor.

He was sent at sixteen to Sura, put under the wing of a Jewish trader from Damascus who had patronage from the court of the great caliph. His father had a letter from Baghdad, which Moshe visited briefly in his sixteenth year. Apparently, he had taken up the study of medicine and was held in esteem by the leading practitioners of that art, both Arab and Jew. When he was twenty, he was sent to study in Cordoba, just before that part of the Arab empire became independent of the authorities from Damascus.

Rachel was twenty years old when she heard rumors of his return to the village of his birth. She had never seriously entertained marrying anyone else. Though she had not seen him since he was a wild young boy and she was a baby of four years old, she had respected the rules of their betrothal. Rachel knew that he would come back to the village a wise young man, sophisticated and worldly, used to soft beds and fine foods and witty talk.

But if he was coming back, it was clear that it was God's will that she love him, and that she must learn to follow his ways, no matter how foreign, no matter how strange.

THE FAMILY OF HAIM BEN-SAUL OF VERULAMIUM
488–756

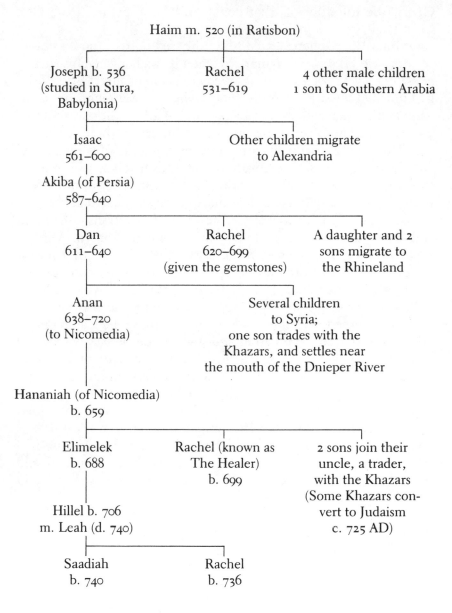

Haim m. 520 (in Ratisbon)

Joseph b. 536 (studied in Sura, Babylonia)

Rachel 531–619

4 other male children
1 son to Southern Arabia

Isaac 561–600

Other children migrate to Alexandria

Akiba (of Persia) 587–640

Dan 611–640

Rachel 620–699 (given the gemstones)

A daughter and 2 sons migrate to the Rhineland

Anan 638–720 (to Nicomedia)

Several children to Syria; one son trades with the Khazars, and settles near the mouth of the Dnieper River

Hananiah (of Nicomedia) b. 659

Elimelek b. 688

Rachel (known as The Healer) b. 699

2 sons join their uncle, a trader, with the Khazars (Some Khazars convert to Judaism c. 725 AD)

Hillel b. 706 m. Leah (d. 740)

Saadiah b. 740

Rachel b. 736

Part Four

Nicomedia, 756

Chapter
19

"Wake, mistress, you're wanted," said the voice in her dream, and Rachel turned about to see a resplendent figure approaching, standing on a litter carried by a dozen slaves. He was red-haired and broad-shouldered, and though Jews were forbidden to bear arms, he wore a sword in his gold-buckled belt. This was her bridegroom, and he was coming to her, at long last, coming to her in her dream.

"I'm sorry, mistress," insisted the voice. "You must get up."

The servant shook her gently, blinking rapidly and deliberately against the frightening glimmering of the healer's jewels in the lamplight. Rachel wore the diamond, ruby, and emerald inherited from her great aunt on a short, heavy gold chain about her neck; these were but a small part of her healing stones. She possessed several moonstones, a jasper, an onyx, many amethysts, toadstones both black and white, as well as sapphires, carnelians, chrysolites, and a single topaz given to her by a Greek merchant of Smyrna, who claimed that it had been blessed by St. James-the-Lesser.

"Mistress, I'm sorry, there's a little peasant girl—her brothers are waiting—they say she's boiling over—the blood is coming out of her nose—she smells of fire—"

Fully awake now, Rachel shrugged off the remnants of her dream. It was dark beyond the pale circle of lamplight, and she could feel the fear in the servant hovering above her.

"No fear," said Rachel softly, intoning the Aramaic she had

259

learned from the mystic scrolls. "No fear, no beginning, no end. Praise be the Lord for having brought me to wakefulness in this moment."

The servant, who had worked for Rachel's mother, had lived with her family for most of her life, had held Rachel in her arms when she was an infant, could still not hide the awe she felt in her presence. Everything about the young woman seemed preternatural, otherworldly. As she lifted her feet from the bed, as she blessed and drank the water from the silver bowl, as she touched her palms to the eastern wall of the room in reverence to the site of Jerusalem's fallen Temple, as she brought her lips to the *mezuzah* affixed to the doorpost, she never seemed less than a creature of light and air, of radiance, health, purity.

"Have they come with a wagon?" said Rachel, speaking in the elegant Greek of Byzantium. The servant spoke a harsher vernacular, native to the hill country about Mount Olympus. Each understood the other of course, but their speech identified them, placed them firmly in the particular classes to which they had been assigned by fate.

"Yes, mistress. And Saadiah is with him. He has put on his sword, though your father has expressly forbidden him, and he will go with you. Your father had not been roused, but if you are ready, I will go to him—"

"No need," said Rachel. "Saadiah will be protection enough."

Her brother was sixteen, her only sibling. Their mother had died within a week of his birth, a youthful, musical girl, forever singing in Rachel's memories. She had been fair, and Saadiah was fairer still; he looked as if he had been the product of fierce blond Northfolk, while Rachel had the black eyes and delicate features of the Greek aristocracy—the tiny privileged group that remained the single constant in nearby Constantinople's enormous multiracial population. But he was no more akin to Frisian sea bandits than she was to Macedonian royalty. Regardless of the color of their skin, the cast of their faces, the little world about them—the hamlets and villages that led to Nicomedia, and beyond, to the imperial city of Constantinople—knew them by a thousand signs as Jews, members of the accursed, doomed race.

A million people lived in the capital of the empire. Every tribe and every race and every people had its representatives in the shops, in the baths, in the palaces; Syrians and Armenians, Bulgars and Slavs, Khazars and Lombards and Greeks, even Persians and

Arabs, hiding their feared nationalities behind local costumes, painted the city with a hundred languages, with black skin and gold hair, with clothing of silk and wool and fur in every color of the rainbow. But among them all only the Jews were singled out for special humiliations: not only were they forbidden to bear arms, but they were forbidden the use of any baths used by Christians; indeed, all contacts between Christians and Jews were discouraged by legislation. In a time when the healer's art was closely associated with spirits of good and evil, doctors were often members of the clergy, and Jewish physicians were forbidden to be employed by Christian patients.

But Byzantine law and Byzantine practice were two different things. Though law had denied Jews the privilege of living behind the walls of Nicomedia, the city not only had Jews, but a small Jewish quarter; in Constantinople itself the Jews lived both in an official quarter and in mansions facing the sea. And if Jews were forbidden to bear arms, it did not prevent the famous Callinicus, a Jew from Syria, from giving his invention of "Greek fire" to the state, and thus saving it from annihilation by the Arabs; his descendants continued to manufacture the liquid fire—its ingredients a closely kept secret—that was the emperor's greatest weapon, even if they themselves could not legally carry a dagger in their belts. As for Jewish physicians not being allowed to practice in Christian households—it was well known that almost every emperor since Justinian used Arab-trained Jewish physicians; even hysterically Jew-hating monks were known to submit to the cure of Jewish doctors, often at the command of their abbot.

"Cover your head," said Saadiah, as Rachel stepped into the front room of the tiny house. His sword was large and clumsily decorated; it was a gift from their great-uncle, from the land of the Khazars, a fierce people known more for horsemanship and ferocity than any delicacy with artwork.

"Good morning, brother," said Rachel, feeling the tension in his boyish figure from four paces. She would be his responsibility. No dishonor, not in word or deed, must come her way this evening, or his own life would be forever worthless. She tried to send her spirit of calm and acceptance across the little space between them, but she felt him reject any attempt of softening. He wanted to be hard as steel, eager to fight fire with fire. "Remember," said Rachel. "They are simple people, and you must not take offense easily."

"They are simple people who would kill us while we sleep," said

Saadiah. "If they burn with fevers, what does it concern you? There's enough sickness for your talents right here among our own."

Saadiah's hatred was a difficult thing for Rachel to contemplate, but she understood its origin, even if she had none of it in her own heart. Their family, though of priestly descent, though replete with stories of past power and opulence, was not one of those Jewish families who lived in a two-story house of stucco-covered stone in Nicomedia, or in a garden-nestled palace in the capital city. Their father Hillel was poor, and would have been much poorer if not for gifts showered on his daughter by grateful patients. The Jewish restrictions weren't felt keenly under the gaze of magistrates, but rather under the hatred that it encouraged in the masses. Slum dwellers living on the dole in the cities and peasants living on some mighty landlord's favor in the outskirts knew that Jews were singled out, scorned, hated as the murderers of their Lord. It was the Jewish poor who received the brunt of their anger; and it was Jews like Saadiah who beat back this mass hatred with a compulsion to shut out the Gentile from every part of his life.

The brothers of the sick girl had come through the rainy night without shoes, and when they guided Rachel with clumsy hand motions to their wagon, she could smell their unwashed bodies and fetid breaths like that of some dangerous, bestial species. But she stilled the revulsion she felt for their uncleanliness. She would recommend a strong mint tea for all the members of the girl's household. They would drink it for their health, and it would not harm them; but it would do more to kill the stink that came from their rotting gums than for any possible contagion from their sister's fever.

Rudely, Saadiah spoke to his sister in Hebrew throughout the noisy trip: the horse cart seemed a hundred years old, and the horse not much younger. The younger brother held an icon, a clumsily executed picture of the Virgin Mary, in his hands, and never stopped mumbling prayers to it as his taciturn older brother drove out of the Jewish village and into the muddy roadway outside of it.

"Perhaps he's never heard of the imperial edict," said Saadiah sarcastically.

"Do not speak of it," said Rachel.

"It's unlikely that they are capable of understanding Greek, my sister. Even with twenty icons in their filthy hands, and six hundred angels working overhead, these pigs wouldn't understand a word of the sacred language."

"Hebrew is not a sacred language if it is used to speak the evil tongue."

"I speak no evil tongue if I tell the truth about Gentiles who would use you, and then kill you like a dog."

"Brother," said Rachel. "Listen to the words of the rabbis: 'Silence is good for the wise; how much more so for the foolish.' "

"Do not do that!" said Saadiah, suddenly so angry that she imagined his face growing red in the overhanging blackness of night. "I am not foolish! I am responsible for your safety and I will not be mocked!"

Rachel could feel the horse cart slow, could sense the worry and bewilderment coming from the peasants up front. "I am not mocking you, Saadiah," she said. "I am only trying to maintain some peace in this cart."

"Icons are illegal. The bishops issue edict after edict. Monks have their noses cut off, their eyes torn out of their heads for carrying around such a thing as our peasant friends carry—what do you think they would do to two Jews in their presence?"

"Saadiah," said Rachel. "Their sister is sick, and they are praying the only way they know how. Now I want you to please be silent, because I too must pray, to prepare myself for what I must do."

"Go ahead," said Saadiah. "You pray." It was not so dark that she couldn't see his hand reach for the hilt of his sword and grip it with all the strength of his frustration. But Rachel was able to survive his bad temper. She had the gift of inner calm, of being able to remove herself from the world of crossed desires, unreachable ambitions, terrible envies. She kept open her eyes, and watched the night fade away, chased by tiny ribbons of dawn. The morning star watched over them, its path the clue to a myriad of futures; the moon, in its third phase, lost its glorious radiance with a steady rhythm that seemed to spring from the turning of the horse cart's wheels. She wondered if the sun would rise before they would reach the peasants' home. The little girl's fever would surely be easier to bear with the door to the hut thrown open to the light and the air.

"Madam," said the younger brother, clutching his icon. "Please help us."

They had arrived at the outer ring of two circles of cottages, flimsy and flammable, their straw-thatched roofs and straw-strewn earthen floors excellent only for breeding disease.

"Touch the emerald," said Rachel in Hebrew.

"I will wait outside the hut," said Saadiah.

"There is disease inside and outside," said Rachel, and she fixed her black eyes on her brother, and quickly he touched the stone about her neck with the tips of ten fingers.

"All right?" he asked her, and only when she had nodded did he remove his fingers from the powerful stone.

There was a small crowd outside the hut of the sick child. Toothless old peasants, swaying to some interior prayerful rhythm, clutched images of saints and martyrs; hulking young men held aloft huge Greek crosses; kerchiefed women, barefoot and shapeless behind layers of tattered shawls gripped candles to throw back the last shards of night.

Saadiah jumped down first, his hand on the hilt of his sheathed sword. But there was no danger, not from this crowd. They pushed each other back from the doorway, many of them crossing themselves, mouthing incantations against the Evil One, but all of them glowed in anticipation. Even Saadiah could sense the strength of their expectations.

"The healer," said one of the old women.

"Praise the healer," said another.

In half a moment, as Rachel alighted from the ancient cart, it seemed as if the evil-smelling crowd would come close, would extend their hands and try and touch the Jewess. But there was nothing evil in their intentions. They had the collective tenderness of a pack of children for some friendly creature they were seeing for the first time.

"Get back," shouted Saadiah, drawing his large sword in one practiced motion. The crowd, used to the casual intimidations of their age—aristocrats from Nicomedia or the capital riding in gold-plated carriages or slave-borne litters routinely sent servants with sticks ahead of them, to beat away peasants and livestock from their path—stepped back, without any sign of resentment or hesitation. In a harshly consonanted vernacular that was nearly incomprehensible to Saadiah, the younger brother of the sick girl shouted at the villagers, and they stepped back yet farther, some of them bowing at the same time to show their respect.

"Say nothing," said Rachel to her brother in Hebrew. "Be patient and strong, and politely refuse their food and drink."

Saadiah was about to reply that he knew enough how to comport himself in the presence of Gentiles, but his sister had already stepped into the uninviting confines of the hut. He heard a single musical note, as if a harp string had been pulled as she'd stepped onto the earthen floor, but realized that it had been not the sounding of an instrument, but a cry of relief from a human throat.

"You have come," said the girl's mother, her weather-beaten face lit from behind by a score of candles. The unusual amount of light, like the exclusion from the hut of chickens and pigs and the child's eight siblings and three orphaned cousins, was not out of consideration for Rachel, but for fear of the demons lurking behind the face of every disease. No one spoke of contagion, but of the insatiable appetite of the black spirits. Once under the skin of one child, they would wait for another to get close. Only the candles and the crosses kept them from leaping promiscuously about the length and breadth of the cottage.

The girl's father, a squat blond man of no more than thirty years, knelt before an icon of surprising beauty. So many candles illuminated the brightly colored portrait of the Virgin and the Christ child that for half a moment Rachel's eyes were drawn to it, in spite of the urgent pain that called to her from the child's heart.

"Yes, of course," said Rachel, removing the short chain from which the three jewels of her namesake hung about her neck. She held the chain tightly in her hands, and slowly moved it, so that the jewels sent their coruscating light into every corner of the room.

"Yes," said the child's mother, as if already she could feel a lessening of the evil spirits' strength in the hut. The child's father said nothing, remaining lost in prayer before the icon. Rachel understood why the emperor, and the clergy he was able to control, had forbidden all graven images; the Christians, after all, still followed the Torah of the Jews, though they called it the Old Testament to distinguish it from the Gospels, or New Testament. And God's message had been clear enough, forbidding any "image of any figure, male or female, the likeness of any beast that is on the earth."

Those monks and priests who risked death and mutilation to keep their elaborate pictures of Jesus and the saints adorning their churches and monasteries, tried to foist blame on the icon breakers away from the emperor's party and onto the hated Jews—as if it were the Jews' fault that Leo III had decided to rid East Rome's

Christian worship of pagan influences. Though no Jew persecuted a Christian who worshiped any image of angel or man—how could he?—they became associated in the minds of the less educated clergy with the Iconoclasts, the breakers of their sacred images. Yet here was Rachel, a Jewess, in the home of an icon worshiper, not to break any images, not to attempt to explain to the peasants that the picture had originally been drawn to suggest the unseen spirits they represented and was itself no more holy than any piece of paper or bit of clay or elegant remnant of tessellated floor. Rachel was here, on the contrary, to present another image to these people: not a portrait, not a frieze, not a plaster sculpture, but an image without clear delineations, without limits. The Jewess was here to combat death and demons with light and radiance, with jewels that would send their healing rays not only through the gloom of night, but through the fetid smells of sickness and poverty, through the smoky sputtering of candles, through the muttering and murmuring of anxious souls.

Rachel presented them with an image, of a knife cutting through water, of a shout tearing apart the quiet, of incense overcoming all the noxious realities of life with inescapable sweetness. She turned her jewels to every corner of the room, and she cast her image of health, ineluctable, unknowable, an image without end.

"Peace," she said in Aramaic. "Light. Love of the Lord Most High."

Never once did Rachel think of her incantations as proselytizing, as bringing a Jewish custom into a Christian household, for her words came from no book of Jewish prayer, and her cache of jewels had not been blessed by any rabbinical court. She knew that she took her strength from the One God, that the power of her jewels derived from His grace. But her gems and her healing were as much a part of the world about her as the trees and the sea and the mountains. The One God allowed her to heal as He allowed the mountains to reach for the sky, to bury their heads in ice and snow. Even among the Gentiles there were healers, men and women both, whose hands and words and rites removed pain and disease and the specter of death. St. Luke had been a powerful physician; St. Nino had cured the queen of Iberia with the touch of her hands. There was no doubt in Rachel's mind that such powers as they had, she had, and that they all came from the same source. Like the warmth of the sun, that source was available to anyone, pagan, Christian, Moslem or Jew, anyone who knew how to open oneself to accept the Lord's great gift.

"She was burning up before, but now the fever is less, but she shakes. Look at her fingers, look at her feet, she has the shakings —and her skin is so pale, and she is wasting away—I give her the best to eat, fresh eggs, raw and boiled, hot bread, wine and water, vegetables raw and boiled. I've put mint on her chest, I've put the cross of God on her lips, I've fasted two days, and my husband has touched no spirits since her fever began, no spirits, no meat, nothing but black bread and water from the creek."

The young mother looked up at Rachel sharply, as if to discover any condemnation in her sorcerer's black eyes. "I've done what I could, and I prayed all night, and finally, in my sleep, I heard clear as day, the angels called for you, they called for the Jewess who is the healer, and even the priest said it was all right, he said I should call on you, if you would be so good, to try and save the life of my girl."

"How long has she been sick?" said Rachel. Slowly, she replaced the chain of jewels about her neck and secured the heavy gold clasp.

"The fever has been for eight nights, but not always bad. She's been better and she's been worse. She's gotten up and then become tired. She only started to shake like that today. And there's the blood too. The nosebleeds, as if she'd been hit by one of her brothers—the blood just comes and it doesn't stop. Is that a ruby?" The young mother was pointing to the brilliant stone on Rachel's chain.

"Yes."

"Forgive me, but my mother once said that it was a blessed stone, blessed by St. Peter, but that it was not to be used in the case of fevers—"

Rachel met the woman's eyes and could see the frightened glimmering of doubt and hesitation. She wanted to be mastered, to be told that she must not think and that she must not question. Rachel could see that she had but one step to take before the mother would be as easy and open to the source as she was herself.

"St. Peter's stone is the jasper, not the ruby," said Rachel. "And you must remember that I wear certain stones, and that I carry others, and that my only desire is to heal. Now a ruby worn against the skin should be removed in the case of fever, yes—but I have not pressed the stone against your daughter's skin, have I?"

"I'm sorry, madam—"

"Silence, woman," said Rachel. "You have questioned my skill, so I must now explain myself, and then we shall have done with questions once and for all. It is necessary that you believe, and then you must not understand everything, you simply must accept—"

"I do understand, and I humbly ask your forgiveness—"

"Listen," said Rachel. "I wear three gems, blessed by my namesake. Together they fight the presence of evil spirits. Already they are hurrying from this place. They have tried to stir you, and a protest came to your lips, but they have lost—they are going—listen—do you hear their black wings—?"

"No, yes—I hear what you hear, madam, but you must tell me what it is because I know nothing of the signs—"

"They are going from here, listen—listen," said Rachel.

"Yes, madam," said the young woman.

"Boil up a cup of water, at once," said Rachel. "Boil it until half the water has bubbled away in clouds of steam."

"Yes, of course," said the woman, happy to be able to do something with her hands. Rachel spoke to her from across the room as the woman hung a pot over the fire, her husband still oblivious of everything but the serene faces of the icon. Softly, insistently, Rachel explained to the woman the efficacy of the gems she wore, while all the while she examined the child, alone on the huge straw-filled mattresss, usually the sleeping place for every man, woman, and child in the evil-smelling cottage. Touching the girl's pale forehead, she was surprised at its coolness—her eyes were feverish, but the fever was not apparent to her touch.

The child was watching her, and as Rachel continued to speak to her mother across the room, Rachel could feel a lessening of the child's tension. Slowly, she explained how the ruby's red light gave spirit to the blood, taking its power from the sun itself. Because she had shone the ruby about the hut so that its reflected light had reached every corner, the cottage would be safe from lightning, floods, and infestation by worms.

Rachel didn't add that the ruby was good for air infected by disease, thinking that it might insult the woman's housekeeping. Among the Jews, there was much less sickness than among the poor Gentiles, simply because Talmudic Law insisted on weekly bathing, and on the ritual washing of hands before every meal.

Together with the rabbinical dictates on cleaning for the Sabbath and festivals, particularly Passover, when the entire household was turned upside down in search of any particle of bread, even the poorest Jewish cottages were hygienic compared to those of the peasant population. Even among the rich denizens of Constantinople, where Roman baths were as available as they had been in the west half a millenium before, there was a greater attention to the cosmetic aspects of cleanliness than to the earlier Romans' religious need for purity of body as well as soul. Heady perfumes and luxurious embroideries covered many rich men's bodies, prone to the same diseases as the malodorous peasantry.

"The water is boiling, madam," said the child's mother. Rachel advised her to watch the water closely, as the heat would slowly remove all that was evil from its pure contents. She told her about the value of emeralds, how they would help the child gain weight and would calm her poor digestion. The diamond, of course, was famous for its ability to quiet convulsions and tics. Rachel moved the necklace about her throat, so that the diamond faced the child, and as the child caught the stone's fire in her eyes, Rachel saw the trembling tips of her fingers quiet.

"You have a little fever, child," said Rachel, "and I will take it away, if you help me." She was addressing the child, and though the child heard her clearly, and wanted to do what she was told, she was too frightened to speak. When she opened her mouth, her lips trembled in the same frightening irregular rhythm that characterized her fingers and toes. So agitated did she become that the trembling in her lips moved grotesquely to her cheeks and to her right eye; the pretty face was suddenly disfigured by a tic that twisted this eye into a rapid pattern of opening and shutting.

"Tomorrow," said Rachel to the mother, "no matter how feverish, you will boil water and bathe your daughter. You will scrub her clean, you will do this no matter how much she cries."

"Yes, madam," said the mother. Rachel could not discern whether the overpowering smell came from the mattress or from the child herself; it was not only a human fecal smell, but an animal smell, perhaps a residue of the animal wastes that had been pushed to the corners of the cottage. Her father liked to say that no peasants went to hell because Satan couldn't stand their scent. Rachel hoped that a bath would do more than scrub away the filth and smells of years; she hoped it would strip away the incapacitating prison of fear that ringed her frail body, that allowed the demons to lay claim to what rightfully belonged to the Lord.

The mother abandoned the fire, hearing her child begin to whimper. "Why is her face twitching, madam? She wasn't doing that before!"

"Bring me the boiled water," said Rachel.

"Yes," said the mother, and brought over the iron pot, holding it with two filthy rags. Rachel asked if there was a cup in the cottage and the woman brought this over, and even in the bad light of the spluttering candles and the new day twisting through the doorway, Rachel could see the filth that encrusted the crude vessel of clay.

"We will use this," said Rachel, and she took out a silver goblet from her jewel pouch and placed it on the earthen floor. The peasant woman looked at this with wonder, so that Rachel had to repeat herself, speaking more firmly still. Slowly, the woman poured the boiling water into the goblet, and then Rachel told her to move back. "Sit your daughter up. Hold her," she said.

Rachel removed a topaz, light pink in color, with the transparency of glass, and dropped it into the goblet. "The gem will take away some of the heat, so that she may drink." The child was sitting up now, and Rachel held the goblet, hot from the water inside it, and brought it to the child's trembling lips.

"Look at my diamond, child," said Rachel. "Look, and drink of the water, pure and simple, the gift of heaven."

"Drink," said the mother more sharply. Awkwardly, the child held her hands to the sides of her head, as if to force the trembling to still. Her mouth open, she allowed the hot liquid to pass her lips.

"Hurts," she said, stuttering the word.

"Look at the diamond," said Rachel. "Look, and drink. Look and drink." Once more she brought the goblet to the child's lips.

"Drink," said the child, and this time she stuttered less. The mother noticed that her daughter's hands trembled less where they held her cheeks, and that the twitching in her toes had stilled altogether.

"We are fortunate that the moon is in its third phase," said Rachel. "That is when topaz is most effective."

"Most effective for what?" said the woman.

"Just see that she drinks every last drop," said Rachel. She took out an orange stone from her pouch, small and bright. In the candlelight, it had as much fire as the diamond she wore about her

270

neck. "This is jasper. She must hold this against the skin of her chest. It will take away the fever. It will take it completely away."

Rachel stayed with them until an hour past sunrise. The child drank the boiled water, and held the jasper against her chest, and gazed reverently into the stones about the healer's neck. She had been agitated, increasingly worried about her parents' fear, about being set alone on the large mattress surrounded by candles; it had been horrifying to feel her body twitch uncontrollably, as if the devil had really taken control of her just as her brothers used to warn her he would. Such shaking had happened to other children, especially young girls, usually after having been sick with fever; and often the shaking was just the precursor to worse: weakness, loss of appetite, a desire for sleep that would lead finally to a gentle drifting away to death.

But the child felt her fear dissolve in the presence of Rachel. The jasper removed what was left of her fever as the topaz had taken the heat from the boiling water; the terror and irritation that brought on the twitching dissolved in the radiance of the healer's gems. When Rachel took the jasper back from the child's hands, she fell asleep at once. Neither the tips of her fingers nor the muscles of her face moved in any irregular fashion. Only the toes shook, and these were calmer than before. Rachel assured the mother that this would soon end.

"But you must bathe her," she said. "And keep her quiet. Let her alone to sleep, and when she is not sleeping, to lie or sit quietly. She is not to be teased or given work of any kind. If she is allowed to find peace, she will be well, and she will never be sick again.

Rachel bent over the sleeping child and placed her lips to her cool forehead and kissed her. As always at this moment of departing, she felt the beginning of a wave of exhaustion. Though she had lifted no great weight or walked difficult miles, the process of healing always left Rachel desperate for sleep. She didn't understand why this was so, for the skills she employed were physically easy; the placement of stones, the laying on of hands not only required no exertion, but were done instinctively, prompted by the love that flowed from her to anyone who was ill. Still, the exhaustion was real, a tangible force kept at bay only as long as she was with the patient, giving of her love, healing.

Rachel forced herself to walk slowly, as if speed might collapse her legs. Stepping across the cottage's threshold, she steeled herself for the blast of Asiatic sunlight and allowed her brother to grab her elbow, to steady her.

The child's mother tried to kiss the hem of Rachel's tunic, but Rachel was not so tired that she would allow this. Saadiah refused the copper coins offered them by the hysterically grateful woman, and practically lifted his sister into the cart. Without a word, the peasant brothers turned the cart about and drove back toward the village of the Jews.

As she drifted off to sleep, Rachel wondered if the child's father, lost in prayer before the icon, knew yet that his daughter was well, that the pain had been removed from her soul. She imagined his wonder and joy at coming out of his meditations, from the brightly lit faces of the Virgin and child, from a heart beseeching the Lord of the World for life for his daughter, and finding her, still, no longer feverish, her lips twisted not by some malevolent demon, but by the gentlest of smiles.

Such a smile rested on her own lips as she descended deeper into sleep, returning to the dream from which she'd been awakened in the hours before dawn: her bridegroom, red-haired and strong, was coming to her. Beyond the anticipation in his blue eyes was a reflection of the child's smile; beyond his desire was approbation and fellowship, for he too was a healer and a lover of the well-being that God extended to the creatures of the earth.

Chapter
20

Moshe Bar-Amnon felt the muscles of his neck constrict and his heart begin to race; it was painful to take a breath. Moment by moment, his breathing grew more shallow, more rapid. It was like the time he had studied medicine in Cordoba, when a disease had struck at the lungs of the city's slum dwellers. The wasted bodies, glassy eyes, and painful attempts to draw air into ruined lungs had infected his spirit. Treating the sick, he developed their symptoms, though they disappeared the moment he went to sleep. His master, Ibn-Ezra, himself a follower of the teachings of Asaph Ha-Rofe, removed Moshe's symptoms with a night of excess: a half hour in the vapor bath, a dozen cups of Syrian wine, and the most expensive prostitute in the city.

Soon, Moshe learned to shrug off the sympathetic pains a young physician often develops when studying or treating disease. In fact, like many physicians, he developed a remarkably strong constitution, seldom falling ill with a fever or even a sniffle. In Alexandria, where he had gone to study and practice after Cordoba, he met a Persian Jew who had studied for many years in India. The Persian had studied the famous medical treatises of Caraka and Susruta, and learned the Indian technique for cutting into the bladder to remove stones.

"But," the Persian Jew had told Moshe, "more important than any surgery, I learned their way with the universal forces."

Moshe, like every student of Greek and Indian medicine, knew how the former divided bodily substances into four humors—blood, phlegm, choler, and melancholy; the Indians believed that the body had three elementary substances—spirit, phlegm, and bile. Both believed that the harmony of elements was what led to health.

But the Persian Jew was not talking about balance. "They believe that one can accept or reject disease. That the strength of the soul is more important than the strength of the body. How else explain why a plague takes many who are strong and leaves some who are weak?"

"But a plague takes the saintly as well as the evil," Moshe had said, but the Persian Jew interrupted impatiently.

"I am not talking about good and evil," he had said. "I am talking about an attitude to disease. The Indians have physicians who can perform surgery when they're in their ninth decade, because they refuse to let the sickness of old age take their strength. That is what I learned from the Indians: harden your soul to disease, because your soul is by nature meant to live in a healthy frame."

But Moshe had not so much hardened his soul to disease as he had to his humble origins. He knew that the constriction he felt in his throat was not the result of sympathetic symptoms, but of the confusion in his soul; a confusion that had begun when the ferry had taken him across the Bosporus to Nicomedia, when the familiar coastline appeared out of a gentle mist, and the landscape of distant mountains lit from the east by the rising sun struck him with force: he was going home.

To his father, Rabbi Amnon, who partially subscribed to the Talmudic saying, "The best of physicians is destined for Hell."

To his fellow villagers, who cured eye disease by rubbing spittle past the eyelids, and treated worms in the bowels with plucked maidenhair, swallowed with seven white dates.

To his mother and her fanatically religious family, who subscribed to the belief that disease was God-given, and should not be combatted, but accepted as justice for some past or future sin.

And of course to his bride-to-be, a creature about whom he knew almost nothing, and whom he had last seen when she was a giggly child of four, with hair as black and as thick as an Arab's. Perhaps she would agree with the great Rabbi Akiba, who suggested that a man should embrace all his misfortunes with happiness, as an excess of punishment in the world surely meant a compensatory multitude of rewards in the world-to-come.

"Perhaps she is pretty," said his servant Cyrus, as their hired carriage left the heavily rutted road from Nicomedia, turning into a yet more rudimentary path, lined with trees whose roots threatened to tear off their wheels.

"She is twenty. In my village that is an old woman."

"In my village too," said Cyrus, who was a Jew from Persia, born a slave, sold to traders who sold him his liberty. He spoke Persian, Arabic, Aramaic, Latin, and Greek, but not a word of Hebrew, not even the most rudimentary of prayers. Cyrus thanked no one but himself for his liberty. He had seen Arabs slaughter Persians, Greeks slaughter Arabs, Avars slaughter Greeks. In Alexandria, where he had met Moshe, he assisted at the dissection of animals and helped administer alcohol and opium before surgery on humans. But he knew neither Torah nor Talmud, nor any philosophy of the Greeks, and most doctors, Jew and Gentile alike, found his impudence unwarranted and unbearable. Moshe found him a delightful companion, tireless, loyal, and unafraid to speak his mind. "But you're the one who wanted to come back to this dung heap. If it was up to me, we'd have never left the fleshpots of Egypt. I always prefer fleshpots to dung heaps, but that's probably because I'm such an uneducated man."

"My father is old," said Moshe. "I have not seen him since I came of age in Smyrna, at that pious old academy. That's eleven years. Even if only to kiss his hand and ask his blessing—"

"Stop your nonsense," said Cyrus. "You're going back to claim your bride and settle down as the village rabbi. You can do a little doctoring on the side, drain a few gouty feet here, bless away a few headaches there, and before you know it you'll have ten or twelve little children and a long white beard, and when they ask you about Galen and Hippocrates, you'll say you never heard of them."

"Cyrus, I hope you'll remember to speak more politely to me when we're in the company of others," said Moshe.

"Yes, Your High and Holy Majestic Lord of all Scalpels, Medications, and Brothels," said Cyrus. "I shall be like an abject slave and speak only in the crudest Greek, with my eyes lowered to the ground."

"Cyrus," said Moshe. "These are not city dwellers, you understand. They are my family and my friends and—"

"Yes, master," said Cyrus, clasping his hands in histrionic subjection. "But if you go ahead and marry this black-haired creature, what will become of me? I understand they hang nonreligious Jews in this part of the world."

"Not hang," said Moshe with as serious a face as he could manage, "Castrate."

Cyrus was still laughing as a messenger from Nicomedia overtook them on a powerful Arabian horse. He was armed with sword and lance, and wore the imperial colors. The driver of the hired carriage slowed to a halt as soon as the man lifted his black-gloved hand.

"Are you the Jew called Moshe, son of the rabbi called Amnon?" said the messenger.

Cyrus spoke before Moshe had a chance to harness his indignation at the man's preemptory tone. "My master here is the noble physician, Moshe Bar-Amnon, known and honored throughout the Caliphate, where he has studied and practiced only to come back and serve the emperor."

"You're wanted in Nicomedia," said the messenger, not a whit chastened by Cyrus's words. "The bishop has sent for you."

"Has he?" said Moshe, finally finding the words to carry his anger. "How do I know that? Perhaps you're a bandit, or an Arab, or a liar—or all three."

The messenger, on horseback, started to draw his sword but Cyrus was too quick for him: His own long-bladed, thin Syrian sword was already in his hand, drawn under the voluminous folds of his traveler's mantle; standing at the edge of the carriage's threshold, he held the blade to the messenger's throat.

"If your horse moves, you die. If your blade moves, you die. If you insult my master, you die," said Cyrus. "Now, brave messenger, get down from the horse."

The messenger did as he was told. Cyrus and Moshe stepped down from the carriage, their driver watching from his seat as if this were some sort of bizarre new show in the Hippodrome. Cyrus happily kept the point of his blade at the man's throat.

"Now suppose you begin again," said Moshe. "But this time deliver your message properly, or my servant will certainly kill you."

"Yes, sir," said the messenger. "You're completely right. And I am sorry for having given offense."

"My master is not interested in the apology of a dog. He just wants the message, given in the appropriate way."

"Yes, sir," said the messenger.

"You don't have to call me 'sir,'" said Cyrus. "I'm just a servant, you idiot. Now speak out what my master had demanded."

The messenger willed himself to be calm. Looking past Cyrus, trying to ignore the blade at his throat, he squinted at Moshe, the fiery red beard and hair backed by the early afternoon sun. As if delivering his message before the imperial court, he shouted now, "Great Moshe Bar-Amnon, Physician of Alexandria, I bring you greetings! Sir, it is my honor to—"

Cyrus interrupted the messenger, bringing the blade infinitesimally closer to breaking through the skin of the man's neck. "Idiot, you have not told my master in whose name you speak!"

"I beg your pardon," said the messenger. "I have been sent by the bishop of Nicomedia, himself a physician of Constantinople, and founder of several hospitals for the poor. It is he who sent me—"

"Enough," said Moshe. "What does the bishop want with me?"

"Great Moshe Bar-Amnon, Physician of Alexandria—"

Once again, Cyrus had to bring his blade closer. "You're not listening very well, idiot, are you? What is the message? Skip the honors!"

"I'm sorry, it's just that the honors were what I left out before—"

"Let him speak, Cyrus," said Moshe. He came closer to the messenger now, and as he did so, the messenger grew unaccountably more frightened. Only the patriarch and his priests wore beards with impunity, as the emperor had forbidden them to all his other subjects. Jewish traders who came to market day in the smaller cities and towns risked having their beards cut off, often at the instigation of the less educated clergy—those same members of the Church who refused to abandon their icons and blamed the Jews for their suppression.

But this Jew had a presence altogether different from any of the petty traders and peddlers he was used to seeing in the villages near the capital. It was not only his unusual coloring and his martial stance and stride; it was the look of contempt in his eyes. This Jew despised him, and not in the way of his servant, who was simply looking for mastery. This Jewish physician found him small and insignificant, and his eyes expressed a complete indifference to his existence. But it was more than this too. The eyes not only indicated a power behind them but were a power in and of themselves. The messenger felt disoriented simply trying to meet Moshe's steady gaze.

"Great Moshe Bar-Amnon! Forgive me the unintentional dishonor of not calling upon you when you first arrived in our city! But it is only today that I learned of your arrival and your immediate departure for your native village!"

"Do you want the lout to keep on shouting?" said Cyrus. He spoke this time in Arabic, so that Moshe didn't bother to answer; leaving it as a joke between the two of them. The messenger continued.

"It would do me great honor to have you return to my palace, as my honored guest, so that we may talk of medical matters of our mutual concern!" The messenger stopped here, as if he had arrived too suddenly at the end of his master's words.

"Is that the complete message?" said Moshe.

"Yes, sir. It is the invitation of the bishop, yes."

"Tell the bishop I will be pleased to visit him within a week's time. I shall send notice of my arrival a few days before."

"No," said the messenger. "I am sorry, but you must come now."

For a moment, even Cyrus was taken aback; he had thought the man's spirit already broken. "You've heard my master," said Cyrus. "He said that it will be next week."

"All right, all right," said the messenger. "Yes, sir."

"Shall we allow him to leave," said Cyrus, "or shall we have him announce our entry into your miserable little hometown?" Once again he was speaking Arabic, but Moshe hardly heard him. He was concentrating intently on what was in the man's eyes.

"You, messenger," said Moshe. "You've lied."

"No, sir." In spite of himself he was drawn to Moshe's eyes, though it was dizzying to look there. "No, sir. It's no lie—"

"Look at me," said Moshe, and for a moment, the messenger forgot there was a sword held to his throat, so riveted was his attention on the red-bearded man's pale eyes. "The bishop asked you to invite me to his palace. But what did he say to do if I refused the invitation?"

"Well—you didn't—"

"I am not coming back with you—"

"You must!" said the messenger. It was as if Moshe had reminded him of a task that he must needs accomplish, no matter what the cost. He started forward, and Cyrus's blade reminded him why he must not move. The blade pricked him, and he drew himself back, holding his hand to his neck. There was no fight in the man, only confusion. Moshe could see this at once, because for him confusion, indecision, hesitation were all part of the mystery that led to disease in men.

"Please, sir. I am sorry, sir. The bishop meant no disrespect. I mean no disrespect. But the bishop has urgent need of—"

Moshe was now so close to the man that he could feel the physician's breath against his face. "Did the bishop authorize you to employ force to bring me to him?"

"He said that I must not harm you, no matter—"

"Not harm me," said Moshe. "You've answered my question."

"No, sir—please believe me—"

"You are well-armed for a messenger—"

"Please, sir. The bishop is your friend, but there is urgent—"

"He told you to bring me to him at the point of your lance if need be," said Moshe. "Is that correct?"

The messenger wanted to contradict, but he could see that it was pointless. This man was not a doctor, but a demon. He knew all things, and his eyes could turn a man to something spineless and cold. "Yes, sir," said the messenger. "But he was very strict with me. He said to treat you with honor, though you are a Jew."

"Though I am a Jew," said Moshe Bar-Amnon.

"You're the one who wanted to come home," said Cyrus.

"We are still going home," said Moshe. "Let him alone, Cyrus," Cyrus lowered his blade and the messenger stepped back quickly, reaching for his horse's tether. "Tell the bishop I will come, as it is so urgent. But not until tomorrow. I must sleep one night in my father's house."

"Yes, sir," said the messenger. "I will surely tell the bishop." He rode off at a gallop to Nicomedia, while Moshe and Cyrus continued on their way. In less than an hour, they were greeted at the outskirts of the village by a cacophony of stray dogs. As they turned about the community smokehouse and entered the dusty main street, lined with modest houses of one and two stories, hidden behind low courtyard walls, the sound of the dogs was overshadowed by chanting.

"Look," said Cyrus. "Is that the synagogue?"

279

"Yes," said Moshe. He was not abashed before his servant, but the confusion in his soul, momentarily stilled by the messenger's demands, was now brought back in force. There, on the wide porch that fronted the wooden synagogue, were a group of at least two dozen, all of them dressed in their bright Sabbath colors, the men bearded and broad, and a few, those of his mother's family, standing out from the rest because of their red and blond hair.

They were singing, and Cyrus didn't bother to ask what this was: he had witnessed the honors given his master by other communities, Jewish and Gentile alike, and more than a few sang songs of welcome, praising their God for allowing the great man to come to their poor town.

"Be civil, Cyrus," said Moshe.

"Of course," he said. "But how soon can we take the bishop up on his friendly invitation?"

It was only when the carriage had pulled much closer to the small crowd on the porch of the synagogue that they could see what marked its center. There were two chairs, upholstered in some sort of heavily embroidered fabric, and one of them, the empty one, was slightly larger than the other. The smaller one was occupied by a black-haired young woman dressed in a spotless white tunic, with jewels of unexpected magnificence gleaming from a chain about her neck. It was only when the carriage had stopped and the welcomers had ceased their singing that the young woman had the courage to raise her head.

"Rachel," said Moshe, speaking the dear name softly to himself, recognizing her black eyes and beauty from across sixteen years, recognizing the child he had been betrothed to all his life, shaken by a rush of memory and kinship. This was why he had come back: not to kiss his father's hand, not to exhibit his worldly grace to his backward village; a preternatural instinct had urged him here, if only to take a look, to pause for an instant and stand before the woman that tradition had claimed for him. Moshe nearly stumbled as he got down from the carriage, so wild and irrational was his desire to know this woman, so sure was he that whatever confusion of soul had brought him across half the world to see this day would soon be made clear.

Rachel, for her part, could not even voice his name. She remembered nothing of the boy of eight, save the stories told about him by jealous classmates and proud family members; that and his red hair. But she remembered the man, remembered his shape, the breadth of his shoulders, the wild power in his blue eyes as they searched for her in her dream. As he came close, she touched the diamond on her chain, to steady her nerves and render her feelings invisible. But for once, the great stone didn't work: her hands shook, and the very ground seemed to quake beneath the synagogue porch as she tried to rise out of the chair; and when she tried to open her mouth to speak out words of greeting, tears began to run from her eyes.

"Rachel," said Moshe Bar-Amnon. "I have come back to honor our contract. I have come back to make you my wife."

Chapter
21

They washed their hands, blessing God for commanding them to do so; they blessed the Lord for bringing them bread out of the earth; they lit many candles, beseeching the Lord to forgive them the extravagance outside the Sabbath day; they blessed God for bringing home their son, their cousin, their bridegroom, and having kept him in health to reach this day.

"Rachel," said Moshe, addressing his betrothed from his seat of honor at the head of the long table laden with meat and wine, "I don't see you eating any of this wonderful feast."

The meat was too lean, the vegetables oversalted, the bread not nearly as fine as that of Alexandria, but praise was certainly due the figs and dates, the pistachios with which he used to gorge himself in his youth, the fine embroidered tablecloth already stained by the drinkers of the thick wine from Chios. By the unrestrained appetites of the others, Moshe understood that this was no everyday meal, and was probably more copious than anything served up on the Sabbath itself. The men, most of them bearded, in spite of the imperial edict of 756 which forbade facial hair to all men outside the Orthodox Church's clergy, seldom lifted their heads from their plates. Unlike Rachel, the women took little rapid bites, like voracious birds, their faces reddening with the unaccustomed pleasure. Moshe wondered if his parents had broken into their three-year supply of food, kept in the cool communal storeroom: all subjects of the emperor living in and around Constantinople were required to set aside great quantities of basic foods, as the threat of siege to the capital by Arabs or Persians or northern barbarians was always alive.

"I do not eat meat, Rav Moshe," said Rachel, barely looking at him as she spoke, as if not wanting to take up too much of his attention. But even if she hadn't spoken a word, he found it difficult to look away from her. She wore no transparent silks, hadn't plucked her eyebrows or rouged her lips, her hair wasn't pulled into coils on either side of her head, laced like that of the great ladies of Constantinople, with strings of pearls and chains of gold; yet her beauty was impossible to avoid. The thick head of black and wavy hair, artlessly framing the gentle face, the steady, strangely benign look in the black eyes, the very pale skin, nearly wan against the blackness of her hair, all contributed to a kind of ethereal loveliness, unplanned and modest, as if she had no recognition of her own physical nature. Moshe wondered if no one in this town could have told her that she was beautiful, that the light in the room seemed to vibrate about the crown of her head, so vivid were her features, so remarkable was the harmony of beauty and spirit within her earthly frame.

"Not even on the Sabbath, Rachel?" said Moshe. Before she could answer, he went on quickly: "And there is no need to call me 'Rav.' Even among strangers, I feel unworthy of that particular title."

"Yet you do not seem to mind being called 'doctor,' my son," said his mother. His mother's uncle, a tall, very old man with a long gray beard shot through with red, laughed out loud at this, laughed until he gagged, and Moshe had to get up from the bench and slap his great-uncle's back with force.

"Thank you, Doctor Moshe," said the great-uncle, and he began to laugh again, so wild with mirth that Moshe felt himself stiffen into anger. He knew that many found his manner arrogant and overbearing, and here, among his own family, he tried to keep his manner subdued and respectful. But there was no respecting this old fool, great-uncle or not.

"If you want to kill yourself laughing at a name, you will very soon succeed," said Moshe.

Rabbi Amnon, Moshe's father, spat at the sound of these words, to avert the possibility of their turning into reality. "My dear son, I'm surprised at you," he said.

All of a sudden, men and women were turning about, joining the rabbi's action. For half a moment, it seemed to Moshe as if he'd been transported into some world of the deranged: his mother spat, his cousin spat, Rachel's fiercely dark father spat; he had to restrain himself from mocking them, from citing the Talmudic injunction against superstitious practices and beliefs. But his father had only begun his protest.

"One mustn't tempt the evil spirits with such frivolous talk," he said, but then caught up his words sharply. He had suddenly remembered that Moshe was not only a virtual stranger, but a wise man, a sage, praised by the famous rabbis of the Babylonian academies and therefore of greater authority than himself, a simple scholar, the leader of a simple congregation who made his living selling kosher wine.

"Forgive me, my son," said Rabbi Amnon. "It is not seemly that I should be lecturing one educated in Pumpeditha."

"You are my father, and you can lecture me and criticize me all the days of our lives," said Moshe.

"That is true," said Moshe's mother, her tone sharp, as if prepared to castigate her son now that he had allowed his father to do so. Indeed his mother had seemed angry at him almost from the first moment of his arrival, as if something about his manner, or his face, or his speech, had irritated her. "No matter what honors given you by the Arabs and the Christians and the pagans, you must remember who gave you life."

"I have never forgotten, Mother," said Moshe, aware that his voice was taut, that his temper was rising. It made matters worse that he felt her anger justified: he knew that his heart shrank at the sight of his village, at the fact of his parents, elderly and unenlightened. Although he loved them, his love was based on a childhood memory; and as an adult, he had become hard, superior, impatient. "I will be more careful how I choose my words," he said. "The last thing I wish to be is an ungrateful son." Deliberately, Moshe turned to Rachel, forcing the lines of his face into a milder pose. He had not finished his little exchange with her on the subject of her diet. "I'm afraid we were interrupted," said Moshe. "I asked you about your reluctance to eat meat—"

"It is said that *you eat the meat of the pig*," said his mother, her

284

tone a step sharper than before. Moshe heard the words as if they were sharp stabbing pains at the back of his neck. "It is said that *you performed surgery on the Sabbath*. That *you carried gifts to the pagan temples on our own Holy Days*."

Moshe, unwilling to turn his eyes back to his mother, continued to look in Rachel's direction. Her pale face flushed, and her eyes seemed to glisten as if from a nearly invisible layer of tears. Clearly agitated, she raised her fingers to the diamond at her throat, and Moshe, instead of listening to the litany of his mother's accusations, found himself marveling at his betrothed's beauty: the jewels she wore were spectacular, but hardly caught the eye against the competition of their owner. Suddenly, in this confused moment of recoil and attraction, castigation and desire, he remembered about the jewels around his betrothed's neck. She had inherited them from another Rachel, known as the Healer. Indeed, more than once his father's letters had mentioned how appropriate it was that the young doctor would be marrying the new healer. As his mother continued to rail at him, he wondered if Rachel perhaps might be not so very different from those who had spat superstitiously on the ground. Perhaps she would sleep with a diamond under her pillow, so that God would grant her a fertile womb; perhaps she believed that hemonis led to divine inspiration, that heliotrope held to the forehead gave one the gift of prophecy, that a jasper cured palsy, that an onyx worn next to the skin led to nightmares, while a turquoise held to the ear gave rise to the murmuring of angels and the gift of sleep.

"Why do you avert your eyes, my son?" said his mother, though Rabbi Amnon was sharply urging her to cease. "I am addressing you, not your pretty bride-to-be. The Lord God will forgive you if you offer repentance, if you follow the commandments, if you will stop your pagan ways—"

"He has not said that any of your accusations are true," said Rabbi Amnon. "Do not forget what the sages tell us, the sin of slander murders three people: he of whom you speak, he to whom you speak, and he who speaks."

The great-uncle spoke now too, his eyes lighting with the chance to exhibit his erudition. "The law is very explicit," he said excitedly. "He who utters words of slander shall be stoned to death."

"Oh, no," said Rabbi Amnon. "I am afraid you misread the page. That sentiment was a minority opinion. Clearly, the sin of slander is great, but the sages only meant that the sin was so great that it is equivalent, in a moral sense, to those crimes that were punished by stoning in the days of the Temple."

"I have not slandered anyone," said Moshe's mother. She shouted at her son: "Tell them if I have slandered you, or told the truth so as to lead you to righteousness."

"Whoever speaks slander," said another ancient cousin at the table, as if rising from a deep sleep to utter a final proclamation, a summation of all his earthly wisdom before departing for the eternal rest, "is as if he has denied the very existence of the One God."

Another cousin, this one younger than the others, and with the tight lips and narrow eyes of the zealot, insisted on being heard. There was little thought anymore to what Moshe's mother had said about her son. This was an impromptu study-hall session, competitive and insular. The real world ceased to matter. All that was important would be having the last word. "The Talmud says that the speaker of slander shall be cast to the dogs. Wait, I'm not finished. The Talmud says too that whoever slanders another is committing a crime equal to those of idolatry and unchastity and murder. Let me finish, I have more to say on the subject. I have studied this subject just last month, and heard Rav Nachman of Durazzo debate another great rabbi, I don't remember his name, from Selybria—both of them were beardless, but could quote long sections from the Gemara—never faltering—"

"Silence, you idiot," said Moshe, his anger finally on all of them —on his mother and father, his cousins, old and young. But he kept his pale eyes only on the last speaker. "How dare you go on like this, when you yourself charge my mother with every word you speak? You are guilty of slander whether or not my mother is. You speak the evil tongue. You have a demon in your throat, and I will remove it with my own hands if you speak another word."

"Your mother has only asked that you tell us the way you have lived, my son," said his father. "She does not mean to charge you with crimes, but to show you the way back to the ways of your own people. We hold the position of the physician in the greatest esteem, but before you were a physician, you were a student and a follower of the Torah, and the way of the sage is far better than the way of the physician, for the physician heals the body, and the sage heals the spirit."

"Only speak, son," said his mother. "Tell us that you do not follow the ways of the pagans."

"Mother," said Moshe. "I must be very careful of how I speak, so that no one can misunderstand my words." It had been a long time since he had sat in a room full of Talmudists, and his prodigious memory, laden though it was with the accumulations of symptoms and their cures, found the passage they would need to hear: "The tongue can be the most dangerous part of the body. Of all the limbs of the body, it alone is horizontal, while the others are vertical; the other limbs are outside the body, while the tongue is inside the body. And do not forget, the rabbis warn us, that the tongue has been placed in a house with two walls, shut behind a wall of teeth, surrounded by lips that must know when to be sealed."

"You have not answered my questions!" said his mother, but now Rabbi Amnon took his husbandly prerogative and commanded her silence.

"You will not learn, if you do not listen," said Rabbi Amnon. "Your son speaks with the tongue of gold. There is no evil spirit in him. His heart doesn't know evil ways. Perhaps because he is a physician, in the interest of preserving life, he has performed true acts of mercy. To those uninformed and malicious, a doctor's duties might seem like the works of an unbeliever. But listen to your son. Observe his knowledge. By saying what he has said, you should know him for good and just, and not bother him with trivial details and petty accusations—"

"To profane the Sabbath is not petty!" said Moshe's mother. "I want to know—"

"I have forbidden you to speak," said Rabbi Amnon with great dignity. Moshe was about to intercede, to rise from his seat and explain how he didn't violate the Sabbath—except when necessary to sustain life, that he never ate meat that was not kosher—but he would gladly do so if the alternative was starving. He had expected his family and friends to be simple, even backward, compared to the men of Cordoba and Alexandria, but he had wanted to try and accept them for what was good and noble within their souls, instead of what was ugly and small. It was one thing to believe, for example, that Jerusalem was the center of the world, that the three great rivers of mankind—the Nile, Euphrates, and Ganges—all flowed from a single source in the Garden of Eden, thus defying all the rules of nature and facts of geography; it was quite another to fault a physician for saving a life, or attempting to do so, simply because it was the Sabbath or a Holy Day. Moshe had been prepared to allow them their myths, their superstitions, their ignorance, their prejudice. He had been ready to avoid telling them what he knew of the shape of the world, of the sophisticated geographical and astronomical discoveries of Chinese and Indians and Arabs, of the intellectual radiance of ancient Greece that was still the complement to a liberal education in the Caliphate.

But suddenly he was ashamed of all of them, ashamed not of their ignorance, but of their clannish desire to exclude themselves from all knowledge of the outside world. Once the Jews were the people of the Book, students of the Torah, drawing their sustenance from its straightforward teachings, its elegant poetry, its powerful stories of righteousness triumphant over evil. But they had turned from the Torah in Nicomedia and lavished their attention on the Talmud, that enormous preserve of folklore and wisdom and laws, the product of seven hundred years and countless scholars' debate, a collective masterpiece, dense and articulate, labyrinthine and clear as crystal. More than anything else it was an elaborate commentary on the Mishnah, itself a gloss on the Torah; the sheer effort to master this wealth of material had shut them off from other directions, other possibilities of knowledge. It was not that Moshe thought ill of the Talmud. He had been a master of its intracacies from early childhood; it was his knowledge of its law that had shown the village his intellectual power and that had given them the impetus to send him off to further studies. Indeed, his early training in the Talmud's inimitable system of earnest and painstaking debate, always resorting to primary sources, logic and precise definitions, had formed his mind, given him an apparatus that had allowed him to address the medical texts of Greece, India, and Rome with sharp insight and organizational clarity.

But what vexed Moshe was the wastefulness of human thought and energy that was poured into deciphering the massive text, expounding on it, adding to the already tremendous volume of commentaries, written and oral, hoping to discover in the seven-hundred-year-old opinions of a Babylonian rabbi something of relevance to the present. Even as his father continued to defend him against the opinions of his mother and others of her family—Rabbi Amnon cited the Talmudic passage that declared the rescue of a life more vital than observing the letter of the Sabbath laws—Moshe felt his anger grow. He would interrupt him, and tell him that the Talmud was often right, but that it was often wrong too. It was true that the Talmud allowed physicians to treat patients in danger of death on the Sabbath, but at the same time it cast aspersions on the whole class of doctors as mercenary and inexpert; while it correctly indicated that impurities in the blood were the chief agents of disease, it was filled with wrongheaded medical knowledge too: it was not true that a copulation in the daytime led to a birth at daytime, or that a multicolored scorpion crushed into dust provided a remedy for cataracts.

Though Moshe had gotten to his feet and was prepared to finally speak out his heart, regardless of the consequences, he turned in the noiseless confusion of bad feeling to Rachel, as if he might be looking at her for the last time. She would find him irreligious, disrespectful of his elders, and unworthy of being her husband; and he would not stoop to convince her to throw away her superstitions and shackles to true thinking and go with him to Constantinople, or Cordoba, or Baghdad. But he was surprised to see that she too was rising, and that her eyes were wild with pain.

"Someone is ill," she said.

No one had a moment to comment on her premonition. Cyrus, Moshe's servant, was hurrying into the dining room, shouting for his master as if there was no one else at the table. "Doctor," he was saying. "At once, hurry—they're waiting—"

"What is it, Cyrus?" said Moshe, glad of a chance to leave, but letting his words ring with impatient annoyance, as if leaving was the last thing he wanted.

"Outside, master," said Cyrus. Coming closer to the candlelight, Moshe could see that his servant was white-faced, that the supercilious manner was cowed by urgency and fear.

"It is very bad," said Rachel. She had come from her place at the opposite end of the table and spoke directly to Moshe. "It is good that you are here, because I am afraid that it is something evil and strong."

"Is that why you touch your jewels?" said Moshe.

"Master, this is no time for talk—" Cyrus interrupted himself and grabbed Moshe's arm as if it would be better simply to force him outside and explain the reasons why later. With a strange delicacy, Rachel took hold of Moshe's other arm, not with the shy touch of the bride-to-be, but with the firm grip of the possessed.

"Your servant is right," said Rachel. "Let us hurry. There is reason."

Everyone at the table had stood up now, and as Moshe was led out by Cyrus and Rachel, they followed slowly, standing at the open door to the dark street outside. There were soldiers on horseback, two dozen at least, and perhaps half of them carried torches. They surrounded a large wagon, covered with thick hides. Whatever they were guarding inside, they feared; the soldiers kept their distance and seemed to cluster about their own blazing torches, as if the light would beat back danger.

"It is very bad," said Rachel. "I am afraid." But she didn't show fear in an ordinary way, Moshe thought. Her grip on his arm loosened, as if her strength was being absorbed elsewhere. All her concentration was not, like the soldiers, put to backing off from the source of fright inside the wagon, but to going to it, understanding it, giving of herself to stop its pain.

"We must flee, master," said Cyrus. He pulled Moshe so suddenly that his arm slipped easily out of Rachel's grasp. Cyrus whispered fiercely into Moshe's face: "We must get out of here."

"What?" said Moshe, his attention drawn to where Rachel was walking with quick little steps toward the wagon, her hands reaching up to the jewels about her neck. The soldiers moved back on their horses, to let her through.

"We wouldn't come to him, so he sent it to us—"

"What are you talking about? What did he send? Who is he—?" Moshe pushed Cyrus out of his way. "Rachel, wait for us!" he said, but Cyrus stepped in front of him in the shadows between the line of modest houses and the dancing circles of torchlight coming from above the soldiers' high mounts.

"Plague," said Cyrus, hissing out the word.

"There is no plague here," said Moshe.

"There is plague in that wagon, and the bishop of Nicomedia has sent it to us."

"Cyrus, make sense. There hasn't been plague in this part of the world for a hundred years—"

"Master, I have seen plague in Egypt, and I know what plague is and what it looks like, and the bishop has sent you a half-dead peasant as a sample. There is plague in Nicomedia and he wants you to treat it. And I'm telling you, let's get out of this town, out of this country as fast as we can. I feel the air thickening already—"

Rachel, unassisted by any soldiers, pulled herself up onto the wagon and thrust aside the hides that covered it. A light glowed from inside, and for a moment, Moshe could see Rachel's face, staring intensely, but with a curious gentleness, as if she were a saint on a clumsily executed icon.

"You may stay here, as you are so afraid," said Moshe.

He hurried up to the wagon, walking with his long stride and fierce gaze. Several soldiers saluted him, and several others bowed and mumbled benedictions. One of them was the messenger who had stopped them earlier that day.

"May the Lord be with you, master," he said.

"Yes," said Moshe. As he stepped up to the back of the carriage, he heard the horse nearest him shy and his rider sharply still him. The messenger spoke as Moshe thrust aside the hide and entered the moving quarters of the sick man. "The bishop extends his welcome, doctor! If you so desire, we will escort you to Nicomedia tonight! If it pleases you, and if it pleases you only, sir!"

Two candles illuminated the man on the pallet on the floor and Rachel, crouching over him, with the chain of jewels off her neck and held up to her forehead, with the diamond pressing against her skin.

A sour smell of vinegar rose up from the straw-strewn floor, as if great vats of the stuff had been overturned within the confines of the covered wagon before laying this half-dead peasant to rest. Moshe instinctively held his breath. Some infections, he believed, were carried through the air. Vinegar was widely used as a preventative against catching the plague. Even in the palaces of Alexandria, it was sprinkled on marble floors when news of plague in any part of the east reached the great city. Some sprinkled rosewater instead, but most felt this to be less efficacious. There was a feeling that one had to fight the coming disease with something rank and vile that would turn back the demons with their hands reaching for their noses and mouths. Some doctors prescribed a powder of sulfur, arsenic, and antimony, but Moshe felt that this might have a better chance of killing the healthy than harming the unseen agent of disease.

Moshe stepped up to Rachel to share her view of the patient. One of Moshe's greatest influences as a student had been the works of Asaph Ha-Rofe, the sixth-century Jewish physician who had lived in the Galilee, in a community of devout Jews, dedicated to the worship of their God and to the healing of the sick. Moshe wasn't devout, but he had been moved by Asaph's courage: he never flinched at treating a patient, no matter how diseased, convinced that a physician was doing God's work and that God would not let him become infected. Indeed, Asaph believed that many diseases were the direct results of sin, and that the prayers of the afflicted, as well as those of the physician, would lead to healing. Moshe despiritualized this concept. Diseases were the result not of sins, but of incorrect living, and if the doctor lived correctly and enjoined the patient to live the same way, the body could return to this normal stage of health. And Asaph had been very specific about the way of correct living: a regular schedule of exercise, massage, baths, sunshine, fresh air; a decent balance of eating and drinking, including fresh water from clear-flowing streams; an absolute moderation in bodily functions, with everything from sexual intercourse to the rhythm of breathing before lying down to sleep prescribed. This same Asaph had described the laws of Kashrut as dietary preventions to disease, the laws of the Sabbath as an injunction against overwork, both physical and mental, the cycle of the holidays as emblematic of man's need to live in God-ordained regularity, in harmony with His seasons. It was the physician's duty to act as a guide back to the path of regularity, normality. Even when confronted by the dread specter of a leper, Asaph had been without fear. The man was God's creature, and the physician must do God's work and try and return him to the world.

"He is very much afraid," said Rachel.

"Perhaps you should stand back," said Moshe.

"Do you need to get closer?" she said. Moshe wondered what she could mean by this and then started at the realization that she had moved her necklace from where it had been pressed against her forehead and placed it directly over the man's heart, and her own hands now rested on the bare skin of his chest.

"I don't think it wise to touch the man," said Moshe sharply. He was still somehow removed from the scene of healing, towering over Rachel where she crouched over the man.

"No," said Rachel. "I must touch the man, Doctor Moshe."

Now Moshe found himself crouching. He was a physician after all, he reminded himself. He was girded against disease. There was no certainty yet that this man had the plague. And there was no sense of fear coming from this young woman, his betrothed, even as she touched her lovely fingers to the peasant's chest.

"It is dangerous to touch the man if one doesn't know the nature of his illness," said Moshe. But now his voice was less sharp. It was as if she had communicated something to him without the need of words: she was protected, even as he was protected; God wouldn't strike at the healer in the midst of giving aid to the sick. But Moshe wasn't at all convinced that this lovely young woman, laden with the superstitions of Byzantium and the Jews of Asia Minor, and somehow connected with a special story of her ancestors, had any effect at all on the sick, or that her calm and loving manner would protect her from the infected skin and breath and clothing of the filthy peasant. "Perhaps you should step back while I examine him."

Rachel hesitated for a moment. She could feel the terrible sickness in the shut-eyed man on the floor, could feel the welcome of his skin as it reacted to the touch of the gems and the warmth of her love. But this man was her groom, and a famous doctor. She would defer to his knowledge; after all, there were many who had died under the loving care of her hands. And she had never experienced the particular kind of pain that the peasant suffered. It was something sharp, and deep, and rapid, like a knife wound near the heart in a very healthy body; this pain wouldn't last. It would either devour the man swiftly, or evaporate, like water under the rays of the summer sun.

"Of course," she said, moving out of her crouch and backing away from the man, taking the necklace of jewels with her. Moshe saw the cold, supine body start as Rachel broke contact. For half a moment, it seemed as if the shut eyes would open, like those of a severed head rolling from the executioner's platform, and staring with a final passion at the dust of the world. But this was just his imagination, he told himself. The peasant was in a deep sleep, dreamless and dull. Moshe felt his life pulse, faint and irregular, and hoped that the dying man would prove to have suffered from a bad heart, or a damaged lung—anything but the plague.

"He is very cold," said Rachel.

"Yes," said Moshe. Delicately, he lifted the man's heavily muscled arm and pulled back the grimy linen blouse.

"It is bad," said Rachel.

She could not see what Moshe saw at that moment, from his low vantage point over the dying man's body. But she could feel the sudden shift in Moshe's attention, from apprehension and concern to terror. "There is something that is very bad," she said, taking a step closer to her bridegroom, instinctively wishing to share his trouble, to take it on her shoulders and ease his burden. But Moshe was unaware of her having spoken at all. Under the man's armpit was a grotesque boil, the size of a small orange. This was known even in those years as a bubo, from which the bubonic plague took its name.

"You had best leave," said Moshe to Rachel, without turning to look at her. "Go outside and breathe the cool night air. Go."

In a daze of fear, he stripped away the man's leather trousers, tearing at them without thought. Besides the bubo, even in the bad candlelight, he could see the dark masses under the skin, where blood had burst and settled in grotesque designs. But he wanted to expose the groin. The bubo in the armpit was perhaps not a bubo at all, but a filthy boil, some reaction to a cut or a bite of a snake or poisonous insect; but in every case of plague he had ever seen in Alexandria, there had always been the bubo in the groin, sometimes as small as an olive pit, sometimes as large as a melon. Clumsy with speed, he exposed the groin, and found the boil, swollen with poison, as large as an egg.

"Plague," he said, and then he said it again. He was not speaking to Rachel, but to the four corners of the room, to the greatest fear a physician might face, a disease recognized, understood, but known to be nearly unstoppable.

This was why the bishop had sent for him. If this peasant was dying with plague, then Nicomedia was filled with it; and if Nicomedia succumbed to the disease, then so would adjacent Constantinople, and with it, the entire empire. Just as plague had nearly collapsed the empire in 542, and again in 566, it could do so in 756; and with even greater vengeance. There had been no new ways discovered to treat the scourge, only greater ways to transfer it from one filthy population group to another. With plague came isolation, poverty, riots; in its aftermath came the preying barbaric hordes, eager to take advantage of decimated armies and undefended city walls.

"Is there a way to heal him?" said Rachel, speaking softly, but so close to him, that her voice broke through his despair.

"No, no," said Moshe. "Please, you must leave, you don't understand. This is plague. Do not tell anyone. There will be panic. But my servant was right. This is plague."

"Is there a way to ease the man's pain?" she said insistently, because she could feel his agony reach out to her, like a lover calling for his beloved from the far side of a dream.

There were treatments, of course, many and largely useless, and Moshe had studied them all, had worked with men far older and more experienced than he, men who had traveled deep in the heart of Asia, where the disease was said to live, eager to strike out into the world at large whenever a volcano erupted, an earthquake struck, or floods broke through the desert lands. But this man was beyond help. Moshe knew if he bled him there would be a macabre green scum obscuring the blood, putrefying the atmosphere. Lancing either of the man's boils would simply add to his pain, hasten him over the threshold to death. It would be as humane to slit his throat. When the body was cold, the plague had already beat back the forces of life. No physician could do more than pray for the man's soul.

"I think the wretch is past feeling," said Moshe. "He will soon be dead."

"No," said Rachel, not contradicting the doctor's prediction but responding to the pain that was all about them, a pain vivid with colors, red and vermilion and black shot with threads of purple. Without thinking, she thrust Moshe aside, crouching before the man, the necklace finding its place on his chest, her fingers reaching for his cold blue-tinged lips.

"Get away from him!" said Moshe, horrified now at her recklessness. The man could still have enough life to form a cough that would send bloody matter into her face, that would infect both of them and thereby take the germ of Nicomedia into the Jewish village, sowing further destruction. No wonder the soldiers stood back under their torchlights, no wonder Cyrus wanted to leave the village, wanted to get out of the country. Death was all about them, like a sea in a storm, with waves and whirlpools coming from every direction and all at the same time. He pulled her back from the peasant with such force that she fell over and away from the man, landing on her side in the vinegar-soaked straw. But the jewels stayed where she had placed them, gleaming in the candlelight on his pale chest. "You must listen," said Moshe, going to help her to her feet. "He is dying, but he is infected, and we must leave him, and get away from here at once. Both of us."

But Rachel wasn't listening to her bridegroom. She could feel the man calling for her touch, even if it would be for one last time, one brief moment. So powerful was her concentration on the peasant's body that Moshe felt his head turning from Rachel to where the dying man lay on the floor; and there he saw an incredible thing.

The peasant's eyes opened, wide and clear. When he raised his lifeless arms Moshe knew that it was a cry from the heart, the seat of the soul, and that all that was left of the man's strength on earth was calling out to Rachel, was beseeching her for her embrace. In silent awe, he watched the young woman throw herself on the filthy peasant, watched her fingers clasp his cheeks, watched her eyes absorb the plague victim's stare, which so many believed to be deadly in itself.

When the man died, a few moments later, it was not with a sudden twitching agony, but with a gentle acquiescence, as if the presence of Rachel had allowed his crossing to the afterlife to be as simple as a step across a narrow, gently flowing stream.

Chapter
22

The peasant's corpse was driven out into the countryside. There, in an open field, the soldiers set the covered wagon on fire, stopping only to release the horses. Later the soldiers would swear that the flames reached toward the sky in the shape of a man, huge and luminous, and that emaciated arms of fire, long and limned with a ghostly radiance, held on to the burning wagon, as if to keep their hold on the earth. But soon there was no shape to the burning, only the groaning and creaking of wood and bones. The soldiers galloped back to the Jewish village, hurrying the distance between the plague ghosts and their own threatened souls.

Though it was past midnight, torches and lanterns burned from the open doors of the modest dwellings, and shrouded faces peered out into the night. In front of Rabbi Amnon's house, the great doctor Moshe was saying good-bye to his mother and father; he spoke without warmth, throwing his words over the length of ten paces.

"May I embrace you, my son?" said Rabbi Amnon.

"You may embrace me with your love, Father," said Moshe. "But do not come closer. We do not know how the disease enters the body."

"But you are not sick," said his father. "Only God can make you sick, and He allows physicians their health so that they can treat His creatures."

Still, he did not come closer. Moshe's mother watched father and son from the threshold of their house. Here, where so much joy had been anticipated, was now only gloom and trepidation. She knew that her son would never return to the heart of his family, to his roots in their tiny community. He was called away, almost in the instant of having arrived; she would not venture to guess whether it was to answer the demands of the Lord or of His fallen angels. The soldiers' torchlight illuminated the waiting carriage, sent by Bishop Giles of Nicomedia. Moshe wondered if the carriage was infected, if its very wheels ground the city's disease into their dusty village streets.

"Moshe Bar-Amnon!" The shouted name brought the valediction between son and parents to a close. It was Hillel, Rachel's father, and even in the poor light, his tears were as visible as his terror. "I give you my children. They are in your care. If it is the will of God, I shall see them again. Forgive me if I have ever offended you, or if I do so now, but I must ask you: do not anger the devils, do not taunt them. They are powerful, and only the Lord can fight them, and in His own time. Do not bring their hatred upon us."

Moshe had known that he would be unable to prevent Rachel from accompanying him into the place of death; more than that, he wanted her there with him. Learned as he was, he understood that the One God had shared but few secrets about the human body with physicians. Although he despised superstitions, he accepted the possibility of unseen spirits, just as he accepted the existence of an invisible God. And he had seen the peasant's lifeless being invigorated by a spirit, even if only for a moment.

"There is no need for young Saadiah," said Moshe.

"I have kissed my sister, and held her in my arms," said Saadiah, his hand on the hilt of his sword. His words were loud, but his lips shivered. Moshe understood the fear. Men were always more eager to meet death at the point of a sword than through some malevolent force, turning the body into a battleground between spirits of light and dark. "I am as likely to have the disease as you or she."

"You are as likely," said Moshe, "as your father, who has breathed the air about you, who has witnessed the wagon with its dying man, who has felt the wind raised by the soldiers of Nicomedia as they hurried past."

"My brother is not sick," said Rachel. "He simply wants to accompany me."

"I must not be allowed to stay in the village," said Saadiah stubbornly. "My sister must be accompanied, yes. But all of us are risking the health of this place unless we leave at once. Ask my father. He knows that I've kissed Rachel. If she is sick, I shall share her sickness. If she is not, then I shall live or die as the Lord demands."

Moshe tried, even at that late hour, to explain something of what he knew about the contagion of plague. But very quickly, he realized that his words must sound foolish and empty. There were theories, but even their adherents knew that they explained little: some imagined that the illness was transmitted by a poisonous cloud and not by personal contact; others believed that only a cough or a bit of infected blood or the rotting flesh of one already dead could bring about a new plague victim. But none could explain why this unseen cloud selected some for death and others for life, or why some who had held the dead in their arms would remain healthy, while others, in a neighboring house, would die in their sleep without ever having touched a sick body. Astrologers hypothesized planetary movements as the prime movers of poison clouds; other stargazers believed that only those born under unfavorable stars could die from the plague, regardless of the density of any dread miasma over their city. The great Galen of Pergamos, codifier and analyst of Hippocrates' medical work, believed that plague resulted from infected air, the result of corpses left to rot in open fields; some were more susceptible than others to the disease, according to their temperament. One's temperament was a result of the differing balances of the four elements—blood, phlegm, choler, and melancholy—in the body.

"What you're saying is that you don't know who's sick and you can't guess who's going to be sick," said Saadiah.

Moshe fixed the boy with his most authoritative stare.

"I am trying to say that it makes no sense to leave this village, in order to save it or safeguard it. I am not leaving for that reason. I am only leaving to see if I can be of some help in Nicomedia; that is also the reason that your sister is leaving. She and I are not running away because we think we're sick and want to isolate ourselves from the people here."

"I am going because my sister is not married," said Saadiah simply.

Moshe shook his head in amazement and turned to their father for his support.

"It is not seemly otherwise." said Rachel's father.

"Seemly," said Moshe. "You don't understand. We are going under imperial escort to the bishop's palace to offer our services in the name of all that is good and holy—"

"I am going," said Saadiah. Moshe thought it strange that his sister didn't try and urge him to remain. She seemed unfazed about the whole argument, as if her thoughts were well beyond the little scope of their words on this black night. Perhaps, Moshe thought, she was already seeing ahead to the city, and to what awaited them there. For a moment, he had half a notion to forbid any of them to come with him, though he would have feared for Rachel's safety now that it was known that she had touched the plague victim. More than one town had hacked its infected members to death, burning their corpses with speed. Even the possibility of infection in a healthy-looking person had been known to bring God-fearing men and women to the act of murder. Everyone knew the tales of the Great Plague of 542, when Persian soldiers had smuggled past the walls of Constantinople pieces of rotting human flesh, bits of the corpses of their own plague-ridden countrymen, and thereby infected a million and more people in Justinian's empire. Moshe had no perfect faith that the people of this religious village would never turn on their own healer; he had seen what the threat of an epidemic could do to otherwise civilized people. He convinced himself that he was behaving well, rationally, not simply wanting her along out of his own fear; not simply because she was lovely and light and healthy and where he was going was ugly and dark and diseased.

"It is all right if he goes," said Rachel. "Saadiah will not be sick."

"How can you say that like that!" said Moshe, exasperated by her calm, her omniscient sentences, so modestly voiced. "You don't know who will live or die, any more than you can know that touching your jewels is going to make the sick well."

"Quiet, doctor," said Saadiah. "You are speaking to my sister! You'll treat her with respect, or you will answer to me!"

"How dare you speak like that to the doctor?" said Cyrus, coming suddenly out of the shadows, his face no longer fearful, but relaxed back into its ordinary cynicism. His dagger was in his hand, its blade catching the soldiers' torchlight. But none of the soldiers intervened, or even approached their circle. What Cyrus spoke was foreign to their ears, and all of these Jews had now had some form of contact with what they most feared. "And put your sword away," said Cyrus. "Before I use it to cut something off your body that you might need later on in life—"

"I thought you'd be long gone," said Moshe to his servant. "I thought you'd be halfway to Persia by now."

"No, you didn't, great doctor," said Cyrus. "You know how I love it when things get exciting. Few things are more exciting than a city struck by plague."

"We don't know that," said Moshe. Rachel was looking at him now, and he could see that she was holding her tongue, that she was about to say that of course they knew that—that she knew it at any event. But he was wrong; he had little skill at reading minds, particularly one so straightforward as Rachel's. For what Rachel was looking at was a man she loved, and she was seeing past his words, alternately noble, sophisticated, joking, carping, sweet—an entire armament of words that had nothing at all to do with his true feelings. She was amazed at this.

For Rachel saw the man clearly. He was a doctor. He wanted to heal the sick, exactly as she did. There was great courage in his heart, and self-sacrifice. When the peasant had slipped away from the earth, she had felt Moshe's soul go out to him, not only in pity for his death, but in horror and sorrow at the deaths to come, at the deaths he saw as clearly as she. As they all four entered the silken comfort of the bishop's carriage, and Rachel watched the way Moshe asserted his strength with her brother, pretended a superficial relationship with the servant who was his truest friend, and continued his somewhat stilted formalities with her, she wondered when all such indirectness would end. Someday he would have to tell them all the truth: that he was glad of Saadiah's brave company, that he was touched by Cyrus's loyalty and devotion, that he wanted her with him not as a healer, but as his beloved. Rachel was astonished that the great man found her beautiful, that beyond the gulf of experience that separated them was an attraction so powerful that all the horrors that awaited them in the neighboring city were displaced by their closeness in the carriage on the still night roads. But she could not be indirect. It was not within her to dissemble, to tear the love from her face, the fear from her eyes, the faithfulness from her steady frame. And she had a need to tell him what was in her heart.

"Moshe," she said, speaking in Hebrew, in a whisper that she hoped the sleeping Cyrus and Saadiah could not hear. "Let us marry before we die."

She watched his pale eyes as the words struck him, exacerbating his desire, like salt in a bloody wound. He was nonplussed, and could think of nothing to say. His heart raced as he raised his elegant fingers to his red-bearded face. "Moshe," she said. "Please." And she took his fingers and placed them against the diamond, the central stone in her necklace, the jewel that lay against the pulse in her throat. He allowed her to bring the tips of his fingers to the stone, and incredibly, instantly, he felt calmer. Hurrying into a place without hope or reason—a city struck by plague—his nervous heart steadied, his chest grew warm, as if from an abundance of love.

"Yes," he said, not knowing what he was agreeing to, understanding only that the touch of her hands to his made the contact with the stone infinitely pleasurable, that the tiny moment in the carriage was good and that he wished it to go on. He wished to ride like this, their hands united over the diamond, their eyes locked in an embrace that would never end. "Yes," said Moshe again, and he was afraid to move his lips to hers, afraid to let his hands drop their contact with Rachel or the stone, afraid to do anything that would take them a moment closer to the walls of the city, a moment farther from the dream they now shared. "Yes," he said again and again, until the word was a whisper, until the affirmation of their love was so ingrained in her heart that it lost its voice, it slipped noiselessly into her life, as much a part of her as skin and eyes and teeth and tongue.

They passed through the walls of Nicomedia just after dawn. The heavy carriage moved slowly through the well-paved main streets, avoiding the narrow alleys of the slum quarters. It would be the poor who fared worst in the event of plague, Moshe knew, their bodies already weakened by poor water, inadequate food, and the filth and cold and damp of their homes. Once the great cities of Byzantium had shepherded their poor into slums beyond the walls, miserable collections of tiny hovels with beaten earth floors and thatched roofs. Now the poor lived inside the walls, not in houses, but in giant blocks of flats, some as high as nine stories; these tenements were so close together that the rooftops often connected high above the muddy alleys, blotting out the sun and cleansing rain. It was in these dark alleys that the laws of empire were flouted: offal was tossed into the mud, sewage was poured from open windows, pigs and goats rooted about in the muck, and whores, thieves, and murderers plied their trades.

Saadiah woke with a start, his hand still on the hilt of his sword. He looked from Rachel to Moshe to the glimmering wall of rich houses, the upper windows catching the rising sun. "Where are we going?" he said, his words accusatory, directed at Moshe, as if he might be behind some plot to steer the carriage down an abyss.

"We are going to see the bishop of Nicomedia," said Moshe evenly. Smiling, he tried to turn about the boy's dread with a good humor he didn't feel. "And good morning, my future brother-in-law."

Saadiah answered nothing to this, but continued to stare out at the neatly aligned brick houses, their sloping tile roofs surmounted by huge gold crosses. City dwellers used the family names carved in the walls of the homes fronting on the wide streets as geographical reference points. When the streets grew dark, the sameness of the well-made constructions, the identical rows of rounded windows gleaming from the second floors, the smooth brick facades broken by ornate balconies bearing flowers of the season, made it difficult to know which of several rich quarters one might be in. But Saadiah had been to Nicomedia before, had visited here with his cousin, the son of his father's uncle, on a trading trip from Itil, the capital of the Khazars. They were in an Italian quarter, he was certain; Saadiah recognized the name of the merchant of Ravenna with whom his cousin had done business carved in the sun-bright wall. When he looked up at the crosses, he saw that they were western-style, with short arms.

"This is not the way to the bishop's palace. The bishop's palace is on the south side of the city, high on a hill, overlooking the sea." Saadiah was insistent in his fear, turning to his unflappable sister, and even to Cyrus, now moodily awake. "They are taking us to the wrong part of the city! I know what I am talking about! Ask them! They are tricking you!"

"They are taking us to the bishop," said Moshe. "Perhaps not to his palace, but to another house, far from the sight of the sea."

"That makes no sense," said Saadiah, annoyed by Moshe's lack of concern. "Perhaps they needed some Jews to use as scapegoats

—to pick us out as the bringers of the plague. They will try to harm my sister, burn her as a witch. The people of the city have heard of her, after all. Those who haven't been cured by her touch fear her. Some believe her to be in league with devils, but you must tell them that all that is false. We are not superstitious people, simply religious, faithful to the ways of our God. You must tell the driver! Please, you must tell him at once!"

Moshe slapped the boy twice across the face, his hand moving so fast that it was impossible to anticipate, and when he had finished, the others stared at him, as if unsure that the event had transpired at all. Saadiah stopped his tirade, and Moshe fixed him with his hieratic stare.

"Look, boy. If this city is indeed suffering from the beginning of a plague, the whole populace will be babbling like you. They will want the blood of the lepers, and then the blood of the slaves from the north, and then, as always, they will be after the blood of the Jews. If you cannot control yourself, you will leave here at once. I will see to it that you are taken out of the city, away from your sister, and then you will no longer have a home. Not in your village, not in this place of plague, nowhere. You will be quiet, you will be grave, you will be respectful and worthy of respect, or you will not be part of this group."

Cyrus spoke up as his master caught his breath. "The boy will behave now. It's just that he needs a good pee in the morning, master." Moshe smiled at this, as Cyrus kept his face grave, and spoke in Persian, a language that both assumed was foreign to Rachel and her brother.

"As your doctor, I think I can recommend a good solid pee for both of us," said Moshe. The entourage of soldiers had halted suddenly, and the carriage now slowed before gilded courtyard gates, breaking the monotony of the brick walls. Unlike the other houses on the wide street, this mansion had an entrance wide enough for a carriage to enter from the front or rear, and as a porter released the gates, Moshe could see the huge iron door to the mansion on the other side of the courtyard's garden. The door's bronze nail studs were arranged in an elaborate, floriated cross, so elegantly detailed that Moshe was surprised that clerical authorities hadn't ordered it removed from the door as a violation of the anti-icon laws. The courtyard was deep and very wide, almost like that of a country villa, with outbuildings for cattle and chickens, cisterns so deep they could certainly hold a three years' supply of water for a dozen families.

A small bald-headed man suddenly caught Moshe's eye as he hurried from a low building, probably the bathhouse, dressed in a black tunic, the gray-black beard identifying him as a member of the clergy. "Whether or not we are at the bishop's palace, we are in the presence of the bishop," said Moshe. As he stepped down from the carriage, he felt Rachel start behind him. "What is it?" said Moshe, turning back to the carriage, to his betrothed's quiet black eyes.

"You must not be afraid, Moshe," said Rachel.

"I am not afraid," he said, practically snapping out the words. But then he shook away his crossness, looking up at the artlessly beautiful face. "I can never be afraid when I am with you."

Bishop Giles took long steps for a short man, and he hurried without noticeable exertion. He seemed to glide across the courtyard, as if the soles of his sandals barely touched the ground. But it was not the bishop, a good man crazed by inaction, shackled by a lack of knowledge, that Rachel saw as a source of fear. It was the city at her back, beyond the courtyard gates, east and west and south, to the brilliant, life-teeming sea. All around her, she could sense the fearful awakenings magnified by a common sorrow and a uniform dread: did someone else die in the night? Was my body now infected, to begin a pain-wracked descent to death?

"Welcome," said the bishop. "Welcome, great doctor Moshe bar-Amnon."

"Thank you, Bishop Giles," said Moshe, for the man in the simple tunic could be no one else. Even exhausted, the little man had the authority of a prince, and one used to peering into the mysteries of science and of the spirit. "I am happy to be here at your bidding."

The bishop smiled a bit queerly at this, as if about to suggest that only a madman would be happy to come to Nicomedia, willingly, at this moment. "May the Creator of all that moves on this earth keep you in health and help you to assist us in this time of our troubles."

The bishop had green eyes, overwhelmed by enormously dilated pupils, though the sun was already bright. He spoke mechanically, as if the greeting was a formal one he had long since memorized, like a prayer intoned by one without faith.

"Your patient has departed this earth," said Moshe, referring to the peasant whose corpse was long since burned by the soldiers.

"There is a rush to leave this earth, great doctor," said Bishop Giles, and now Moshe detected a further unpleasantness. Beyond the insincerely expressed greeting was a hostility, but whether it was directed at himself, or at the world at large, he had yet no idea.

As Rachel took her place by his side, followed by Saadiah, his boyish hand poised on the hilt of his Khazar sword, and Cyrus, looking appreciatively at the mansion across the courtyard, Moshe began to introduce them: "I am accompanied by Rachel, daughter of Hillel, and her brother Saadiah, and my personal assistant Cyrus—"

"I am Bishop Giles," interrupted the bishop. "Do you know what that means?"

We have been invited to a plague-ridden city by a madman, thought Moshe. But he stilled the rising anger in his chest, remembering the touch of Rachel's hands as she brought his fingers to the stone. "Yes, of course," said Moshe, smiling pleasantly. "You are the spiritual leader of this city—"

"It means that I am named after St. Giles," said the bishop. "St. Giles, whom women pray to, to end their sterility, and to whom priests bend their knees to free their flock from demonic possession. St. Giles! I had better be named after St. Basil, who founded hospitals, or after Cosmas and Damian, who are the patron saints of Christian doctors. They were beheaded, great doctor Moshe, did you know that? Beheaded during the persecutions of Diocletian more than four hundred years ago—and now Diocletian burns in hell, and Cosmas and Damian sit in heaven and look down at us in our confusion. Or perhaps I should have been Bishop Luke, after St. Luke of Antioch, who was a doctor as well as an Apostle of Christ. But St. Giles? I don't know. I don't know if what we have in Nicomedia has to do with demons. I am confused, doctor. That is why I sent for a Jew. I want no theology for this morning. I want the science of Hippocrates and Galen and Asaph Ha-Rofe. I want all the knowledge of Arabia told to me at once, in half an hour, so that we may go into the city and heal what some devil has brought upon us, some enemy of God."

The bishop finally caught up his words sharply and turned about, so quickly that it could have easily been meant to give offense. But almost at once, he turned his head over his shoulder and said:

"Well, come on all of you, let's not stand around all day. You must be anxious to know if it is quite as bad as all that, or if it is only that I am completely mad."

They hurried after him, ignoring the strange courtesy of the liveried servants—who performed little bows to each of them— every one of them in clothing richer than that of their master. The bishop hurried them inside and up a marble staircase to a long gallery overlooking the wide street. The lack of traffic, pedestrian or otherwise, was as frightening as the bishop's bizarre behavior. At the end of the gallery was another staircase, this one of deeply polished wood; if there was a wife in this home, this would be the way to her domain of serving maids, nursery, receiving rooms for her aristocratic friends—ladies who could remove their veils only when they'd been led past her door.

"Rachel, daughter of Hillel," said the bishop suddenly, turning to her as they entered an elegant sitting room, lined with uphol- stered benches and plaster walls. A single eastern cross dominated the room; holes in the plaster indicated where icons had once been displayed, before the anti-icon laws had banished them to store- rooms or destroyed them in the emperor's fires. "Yes, of course. I know that name. You are the famous Jewess. The one who has the gift of healing."

He looked at her through his strangely exhausted eyes. "And your jewels. Not very much in the tradition of Hippocrates, I'm afraid. But very much the fashion of today. You must be careful that someone doesn't rip your emerald from your chain. They are powdering emeralds, all the rich are anyway, beating them to dust and drinking it down with wine." He paused for a minute, looking at the cross on the plaster wall. "They die anyway. Isn't that right, doctor? Powdered emeralds and wine? Not very effective against the plague."

"When was the first victim reported, Bishop Giles?" said Moshe.

"Four days and four nights have passed. Do you see anything in the way of a boil on me, doctor? It is usually four days to a week from the time of the boil to the moment of death. I can thus look forward to at least five days of life—one day to discover a boil, and four days to suffer its horrors—"

"Have there been any other victims?" said Moshe.

"Of course," said Bishop Giles. "Where there's plague, there's two—and four and ten and one thousand."

"But how many are there?" insisted Moshe.

"I haven't got a decent count of the bodies. At least twenty dead. In the past six days. But there could be a thousand dead in the slums, stuck in the mud, infecting our air."

"I only ask, Bishop, because there are ways to try and prevent the disease from spreading."

"You are in grave danger," said the bishop suddenly, looking directly at Rachel. "All your people are in danger. The poor have already made complaints. A man is ready to swear that the Jews have brought poison to the city wells—that your people have infected us with the plague."

"The best way to prevent illness," said Rachel, as if the bishop's frightening words had had no more import than a mote on a butcher's balance, "is to remain tranquil."

"She is lecturing me," said Bishop Giles to Moshe, as if struck by the wonder of this. "That is very interesting, my dear. Tranquil. It is very good advice, particularly as it comes from the famous healer. I, of course, took other precautions. My palace is at the edge of the sea, where the corrupting mists—if there are such things as corrupting mists at all—rise up from the surface and settle into our lungs. I thought it best to get away from the coast, though no place in this city is far from the sea; and I wanted to be away from the south winds. The south winds are what the doctors of Alexandria claim to be the most dangerous, the most likely to blow the miasma upon us."

"Rachel meant no disrespect, sir," said Cyrus, allowing himself to speak without having been spoken to as Moshe had introduced him not as his servant but as his assistant. "She is medically learned, and even in my simple studies in Egypt, I learned that in the case of plague, mental attitude is a significant factor in prevention of the disease. Doctors are warned not to allow themselves to grow melancholy over the passing of their patients. If one loses tranquility in a welling up of sadness, it creates an imbalance in the four elements. Sadness can lower the body's temperature. A lower body temperature will dull intelligence, kill the spirit in one's bones, until your body is like an empty shell, waiting for the plague, eager for it to take its prize."

"All right, Cyrus," said Moshe. He had heard all too clearly the bishop's warning about the threat to the Jews. Already he could imagine the sacking of the rich houses of the Jewish merchants;

308

then, their hate-lust still hungry, a mob of murderers on horse-back, rushing past the city wall, eager to crush old skulls, rape young women, torch the flimsy houses of the Jewish villagers. Their friends and neighbors dead or dying, their own bodies apt to turn against them at any moment, it was perfectly logical that a last reserve of strength would be called upon to slaughter the descendants of the killers of Christ. Moshe had witnessed the effects of mass sickness before, in cities where the Jews lived as minorities. Sometimes the mob attacked the lepers first, or the colony of foreign traders from countries with whom they had once been to war. But always, eventually, they would remember the Jews within their midst: secretive, unwilling to assimilate, elitist in their vast book learning, they were targets of envy, resentment, and hatred. The supreme illogic of well poisoning would make perfect sense to the mob in Nicomedia, if the plague had indeed struck, and was spreading.

"Oh, please, great doctor," said Bishop Giles. "You need not interrupt your assistant. He sounds very learned too. All these wonderful medical ideas will prove very useful, I am sure, if there are people left alive in the city to tell them to. We could tell them to stay calm, even when the blood oozes thick and green, even when the stench of the rotting flesh is so vile that it brings tears to the eyes, even when the three children of a young marriage are tortured in a slow, painful death before your eyes—I will simply tell my flock to be tranquil. Not to be excited, is that correct?"

"Let us go," said Rachel to Moshe.

"Ah, the healer is already anxious to return to the heart of her people," said Bishop Giles. "I am not surprised. I will only need the good doctor's assistance anyway, if he will be so kind. If you doctors know anything, it is to describe what you don't comprehend."

"Rachel is not going to return to the village, Bishop," said Moshe.

"Where, then?" said Bishop Giles.

"I must go to the sick," she said.

The bishop was taken aback by what he imagined to be her courage. "That is good," he said. "I am glad you are not running so fast. We will have a patient soon enough. In a covered wagon, washed in vinegar so that we may bear the stink. I will have tunics washed in rosewater, that we can afterward discard. Perhaps such

309

things really do prevent the spread of the disease. I only know that I have no boils yet, and that I have looked at two dozen patients and fifteen or more have died, and every one has passed away for some reason that only God can fathom."

In those days nearly every Jewish doctor was a rabbi as well; almost every Christian physician was also a priest. In those cases where the physician was not a clergyman, particularly in religious Byzantium, the sickbed was first visited by the priest. The blessing was more important than the little the physician could do; there was a clear understanding that while the physician knew little enough, and usually tried to bring the body back to its own natural balance and harmony, he could not hope to do this without God's help. Obviously the physician had no place in the sickroom until the priest worked his prayers over the diseased body. If God wished to allow the physician to help cure one of His creatures, it would only be after the man's spirit had been attended to. Bishop Giles had studied medicine, but did not fancy himself a fully qualified physician. Yet the aristocrats of Nicomedia, and many of neighboring Constantinople could not imagine anyone else's hands examining their bodies; these hands were imbued with the power of the bishopric, the strength of belief.

"I am sorry," said Rachel. "There is no time for a change of tunic. I must go at once."

"Rachel," said Moshe, letting out a snort of laughter, as if to discard her intention as some sort of girlish impetuousness, and at the same time blocking her way. "We are going to join the bishop in examining the patient when he arrives."

"No," said Rachel. "If you would open your heart, you would feel the need all around us. There is something that can be done, and it must be done at once."

This time Moshe didn't block her way. His betrothed wasn't criticizing him, but simply followed an inner compulsion, a force that could only derive from what spirits of good existed in God's world. Even the bishop's exhausted, ironic face twisted into lines of wondering respect. She walked out of the sitting room the way she had entered, the sunlight dancing in the waves of her hair like a crown placed too loosely on her head. No one thought of leading her to the staircase, directing her to a carriage, offering her an escort to some sufferer of the disease. She had no hesitation, no shackles of doubt about where to go, and once there, of what she would be capable. No matter how horrible the source of pain, the cry from the heart would lead her to it; no matter how hopeless the illness, she would place her hands, and her jewels, and the substance of her faith in the service of healing.

Chapter
23

They all followed Rachel.

Saadiah was the first down the staircase, his hand still on the hilt of his sword, as if lusting for a chance to die in preserving his sister's honor. He was followed by Moshe, his legs so clumsy with anticipation that each stair felt as if constructed of wet sand. Cyrus followed his master, wondering if he would have enough strength to slit his own throat once he had contracted the disease. Finally the bishop came, careful not to tempt the plague by raising his body temperature, but not wishing to lose sight of the procession. He forced his sleep-deprived body after them, step by step, wondering if there was anything he could learn, anything he could suffer that would have value in fighting this scourge of God.

She was at first not aware of being followed, not even by her loved ones, because every part of her waking mind was directed to a particular source of pain. There were distractions, of course, and her open eyes might have witnessed a soldier's face, a fearful pallor rising up from beneath skin burned by wind and sun; or a dissolute reveler, unsteady in the morning sunlight, not comprehending why the streets remained empty of the ordinary traffic of men and letters and carriages. She might have heard the bishop's driver offer her transportation, or the lone monk walking the street, his face obscured by a "smelling apple" held to nose and mouth—this was an antiplague concoction of black pepper, red and white sandal, roses and camphor, molded with gum arabic into the shape of an apple—shouting at her immodestly dressed figure.

312

"Cover your face, you godless creature!" shouted the monk, for Rachel was without her veil, and the monk was without restraint. In a universe that suddenly seemed on the verge of anarchy, he would at least try and enforce a few last rules of civilization. But Rachel was pulled quickly past the monk, past the wide paved streets unused to fear and the threat of misery; though there were cries for help from individual homes behind their elegant walls, none were as urgent as the one she already followed.

"Rachel, wait," said Moshe, running up to her as she turned south, toward a narrower street, winding up a little hill lined with shops, all of them shut tightly this market day.

Her betrothed touched her, and she could feel the urgency in his hand, in his voice, the concern for her well-being, and this pleased her. But she could not stop her forward motion.

"Rachel, we are coming with you," said Moshe. "But you must take some precautions. Please, listen to what I say. Do not touch anyone directly, particularly in an infected spot. Do not breath deeply in their homes, and try and cover up your nose and mouth with your cloak. Be especially careful if anyone is coughing—"

"Moshe," said Rachel. "I am glad that you are coming with me to heal the sick."

He was a great doctor, she knew, and she respected his judgment, but there was no way for him to understand completely what drove her, what gave a surety of movements to her hands, what impelled her from a placing of jewels to a laying on of hands, to a silent shut-eyed prayer. Rachel felt a love between them, a commonality of feeling for the sufferings allowed by God in His world, but she understood too that no matter how she and Moshe would grow together, he would never see what she saw, never feel what she felt.

What she had within her heart was a blessing, of course, because it gave her the chance to do good; but it set her apart too. While everyone around her—be they physicians, or rabbis, or saints— looked for causes, results, logic, facts, and understanding, she simply kept her senses open to the spirit that moved all creatures. There was no need for so much thought, for it clouded feeling. In looking and searching for a pattern, one only confused what must needs be simple. To try and explain how she was impelled to heal would be like attempting to teach a wild animal to run by shouting instructions or drawing pictures. The animal knows how to run: if it has been kept all its life in a cage, it only needs to be let free. Not even a push or a shout is necessary. Once the bars are lifted, and the beast steps into the wild, the spirit will fill its heart, will power its limbs. It will not look for understanding. What it needs to be will overwhelm its tiny soul. Rachel wished that others would allow the spirit to overwhelm them, for every man and woman had a soul and a strength more powerful and precious than that of any animal. But she knew that most refused to allow this, even wise and good men like Moshe. They hardened their hearts in trying to see; in trying to understand they kept knowledge at bay; they were like lions afraid to run through the night, kings of the jungle imagining terrors that weren't there. How she would love to tell dear Moshe that there were answers all around, but to attempt to pluck them from the air was fruitless; it simply made them dance in the air, forever out of reach. They would come not by effort, but through faith, by a relaxing—not an exercising—of will.

"But you must listen to what I say," said Moshe. "Please, you must not expose yourself to unnecessary danger. There is only a limited amount of good that can be done, but what we can do we shall attempt with courage, but that doesn't mean—"

"Fire," said Cyrus, looking over his master's head up the rising street, even as Saadiah drew his sword. The bishop, out of breath from the fast pace, shouted at them to stop.

"Let us go back," he said. "They must be burning the Jewish quarter."

But Rachel didn't hear, or had heard the warning as if it were the inconsequential details of a child's nightmare. Beyond the fire was a need, and if it pulled her there, no fire, no mob would bar her way. Moshe took her arm and repeated the bishop's warning, but Rachel was already turning off the narrow street into one yet narrower and steeper, with great holes marring the surface, where paving blocks had been excavated for more appropriate sections of the city.

"Rachel, listen," said Moshe. "We only want to help the sick, to see the symptoms of a victim of the disease, but that can be accomplished without danger—"

"There is no danger outside," said Rachel. She could feel him stifle his fear, a fear that was born within his own logical mind, a result of details she ignored: the bishop's story of the anti-Jewish feeling, the fire over the hill, the unknown numbers of people already sick, already hopeless, already driven

314

from sickness to self-loathing to mass hatred. Without thought, she touched his hand, and he started at its warmth; on the cold and clammy day his own fingers were numb, his lips shivered in the unpleasant mist.

"Where is she going?" said the bishop, all his authority stripped from him now that he was out of his vestments, without his complement of soldiers, without the rich trappings of his office. He was afraid of the mob. When nature turned its wrath on men, men often turned their wrath on the clergy, as if it were their ineffectual prayers that had brought calamity. It was bad enough that half the peasants were icon worshipers, and could erupt into madness at any isolated symbol of the icon breakers—no better living symbol existed in Nicomedia than the bishop, unless it was the bishop accompanied by four Jews—but to be wandering with Jews in a plague-ridden city with a mob already maddened by blood and fire was to ask to be torn limb from limb. Still, he was following the dictates of his conscience, his duty to his flock, no matter how savage, how ungrateful. This was a famous doctor, and with him a superstitious Jewess whom the peasants held in awe. It was better to follow them than to sit and wait for the boils to erupt in his groin, defenseless and faithless.

A goat stuck its head out from an adjacent alley, before shying back from their approach. Its bell was as ominous as the fire that now seemed to be coming from two directions, and with it, a low rumble, the collective voices of a mob. "This is bad," said the bishop to Cyrus. "The bell, the mist, the fire—all are portents of plague."

Cyrus, though out of breath from the pace, was as ever eager to exhibit his medical lore. "So is blood from bread freshly baked," said Cyrus. "So are earth tremors. So are sudden shifts in the wind, bringing moist heat to a dry climate—"

"We are not in a dry climate," said the bishop, remembering that he was talking to a fool. "We are in a perfect climate for the plague."

"No," said Cyrus. "Not perfect. It's a bit cold, and there are no earth tremors." He smiled giddily, as if nothing would please him more at that moment than the earth opening wide, to prove that his listing of plague portents was accurate.

Once again Rachel was turning, and now the alley she took was unpaved and muddy. Regardless of their fear, they all kept their eyes to the ground to avoid the ruts and offal and garbage not yet discovered by the pigs. Somehow they had come in short steps and quick minutes from luxury and light to poverty and darkness, the natural element of disease. The sun was obscured by the overhanging reaches of the top-heavy tenements so that the alleys were like incomplete tunnels, with just enough holes to let in the mist and the gray hint of daylight. They descended and rose, held their breath against odors difficult to breathe, stepped over shallow troughs which were meant to be sewage canals leading to the sea but were instead collectors of rainwater and animal excrement and garbage that the poor used for washing their clothes and watering down their sour wine. Soon the fire and the mob no longer loomed ahead and around them. They had entered the underbelly of the city, so far beyond the reach of hope and promise that even rage was a muted cry here, even anger was but a silent murmuring despair.

While the rich had marble lavatories, bathhouses large enough to fill with a ten families' brood of a hundred lice-crawling children, here the poor shared a communal outhouse, serviced by a slave, whose office was perhaps the lowest in all of Nicomedia. Yet strangely, everyone knew that God kept the outhouse keepers alive during the last plague. Though it was a hundred years ago and longer, the legends of the poor who had survived, saved by the grace of God, or the inability of the contagion to enter their evil-smelling dwellings, had remained in contemporary legends. In Egypt, during the threat of plague, Cyrus had known of rich men who had quartered themselves in tanning factories as well as out-houses, breathing deeply of the terrible air; like those who believed the peasant unwelcome in hell, they believed that the mysterious agent of the disease would not deign to enter such miserable sur-roundings.

But now, sidling about the noxious presence of a real outhouse, not one in some legend of salvation, there was nothing safe about it. Even Rachel seemed anxious not to touch its rotting surface as she hurried past, turning through the darkening mist to a crumbling flight of stone steps.

"Where are you going?" said Moshe.

But she no longer had the words to answer. There was an urgency such as she had never felt, as if the pain that summoned her was not that of one isolated human soul, but a seed for a multitude of hearts that must be succored, lest a hundred lives be destroyed, or a hundred thousand. The steps ran around the outside of the tenements, from which the sounds of children issued, complaining and insistent; but a lassitude hung over the place, as if invisible chains held the natural spirits of the entire slum in awkward stasis.

But the presence of five people hurrying up the steps of their tenement was more than the children, whose inactivity had been ordered by parents and priests, could bear. They came out of their filthy warrens, barefoot and pale, chattering questions and hurling insults. No one could know who these people were—a woman without a veil, a man with a red beard, a boy with a sword, a foppishly dressed servant, a bishop without any mark of office— but all could see that they were not of this quarter. It took a moment for them to be surrounded, not by a dozen, but by a hundred, children hardly big enough to walk, and others as tall as any adult, and all of them curious, insistent, full of an energy that ran through their bones and rags and hungry frames.

"Stand back, children," said the bishop, raising his hands in the signs of his priestly office. But neither the five-fingered salute to the heavens nor the rapid drawing of the cross in the murky air had the slightest effect on the crowd. They were upon them swiftly, holding on to their tunics, making it impossible for them to move.

"Make way for Bishop Giles!" thundered Moshe suddenly, not looking into every corner of the mob, but only straight ahead, at one curly-headed tot, who lurched back so quickly that he nearly started a stampede. Deliberately, Moshe leveled his intimidating gaze at one after another of the children, each one stepping back as if he had been hit with the master's rod. Moshe spoke again, his words as round and uniformly loud as any preacher's: "Your bishop has come to give his blessing! Make way for Bishop Giles!"

There was enough of a pulling back so that Saadiah could draw his sword, and now he too shouted the bishop's name, and the fierce weapon seemed to catch the reflected glory of the bishop's office.

Cyrus followed suit, enjoying the charade of pomp, bending and scraping before the man on his left, who was shorter than any of them save Rachel: "Make way for the miracle of his blessing!" said Cyrus. "The bishop of Nicomedia is among you—all hail Bishop Giles of Nicomedia!"

Perhaps they were confused, none of them having been close

enough before to the great man to possibly recognize him now; indeed, many of the children imagined the bearded Moshe, with his hypnotic stare and booming tones, to be the bishop, and the small, exhausted man behind him to be a servant or retainer. But Bishop Giles too had resources, once they were brought to the surface.

"Step back, children!" he said, and there was no longer a need for shouting. He had turned his hand about, so that his bishop's ring flashed in the diffuse light. "Step back so that you may be blessed!"

Beyond the children were a few adults, some armed with sticks and cudgels, and now suddenly openmouthed at the sight of the august strangers. A young woman with a baby at her breast spoke in a thin, tearful voice. "There is sickness here, Father," she said, imagining the bearded Moshe to be a priest, and not able to see the bishop through the crowd about them. "I have asked the children not to move, to save their bodies from the death demon, but they defy me."

"No one will defy me," said Bishop Giles, his voice growing more confident, even as the children began to believe him to be of the Church, and of high office. "I am the bishop of this city, and my authority extends from God's rule. If there is disease, we shall fight it. If there is plague, we shall beat it. But first you must learn to obey. The willful spirit invites disease, as it invites the devil. You must be quiet, speak only when necessary, move only when essential. The plague looks for weakness, exhaustion, so that it may enter your bones. Defeat it with the wisdom of your elders. Eat light meals, drink only water that has been boiled, sleep only on your side so that no contagion may enter your open mouth. Do not dwell on your sorrows, or they will increase your bodily heat. Avoid touching the dying or dead, but remember that your responsibility to the living includes the burning of corpses whose lives have been taken by this scourge of God. We can root out evil if we remain prayerful, faithful, and obedient."

There was not a sound from the crowd now. Most no longer had their eyes on the speaker, as if this might be construed as mark of disobedience. As they lowered their gaze, the bishop commanded them to bow their heads to receive his blessing. For a few moments, Moshe was moved by the emotions of the man, though he was of another faith, an incomplete physician, a bigot. Tears came

318

to the bishop's eyes, and beyond all the sarcasm and cynicism and defeat he had voiced earlier in the courtyard and mansion, was a sincere plea to the unseen God. Bishop Giles, if not always a believer, was a believer at that moment, moved by the sight of God's children, suffering and omnipresent, all bearing human souls, the future parents of the race, exemplars of the miracle of human life that he tried never to take for granted.

"Trust in our Lord," concluded the bishop. "Trust in our salvation."

There was a long respectful moment to cap the hopeful prayers. It seemed that every man and woman in the crowd shared the bishop's trust and faith and spirit. But then all at once, the spirit of the crowd shifted.

"They are Jews," said an old woman from a higher part of the decrepit staircase. The silence hung in midair, like a balance beam, waiting for a particle of dust to decide which way to fall.

Then a young man spoke. "They are the Jews come to poison our food as they've poisoned our wells."

It was at that moment that Moshe realized that Rachel was gone.

"Stand back," said the bishop, angry not at the danger to his person but at the indignity to his office. Saadiah, pushed back against the bishop, drew his sword and raised it overhead. "I have come to give you my blessing," continued the bishop, and something of his anger penetrated the crowd, giving them pause more than the sight of Saadiah's blade. "I have come to give you my blessing and, together with this, have brought you friends and fellow citizens, Jews trained in medicine, who want, even as I want, even as the Church wants, to see that no harm comes to you and your community."

"Why has no harm come to their community?" said the old woman who had first spoken from her high point on the stairs. "Why has not a single Jew fallen victim to the plague?"

"There are so far few victims of the plague," said the bishop evenly, with courage. "No one can yet explain why one is overcome with the illness, and I doubt that anyone here can speak with authority as to whether or not a Jew in Nicomedia has caught the disease, when we are so far not even sure that disease is among us—"

"As no one can say that you are not a Jew too," said the old woman. "A Jew pretending to be a bishop, just as our emperor has pretended to be a Christian, yet he allows the Jews to break our icons—"

There was an immediate mumble of approval from the crowd. They were so close upon them now that Saadiah could have barely lowered his sword without slicing into someone's head—but he would have been unable to choose; and the boy recoiled at the thought of murdering a woman or a child.

"The Jews have not instituted the anti-icon laws," said the bishop sharply, but the anger was somehow diluted this time, as if he no longer had the strength for it. He was not among his ordinary congregation, educated Greeks who called themselves Romans, those who ignored the facts that great Rome was now a ravaged shell with a tiny population of scavengers, and that an empire built on the backs of conquered peoples by a pagan race of warriors had been replaced by one subservient to the dictates of a Christian clergy; these slum dwellers were not remotely akin to the educated and sophisticated Christians who understood well why the anti-icon laws were first promulgated. Christianity, they believed, would mean nothing if it was allowed to slide back into paganism: for the bishop, the icons were of a piece with idolatry, with the vestigial remains of a score of incompletely stamped-out cults and nature-worshiping creeds. For the slum dwellers, their icons were as worthy of honor as their ancestors, as much a part of their homes and lives as had been the household gods of the Western Romans. Fierce in their love of the Christian deity and the Christian rite, they refused to believe the calumnies heaped on their familiar images by an aristocratic clergy. They loved their Lord Jesus, they accepted His teachings, but they rebelled at the proscriptions heaped upon them by emperor and patriarch as to how they could exhibit that love.

"The anti-icon laws derive from the emperor and the patriarch, whose authority is granted them by God," continued the bishop. "If you doubt the anti-icon laws, you doubt Gospels and Church and our Savior—"

"The Iconoclasts are Jews," said another voice from the stairs, interrupting the bishop, and immediately setting up an ominous chant. Perhaps not a soul among them could have articulated the reasons why the Jews were blamed for the anti-icon laws of their own clergy. But all knew what was essential to know about Jews: they were strangers, they kept to their own communities, they didn't marry out of their faith, and because they were responsible for the death of Jesus Christ, they were doomed to wander the earth as despised souls all the days of their lives.

"The Jews are Iconoclasts! The Iconoclasts are Jews!"

No one had thrown a stone or touched any of them, not the bishop, or Saadiah with his raised sword, not Cyrus or Moshe. But the mob was screaming, building to a madness. They were filling themselves with the sounds of anger, filling themselves with a hatred that would soon need to be expressed with violence. Moshe was too distracted to think of a way out, either through guile or bluff or fury; he was searching for Rachel within the crowd, and it was he, without intent, who struck the first blow, and this only because he thought he had caught a glimpse of her far up the stairs, and someone deliberately barred his way.

Had Moshe been short, or dark, or quiet, the violent thrust of his hand might have passed unnoticed, for the crowd was no longer simple rings of children, with their elders pressing about the edge, and all of them intent on an inner circle of aliens; the crowd was a dark, confused mass now, with Moshe isolated a few steps from Cyrus, and both of them higher than the bishop and Saadiah, and all of them crowded about on four sides with every size of child and adult, some mild and curious, others wild and frenzied, some fatigued and sickly, some fired up with sour wine on empty stomachs. He was tall and red-haired and bearded in a crowd that held no one like him, not in size or color, and when he thrust aside a pimple-faced youth, the boy screamed as if he had been touched with a hot iron. Everyone in the mob could see the action as if Moshe had been alone on a stage, addressing an amphitheater's multitude. The boy wouldn't let up this screaming as Moshe continued up the stone steps, calling sharply into the mass of bodies for his betrothed. The boy's unnatural cries quieted the others. There was a lessening of the chorus equating the Jews with the Iconoclasts. A silence, ominous and dark, swept through the crowd, affecting even the tittering of children. It was as if a single huge body, composed of many conflicting parts, was attempting to silently reach a common decision. Only the pimple-faced youth wouldn't shut up his wild expression of pain, but his cries only served to emphasize the others' silence.

Many now got out of Moshe's way. But there were those who were given courage by the press of bodies, anonymous and strong, and these stepped in his path. When Moshe tried to avoid their bodies, they moved with him, and finally someone reached through space and took hold of Moshe's wrist. Moshe twisted out of the man's grasp, and the man, shocked by the Jew's strength, let out a gasp. All of a sudden the silence about him ended. They shouted at him wildly, as if he were a stray dog who might respond to human snarls and threats and cries. Some raised their clumsy hands, until he was forced to strike out again, and some hit back, first two, then three, then a dozen, and he could taste the blood at the corner of his mouth, even as the image of Rachel disappeared in the bad light at the top of the tenement stairs.

"Let go of me, you fools," said Moshe, aware that Rachel was unreachable, that a hundred hands were filthying his skin, tearing at his beard, trying to pull him off his feet so that he could be trampled into the stone. He remembered that he hadn't explained to them fully why he was here, or why it was that Jews were seldom hurt by an epidemic to the same extent as these slum dwellers. A fist moved toward his chest, toward the place where God had seen fit to carry the heart of man, and instinctively, Moshe blocked the blow and drove his own fist into the side of his attacker's head. But there were too many hands, too many blows, too many demons trying to pull him down to his death. It was all he could do, against the pain, to remember what he was doing in this terrible place: not because he was a lifesaving doctor, not because he was a well-poisoning Jew, but only because of Rachel. She was here, and he had followed, and now they were to be twisted into some part of an immense fabric created in the mind of God.

The voices of the mob were wilder now, punctuated with little cheers, as they dragged Cyrus into a corner, and someone stabbed him in the back with a rusty blade, his blood coloring their rags. The bishop had taken a defiant stand, his arms crossed to show the contempt with which he held their sacrilegious persecution. A fist landed squarely against his nose, and another in the side of his head, but unlike Moshe, he didn't fight at all, he didn't look up to see if Saadiah's terrible sword was flashing; he was content to let them pull him to pieces if that was the will of their God and his.

Saadiah's blade remained overhead, his eyes turning first to Cyrus, as he crumbled to the ground, then to the bishop, who took the blows of the slum dwellers as if he were a champion, a boxer and a wrestler both, immune to physical pain. Moshe was gone from sight, several paces away, the center of a screaming throng. Still, no one touched the boy, though many were close enough to be struck by his sword. Saadiah turned and turned, the sword in the air, unable to strike, unable to select a first victim. Frantically, he looked beyond the knot of men obscuring Moshe for a glimpse of Rachel, for a sight of her relaxed, composed face, radiating calm. But she was nowhere to be seen. It was as if the sounds of violence and anger had obliterated her presence, had made her vanish into the air, like a grain of sugar tossed into the salty sea.

"Rachel," he said, as if he were bidding her good-bye, and he turned about faster and faster now, as if facing every possible attacker, child and man and woman, eager to slay one, if only he could decide who was worth the task. Out of the corner of his eye, he saw that the crowd about Cyrus was moving away, as if disgusted by what he had become. Almost at the same moment, he was pushed for the first time, but without violent intent. The crowd about the bishop was backing away from him, trying to dissociate themselves from his wounds, his blood, his anger. The bishop, still standing on his feet, raised his head to look up the stairs; Saadiah could see that his eyes were filled with blood. Paces away, the crowd stilled, as if all had been doused by icy water. Moshe, bent over and bloody, groped for the side of the building so that he could steady his powerful frame. Strangely, he felt little pain, as if his body were holding any hindrance like this in abeyance because he had too many battles left to fight, like the soldier shot through with arrows, who felt nothing but the fury of battle as he defended himself with heavy sword and shield against a score of attackers. Only when the danger was over would he feel the arrowhead twisting into muscle and bone, and allow his eyes to blind with the agony he had so far refused to acknowledge.

Then, like the tinkle of a silver bell, he heard a small voice.

"Healer," someone said, and someone else added, "Bless the healer," and then a third voice, softer than the others, "Forgive us. Bless the healer." Someone in the crowd had recognized her or else the cry had come back from the sick boy's family whose room she had entered, her arms wide with the power of sympathy. A few now dropped to their knees, forgetting that she was a Jewess, that she had been part of the Iconoclast bishop's party. They had prayed for a miracle, not for a doctor or a priest but for something more, and now they lowered their heads in shame. Rachel the

Healer was among them in their time of need and they had nearly thrown themselves like beasts upon her sacred flesh.

Moshe, straining to see her past the bowed heads, saw the deflected sunlight break through the mist and catch the three jewels in his betrothed's necklace. He blinked, as the mist descended, trying to see who held the jewels high over the crowd, like a magician's rod. At the same moment, he felt an enormous relief, almost a pleasure of anticipation. Ludicrously, he smiled, and instinctively he brought his hands to his chest. It was not the healing rays of diamond, ruby, or emerald that had suddenly filled his heart with warmth and light. It was Rachel's presence, on the highest step. All along the crowded staircase, men and women and children dropped to their knees, crossing themselves. They were contrite, even abashed, but at the same time, hopeful; hopeful in a way that had seemed impossible only minutes before. Moshe wondered if anyone but he could have loved her for her beauty, as her eyes met his, as calm and modest and dignified as when he had first returned to their village. She was not, after all, an icon. Rachel was a woman, and he rejoiced in knowing that she demanded his love, even in the midst of chaos and despair.

Chapter
24

Standing in the shadow of Rachel's skill, Moshe understood that he had never known anything of value about
the human body. Everything in him that was arrogant was
modest in her, everything in him that was tentative and tempered with the possibilities of failure was in her sure and simple,
directed by faith and sympathy. There was no cure for the plague,
and so it exasperated him, no simple theory of how it came to be,
and where it might next strike, and how precisely to safeguard
against getting it, and so it intrigued, mystified, terrified him. He
was a great doctor, learned in medicines and in wielding the sur-
geon's knife, but neither potion nor scalpel was adequate to fight
this God-sent curse. Something greater was necessary, something
that didn't touch at the superficial part of disease, but struck at its
center, at its very core.

The bishop hadn't known how many were sick when he had first
sent for Moshe, nor did Moshe now have any idea of how many
were plague-ridden, even in this isolated poorest quarter of the city.
It was difficult to separate the hungry from the diseased, the hopeless from those wracked by fever. Certainly he could examine
bodies, he could touch and feel and smell human flesh, calling on
years of study to aid him in classifying disease, prescribing treatments. But he knew nothing of the human spirit, he knew nothing
of giving strength to the soul.

"They are all going to die," said the bishop sadly, as Moshe redressed his wounds, under the respectful eyes of half a dozen soldiers. Only an hour after Rachel had stopped the mob from pulling them all to pieces, the bishop had been traced to this miserable slum. Now the emperor's soldiers filled the tenement and surrounded the entire impoverished quarter, but Moshe knew that even the might of ancient Rome couldn't hold back the invisible agents of disease. They could have helped Cyrus, perhaps, could have stopped the hand that plunged the dagger into his back; and perhaps their presence could hold back a new wave of hatred if Rachel's magic proved ineffective, and one by one, fathers saw children fade, mothers saw daughters beautiful and pure wax grotesque, too awful to hold in their arms. Then the slum dwellers might pick up stones and curse the Jews in their midst, might dare attack their bishop as a useless intermediary between themselves and their god; and the disciplined soldiers of East Rome knew well how to deal with rabble.

But for now, the soldiers had nothing to do. They waited, like everyone else, for a miracle or a catastrophe, for a fresh wind, or a complete miasma—one that would rain blood, and swallow them all, and put an end to uncertainty.

Rachel had been with a plague victim for three days since her presence had stilled the angry mob and filled their hearts with humility and hope. Moshe had seen the boy in the adjacent room, a big-eyed child of five, olive-skinned and frail, with the curly-headed insouciant features of a pre-Christian god.

"If it's God's will that they die, they die," continued the bishop. "Christian or Jew must all agree on that subject. Whenever there has been a plague, it has always been to answer some unbeliever, daring to thrust his deceit and avarice, lechery, drunkenness, and irreverence straight into the face of heaven. Look at these people all about us. Do you have any doubt that God means for you to be able to save them? If there is no obedience in a people, if they do not show respect to their own bishop, how can you and your medicine and your bride possibly combat His desire?"

A cry broke out from the adjacent room, high-pitched and weak, not an appeal for help but a release of some preternatural pain. Moshe had examined the sick child, had observed the buboes under the armpits, the swollen excrescence in the groin. He had touched the beautiful forehead, holding his breath against the evil smells that rose up from the boy's unhappy body. If ever a physician had reason to be repulsed by his calling, it was now, seeing the evidence of baleful death, ugly and shameful, in so young and lovely a frame. How could God allow the little boy's sweat and spittle and breath to be so overwhelmingly fulsome? What heavenly reason was there to bring so perfect a creation to such ugliness? What sin could have been committed to make sense of the boy's torture? And certainly, the bishop's words had a weighty validity. If God Himself had raised the buboes on this frail body, had caused the urine to run thick and black, the lifeblood to turn green, had taken His own creature and twisted it into a feverish knot of earthly pain, what could Moshe hope to do to restore health, well-being, happiness?

"One cannot predict the will of God," said Moshe.

"A wonderful answer for a Jew," said the bishop. He started in pain as Moshe rubbed an ointment along the torn flesh of his cheekbone. "If a man dies, it is God's will. If a man recovers, it is God's will. If a doctor cures a man, that too is God's will, just as it is God's will if the doctor cannot do a thing to help a man recover."

Moshe had seen that Rachel had no qualms, no hesitations as to how to deal with the patient. There was no talk about how to justify the sickness in God's world, no attempt to imagine why God had selected this child among so many others for such agony. While Moshe stood at the boy's side, trying to conquer fear and revulsion, unable to offer a single suggestion as to how to alleviate the boy's suffering, Rachel had thrown herself upon him, pressing her lips to the feverish skin. It made no sense, of course: there were no cures for fever based on a kiss, no remedies for plague connected to a string of jewels placed lovingly along a patient's chest. But like a stone thrown into a gentle pond, he felt the ripples of her love and caring extend to himself, to Saadiah, to the boy's family, ringing the raised pallet with clasped hands. All of them hushed, not in fear or admiration at her disregard of contagion, but with the awe of children at watching a star fall to the earth. They felt her force, they understood that there were things in the world beyond their ken, and they accepted this. Somehow, of all the suffering children in this tenement, of all the men and women in the city of Nicomedia who had come down with the disease or who had been felled by the fear of its inevitability, she had been drawn to this single boy. As she tried to comfort him, the sense of her power swept past the room and ran through the miserable quarter, and beyond, into the fearful city. In a superstitious time, in a place where everyone had seen or touched a demon, either flashing up from a smoky hearth, or floating through a mist from the sea, or lingering in the dawn after an exhausting dream-filled night, it was easy to imagine the young Jewess, fighting not for a single soul, but for every soul in the city. Indeed, it must be a demon, and not a disease, who struck back at her goodness with every weapon at his command. For endless hours, she remained absolutely still, her lips pressed to his forehead, her hands placed over the jewels she had strung across his heart; and every cry that came from the boy's lips seemed to be the cry of a prisoner, slowly losing his chains.

The boy's family knew—as the whole quarter knew—that the young woman wasn't simply trying to pull the boy back from death, but was fighting to destroy forever the demon who had come to the city, the demon who threatened to engulf them all. She had not chosen this boy as their battleground, but the demon had. They wrestled over his soul, and whoever would win the boy, would decide the fate of them all.

Moshe stayed by her side as long as he could. There were other people in need of his help, of such help as he felt he could still give: reassuring families that a pressure in the temples was not a sign of the plague, that an old icon found in three smashed pieces behind a chamber pot would not lead to divine retribution, that a simple boil was the result of filth and sweat and not a bubo, sent by God or the devil or a fate in which neither was concerned.

And of course, a doctor in a slum never has to look far for tasks. At every turn were sores and infections, stomachs ruined by polluted water and rancid food, broken arms and legs incorrectly set, deafness waiting to be cured by a deep cleansing of the ears. He gave out such medications as he had with him, he spent long hours explaining why one must not drink from water that has received human waste—indeed, the local Jewish prohibition against sharing the city's drinking water, and relying on their own wells, was what invariably saved them from a score of diseases—why bathing the body was as much a duty to God as to their bodies. There were many who visited with him, and who bowed their heads before the bishop to receive his blessing; but all knew what weightier event was transpiring in the adjacent room of the slum dwelling.

A day went by, and then another, and then a third, and though Rachel had taken food and drink, she never left the boy's side; the fact of her struggle suffused every action in the quarter, weighed on every soul in Nicomedia. What did it matter what little cures Moshe performed, what gentle blessings the bishop uttered if Rachel could not keep up her strength? People still ate and drank and made love and dreamed of the future, but all the while, limning every thought, was the fact of the struggle: if there was hope in the city, it could be shattered in an instant. All waited for Rachel, for the boy to come to life, for the demon to burn up from the souls of his feet to the horns on his head.

Moshe visited his betrothed as often as he could. He too had begun to ignore the fears of contagion, catching the fatalistic spirit of the people about him. Either Saadiah or he, by unspoken arrangement, was always with her; both slept in the sickroom.

But it was deeply unsettling for Moshe to watch over her.

Once he had begun to accept the possibility of her powers, he began to fear for their use. The refusal to sleep would have drained anyone's strength, but clearly, more than simple energy was being extracted from Rachel. She was pale and drawn, and while the black eyes burned in her lovely face, there was a dimming of her presence. No longer did she inspire calm, but rather its reverse; there was something reckless about her figure, something desperate and full of fear. She no longer seemed a creature that was of one piece with fate, but was instead one who dared challenge it. It was as if she'd gotten too close to the sun, and her wings were burned, as if she'd run the distance from Marathon to Athens with victory and death both ready to erupt from her lips.

Moshe wanted to share the burden, but there was nothing he could do. He stood behind her, he begged her to rest, he told her he loved her and that one day they would be man and wife, and have a family of ten children, each one strong and bright and healthy. Perhaps she listened. Saadiah said that she did, that she heard everything but could not speak, so deep was she in the act of healing. It was like being in a waking sleep, placing oneself in the realm of nightmares and fighting them down with the gentlest of dreams.

When Moshe left her to attend to the simpler wounds, he felt a certain relief, going from a world whose lineaments he couldn't fathom to one in which his skill was welcomed. And more importantly, he would be away from Rachel's struggle. Every time the sick little boy let out a cry, he felt her strength flow with sudden

ferocious energy, like a mother summoning her last breath to protect her child; and then a moment later the cry would finish, and
Rachel's strength would lessen as rapidly as it had grown. Worse
than this was the feeling that the cry and the struggle to be able to
bear the boy's pain took something from her that she could not
replace—not with food, or drink, or sleep.

"I must go back to her," said Moshe to the bishop, finishing their
talk and the redressing of his wounds.

"You haven't responded to my wonderful statement," said
Bishop Giles. "How can you and your medicine, or I and my
prayers, change the course of God's intents and desires?"

"I don't know," said Moshe, barely hearing the bishop. He felt
impelled to join his betrothed in her struggle in the adjacent room,
and he hurried there just as the little boy let out a cry, so wild and
helpless that Moshe and everyone else in the room started in a
moment of reflected pain. Moshe moved closer to Rachel, touching her arched back where she stood, shut-eyed and remote from
the world, over the boy.

"Rachel," he said. "Darling."

She hadn't spoken for many hours, and then not more than a
word or two of simple thanks. Therefore it was shocking to see her
suddenly straighten, let go her hold on the boy, and turn with tear-
filled eyes to Moshe. "I'm sorry," she said. "It won't be what we
wanted. We will never marry. We will never have children."

For a moment, it seemed as if she would fall, and Moshe carefully took her in his arms, even as the others crowded about, unable to understand why she had left the still body after so many
endless hours. The boy's mother was the first to voice her fear:

"He's dead! Dear God, he's dead! We're all doomed, he's dead!"

But Saadiah, even two paces away, could see that the boy was
breathing. Indeed his breaths seemed to be coming in easier
rhythm. Before he could say anything, the mother was on top of
her son, clutching at his hand, bringing her face to his forehead.

"He's cold," she said, but the words weren't harsh or accusatory
or sad. They were full of wonder, the first tentative steps toward
gratitude. The commotion meanwhile brought the bishop in from
the adjacent room. He pushed his way through the family and
friends.

"He's not dead," said the bishop, placing his hand to the boy's
forehead. It was easy to forget to refrain from touching a plague

330

victim in the desperate atmosphere of the room. "I believe his fever's broken. Doctor, please come take a look."

But Moshe couldn't turn his concentration from Rachel, weak and smiling in his arms. She had stopped her apologizing, and now her eyes began to close, over her tears.

"Saadiah, help me," said Moshe. "Quickly."

They put her flat on a pallet, and she opened her eyes for half a moment and tried to speak, but the effort was too much for her.

"What's wrong, what is it?" said Saadiah. "Do something. You're the great doctor. Do something for Rachel."

"It's a miracle," said the bishop. He had exposed the boy's armpit, and as he did so, he held his breath against the horrible smell of the buboes, which were discharging their fluid. The boy opened his eyes, and they were large and black, like Rachel's, and curious, intense with an energy to know what he had missed in the days he had spent near death. Moshe heard the bishop as if from a great distance, though they were separated by two paces, and the bishop's voice was loud with joy. "It's a miracle. Praise the Lord! Doctor, come look, the boils are discharging. They have become small! The fever is broken! Your bride has won! The demon has left, and your bride has won, and the plague is vanquished!"

The others took up the chant. "The plague is vanquished!" they sang, and they ran out of the room and into the interconnecting warrens of the tenements. Soon the news would run down into the muddy alley, twist out into the greater streets, find its way past the half-burned Jewish quarter into the quiet, fearful homes of the seaside city. As if in answer to Rachel's demand, a mist would rise, the sun would break through high clouds, and an unusual spell of dry, brisk weather would grace Nicomedia. Within the slum, ten bodies would be found, victims of the plague, and their foul rotting corpses would be burned with a finality that excluded fear. For the boy would live. And the legend would take root, of a woman who had fought the devil, and bested him. Even if plague still lived in the city, it would not be able to sweep its citizens with life-defeating fear. All would know that sickness could be turned about, that hope and faith were stronger than any adversary.

But for the moment, hope and faith were themselves turning to dust in the sickroom. Moshe was unable to look at the boy, so surrounded with ecstasy and gratitude and a release from fear. All his attention was directed at his bride, her strength and will fading before him. Soon, he and Saadiah were joined by the boy's mother, on her knees, before Rachel's still and silent form.

"No, it is not possible. God will save her, master," she said.

"Isn't there a medicine?" said Saadiah.

Rachel hardly breathed now, and though her lips remained in the slightest of smiles, they were turning pale. The bishop turned from the boy and stood over her, not understanding how she had managed a cure or why she herself was succumbing to death. "Perhaps it is simple exhaustion," said the bishop. "Perhaps it is just a heavy sleep, after all. She has worked harder than a slave, without sleep, without rest, with little food. Perhaps she will sleep and she will be well."

"Do something," insisted Saadiah. "Why don't you bleed her? That's what doctors do at a time like this, even I know that. Bleed her before she dies!"

"Bleeding will not help," said Moshe. He knew this as he knew that the boy would have died without her touch, without the giving of her love that had left her weak and empty, drifting to heaven.

"If bleeding won't help, do something else," said Saadiah. He turned on the bishop, imploring him. "There are things, potions, powders—there are methods, there are words, incantations, spells —there are prayers. Shall we pray for her? We must do something!"

Through all the noise of Saadiah's frustrations, through the bishop's prayers for her well-being, through his own plunging despair of inadequacy, Moshe heard a single sound: the open-eyed boy let out not a cry, but a single childish snort, an expulsion of air that was half joyful, half wondrous. Not ready to speak, he was eager to let it be known that he was with the living.

"Yes," said Moshe, and suddenly, he bent over Rachel and kissed her forehead, though she was not yet his wife, and before Saadiah could react, he was up and away from her, going to the boy whose stench still sullied the room. With one swift movement, Moshe removed the string of jewels from his chest. Turning about, he gently placed the jewels below Rachel's neck. Slowly, everyone in the room, except the boy who had first brought them there, gathered about Rachel as Moshe placed her still hands together, over the diamond in the center of the chain.

"Be strong," he said in Hebrew. "Rachel, darling, take the strength of all the good you've done in the world, and be strong, be strong."

Some, like the bishop, knelt in prayer. Saadiah remained on his feet, staring at his still, shut-eyed sister, trying to conjure up a hundred memories of her singing, running, and laughing, with the wind pulling at her hair.

Moshe tried to do what she had done, and this was difficult for him, perhaps the hardest thing he had ever done, because it necessitated turning his back on everything he had learned, everything he had worked so hard to know as a doctor. Belief was needed, and he searched for it. There was no doubt that she had accomplished what he had not been able to, and now he tried to share her vision of the world. He tried to shut out the potions and treatments, the special operations, the bleeding and purging; he tried to shut out logic and replace it with feeling.

But he could not do this. Even with the strength of his love, he could not forget, he could not turn his reason to dust. Deep in his heart, he knew there must be some reason why the boy had recovered, some secret of air or fire or earth or water. Moshe loved Rachel, and he wanted to dissolve his mind in that love so that he could be free to duplicate her faith, free to let the possibility of her healing overtake him, so that it would work its magic on her, but he couldn't. A fury took hold of him, and he tried to contain it, but his temper proved too strong. The vision of those about her bed, abject and humble, bowed by superstition, enraged him. He was full of love, and love only, and he wished to say good-bye with his heart at peace.

With a cry of pain, he lunged at the still hands and would have torn them off the diamond on her still chest.

But the hands wouldn't budge.

Moshe, flabbergasted, got to his knees, placed his hands more firmly on hers, and tried to separate them, the moment of his wildness past. He thought she might already be dead, and the body passed too quickly to the stiff strength of a spirit-deserted corpse.

But clearly, he felt her breath against his cheek as he held her hands. And the hands were warm now, and strong. When he tried to pull them away, they were like steel, holding the diamond with such force that no man in the city could have separated her from her stone.

"Rachel," he said, slowly easing his wild grip.

She opened her eyes then, blinking against the tears, and she whispered his name, and soon after that she fell asleep, her heart beating with the steady rhythm of the young and strong. Moshe placed her now gentle hands on the diamond, centering the string of jewels along her breast, with the diamond resting carefully over her heart.

There was no logic in his heart, no anger, no understanding. Moshe was simply grateful. He had wanted her to live, and some concatenation of magic and desire, some inexplicable force had given her strength in spite of his doubts, in answer to his love. Moshe would continue to look for structure and reason in the mad tapestry of the universe. But never again would he shut his heart to what his mind couldn't fathom. Somehow, there was a sun in the heavens, a God invisible to the world. As long as there were people in pain, he would follow his calling, he would consult his books, examine the physical evidence before his eyes; but he would accept that what he was doing was at the surface of things, tolerated by deeper forces only because his dogged work was well intentioned, human.

Still, kneeling next to his future bride, he felt no limitations on his soul. He loved her, and she breathed the bright colors of life back into her skin. Rachel would wake and live, and together they would bring not ten but eleven babies into the world, each of them strong, each full of hope and promise and faith and dreams.

The Family of Saadiah
Ben-Hillel of Constantinople
756–1096

Saadiah remained close to his sister Rachel all his life. Though his urge for adventure led him to join his cousins in the land of the Khazars, he made his permanent home in the Jewish quarter of Constantinople, to where Moshe and his bride and their growing family moved a few years after the plague had been vanquished in Nicomedia. But it was on trading expeditions to the northern Caucasus, to the Greek colonies in the Crimea, to the remote Bulgar trading stations along the Volga River that his heart came alive; if not for Rachel, he would have left Byzantium forever.

Saadiah's son Hillel, and later, Hillel's son Kallai, had no such strong reason to remain in the capital of the empire. Khazaria was a remote, rough-hewn mountainous kingdom, its fair-skinned, big-boned people as wild as the Slavs they captured for the slave trade, as brave as the illiterate Rus people, as primitive in cultural matters as the Alani and Goths and Magyars whose destinies they ruled by the sword.

But the Khazar aristocracy, and the *kagan* himself, were Jews. They were Jews by conversion, Jews who had once flirted briefly with Islam, and who included pagan rites a thousand years old in their attempts at fulfilling the complicated Jewish ritual. But even if these elements of shamanism and ignorance had prevailed in Itil, the Khazar capital, even if the leavening of imported rabbinical scholars hadn't been able to found proper synagogues and schools among the converts, Saadiah's son and grandson would have chosen to remain among them. Here, as nowhere else in the world, were Jews who minted their own coins, who exacted tribute from their neighbors, who granted religious tolerance to their citizens instead of having to beg that favor for themselves. Here the ruler was Jewish, and the common people prostrated themselves before him as he made his way in state to the synagogue to offer his prayers to the Greatest King. In Khazaria Jews walked as tall as they wished, talked their convictions out loud, disregarding who might be listening over their shoulders. In Khazaria Jews were thieves as well as soldiers, vagabonds as well as moneylenders, peasants as well as traders in gems. But above all, in Khazaria Jews weren't despised, outcasts, symbols of degradation. In Khazaria, Jews were free as they had been nowhere else since the Roman conquest of Judea.

When Hillel ben-Saadiah married the daughter of a rabbi from Damascus, he insisted that the ceremony be in Itil, where he chose to live. Kallai, the only product of that union, married a Khazar girl, a Jewess whose grandfather had converted to Judaism eight decades before her birth. When Kallai visited Constantinople, it was all he could do to restrain himself from drawing his sword at the hundred indignities forced upon the Jews of Byzantium by imperial decree, indignities that local Jews had learned to bear without complaint. Nearly everything about the Jewish community of the city angered him, whether it was the impieties and excesses of the sophisticated merchant class, or the zealous fanaticism of his own relations. Only his ancient great-aunt Rachel, and the stories of the illustrious ancestors who shared her name—heroines, martyrs to their principles and their faith—inspired him. When she died at the nearly legendary age of ninety-six, Kallai was thrilled to discover that the honor of bearing her name had passed to his own child, as he was the male heir of her brother Saadiah. With the name came the gift of her jewels, which superstitious people claimed to have powers of healing. But his own daughter died in childbirth at the age of seventeen, and Kallai's son Benaiah's daughter, given the same great name, died in childbirth at the exact same age. Still, the power of the name in family legend was stronger than even two generations of misfortunes could erase.

Joab ben-Benaiah's daughter lived to eighty-four and was said to have given birth to fourteen children, most of whom emigrated to the land of the Magyars in search of new trading opportunities. This Rachel's brother Baruk went much farther west than his sister's children, joining the little, thriving Jewish community in Cologne, on the Rhine.

Baruk's sons flourished in the Rhineland, and soon cousins from Khazaria joined relations newly settled in Mainz and Worms and Speyer. Most were traders, importing silk from Thebes, leather from Byzantium, glass from as far as Aleppo and Tyre. Baruk's youngest grandson, Yakov, bought the right to name his child Rachel from his two older brothers, who had little use for ancient traditions—or necklaces—and named his newborn baby after the great-aunt who had lived and died in Khazaria, and whom he had never once seen.

As long ago as 899, when Baruk had first migrated to Cologne, the Rus people had been threatening the Khazar kingdom, in their need for an outlet on the Caspian Sea—known for half a millennium as the Sea of the Khazars. In 913, and again in 943, the Russians made successful raids down the Volga River, and more and more of Baruk's distant relations migrated westward. By 965, when Itil itself was decimated by a Russian horde, the far-flung family had one unifying strength: the legend of Rachel, "their" Rachel. She and they were descendants of the priestly family who had braved the might of Antiochus: she and they were *Cohanim*, and in their veins ran the blood of the Maccabees; and further back than this—through his favorite daughter—the blood of David the King. The family settled in Prague, and further west, in the Danube River cities of Augsburg and Regensburg, in the growing cities of Paris and Troyes along the clear-flowing Seine, and in little trading towns along the lower Rhone, from which they corresponded with learned Jews in the great cities of Spain. But all remembered to append "*ha-Cohen*"—the priest—to their name, and most remembered that a branch of the family still passed on the name Rachel, from the spirit of the dead to that of the newborn, in an endless chain linking past and present and future, a straight line driving sense and meaning into the chaos of history.

Ezra's son Ohel disgraced his family by becoming rich in the slave trade, selling pagan Slavs at the great Danube market of Raffelstetten. His daughter, a willful child born in the much feared

337

year of 1000—when men anticipated the destruction of the world —was given the heroic name, and did everything she could to disgrace it. Her lovers were Jewish and Gentile, residents of Prague and Paris and Cologne, and when she died in 1069, the news took six months to travel to Mainz, where Barzillai ben-Ohel-ben-Ezra lived a simpler life, but only a little less self-indulgent. Until his death at the age of seventy-five, he fascinated the aristocrats of Mainz with his exploits in love, at swordsmanship, and with the wine cask. He fought a threat of excommunication from the rabbis of Mainz by erecting the city's largest synagogue, and by supporting an academy of Babylonian scholars newly moved to Jerusalem, buying them the protection of the city's Seljuk rulers.

Barzillai had two children, Ohel, named after Barzillai's father, and Rachel. Rachel learned at an early age to ignore the humiliations forced upon her mother by Barzillai's open infidelities. She frequently spoke to her father's mistresses, women of faraway cities, fair and dark, large and small, beautiful and plain; and she learned from them. The world was vast, and full of murder and calamities, they told her. Volcanoes erupted, and tidal waves swept the earth; storms could level a city faster than an army; disease could fell the strongest, the richest, the most noble of spirit. Only a divine, incomprehensible presence could account for the infinite fortunes to which the human race was subject. All one could do in this precarious life on earth was be unafraid of its end and live fully the years granted one by God.

Rachel married Yosef, a young scholar of Mainz, handsome and strong, and eager to break the binds of the academy. In spite of the threats of the rabbis, he joined Ohel in the family business: a vast trading company that linked family members along the Rhine, the Danube, the Black Sea ports, and across Byzantium to the endless lands ruled by the Arabs. Eight years after the birth of their daughter Deborah, he was captured by pirates on the Black Sea. One report found Yosef alive, awaiting ransom in Damascus. Another indicated that he was free and awaiting passage home from Beirut. There were rumors of his life or death in Seleucia, Laodicea, and Ephesus. A trader from Brindisi insisted that he met and spoke with other members of that fateful trading voyage, who had only just been released from a Seljuk prison.

But by the spring of 1096, Yosef had been gone for two years, and Rachel had begun to lose hope. Even if he had survived piracy or shipwreck and had fallen into the hands of the Seljuks, their once-excellent trading relations with the east had long since deteriorated. Barzillai had been dead for twelve years; Ohel was beset with financial disaster in the anticipation of the great war that would first sweep Europe on its way to the East. The holy war declared by Pope Urban II in November of 1095 had fired the imaginations of multitudes, men of faith, of courage, of daring, as well as lesser men—those who followed no gods but those of lust and pillage and destruction. The People's Crusade was about to engulf the Rhineland, and Rachel needed more than the faint hope of her husband's return to ensure her life, and the life of their child.

THE FAMILY OF SAADIAH BEN-HILLEL OF CONSTANTINOPLE
756–1096

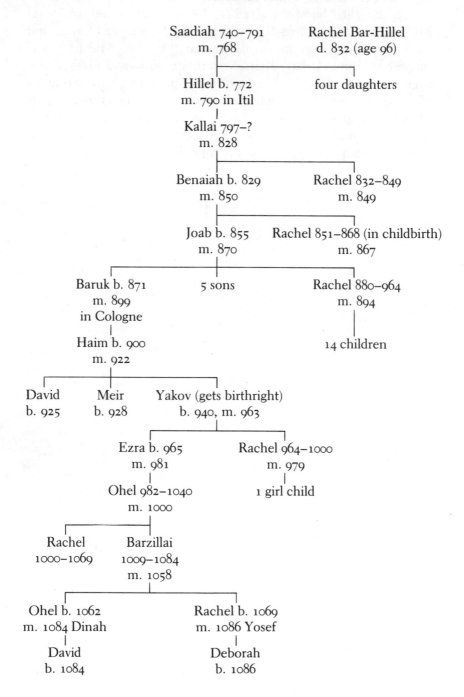

Saadiah 740–791   Rachel Bar-Hillel
m. 768   d. 832 (age 96)

Hillel b. 772   four daughters
m. 790 in Itil

Kallai 797–?
m. 828

Benaiah b. 829   Rachel 832–849
m. 850   m. 849

Joab b. 855   Rachel 851–868 (in childbirth)
m. 870   m. 867

Baruk b. 871   5 sons   Rachel 880–964
m. 899   m. 894
in Cologne

Haim b. 900   14 children
m. 922

David   Meir   Yakov (gets birthright)
b. 925   b. 928   b. 940, m. 963

Ezra b. 965   Rachel 964–1000
m. 981   m. 979

Ohel 982–1040   1 girl child
m. 1000

Rachel   Barzillai
1000–1069   1009–1084
m. 1058

Ohel b. 1062   Rachel b. 1069
m. 1084 Dinah   m. 1086 Yosef

David   Deborah
b. 1084   b. 1086

Part Five

Mainz, 1096

Chapter
25

It was the third day of April, but winter lingered in the wet, river-whipped winds of the high ground near the lord's castle. Deborah, daughter of Rachel bat-Barzillai-ben-Ohel, contemplated the green and red and blue bands of color that circled the threatening tower, reaching for the sun behind black clouds. She had no friends with whom to play this morning. David, her cousin, was at the synagogue school. Hugh, the lord's son, was miles beyond the city walls, working his horse into a lather under the eyes of his riding master. The lord's two daughters were in Frankfurt, twenty miles away, lingering after a cousin's wedding feast.

Even Brother John, her Latin tutor, would have been fun to see at that dull moment, but he was hidden from sight in the monastery, suffering from a fever. Worst of all was that three weeks remained before she could rejoin the five other girls in Rab Shalom's Bible class. Even her mother's influence couldn't rescind Rab Shalom's punishment, banning her from the other girls—and not just during the morning studies, but even in the afternoons, when they were let out to run about the winding alleys and hilly high streets of the great merchant city of five thousand souls. And all because she had spoken of the falling stars, the floods, the famines of the past three years; all because she had voiced the fears that everyone held in their hearts. There were such things as omens and portents, of this she was certain. It was only Rab Shalom's loathing of the influence of Gentiles that had gotten him so angry with her. But didn't Jew and Gentile both live in the same city, behind the same walls protected by the same lord's castle? What did it matter that Hugh had filled her head with the dire prophecies of his bishops; every rabbi in Mainz felt the doom rising up from the depths of the earth.

"You, girl!" cried a stranger's voice from the bottom of the hill, his accent crude and unfamiliar even to Deborah's practiced ear. She hurried to get off the rough rock on which she rested, soiling her heavy wool mantle. "You, girl! Pilgrims' house?"

"Good day, sir," said Deborah very politely, as the man came laboriously up the hill and into view. He was clearly not of the city, nor of nearby Frankfurt. In his ragged leg bandages and short, filthy cloak, it was a wonder he had been allowed through the city gates. He squinted painfully, as if suddenly assaulted by bright light.

"What pilgrims' house?" said Deborah cheerily. She was very disposed to talking, even under ordinary circumstances, but now, friendless and bored, she would be happy to chat away the morning with a ragpicker.

"Pilgrims' house, pilgrims' house!" hissed the man, swinging yellow hands toward her, exhibiting fingernails like talons and fingers marked with clusters of warts.

Deborah could have simply and quickly explained to the man that there was no such thing in Mainz as a pilgrims' house. Though a child of ten, she thought herself privy to great stores of knowledge. Indeed, Deborah believed that if she didn't know of the existence of a pilgrim's house in Mainz, he could be completely certain that no such place existed. She knew all about pilgrims, how one could guess their status in life by the length and quality of their clothes, by the width of their belts, and by the absence or presence of silver in their boot buckles. The pilgrim before her was not only in short threadbare clothing, he was also beltless, his shoes were held together by rags, and she imagined the wildness of his eyes to be a sign of starvation.

It was not surprising that she knew so much. After all, her grandfather had been the famous merchant Barzillai ben-Ohel, and his legacy of legends and lore—if not his money—had come down nearly intact to her generation. Her mother and her uncle filled her ears with stories of travel to the Holy Land in the years before the Turks controlled Asia Minor. Pilgrims, Jewish and Gentile, had arrived in Mainz and other Rhineland cities to begin the traditional route along the Rhine and Danube to the East. Jewish merchants often arranged for letters of introduction to kinsmen and coreligionists along the way or, better still, made it possible for pilgrims to join a trading party that would get them safely through Hungary, past the Byzantine frontier and overland through Asia Minor to Syria and Palestine. But there had been few pilgrims for twenty-five years. Even Deborah's father and uncle were telling her stories of things they themselves had never seen. Occasionally some reckless adventurer would take a band of knights and attempt to brave the chaos of Asia Minor, where war was the only constant in an anarchic life; less frequently, unarmed pilgrims, trusting in their faith alone, would buy an expensive passage from Italy, or attempt the half-year overland trek to Antioch, where they might petition for permission to continue on to Jerusalem. But most such pilgrims were never heard from again. Though they journeyed in the service of their God, pilgrims seemed to be at greater risk even than merchants. And merchants, in spite of the chance for great profits, had attempted fewer and fewer journeys to the east in Deborah's lifetime. Deborah's own father had been captured or murdered two years before on the Black Sea, attempting to forge a new trade route less dangerous than the ones that had been in decline for so many years.

"Pilgrim, pilgrim!" said the man, shouting the words now, as if this would aid in their comprehension. "Pilgrims' house! House. Pilgrim. You, girl! Pilgrims."

"What pilgrimage are you making?" said Deborah, using the elaborate phrase in a rougher version of her own Rhineland vernacular, so that the stranger might better understand. He was certainly not a Jew, or she would have used a version of that same Germanic speech, laced with Hebrew and Aramaic words—an argot peculiar to the Jewish colonies on both sides of the Rhine, but certainly comprehensible to the Gentiles who lived in their areas. Her Hebrew, Rab Shalom notwithstanding, was excellent too, and not because her family was religious; indeed, the descendants of Barzillai were not noted for piety, but for mercantile skills, daring, and extravagance. Deborah had been somewhat late in learning to talk, confused by the abundance of languages and dialects in the household. But now her Latin was as fluent as any budding scholar's; and she could parrot the speech of Eastphalians and Westphalians, Saxons and Silesians, Bavarians and Franconians and Thuringians.

When a Jewish trader from Champagne prattled at her in the soft, eliding of his region, Deborah never faltered, though she could barely follow his meaning: she spoke out phrase after phrase, blocks of words in dialects known and unknown, words twisted from Hebrew, mixed with Latin, overlaid with Germanic precision. There was no stopping her. She would be heard. She would speak, even if no one in the room understood, or cared for her opinion. She would speak, even if her words made no sense, save for the sound of their production from human lips and teeth and tongue. In an age when children kept their eyes to the ground, listening for the commands of their elders, Deborah was like a garrulous, half-crazed old lady grown suddenly small. She had too many stories for her years, she was in too much of a hurry to share her store of wisdom with the world, as if afraid of being interrupted in mid-thought by the Angel of Death or by the demon who had removed her own father from the world.

"Are you going to Spain or Monte Gargano or Rome?" she said, showing off her knowledge of place names—a knowledge she had gleaned from her father's tales, destinations to which he had promised to take her. But of course, he had followed other destinations, different destinies. He would never take her to Venice or to Rome or to Spain, but she would still remember his promises. They were gifts to her, memories as tangible as the marzipan candies her mother lovingly placed in her eager hands.

"You wouldn't be seriously going off to Jerusalem, now would you?" she said. Though he had been clear only on this one point— "pilgrim"—Deborah couldn't imagine the man before her attempting the five hundred miles to barbarous Hungary, let alone the infinitely greater journey of which she sang in her prayers every day. "My father was going to take me to Jerusalem, so that I could touch the wall of the Temple and see how the city turns gold in the sunshine. But you're not one of those who means to go there? It's much too far to walk. You need to take a boat, to sail on the Great Sea. And that's far too dangerous. What's your name, pilgrim?"

"Pilgrim," he said again, leaping on her use of the word with such force that the child started. But she didn't take fright. No one had ever harmed her or attempted to do so in the city on the Rhine.

Most knew her by sight; many knew her name, or recognized her as the daughter of Rachel bat-Barzillai.

"You don't speak our language," said Deborah, sad for the man's poor clothes and lack of words. "But someone let you through the gate, so you can't be a bad man. You want to go to a holy place, I suppose, if you are a pilgrim. The cathedral is that way." She turned about and pointed past the tower of the castle, past the bishop's palace, to the spires of St. Martin's, gray and grim against the dull sky. "But you probably aren't here for that, even though it's famous. Hugh told me the pope was here, fifty years ago, right in the cathedral. And the cathedral is the center of the country hereabouts. There's an archbishop, and that's bigger than a bishop —but you probably want more. Especially if you walked so far."

There were four major destinations of salvation-seeking pilgrims in those years, and only one of these—the most desirable, and the least accessible—was the Holy Land itself. The shrine of St. James at Compostella, in northwestern Spain, was much visited, as was that of St. Michael at Monte Gargano; numerous shrines awaited the pilgrim in Rome, the capital of Christendom, the haunt of the ghosts of Caesars—and a major embarrassment to the world's clergy. Rome, ruined and rebuilt and become a pawn between a shifting array of power seekers, was itself famous for its whores, its drunkenness, its brazen, amoral population. Where women in London and Paris dressed their hair behind scarves and veils, the women of Rome dyed theirs gold and painted their lips and eyes like the women of Constantinople. Nuns who had traveled five hundred miles to be able to approach the relics of an apostle were molested in broad daylight; monks who had left the serenity of seclusion were mocked and abused with no more regard to their calling than if they had been Saracen pirates.

"You, girl!" said the filthy man, who was rapidly losing interest even for Deborah. It was clear that he had no more words in his head than those, and "pilgrims' house," and there could be little amusement in watching him grow angry with frustration. But if Deborah was becoming less interested in him, he seemed to be becoming momently more interested in her. His squinty eyes noticed the fine quality of her mantle, the new leather of her boots, the cleanliness of her person. "Pilgrim," he said again, but this time the yellow hands were grasping in the universal symbol of the beggar. "Pilgrim," he said, and he pulled open the ragged cloak to reveal a large and clumsy cross stained into his tunic. Deborah suddenly smiled, happy that she could understand the man. He wanted money, and he was explaining that he was a holy man and therefore entitled to ask for alms.

"I am sorry, sir," said Deborah. "I have no money." Now she spoke a bit louder, and rolled the syllables together, the way she had heard the traders from Lyons do with their dialect, running words one into the next in a lovely rush of sounds. He didn't dress or carry himself in the manner of the traders from Champagne, but she remembered hearing of the sudden massing together of French pilgrims, serfs and freemen, farmers in debt and younger sons of the nobility, clergy anxious to put aside prayerbooks and pick up swords. They were going on a great adventure, to free the Holy Land from the Moslems, at the bidding of the leader of Christendom, Pope Urban II, and because of the crosses they wore on the clothing, or on their shields, or stained on their foreheads, they were called "Crusaders."

Her mother, hearing of the crimes committed in Rouen and Lorraine, called them what the beleaguered Jews of those cities called them: "*to'im*," aimless wanderers. She wouldn't tell Deborah what the delegation of Jews from the other side of the Rhine had reported to their German coreligionists, for even among the adults there were many who refused to believe in such atrocities. God had been good to the Jews of Mainz, blessing them with prosperity and peace. The lords of the Gentiles, both spiritual and secular, had invited them into their cities, because the Jews brought international trade, financial growth, as well as peaceful and law-abiding citizens. It made no sense that God would allow the wholesale slaughter of His own people. It made no sense that the lords of Christendom would allow the destruction of the Jews on whom they had come to depend for communication with the outside world. Mainz was itself at the westernmost point with the long route to Constantinople, the greatest city in the world. It was no wonder that one out of every four citizens was Jewish—and if the fears of the Jews west of the Rhine were correct, the Crusaders would not only murder the Jews of Mainz, they would destroy the city's life in the process.

"Are you one of the Crusaders?" said Deborah calmly. She knew nothing of murder or pillage or rape, but only that the talk of portents related to some evil that large groups of dangerous men

348

were bringing their way. But this man was by himself, and he looked, not dangerous, but only hungry and poor. "David says that you can't be bad men, because you want to save your souls. Even if you're Christians, you have souls, and he says that Christians are as likely to be good as Jews. But Hugh—Hugh is the lord's son— he's very different from David. He likes to fight, and he's older than David, and he's very nice, but he always thinks the worst of everyone. Like with this. The Crusaders. He says that the people joining are just serfs and slaves and farmers so much in debt that they're selling their children. He thinks only the real armies, under the great dukes, can ever be right and noble, just like himself, because he's a knight too. But if you're not a knight, then it means that you're rabble. Hugh says—"

"Pilgrim," said the beggarman, taking a step closer to the girl, pressing his fingertips to the cross on his tunic. He wanted something, and he was through with talk, and when he moved his ugly hands, he was swift and accurate enough to grab the child's slender wrist.

"Don't touch me," said Deborah, still quite calm, as if the man had made a mistake in manners, and not being of the country, must needs be instructed at once. "I have marzipan," she said, remembering that her mother had given her a few odd lumps to fortify her against the river winds. "Candy," she added, because when she tried to pull her hand out of his grip so that she could find the treat, she realized that he had no intention of letting her go.

Suddenly, she was terrified.

An awful substance, as tangible and ill tasting as tallow, seemed to be rising up in her throat. She wanted to move, but she could not; she wanted to speak, to shout, but for once, there were no words on her lips. Wildly, she tried to push back from him, but he held her tighter and tore at the bronze brooch that held her cloak about her shoulders and neck. He smelled worse than the peasants that crowded the city's markets; his fetid breath blew out at her through a mouthful of cracked, blackened teeth. She didn't understand what was happening, because for all her life, she had been rewarded for good actions, punished for bad ones. What had happened to her father, her mother had carefully explained, had nothing to do with her behavior in this world; it was part of God's grand scheme, and unlike the slap she received for forgetting her bene-

349

diction before eating or the tale spun out for her by her mother after a good report from Rab Shalom. But this beggarman could not be part of anyone's grand scheme. He had been in need of directions, and so she spoke with him; he seemed hungry, and so she would have given him some candy—if she had a copper coin or two, she would have given him that as well.

But now, he acted as if she were his enemy. The brooch was ripped off the cloak, and the thick wool fell to the ground, and the man picked this up with his free hand, pressing his filthy beard against the soft, clean surface. Happily, he looked at the brooch and cradled the wool in his arm, and then looked the girl up and down for what else he could steal: boots, or gown, or leggings.

"No, please," said Deborah, her voice returning, squeezed out around the knot in her throat. The man was muttering now, and she wondered if this was human speech, if perhaps the strength that held her wrist prisoner was the strength of a demon, and that when he was through stripping her of her earthly possessions, he would try to claim her soul.

He wanted her boots first, she realized, and as he squatted before her, he shouted instructions at her in his incomprehensible language, spitting as he spoke, angry with purpose, clumsy with th joy of his new possessions.

"No," said Deborah, no longer polite, no longer afraid, remembering the anger that had swept over her after the discovery of her father's absence from her life. This man was a pirate, like those who had stolen his life, like the men whose actions had been predicted by the stars flung down from the heavens, like the enemies of her people whom Hugh had said would try and burn the Jews of Mainz in their synagogue. "Don't touch me! Get away from me!"

But she couldn't break his grip on her wrist. Deborah found her eyes filled with tears, her knees buckling under her, her backside pushed to the hard cold ground. "Help me!" she screamed. "Leave me be! My mother is Rachel bat-Barzillai! You're not allowed to touch me! I am under the protection of the lord and the archbishop and the emperor! Help me!"

But the beggarman paid no more attention to her than he needed to keep her captive. Quickly, he pulled off her right boot, and then her left. Struck by the sight of a coral-studded comb in her auburn hair, he exhaled an ecstatic explosion of air. But Deborah's hair was too tightly wound around this comb for easy removal; Rachel, her mother, had taken care that no idle tree branch would dislodge the gift handed down to her from her grandmother. The beggarman pulled at the comb, clumsy with greed, wondering at the nature of the jewels he had never seen. His concentration was intense, but he didn't let up his hold on the child's wrist. Deborah was screaming now, her anger magnifying the pain at his pulling of her hair a hundredfold, so that when the grip was suddenly gone, and she was flung unceremoniously back by the force of her own pulling energy, she continued to scream as if the pain had never let up, as if the beggarman hadn't rolled over backward, with blood rising from his filthy mouth like a geyser.

It took her a moment more before she could believe that what she saw was true, and not a dream descending from the clouds, not a wish rising up from the river mists.

The lord of the castle, enormous and strong, had come to her rescue. Hugh's father, protector of Mainz, stern and forbidding, had appeared to stop her pain. She tried to speak, but her lips wouldn't twist themselves about any recognizable sound. She knew the lord despised her. Deborah wanted to understand if she was alive or dead or sleeping; whether the destruction that screamed through the wet air was real.

Now a hand went out to her, firm, but soft as a fine lady's, and as she stumbled blindly to her feet, she heard the lord's dogs, not barking like common curs, but growling, rooted to the bit of earth where the lord had ordered them to stay.

She looked at the dogs, blinking, as if the sight of their taut, muscular bodies, obedient to the stern master of Mainz's great castle, would explain to her how and why she had been saved. But they only added to the overwhelming questions: why the beggarman had assaulted her, how the lord had managed to appear like a knight in a minstrel's tale, why she felt not like a princess saved by her king, but more like a criminal, watching a vision of her own future.

"Come, child," said the lady of the castle, and Deborah turned to look up at the beautiful gray-eyed face, the golden hair visible from behind its virtuous linen scarf. But she turned back to the dogs, still waiting for their master to finish.

But the lord of the castle was not in a hurry. The man who had trespassed onto his land, who had committed crimes against the person of a child of ten, would be punished not only by divine law, not only by civil law, but by the immediate fury of a knight who lived for battle and who regarded thieves and beggars as less worthy of life than rats.

Deborah had all her life seen incidents of violence: a servant slapped, a peasant whipped by a passing carriage driver, a child punished by a drunken parent in the market square. And she had seen the knights in their brilliant colors, coming and going from the local tournaments, though her mother had never allowed her to join the dangerously surging crowds that observed the ritualized brutality from beyond the safety of the nobles' stands. Every day of her life, she saw swords and knives, freshly killed animals, fish gasping in murderous air. Hugh, the lord's son, had shot a hare with a great bow before her eyes: she had cried when he had run to her, the bloody little creature dead around the arrow that had miraculously penetrated fur and skin and bones.

But she had never seen the murder of a man.

The lord's lady held her hand now and brushed her hair gently with her long fingers. She spoke to her softly in the local dialect, though she was herself from a city two hundred miles south. "It's all right, child. Come with me, Deborah. No harm's been done. There, let me help with the boots. You must drink some hot wine. Come, let's go at once, shall we? We will clean you up good as new and take you home to Rachel."

But Deborah's eyes had cleared now, and she couldn't turn them from the sight of the great lord, his blond beard shot with gray, the hair on his head reaching to his shoulders and thick as his own son's, his face as grim as any specter's; methodically, he continued to beat his walking stick into the beggerman's back and neck and face and skull. The beggarman no longer screamed at the pain, but still his body reacted to every blow, jerking and starting and spurting blood and teeth.

"Please, Deborah," said the lady of the castle. She had stooped to help the child on with her boots, and now she had her arm firmly about her shaking shoulders, but still Deborah wouldn't move. The lord was out of his mail and dressed in the simplest of tunics, but even without armor, without his sword, without the rich colors of wool and ermine and silk, he was all powerful, a representative of the ineluctable hierarchies of the world.

"He saved me," said Deborah quietly.

"Yes," said the lady, who had always been her friend. Even when the great lord had turned his face at her approach, even when his arrogance to her had driven his own son into something approaching disrespect, his lady had always treated her with kindness. It was the lady and not her lord who urged her to play with the daughters of the castle, it was the lady who made silly jokes about her son's teasing of the ten-year-old as if the handsome fourteen-year-old Hugh could possibly be in love with her.

"He is killing that man," said Deborah.

"Come away, child," said the lady, more firmly now, as if she had stepped on forbidden ground. Deborah remembered a story her father had told her long ago, long before he began the voyage from which he had never returned. She had complained to him about the lord's hatred of her, and he had assured her that what she was feeling was not the lord's hatred, but merely his stern and rigorous character. He would not smile at her, but he would protect her, as would the archbishop, though she and her family were Jews; she must remember that she was of a people who had been invited to the fair city not out of love but out of mutual respect. The lord would see to the protection of the city and its inhabitants, following laws laid down by the Church and by the emperor and by the barbarians who had come before them, and by the Romans who had been overwhelmed, murdered, and assimilated into their midsts five hundred years before. Deborah's father explained that the lord of the castle wanted to be like a Roman knight, stern and just, but also a Christian, following the charity and mercy of his religion, and also a barbarian, giving vent to his rage without thought or fetters to his compulsions. And just the way the Roman walls first built around the city a thousand years ago still stood in part, but had been added to, built over, made stronger with clumsier design and inferior craftsmanship, so the lord had taken the laws of Rome and added to them the chains of religion, the brutality of pagan justice, the whimsically ritualized rites of late-eleventh-century knighthood.

The lord, her father had told her, had once been approached for justice by two men in a boundary dispute. The archbishop supported one of the men, who had given great funds toward the dressing of an altar in the cathedral. But the lord, stern and just, insisted on torturing both men to extract the truth from them in the manner of his race. One man continued to be firm in his testimony; the other admitted finally to having moved a landmark.

353

This man was the friend of the archbishop, the giver of charity. The archbishop appealed to the lord to be lenient, but the lord was more concerned with being just. He followed the custom of his father and grandfather in these matters, customs handed down in the Rhineland before Christian or Roman had ever set foot on its soil. The man who had moved the landmark was buried up to his neck in the disputed land, his exposed face smeared with honey, so that the birds and the bugs and the vermin came to devour his eyes and nose and lips before he was dead. Even when he screamed to the heavens for the release of a swift sword, the lord remained firm: the law must be followed; the boundary mover must be destroyed by the weakest of creatures, must then be devoured slowly by the land.

All this Deborah remembered, so that she had long feared the lord, and respected him; she had learned to accept his stern indifference as a fact of nature and not as a personal affront. He followed laws and rules and rites and customs, and was foreign to smiles or friendly words or pats on the head. But now he had saved her life. Now the lord had turned his stern face from her to the man who had assaulted her, and he had followed his rules and rites and beaten the beggarman so that the blood ran out of him, so that the life stuff was harried out of his body, so that he would be a broken-boned corpse left to rot outside the walls of the town.

And this was too much for Deborah. She had never asked the lord to go so far. It was enough that he had protected her, as was his warrant. It was enough that he had torn the beggarman's horrible hands away from their contact with her body, enough that he had punished him with blows. But she wanted no murder on her behalf. She wanted no murder at all. It was as if in wanting the lord to hold back his fury, she was trying to prevent a greater fury, the fury predicted by the portents, the rage envisioned in the stars and the floods and the famines.

"Please, sir," said Deborah. "He was hungry and I wanted to give him some marzipan."

As if in proof of her good intentions, she took out a piece of the candy, small and daintily designed, so decidedly gentle in so violent a place, and held it up before the lord of the castle. Slowly he turned from his task and looked down at her from his great height.

"It was only because he was hungry and poor, sir," said Deborah. "He was looking for the pilgrims' house, and then he wanted my candy and my cloak and all my things—he is poor, sir. Please don't kill him, sir. He can have the candy. If he's hungry. It's very good, and warming on the coldest days."

The lord turned his bloodshot eyes back to the rag-clad corpse and then slowly faced about to Deborah. He looked at the marzipan in her hand and took it from her with his bloody fingers. Then he tossed the candy onto the beggarman's corpse.

"He trespassed," said the lord. "He stole. He attacked a child of my city."

"Yes, my lord," said Deborah, remembering her father's story, the man sentenced to being buried alive, his face smeared with honey as a lure to the sharp-beaked birds. She started to back away from him, afraid to turn her back, hoping that the lady of the castle would come up behind her and take her hand and lead her away from her fierce husband.

"In future," said the lord slowly, raising his eyes from Deborah's to where they rested threateningly on the lovely gray eyes of his wife. "In future, you will no longer be welcome here, girl. You will no longer run in the castle grounds, you are forbidden to approach the gates of the drawbridge, you will no longer be welcome as a guest of my daughters or my son. You will remain with your family in your own quarter, and you will have nothing to do with anything that is mine. You are not welcome, you are not wanted, you are forbidden to approach us. Do you understand me, girl?"

"Yes, my lord," said Deborah.

But of course she didn't understand.

She only knew that the ground was shaking, that the moon was falling to the earth, shining a wild, preternatural light past her teary eyes, burning up the inside of her head with heat and radiance.

"Yes, my lord," she said, and she wondered if the lord's daughters would cry, if Hugh would pretend not to notice her absence, if it were possible to die of shame. She was not welcome, and she tried to back away from the force of his contempt, but her legs were weak and her sense of balance confused by the tears, the blood, the pounding of her heart.

Finally, the lady's hand was back in hers, leading her away, stumbling, down the hill toward the center of town. They were not even within the walls of the castle grounds, not even past the drawbridge, but simply within sight of the tower. Carefully, she wondered if that would be permitted. Not attempting to calculate the true meaning of her loss, she tried to salvage some part of her happiness. She hoped that she could still play on this part of the hill, could still lie on her back and contemplate the sky about the tower, waiting for Hugh to come riding up at breakneck speed, racing the long way about to the gates and the drawbridge and the castle that were suddenly denied her.

Even before the lady had let go of her hand at the first paved street, even before her blinding tears had been dried by the wind in the alleys, she knew that the portents were true, that the world was coming undone, that violent men and desperate times were drawing momently closer, crawling up from the depths of the earth. Not the lord of the castle, not the friends of her childhood, not the contours of her life in the city of her birth would ever be the same. The Crusader had come, a beggarman to whom she had offered words and innocence and marzipan, and in his wake was murder, malevolence, and despair.

Chapter
26

The emissary of Count Emich of Leisingen was of small stature and walked with a considerable effort to remain ferociously erect. Whether this posture was a result of a battle wound or an effort to look as tall as possible in his limited frame, Rachel bat-Barzillai didn't know. She was used to the unsettling effect she had on men, Jews and Gentiles alike. Particularly strangers ushered into her presence were shocked into a display of manliness and sophistication; expecting a money-lender, a merchant in the shape of an old widow, they were met with a tall and lovely woman of twenty-seven years.

Rachel was green-eyed, and given to the most direct of gazes. She looked so carefully into one's eyes when speaking or listening that one felt both flattered by her attention and nonplussed by her concentration. The count's emissary had expected an elderly Jewess, in somber clothing, careful to give him respect, express the goodwill of her community, and loudly proclaim its poverty. Certainly he expected no beautiful woman, no ostentatious dress. Her tunic was so low-cut that he could see the swell of her breasts against the red silk undergarment. If it were not for her elegance, she could have been a bride; if not for her gravity, someone's fresh and hesitant bride-to-be.

Beyond the elegance, beyond the gravity, was a sense of power that made little sense to the count's man in the first days of April, in the year 1096. Peter the Hermit's hordes were streaming into

357

nearby Cologne, and already there had been small outbreaks against the Jews of that city, clamoring not only for the silver that would buy arms for their Crusade, but for the lives of the Jews who lent the silver at interest.

As if to defy any threat of monetary extortion, the woman wore jewels. There were parti-colored gems strung in her uncovered, long, and braided auburn hair, in a thick leather belt tightly circling a tiny waist, in a gold necklace that held an emerald, a ruby, and a central, charismatic diamond. If it were not for the fixity of her stare, the count's emissary would have been torn between two lustful images—that of the woman's form, and that of her jewels. But as it was, he kept his gaze on her green eyes, and felt himself ridiculed under the weight of her words.

"I suppose he has some means of guaranteeing this loan?" said Rachel, answering his badly phrased request for funds for the count's journey to the east, to fight the infidel.

"I'm afraid, madam, I don't quite understand," said the count's man. He had not been asked to sit, or indeed to go past the antechamber in which Rachel had met him. She herself had sat almost at once, in a spindly chair, so that he was forced to look down upon her shining mass of twisted and bejeweled hair. It was no wonder that the bishops preached of the temptations of the flesh, of the "devil's snare" that an uncovered head of woman's hair could be to a man.

"What is it that you don't understand, sir?" said Rachel. "The nature of a loan or the desire of a lender for a pledge? It's really quite simple. If you are a merchant, and wish to have money for a merchant's venture, you agree to return to me more than what you've been lent—which is of course at considerable risk, seeing as how you may be lost in a storm, attacked by pirates, or murdered upon arriving at your destination. A guaranteed portion of the profits of your voyage, in the happy event of your return, is the only way we have done business in Mainz."

"I don't understand, madam," said the count's man. "I'm not a merchant."

"Not a merchant?" said Rachel, feigning great surprise. She forced herself to remain seated. There would have been a time when a man such as this, even on a legitimate mission, would have considered himself privileged to be inside the home of Barzillai, or his daughter or his son-in-law. But Barzillai was long since dead, and Rachel's husband was two years missing, and the residents of this house were no longer as proud as lions, even if they had not yet become as meek as lambs. They had been merchants, and still managed to send goods overland and by sea, but the height of their glory had been over since the day, two years after her birth, that the Turks destroyed the forces of the Emperor Romanus of Byzantium near the town of Manzikert.

Ever since that summer of 1071, the Byzantine empire had been a battleground. Normans, Cumans, Turks, Armenians, Venetians, Anglo-Saxons created alliances, fought each other as mercenaries, as parts of the empire's motley forces, or as one or another fierce faction looking to carve out an emirate or a dukedom for their children and their children's children. It was not simply the pirates of Chaka who sailed out from Smyrna to terrorize the Aegean, not just the Turks who raided caravans throughout Syria and Palestine, or the Arab princes who made slaves of Christian pilgrims, or the Christian adventurers who made slaves of Moslem villages; it was the cumulative effect of these and a thousand other anarchies where before there had been trust in an empire, in a trade route, in a difficult but still-open channel between east and west.

Now the route was not difficult, but desperate. Pope Urban's appeal to wrest control of the Holy Land from the infidel was as much an appeal to save the entire Christian east—Byzantium—as it was to break past the walls of Jerusalem.

The last few years had been the worst in Rachel's memory. Men who were not ordinarily superstitious listened to astrologers and midwives and madmen. In the famines and floods that swept away the lives of thousands, they predicted a catastrophe for hundreds of thousands. Looking into the night sky, they predicted mass movements, vast armies running out of control, like bodies without heads, like beasts without souls.

Sometimes Rachel believed her husband's attempt to forge a new trade route hadn't been so much a mad adventure as a deliberate assault on the whole world of fear about them. As each merchant retreated into a smaller territory, a narrower sphere of activity, the general fear grew, battening on the new ignorance. Contacts with the east diminished, vanished. Men forgot that beyond the surface of the Moslem world were riches—in goods, in learning, in the preserved heritage of the ancient pagan masters of the world. Her husband Yosef's failed attempt at coming home with a full cargo on a flotilla of riverboats was mourned throughout the Rhineland. Merchants who had been lured here by dreams of prosperity from as far away as Spain and Italy and Greece, were seen learning the few humble trades allowed to Jews by the laws of state and church.

The children of dead Barzillai, himself the descendant of Jews from Nicomedia—even this suburb of imperial Constantinople was now in barbaric Turkish hands—tried to keep their trade alive. Ohel, Rachel's brother, was able to safeguard—through bribes and threats and treaties with a hundred barons and bishops and thieves —the route up the Rhine and Neckar rivers to the Danube and into Hungary. Still, Rachel's family, used to venturing funds on far greater—and more lucrative—merchant expeditions, now found themselves lending money, associating their name with the commonest of usurers. Rabbi Eliezer ben-Nathan of her own city had long sanctioned moneylending to non-Jews, as long as the lenders owned no vineyards or fields; scores of other Jewish leaders allowed the practice in recognition of laws that forbade Jewish ownership of land, thereby depriving them of an ancient Jewish source of livelihood. Even in those years, there were Christians who found it difficult to imagine that the Jews of their busy merchant cities were once farmers and shepherds; it seemed that the people of the Book must have always lived in cities, thriving on trade and intrigue and moneylending. It was no wonder that illiterate knights and peasants who could only know the people of the Bible from tales told aloud, believed Jews to be a cursed race, inflicted on the Christian world like a disease.

Moneylending must be the Jew's natural occupation, as the eating of human flesh was natural nourishment for a vulture. It made no difference that Christian moneylenders charged four times the interest rate of the Jews; these Christians were violating the laws of their Church, while the Jews were following their innately evil ways. It mattered less that the highest occupations and pursuits in life were closed to Jews, who could never be knights in a martial age or statesmen when the mantle of dead Rome was now worn by the pope, the leader of a Christian Europe, ruled by churchmen.

The Church had forbade usury for its members, but it allowed Christians to borrow from Jews; it encouraged the conditions that created, year by year, an entire class of hated Jewish moneylenders, and a growing pool of borrowers whose best interests lay in their persecution.

The leaders—lay and ecclesiastical—who once invited Jewish merchants to bring the life of trade to their cities, now invited them moneylenders to finance their battles, wars, crusades. Money was needed in a time when serfs fled their liege lords, when harvests were burned by marauding armies, when goods could no longer be exchanged for debts of services. But because Christians were reminded, time after time, of the greatest crime in history—the murder of Jesus Christ by the Jews—it was not with gratitude but with loathing that a loan was demanded. And it was common to remember the crime of the Jews in refusing to repay a loan to one of their race, as if in denying a commercial obligation to a Jew, one was avenging their complicity in the Crucifixion.

Of course, this forced the moneylenders to charge higher rates of interest, as the likelihood of full repayment of loans diminished with the threat of persecution. If a knight refused a debt by waving his sword, a king refused his by banishing all the Jews from his kingdom.

But such intrigues of moneylending were uncommon in Mainz. The city's trade had not declined as precipitously as that of other Rhineland cities; nearby Frankfurt, Cologne, and Worms all had worse economies, more Jewish moneylending, and more anti-Jewish sentiment. Even before the first words of the pope's call for a crusade from Clermont-Ferrand—which the Jews would learn to call *Har Afel*, "the mountain of gloom"—there had been attacks on Jews in Speyer, where the Jewish colony had only recently settled, fleeing from persecution in Bavaria. Jews had been persecuted in Mainz too, but not for many years. Yet men and women older than Rachel could remember terrible times when they had to lock themselves in their houses and wait for the drunken mob to spend their rage against their poverty, their fearful superstitions, their class-locked lives.

Still, for Rachel, Mainz was more than a haven. It was a home, a community to which she belonged as deeply as any citizen. Barzillai had never had to flee the city or ask forgiveness for his religion. He had spent more evenings with the present lord of the castle's father than he had in his own home; the archbishop had not only been a political and commercial associate, but a friend. The famous stories of the persecution and martyrdom of Amnon of Mainz in the early tenth century had taken on a legendary gloss in the comforts and privileges of Rachel's life, at least until the last few years. Though she understood well the animosity toward Jewish moneylenders, though she feared for the safety of her family in the coming waves of Jew-hating Crusaders, she was still unable to allow a man to threaten her for being a Jew in her native city.

"If you are not a merchant, what in the world are you doing here in my house?" said Rachel.

"You are a moneylender, madam," said the count's emissary. "We both understand what that means."

Rachel made a great distinction between lending money as part of a commercial venture and lending money at interest. Often she risked funds in return for a chance of great profits; she hated to lend brass or silver coins, to reap a profit based on how long it took to return them. But of course she made no attempt to explain this distinction. The man was not here to punish her for usury or to win a philosophical argument. It mattered not what sort of moneylender she was, but only that she possessed money at all.

The count's emissary smiled, shifting from foot to foot, trying to fix his eyes on the diamond about her neck, but felt himself pulled by the examination to which she continued to subject him. "It is difficult for poor Christian knights to equip themselves without the help and generosity of moneylenders such as yourself. Surely you know that Little Peter has been very generously helped by members of your race—"

"Who is 'Little Peter'?" said Rachel sharply, interrupting the insinuating speech.

"He is not so little," said the count's man, attempting a flash of wit. "He is rather a great personage. Peter the Hermit, Little Peter, Ugly Peter, Wart-faced Peter—he is known by many names, but regardless of his outer appearance, he is a holy man. Everyone will admit to that fact."

"I know of Peter the Hermit. He is bringing forth the dregs of France and Germany and taking them to my doorstep. And you say he has been helped generously by members of my race? I see. What else do you have to say?" Suddenly, she was up, and out of her chair, her eyes wild with rage. "Stay where you are, little man. I didn't ask you to move, did I?"

"Now, madam, you are talking through me to Count Emich of—"

"Count Nobody, Count No-Person, Count No-Importance!" said Rachel.

"Madam!" said the count's man in a last stab at courage, but the woman was half a foot taller than he, and when she slapped his face, he felt idiotically fearful, as if some trick of etiquette had beguiled him, leading to this ignominy. He opened his mouth and brought his hand up to his face and would have tried to compose a sentence that was no longer circuitous, but a straight-line threat, directly from Count Emich to the richest Jewish family in Mainz.

But then he saw a peasant emerge, as if by some prearranged signal, from behind the heavy drapes that kept the chilly air from penetrating through the north wall of the old house.

"It's all right," said Rachel to the servant. "This idiot of Leisingen is just leaving."

"Wait a minute, madam," said the count's man. "You are making a terrible mistake, and I don't want to be responsible for the consequences." As the enormous peasant came at him, the emissary put his hand to the hilt of his sword, an action that was as automatic to a knight as cringing was to a mongrel threatened with a stick.

But the peasant had either been trained by a weapons master or was blessed with preternatural speed. He slammed his ham-sized palm over the grasping sword hand, crushing it against the sword hilt with such force that the emissary shouted in a shock of pain. Rachel spoke to the servant in their Jewish-German speech, but the count's man understood every word.

"Pick him up," she said. "And throw him down the stairs."

The servant was ready to fulfill this desire, but first finished with disarming the man who had angered his mistress. Swiftly, he pulled the man's arm behind his back, driving him to his knees; holding him in place with his left hand, he used his free hand to draw the sword and toss it across the floor. Haphazardly, it slammed into a large bowl, which spilled its contents of sweet-smelling herbs.

"Wait, madam—listen to me—they're going to murder the Jews," said the man.

"Throw the beggar down the stairs," said Rachel.

Silently, the powerful servant picked the count's man off the floor, disguising the struggle to lift the great weight under a grim smile. He held him in the air, like one of the crumbling Roman mosaics of a contest of long-vanished gods.

"Please, only just listen for one moment," said the count's man.

"It is my fault that I spoke without intelligence, but it will be your fault if you missed a chance to help save lives."

Rachel hesitated, and as the servant staggered under his load, she saw her daughter Deborah, red-cheeked and teary-eyed, burst through the door from the stairwell, panting from the two-flights running climb.

"Mother," she said. "I can't go to the castle. Never again. I'm not allowed to go to the castle." But Deborah, caught up as she was in her monumental problems, could not fail to notice the incredible sight of their servant holding a knight in the air. For once, she had nothing to comment on or question about, but simply allowed her astonishment to fix all the features of her face.

"Go to Cook," said Rachel, speaking sharply in Hebrew, in the tone that left no room for debate.

"Why is he—" Deborah began, but then, even as she said this, her mother barked another order, in the Hebrew-German argot Deborah found so unattractive, and the servant dropped the knight heavily to the ground. Somehow, the man had landed with a semblance of grace, looking up at the big peasant from his hands and knees, like a wild beast ready to leap at the throat of his trainer.

"Go, Deborah," repeated Rachel, as the knight hurriedly got back to his feet, squaring his small shoulders as if they were capable of murderous violence. "You will tell me later—"

"The lord doesn't want me to play—"

"Deborah," said Rachel. "For once, do as you're told."

"Should I go to Uncle Ohel?" she asked, looking over at the knight, at the sweet-smelling herbs strewn all over the floor, at the unfamiliar sword, out of its sheath and dangerous in the room's bad light.

"Go to Cook!" shouted Rachel, and now she placed her hands on her daughter's shoulders and hurried her out of the room, pushing her as violently as the beggarman had pulled her to the ground. Deborah burst into tears, but her mother didn't see them. Deborah tried to summon the words to tell her about the beggarman, the lord and his stick, the lady and her consolation, but her mother was too full of some other event to notice the dirt and the tears in her best cloak, the missing brooch she had left behind on the hill, the wildness of her hair where the Crusader had tried to pull free the coral-studded comb.

"Listen to me, madam," said the count's man, once again standing as tall as he could, his breath if not his confidence back in his rigid frame. "If you love your daughter, you will listen to me in the name of Count Emich."

"Go on," said Rachel. She turned about anxiously, to see if it was her imagination that Deborah was hiding behind the threshold to the adjacent room. "Count Emich has sent you because I am a moneylender, though you are not a merchant. Go on, go on."

Her family had been richer by far in Barzillai's time. Even poor Yosef, before his last voyage, had managed to bring more silver to their household than she and Ohel did in these anxious days. Still, the notion that they were rich lingered in the minds of Jews and Gentiles alike, and not only in Mainz. When the delegation of Jews from Rouen came to Mainz to warn the chief rabbi of the wandering anti-Jewish hordes following Peter the Hermit, they suggested that the children of Barzillai send Peter a great present. When the Jews of Lorraine sent messengers to Mainz, detailing the sad persecution in which two dozen Jews had been murdered, they hoped that the heirs of Barzillai the *Cohen* would send an even greater gift to the emperor Henry IV, so that he would be more likely to protect them. Even when Kalonymus, the chief rabbi of Mainz, decided to swallow pride and principle and send Godfrey of Bouillon—who was assembling an army of soldiers rather than peasants, but still chose to motivate them with promise of pillaging the Jews of the Rhineland—five hundred pieces of silver, he thought first of Rachel and Ohel, children of the famous benefactor Barzillai.

But what money they had wasn't secure in lands, as they could not legally possess land; nor was it secure in gold bullion, which could no longer be owned by Jews. Rachel was rich in debts and obligations owed to herself and Ohel, some from merchants, some from princes, some from the emperor of the Germans. She owned the contents of the house she and Deborah shared with Ohel and his wife and son; but the house, and the land on which it stood, was not theirs and could never belong to them as Jews, by law. When Rabbi Kalonymus had asked their help with the bribe for Godfrey of Bouillon, Rachel sold most of her mother's delicate gold jewelry in lieu of any other way to swiftly raise so much silver coin. Had the emperor, and the princes, and the bishops, and the merchants paid her half of what they owed, had a third of the voyages to which she and Ohel had ventured their capital and their connections returned with full cargoes, they would have been as rich as everyone assumed them to be.

But often Rachel wondered what precious few items remained

between herself and poverty and powerlessness. After centuries of trade and riches, the most valuable, the most portable family possessions were the three gemstones she wore around her neck. According to family legend, they would have been first given to Rachel bat-Akiba by her father in Persia nearly five centuries ago. Whether the gemstones were that old and that traveled, whether they had been used by the superstitious to quell fear and pain and disease, were as clouded in doubt as their own future. Rachel had sworn to her father that she would never part with the necklace, acknowledging his tales of its ancestry and the special legacy of her name. But she knew that if all three stones could give her daughter one more moment of life, she would trade them instantly.

When she pressed the stones in her hands, in the familiar habit of a lifetime, she felt the kindred warmth of all the namesakes who had touched these jewels, who had held the central diamond against the lifeblood coursing to their hearts. But now she also felt their material weight, reminding herself of their power in a chaotic world. Even with currency so debased that gold coins were horded and not traded, even with trade so upset by war that precious silks could not find buyers to risk bringing them from east to west, even with men preferring to pillage rather than to buy, these gems were rare enough, fine enough, beautiful enough to retain their value. They were small, therefore portable, universally desired, thus able to be sold in any corner of the world.

Though their house was in the privileged quarter of Mainz, close to the bishop's palace, close to the lord's castle, close to the walls of the city, but behind the road that led to the gates of the lord's fortifications—a last refuge in the event of invasion by some monstrous horde—it made her feel less safe than these heirloom gems. About her throat was not only portable wealth, instant power, but the goodwill of a score of Rachels. Even if she had to let go of the gems, her namesakes would remain with her, ringing her heart, embedded in her soul.

"Count Emich is sorely in need of silver to pay for his voyage to Jerusalem."

"No doubt."

"He is not an enemy of the Jews. But there are those among his followers who ask the question—"

Rachel interrupted him with a clap of her hands. Having heard the arguments of a dozen extortioners, she knew them by heart.

"The question," she said. "Why fight the infidels in the east when here in the west are the greater enemies of Christianity? Why risk life and limb fighting those who have persecuted Christian pilgrims when here among you are the very murderers of your Lord Jesus?"

"Yes," said the count's emissary. "That is the question."

"Do you believe that I and my daughters are responsible for the killing of your God?"

"Madam, that is certainly not for me to say. I am simply the representative of Count Emich, who is your friend, and hopes to remain so."

"I have never met the count, and I have barely heard of him, as his title is not so very distinguished as you seem to believe." Rachel moved closer to him, and was suddenly desirous of an answer to her question. "We will forget the count and we will forget the reason why he has sent you here until you answer my question. Am I and my little daughter guilty of the crime of deicide?"

"I am here as your friend—"

"Did we kill Jesus Christ?" said Rachel. She hadn't meant to shout, but she had, and in the ensuing silence, she could see the emissary draw up his words, like soldiers being lined up in battle formation.

"Certainly, you will not contest the facts that the Jews rejected Jesus Christ, that the Jews murdered him, and that this murder was not the responsibility of one Jew, but of all Jews—not in one generation, but in all generations. This is the word and the lesson of the New Testament. This is what the Church tells us. While you and your child may be good people, you cannot escape the fact that you are Jews, and therefore guilty of the greatest crime in history. You cannot. It is the word of God."

"You believe this?"

"Yes."

"So why do you not simply kill us? Why do you want me to give your count money so that he may spare us from the mob? Isn't the mob correct in wanting us to die like the dogs we are?"

"You don't understand," said the emissary. "The count is very civilized and understanding. He knows that there are wise and good Jews. He knows that God wouldn't have allowed you to live in this world unless He had a reason to do so. But all the same, it is difficult to fight the arguments of the mob. There are peasants who believe that the Lord has spoken to them, who have seen visions of Christ on the cross, demanding the blood of the Jews. Many believe that they must kill every Jew in the Rhineland before they can touch the soil of the Holy Land. Volkmar's followers are even worse. They know that the Jews are the spawn of the devil, because no ordinary men could have killed the Lord Jesus. What good will it do to fight the Saracens, they say, if the children of the devil remain alive in Christian Europe? You must understand, madam, that to fight such desires is expensive."

"Of course," said Rachel. "To fight the desires of Godfrey of Bouillon's men cost five hundred pieces of silver. Now you have to fight the desires of Count Emich's men, and then of course, there will be the worse desires of Volkmar's men, and meanwhile Peter the Hermit's men are rioting up and down the Rhine. Apparently, they are not sure if Jerusalem is closer to Frankfurt or Cologne, so in the meanwhile they burn fields and attack the virtue of women. But since they do not only attack the Jews—though of course the Jews are their favorite prey—how do they manage to justify that? Is there some reason why they delight in burning a monastery as much as a synagogue? Do they suspect that the murderers of Christ have taken refuge in worshiping His name day and night?"

"Madam, listen, please. Count Emich is a nobleman and a soldier. He is not like the preachers Volkmar or Gottschalk. William the Carpenter and Thomas La Fere follow him, as do the lords of Salm and Viernenberger, Zwiebrucken, Drogo of Nesle—"

"How much money does he want from the Jews of Mainz?"

"The same as they raised for Godfrey."

"That is impossible!" Rachel had snapped at the man thoughtlessly, and now she tried to cool her temper, to let him understand that there were limits to which the Jews could be pushed. She had already physically abused him through her servant. Even if he was a fool, she would try to hear him out calmly.

"Surely you Jews have the money—"

"If I say it is impossible, you will accept that I speak the truth!" Rachel wanted to sit on her anger, but too much of Barzillai's blood ran in her veins. In another moment, she would regret having allowed him to speak at all. She would have liked to have seen him at the bottom of the stairwell, dusty and bruised and beaten.

"Count Emich of Leisingen is a worthy and honorable man. If you shout at me, you shout at him," said the emissary, pointing his finger and waving it before her steady eyes.

"Do not advise me in my own house, sir," said Rachel.

"Count Emich needs five hundred pieces of silver."

"You tell the Count Emich that he is not worth five hundred pieces of silver. Not when it is no longer possible to raise two hundred. Not when every other robber baron is starting his own crusade of pillage. You tell him that if he comes to Mainz to kill the Jews, he will find resistance, and soldiers of the emperor sworn to protect us. You tell him that if he is our friend, he will stay away, and that if he is our enemy come to steal our money, he will be sorry the day he brings his men to our gates."

"Madam, you underestimate my lord. If he protects you, no one will harm you. Not Peter's men, not Godfrey's, not Gottschalk's or Volkmar's. Count Emich has been branded with the cross of God, over his heart—a brand that came in the night, while he slept, and never woke him, never brought him pain. He exposed his chest for his army the next morning. Two thousand men saw the miracle and got to their knees, shouting his name. He is the anointed leader of the Crusade. He will thank you for money to buy arms and feed his armies, and no one will attack the Jews of Mainz, no one will harm you or your people."

He was not tricky or sophisticated, and she had a hundred answers for his reassurances; but still, she wanted to grasp at straws. If there was some chance that he spoke the truth, that the murderers would spare their city and prevent others from breaking into their quarter and setting fire to their lives, she would gladly sell everything in her house, every remnant of jewelry and finery.

But how could she believe him? She heard his twisted words, distorting the anti-Jewish feelings of the New Testament into an even greater hatred. The mob would never leave the Jews alone, because no matter what the Jews did, they would always be hated.

Yosef, her poor husband, had long ago made this clear to her. The Jews were not hated for killing Jesus. All the convoluted talk about the responsibility of the Romans for the Roman execution of a Jewish rabbi—and Jesus was certainly not the first or last Jewish rabbi to meet death at Roman hands—was beside the point. The leaders of the Church knew that Christianity came from Judaism. Jesus was an observant and devout Jew, as were his apostles, as were the men and women to whom he addressed his messianic claims.

But it was the Jews, the Chosen People, to whom Jesus spoke

out his prophecies, his visions; it was to the people of whom he was a part that he shared his dream of peace, goodness, and redemption. The Jews not only rejected Jesus, but remained Jews. They kept alive learning and traditions that were part of Jesus's own life. Their faith didn't crumble, their language survived, their Bible remained read and revered. A thousand years and more after Jesus's death on the cross, the Jews still read from their Torah scrolls, still refused to see the Christian revelations in their holy texts. There could be no reason why the people who were Jesus's own people, the children of Israel—even the descendants of Jesse and David, even the whole tribe of Judah—refused to follow the Son of God, unless they themselves were children of the devil. But if they were children of the devil, why had Jesus been born among them? Why had the apostles been culled from this cursed race?

But general hatred is not rational, nor does it depend on a thousand sophistries. The masses need only remember that the Jews killed their Lord, and it is simple for them to forget that their Lord was one of the Jewish people. The Christian world need only remember that Judas was a Jew, and forget that all the apostles shared his religion. The rabble who followed the hate-crazed preachers through the Rhineland, expecting the towers of Jerusalem to appear just after the next turn of the river, need not wonder why Jesus had been born a Jew. It was enough to know that every Jew had murdered Him, every Jew was a devil's child, every Jew was a bloodsucker, a well poisoner, a demon who must be destroyed.

"Count Emich will protect us?" said Rachel softly, fingering her jewels, wondering if she should send for her brother and together call a meeting of the Jewish merchants of the city. "He will prevent the mob from entering the city, and leave us all in peace? He will swear to this before witnesses?"

"Madam," said the count's emissary, warming to his task. "I will tell the count of your support for his cause and your hospitality to his emissary." Here he smiled at the huge servant as if as part of the truce he was creating, the count's soldiers would tear the servant limb from limb. "The count will protect you from every army in Germany, he will swear to be responsible for your lives and properties, he will do this gladly. For this he needs only the sum of five hundred silver pieces to buy his armor and provisions."

"I will think about this," said Rachel. "I need to talk to the rabbi and the merchants—"

"Of course," said the count's man. He smiled expansively now, sure of his new power. "If I may suggest something, madam. If I were to return to the count empty-handed, he might be less happy than if you could part with something right now, a token, a present."

"A small bribe before the larger one?" said Rachel.

"A present of friendship," corrected the count's man. "Perhaps your belt, with its pretty jewels. Though it looks so lovely around your small waist."

"You admire my belt?" said Rachel slowly, looking to the huge servant behind her, as if wondering how he could have refrained from striking the man in his insolence.

"It is lovely, but not as lovely as the woman who wears it," said the count's man.

Rachel swiftly unbuckled the belt, with its pretty gemstones embedded in the Spanish leather. For a moment she hesitated, realizing that she had already once begun to act honorably in having the man disarmed and knocked down and nearly thrown down the stairs.

"I am very sorry for you that you are a widow," said the count's man. "But not sorry for myself." His smile was nearly a leer now, and when he looked into Rachel's eyes, he started at the hatred there, at the strength of her contempt.

"I am not a widow," said Rachel. "My husband is missing, but only God knows if he is dead or alive."

"I only meant to say that you are beautiful," said the count's man.

"You want the belt," said Rachel sharply, and the count's man saw it lash at him, a snake come to life, saw it reach out and strike his hands, his wrists.

"Madam," he said, but the woman was no longer interested in words, and he had to cover himself ignobly, cowering before her as she struck him with the buckle, beating him until the blood ran and he had retreated, falling backward down the stairs, covering his shame under a mask of fury. "You want my belt," she said to him. "Here's my belt for you and your kind." All the way to the camp of Emich and his followers, the emissary practiced his story, composing a picture not of defiance, but of devilry, hellfire, and damnation, a story he believed in his heart.

Long before he reached Count Emich, the lord's son, Hugh,

returned to Mainz with news of the riots in Cologne. The silver paid by the Jews of that city to Godfrey of Bouillon, duke of Lower Lorraine, hadn't prevented the followers of Peter the Hermit from running wild through their quarter, tearing beards off the faces of old men, setting fire to synagogues, wielding heavy swords and axes for the first time—striking down women, unarmed men, crushing the skulls of infants as if contained in that act was the joyful remission of sins promised by Peter for all the followers of his Crusade.

"They are rioting in Cologne," Hugh told Rachel, looking at her wild face, at the tears in the eyes of little Deborah. "They are burning and killing and there is no one in control. But there is no need to fear. Archbishop Ruthard will never allow such people in our city. And my father would sooner die than let them harm a single Jew of Mainz. And I pledge my honor and my life to the protection of you and your daughter, in this month and year, and for every day that I shall live."

He was fourteen, Rachel remembered, and very much like his father had been at that age. Headstrong, reckless, and in love with the Jewess of the house of Barzillai. Rachel wondered which mad group would descend upon them first, that of Peter, or Volkmar, or Gottschalk? Or Count Emich, whose emissary she had humiliated this day? She wondered if Hugh's father, the lord of the castle, would remember his own old pledge of love, and save them; or if his heart had turned as cold as the world in this terrible April, and as he had banished Deborah from the castle, so he would abandon the Jews to their fate.

Chapter
27

The mass movements of people predicted by stars falling from the Rhineland sky continued throughout the months of April and May.

Volkmar urged fifteen thousand men to Ratisbon and Prague, letting his men pillage in every village along the way; by the time he was ready to cross into Hungary, where he had planned to meet with the larger number of scavengers surrounding Peter the Hermit, it was said that even the lead from the roofs of churches had been stolen.

The preacher Gottschalk, who had once followed Peter's ragged standard, now took his own army up the Rhine and into Bavaria, on the way to Hungary and Byzantium. Those who were not monks or runaway serfs were mostly varlets, the half-wit scum of the armies whose business it was to hurry the maimed and dying into the next world by slitting their throats or crushing their skulls. In an army led by a duke, supported by knights on war-horses, and men-at-arms who could march all day under the weight of swords and shields and armor, these varlets were a necessary evil, a despised remnant who lingered just beyond the fringe of the battle, then hurried forward when their victims lay bleeding and incapacitated on the field. But an army of varlets was a sham. It knew nothing of courage, discipline, or purpose. Gottschalk had gotten them as far as Bavaria by quoting to them the benefits offered to Crusaders by Pope Urban: murderers sentenced to death were granted life service in the Holy Land; serfs were freed from their bondage to the soil; taxes, debts, crimes, and sins were all excused for those joining the Crusaders. Gottschalk would keep them going by allowing their random violence inflicted on Christians, Jews, and pagans alike; all the defenseless were prey, and continuing inducements to remain with the army of faith.

Godfrey of Bouillon's better-disciplined army still remained in the Lower Lorraine, where he continued to extort money from the local Jews; but even so, he couldn't prevent small groups of men from forays into the smaller towns where Jews lived, to add rape and murder to the crimes of blackmail.

Count Emich of Leisingen sent emissaries to other cities than Mainz, other families than that of Rachel bat-Barzillai. Bribes came to him from Worms and Speyer, which must have gladdened his heart; warnings came to him from the emperor Henry, which should have trammeled his temper. But Count Emich felt inviolable, destined for glory, and he wanted no holds on his men's anger or energy. Like the cross he claimed to have found miraculously burned into his chest upon awakening from a joyous, dreamless sleep, like the sacred goose five thousand French peasants had followed into his camp, like the visions of the storming of Jerusalem, of the Second Coming, of the glory he would receive at the Throne of God, Count Emich imagined nothing that was not inevitable, destined.

When his armies approached the gates of Speyer, Emperor Henry's messages were ignored, the bishop of Speyer's threats of excommunication were laughed at. Emich knew that what his men did was what God wanted. Certainly the masses of peasants and serfs, even the minor clergy, believed that the Jews who suffered at the hands of Crusaders were meeting a fate that God had allowed as revenge for the shared crimes of their nation.

When the bishop's resistance to Emich stopped the razing of the Jewish quarter of Speyer, Emich was content with the massacre of only a dozen Jews there, as he was sure that this was what God had demanded, and no more and no less. When a single Jewish girl took her own life rather than be raped by one of his men, Emich didn't punish the man, as he believed that the suicide, as well as the impulse to rape and pillage, as well as the massacre, were all of a piece, and all God's will. Still, he grew angry at the news that the bishop of Speyer had captured some of his men and cut off their hands as punishment for pillage and murder. This he saw not as God's will, but as the bishop's revenge for having his authority flouted by a minor nobleman.

Emich resolved to exhibit his will with greater force upon arriving at the city of Worms.

Here, a day's journey south of Mainz on the Rhine, was a much larger and more prosperous Jewish community. Either out of friendship or because of a bribe, the bishop warned Emich's men from the walls of the city. The count responded by appearing before the gates without a tunic in the May rain, exhibiting the branded cross on his chest to the gatekeepers.

Leaving his entourage behind, Emich entered the city, accused the Jews there of well poisoning, and began the rumor that the bishop was himself a renegade Christian, a secret Jew planning to undermine the faith of his flock.

The Jews of Mainz heard about what happened in the following three days and nights from the few refugees who were able to survive the savageries of Emich and the hatred of their fellow citizens. Whether it was Emich's rumor of well poisoning, or the chance to obliterate long-standing debts to Jewish moneylenders, or the opportunity to ransack the wealthy homes of the Jewish quarter would never be known. But it was clear that some terrible force had been tapped in Worms, something that had begun to be seen in Lorraine and in Speyer, as it had been seen in a thousand other places in a hundred other times.

Emich had spoken of the hateful Jews, and the populace had responded with Jew hatred. Not one, but hundreds, rushed to the city's gates to open them wide to Emich's men. As the soldiers and peasants, camp followers and vagabonds and knights rushed into the narrow streets, they were met by a spontaneous, cheering throng of citizens. The cheers were not for the soldiers' courage at leaving their homes for the distant war in Jerusalem, but for their coming to murder the Jews of Worms.

The bishop had tried to hold back this hatred, had attempted to use authority and reason to stem the tide of violence, but the people of his city had a need to believe the calumnies of Count Emich of Leisingen. Even in the face of the bishop's courage—he opened his palace, a holy place of refuge, to more than five hundred Jews—the mob's hatred couldn't be stopped, nor could its fury. They smashed down the bishop's doors, they knocked over the bishop's guards, then they threw the bishop himself into a corner while they proceeded to defile his palace with murder and rape and mutilation.

"How many died?" Rachel asked the merchant of Worms who stood before the group of Jewish leaders in the main synagogue of Mainz. Her brother was there, as was his wife Dinah, and four other men of trade. The widow of the last *parnus*, or community leader, was there too, dressed in black hat and black veil and black gloves, mumbling prayers as if they were the key to holding back the murderers from their gates. Rabbi Kalonymus, the current *parnus*, was there, but he asked few questions, as he was already quite sure of what must be done: he had been advising flight for more than three weeks, since the news of the far less devastating massacre in Speyer had reached them.

"I know of two dozen who might have lived, madam," said the merchant of Worms. "It is not difficult to subtract that number from the six hundred Jews who lived in Worms."

"It is not possible," said Ohel's wife Dinah, eliciting annoyed glances from all the other merchants in the small and luxuriously furnished room, adjacent to the synagogue's sanctuary. They had been there since shortly before dawn, hoping to come to a decision, or at least a mutual prayer to share with the congregation. But there had been no decision, no direction. Now all were irritable, looking for an outlet for fear and anger. Because it was Dinah who spoke, a woman—and one who was not active in business like her sister-in-law Rachel—they waited impatiently for her to finish, though there was no cause to hurry, no minor urgencies that made sense against the larger urgency of the coming catastrophe. "The people of Worms could never allow such things to happen," she said. "Worms is no different from Mainz. The bishop is a wonderful and educated man."

"They threw the bishop down and stepped on his face, madam," said the merchant of Worms. "Some say that he is dead for his courage. Perhaps the emperor Henry will send soldiers to punish Emich for defying his orders. But all that is of no importance. What is important is that they have murdered us, they have burned our homes and our synagogues, and they have killed every Jew they could find. The villagers came after us with clubs, even after we had gotten past the walls of Worms. Every town, every manor in the vicinity turned on us. The hatred shown us in Worms spilled over and touched every peasant between our city and yours. Not until we could see your lord's castle from below the walls of Mainz did we feel safe."

"You are not safe now," said Rabbi Kalonymus.

"Archbishop Ruthard will order the gates closed," said Ohel, breaking his long silence with a glance at his sister. "The lord of the city has called on his knights and his men-at-arms. The city's defenses are excellent, and the law and the temper of the people are on our side."

From the neighboring great hall, they could hear the hushed mumbling of the morning assembly for prayer. The synagogue, a tall and airy structure, was set in a decline between two rising hills lined with six flat buildings in the Jewish quarter; its main floor extended eight feet below the ground, so that the main sanctuary could rise to an impressive interior height without violating the city ordinances against building any synagogue higher than any church in Mainz.

"There is the chance to give Count Emich seven pounds of gold," said one of the merchants of Mainz, and not for the first time. "We have not fully discussed—"

"There is no need!" said Rachel. "He took money from the Jews of Worms. Ask this man if you disbelieve me! I absolutely refuse—"

"Rachel," said Ohel, speaking as gently as he always did to his sister, his only sibling, "though your anger and suspicion are justi-fied, we must agree to pay the sum. Think of it. If there is the slightest chance that money will buy lives—"

"Money will not buy lives from Emich. It will buy passage out of Germany," she said, amazed at the certainty with which she spoke. "There is no other way to survive this. We must leave, and go elsewhere."

"Where might that be?" said the merchant of Worms. "I had the luck to get this far, and these few miles were treacherous. What country can we get to? What place will give us protection? Who on earth do you think you can trust?"

"Spain," said Rachel.

Even Ohel laughed out loud at this. To get to Spain was as difficult as to fly over the Alps to Italy or to swim the North Sea to the land of the Danes. The Rhineland, east and west of the great river, was overrun by soldiers, most of them united under no other theme than Jew hatred. In Champagne and Lower Lorraine, where enormous fairs had been built around the presence of Jewish merchants, the preparations of great armies for their voyage to the east now led to anti-Jewish outbreaks. In Lyons, where the Jews were so numerous that the market day had been changed from Saturday, the Jewish Sabbath, to allow their participation, rioters had last month stormed their synagogues. In Troyes, home of Europe's most renowned rabbi, Rashi, the population had turned for the first time on their Jewish citizens. If a Jew was unsafe in his own home, he was yet less safe trying to leave it.

Even if one could travel overland through Germany and France, Spain was separated from the rest of Europe by more than a treacherous range of mountains. Here was a vast land ruled first by pagans, then Romans, then Moslems; now as Christian warriors destroyed the Moslem kingdoms, remnants of classic civilization were mixed with a barbarity unknown even to the lords of France and Germany. To visit the shrine at Compostella was a feat performed by only the most daring of knight pilgrims, fearful not only of Moslem armies, but of robber barons and land pirates of a hundred varieties. And in the wake of Christian battles against Moslem kings, victorious Christian armies had turned on local Jewish populations, as if pillaging their homes was one of the perquisites of warfare.

"It would be better to simply trust in our neighbors, remain in our homes, and pray to God," said Ohel's wife Dinah. None of the merchants listened to Dinah, but some answered Rachel, and at the same time: Spain was dangerous, unreachable, inhospitable to Jews.

"There are Jews in Barcelona," said Rachel. "Old families that lived under Moslem rule, and will live under Christian rule just as well. My father imported paper from them, and leather. There is even a distant relative on my mother's side, to whom I have written. My husband hoped to reestablish trade with him."

"Your husband," said a merchant with distinctly sympathetic tones. Yosef's disappearance from the face of the earth was of a piece with Rachel's sudden inspiration to fly to Spain—as practical as importing Palestinian scallions from Saracen Ascalon to Christian Europe.

"Rachel, perhaps it would be better if you went home before the service, drink something hot with some fresh bread," said Ohel. He had never heard her talk of Barcelona, or relations in Spain, or indeed of any dream about going there.

"I am not crazy," said Rachel. "I don't know everything there is to know about Spain, I know very little. But I've been looking for a place to go. Spain is right. I know it."

"How can you know it?" said Ohel, but then all at once he knew, and shook his head slowly from side to side. He wouldn't give her away, of course. It was not his fashion to ridicule his sister, especially when she spoke of an impulse, an intuition, a wordless daydream. Their father had always encouraged her in this silliness, claiming that all her namesakes were gifted with second sight. But for all the visions she had had, nightmares and dreams of fat and plenty, he never once known her to be right—except, of course, when she had awakened in the middle of the night two years before to tell him that Yosef was lost, that he was gone, that no one in Mainz would ever see him again. But then, it was perhaps no great feat to fear for one's husband, traveling through pirate-filled seas.

As for Spain, he was sure that the fanciful image of Barcelona had simply entered her head, even if only to keep out the closer images of Emich and Volkmar and Gottschalk and Peter the Hermit.

"Yes, of course," said Ohel, smiling to cover Rachel's embarrassment. She could see that he knew now that Spain was one of her impulses, her urgent visions pulled from an endless variety of possibilities, none of them connected to logic and reason. "You have written to a relative. I don't remember a relative."

"We are related to the family of Samuel Ha-Nagid," said Rachel.

"What do you mean?" said Ohel, forgetting for a moment the seriousness of their situation, so astounded was he by Rachel's statement.

Samuel Ha-Nagid had been the vizier of Granada, and the military commander of its Moslem army for twenty years, until his death on a campaign against Seville in 1056. Jews who knew nothing of distant Spain still sang his praises, for Samuel had been a poet, a warrior, a statesman, but still found time to lead the Jews of Spain through his religious books and poetic devotions. It was well known that he claimed descent from the House of David—as did half the successful Jewish families in Mainz, or Narbonne, or Barcelona. It had been a standing joke between Rachel and Ohel, how their mother used to claim descent from both the House of David and the House of Aaron.

Barzillai was a *Cohen*, a descendant of the priests of the Temple, and therefore a descendant of Moses' brother Aaron, from whose numerous family all the priests were drawn. Even in exile, Jews who were *Cohanim* assiduously guarded their rites and privileges in the synagogue service, modified from their original holy task in the sacrificial offerings of the ancient Temples. All Jews who were not *Cohanim* were either Levites—descendants of the tribe of Levi, into which Aaron was born—or simply Israelites. Israelites were descendants of any of the other eleven tribes.

One of these tribes, Judah, was the tribe of Jesse, and Jesse was the father of David the King. Both the Jewish Messiah—who had not yet arrived—and the Christian—who had—were said to be descendants of David and Jesse and Judah. The status of *Cohen* and the status of descent from David were therefore much sought after, apparently in Spain as well as in Germany. Few had the temerity to claim descent from both great trees. But Rachel's mother, bowed by Barzillai's infidelities, channeled all her boldness into extravagant claims of genealogical greatness.

"Mother said we were related to him," said Rachel. "And there is the man in Barcelona, Ben-Yizak. He is supposed to be a son of mother's great-uncle Haim."

"Mother's great-uncle Haim," repeated Ohel incredulously. "The only way we're related to Ben-Yizak of Barcelona is that our grandmothers hung out their clothes to dry under the same sun."

"Ohel," said Rachel quietly. "I *believe* that we can go to Spain."

Ohel hesitated, not because he had the slightest inkling that Rachel was correct, but simply to clear his tone of exasperation. He knew that Dinah, always jealous of his lovely sister, was watching.

"Samuel Ha-Nagid is in Granada, not Barcelona," he said. "Besides which he's dead and buried. His own son became the vizier after he died, but the people envied him, and he was murdered—and then there were riots in Granada just like there are in the Rhineland. Who knows how many died there, or if there are even Jews left alive."

"There at least the Jews became viziers," said Rachel. "Even if they were murdered, they had dignity and power. Here all you suggest are bribes and prayers. Listen to me, brother. Even if you have never listened to me before. We must go to Spain, somehow, by land or sea—"

Dinah interrupted with her sweetly modulated voice: "Perhaps on the wings of eagles."

Rachel shook her head, as if to clear it of Dinah's skepticism. Instinctively, she held the diamond stone close to her neck, feeling a current of warmth run from the stone, warming the tips of her fingers and the base of her neck.

"Don't laugh at a gift from God," Rachel said sharply to her brother. "If you have ever loved me, you will listen to me. You must find a way, we must all find a way, but we must go to Spain."

Her speech was so suddenly passionate in the small space of the room that an embarrassed silence allowed the growing chatter of the arriving congregants from the adjacent sanctuary to be heard.

Rabbi Kalonymus brought the meeting to a hurried end.

The congregation was assembled in the sanctuary, and he was wanted to address them, he explained. Carefully he added: "I will leave this city before the end of today. This is what I will tell the congregation. Not to go to Spain, but to nearby Rudesheim. And not forever, for Mainz is my city, and I will return."

Rachel looked at the *parnus*, at the merchant of Worms, and at those of her own city. All were white-faced, the life already drawn from their tired flesh.

"Now let us go and pray," said Rabbi Kalonymus.

But all of Rachel's prayers were centered around flight, and the stones about her throat. She knew that every important Talmudist in the city would share the seats of honor near the ark, reminiscent of the Holy of Holies in the destroyed Temple of the Jews. The women would sit separately from the men, just as they had their separate women's court in the Temple. Even the blessings of the priests were repeated by those members of the congregation who descended from the original *Cohanim*. Before the ark—which was built into the eastern wall of the synagogue, facing Jerusalem, and therefore the original Temple—was the *ner tamid*, the eternal light, the symbolic representation of the Temple's golden menorah.

But Rachel found no sustenance or glory at that moment in the association of the sanctuary with the ancient Temple. The Jews had been a warrior people, proud and ready to defend their honor at the slightest provocation. Now they were reduced to counting their gold bezants, attempting to buy their lives from their oppressors. Rachel was afraid that such men would submit all too easily to *hillul ha-shem*, "desecration of the Name," agreeing to be baptized in order to save their lives. Rabbi Kalonymus would undoubtedly bring up the memory of the famous martyr of Mainz, the great Amnon, who suffered the horror of having all his limbs severed rather than be baptized. For all his courage, Amnon was remorseful that he had even considered the possibility of conversion to save his life. He told his adversaries that they should cut out his tongue for having asked for three days in which to think over his decision. It was then that they had cut off his arms and legs, and he, in his pain, began to compose his prayer to God. Before he died, he had finished the *U-Nessaneh Tokef* prayer, but only in his mind. He was brought into the synagogue, where his lips moved soundlessly, his eyes shut against the pain. His torturers had rubbed salt into his wounds, had laughed at his piety, had expressed the hope that he would live a long life, to prolong his agony. Legend says that the whole community was present in the synagogue, as it was Rosh Hashanah, the holy first day of the Jewish New Year. Everyone had been terrified by Amnon's fate, and they listened carefully for his words, which emerged too quietly to be heard.

But then, just before the *Kedushah* prayer, his words rang out, filling the congregants with awe: "Let us tell the mighty holiness of this day." It was a long time before they realized that the explosion of sound had been his last words on earth. He died moments later, a beatific smile on his lips.

The rest of the prayer appeared in lines of fire, in a dream dreamed by an ancestor of the present *parnus*, Rabbi Kalonymus. Rachel knew its words as well as she knew the Psalms of David. "On New Year's Day the decree is inscribed, and on the Day of Atonement the decree is sealed: how many shall pass away and how many shall be born; who shall live and who shall die; who shall attain the measure of man's days and who shall not attain it; who shall perish by fire and who by water; who by sword and who by beast; who by hunger and who by thirst; who by earthquake and who by plague; who by strangling and who by stoning; who shall have rest and who shall wander; who shall be tranquil and who shall be disturbed; who shall be at ease and who shall be afflicted; who shall become poor and who shall grow rich; who shall be brought low and who shall be exalted."

Rachel knew that she couldn't go into the sanctuary, listening to the tremors of fear, the sustenance offered by legends of martyrdom. She wanted no martyrdom on behalf of *Kiddush Ha-shem*, "sanctifying the Name" in a futile acceptance of death. She wanted to live, and she wanted Deborah to live, and she wanted every Jewish boy and girl in Mainz to reach the full measure of years contained in their human frames—and not meekly accept a fate that would be the result of indecision and passivity.

"Where are you going?" said Ohel as Rachel hurried past him, nearly tripping the fragile and insistent Dinah to the ground. "Rachel, answer me—where are you going?"

But she had no answer other than the memory of Deborah's face when she had finally told her about the attack of the beggarman, no answer other than the impulse that must needs rule her heart.

Ohel caught up to her, reached out, and grabbed her arm.

"I'm going to Spain," said Rachel.

It was the last time he ever touched his sister; they were the last words she ever said to his sad, defeated face.

Chapter
28

In fact, Rachel had no idea where she was going, except that it was away from the synagogue and out into the streets.

She hurried up the steps, past the incoming congregants, many of whom tried to stop her long enough to pay their respects. But she heard no voice, except the one in her head, and that was urging her outside, up the steep paved hill that ran past the Jewish quarter, past the stalls of the fishmongers, past the early morning hawkers of bread and ale and sweetcakes. Rachel was too enervated to notice the wide variety of looks hurled her way by the peddlars and peasants, whose faces usually wore a uniform blankness of humility and patience. Today there was pity and hatred, jealousy and violence and sadness. All the townspeople knew that Emich's men were coming, and what they had done to the Jews of Worms. Mainz was different, many of them said, but there were as many who were determined that Mainz should be no less exacting of their revenge on the Jews' prosperity than their Rhineland neighbors had been.

"Where are you hurrying, madam?" said an old man with yellow and white hair, his speech distorted by the hole burned into his tongue when he was still a youth—this had been his penalty for speaking blasphemously before witnesses. He held up a piece of bread, flat and warm, though the morning had not yet lost its chill, and Rachel smiled at his familiar face and gave him a copper coin for the bread. But she lost none of her momentum, though struck by complaints muttered about her from the many booths and stalls; no one failed to notice her brightly colored clothing and the lavish jewels that had once had the power to heal the sick.

Rounding a corner, she collided with a hunchback, whose handless right arm was a relic of another old crime, but whether it had been for theft, or striking a blow, Rachel had no recollection. The man didn't apologize, and was so rude as he sidled away that Rachel was shocked from her obsessive daze. He had said something about the Jews, something obscene and vile, and the words had wounded her profoundly. She had never before heard an insult directed at her face in her native city.

Suddenly, it seemed that all about her were the maimed and the misfit.

The street was very narrow, and the tenements that rose to six and seven stories inclined toward one another, like strangers bowing in stiff greeting. She was very near the river, but no breeze penetrated the alley, no sense of the peace and continuity that the clear-flowing Rhine gave to her reached through the stench and the grime and the confusion of the poor quarter's stalls. She knew that she had taken a wrong turn, she who had known every street in Mainz since she was a small child, could walk it blindfolded at night, could find her way in a storm with all the lamps extinguished by wind and water. Every other step she took she was confronted by another leering face, one branded with the first letter of "thief," another scarred with one or another of the mutilations reserved for runaway serfs. Faces with wandering eyeballs, without noses, with squints and cataracts and toothless grins loomed up at her, as their lips opened wide to shout insults and threats.

Rachel had to run. She had to find Deborah, she had to sell her jewels and get to Spain. All the words of the merchant of Worms came back to her, words that had built visions of treachery, of friendships violated, of neighbors turning to adversaries in the blink of an eye.

"Deborah," she said, seeing a head of curly auburn hair. But then the sun moved, and the little slice of light in the alley shifted so that the little girl was not Deborah, but an old man, whose red hair was full and shot with white and gray, the color of his beard. She stopped for a moment, wondering where Deborah was; and indeed where she herself was going.

A peasant asked her for a coin, and she gave it to him, and another jostled her, and she started in an unwarranted fear. She found herself pressing first the loaf of bread into one beggar's hand, then the coins in her purse, one and two at a time, until one old hag ripped the bag from her hands, sending the copper coins clattering to the paving stones, where urchins fought each other for the dull little bits of earthly wealth.

Then all at once her fear grew.

She blinked, trying to bring understanding back to her confused mind. Rachel didn't know where she was, how she had gotten there, where it was she had wanted to go at all.

A moment later, a black cloud reached up from behind her eyes and obscured all vision. For a second she saw nothing, heard nothing, though the taste of fear was sharp against her tongue. When she could see, her eyes were looking straight up at the slice of sky between the tops of the leaning tenements.

The horrible faces of the poor continued to blow up before her eyes, as if they were magnified by the content of their anger and their hate. She remembered hearing of the lawful atrocities of William the Conqueror, the Norman who had conquered England thirty years before, and who had quelled the wild behavior of the rabble by abolishing the death penalty: in its place, he ordered the gouging out of eyes, the crushing of testicles, the hacking away of hands and feet, so that men would fear not death, but life lived in violation of his rules.

"Please," said Rachel, feeling the back of her head pressed to the paving stones, the fetid breath of the deformed mob all about her.

Hands tried to pull at the necklace about her throat. She didn't know if she had slipped, or had crumbled, or had been forced down; but she knew now that she was fighting back. Her hands held the central diamond, and her elbows were pulled close in to her neck. She shouted, or tried to, for she couldn't hear her voice in the great din. They could have her clothes and her coins, even the very hair on her head; but she had need of these jewels, for they would get her to Spain.

"Where are you going, madam?" said one voice, clearer than the others, and she saw a sturdy peasant boy reaching out to help her to her feet. She heard a few more phrases, voices of concern. She heard her name, Madam Rachel, Rachel the daughter of Barzillai, Rachel the benefactress who always gave to the poor in the time of their need.

"Please, this is mine, it's very old and important to my family," she said, wondering if he could hear her words, wondering if he was only another specter in a dream.

"Let me help you, madam," he said, and his thick dialect ran over her like fresh water. He was real. He wanted to help her. So did the others, ill smelling, variously shaped, peasants and paupers —they looked down upon her with nothing but concern.

She had made a terrible mistake. No one had thrown her to the ground. Fear had allowed her to fall, fear and haste and confusion. There had been an ugliness all about her, and she had rushed into it, hoping to find in confusion and fear a different direction than the one she know she would finally take.

"Thank you," she said to the peasant. When she stood, she leaned on his filthy arm, she allowed the breath of the poor to blow into her nostrils. Rachel had dropped some coins in her haste to get rid of them; one old woman had wanted more than her share. Everything else had been her imagination. Certainly no one had dared to touch the jewels about her neck, any more than any of them had thought to defile her person.

She began to explain to the young peasant boy about the hunchback who had cursed her, but she remembered now that the mad had license to say what they wished and never be blamed for it. Once again the boy asked her where she was going, and then, at that moment, she saw the red and white floral design that the lord of the castle had always favored on his tunic, mail coat, and shield, brightened by such a sudden showering of light that Rachel imagined she must be falling again or dreaming, unless she had become as mad as the hunchback who had cursed her and her people.

But no, she wasn't dreaming.

This was Monday, a secondary market day, and one that the lord favored in his long and regular walks. On Monday, one who knew Mainz would know where to find him. She had avoided nothing by losing her way in the poor quarter. Rachel hadn't been going to the castle, because she had preferred, somewhere in her mind, to meet him in the street, amid the peasant stalls, surrounded by a cacophony of men and women hawking their wares, all of whom would quiet at his approach and bow their heads in homage.

"Rachel," he said, his voice strange against her memory of it. It had been many years since he had called her that, and the thrill of the simple syllables of her own name on his lips unnerved her. But almost at once, he rectified the mistake. "Madam," he said. "I will speak to you."

In spite of the certainty of the words, he was tentative, speaking nearly in an undertone, attempting a privacy that men of his stature rarely used.

His name, like his son's, was Hugh. Rachel had called him that for so many years that she found it stilted to call him "my lord," now that they were adults, now that they had each married and brought children into the world. But they had taken to a formality of greeting, a careful averting of eyes and stiffening of every feature of face; it was simpler to be "madam" and "my lord," simpler still to be less than that, speak only when absolutely necessary, meet only in the presence of others, best of all never to see each other at all. When they were children, he had come around her home, pretending to be fascinated by Barzillai's stories, but really wanting glimpses of Rachel, and later, time for long talks of knightly love, high ideals of friendship and romance. There had been many such talks. They shared books, legends, tales, songs. She could remember his boyish voice, so changed now by the years into something deep and grave and threatening. Once it had been high and pure-toned, each note distinct and shining, as tightly connected to emotion as lightning to thunder, as sunshine to the heavens.

He was only a few years older than she, but looked older by a decade at least, even when they had been children. He was very tall, and his beard had grown in early, and he had the rough shoulders that he'd passed on to his own son. Barzillai had told him that they would stand him in good stead if the Saracens captured him and placed him in the galleys for life service under the lash, pulling at the long oars through the endless sea.

"Hugh," she said, without thought, and the name caught him so by surprise that his face went a shade darker; not like a blushing damsel, but like a suddenly angered old king. The lord took hold of her roughly, and she could feel the fear rising from his gaily decorated frame. He wore the light mail coat that had been in his family for generations, the old sword that his father had entrusted with Barzillai for adding simple jewels to the gilded hilt. Swiftly, he walked her away from the crowded stalls. Though the peasants fell back, parting like the waters of the Red Sea, she was amazed at their progress toward the river. She wondered where the ground went, the steps, the hills, the twists and turns to the city walls. It seemed like they were moving through space, as if their feet hardly touched the paved ground. It seemed as if time had been twisted around a dream of desire, a dream where one was young and old, child and adult in the same breath, with no logic breaking the spell of images and memories. Rachel could remember a time when they had been like this, floating over the grass, on the high ground that led up to the great castle, but the lord had been a boy then, the son of the lord of the castle, and it had seemed then that life had no urgency, no tasks, no progression. There was no need for marriages, children, alliances forged in blood, based on common backgrounds and traditions and goals.

She didn't know how to tell him that she had been looking for him, that if he hadn't been in the market she would have braved the men at his gates and demanded an audience in the great hall of his castle. Rachel didn't understand the anger she felt in him, but didn't trust it any more than she could trust the fear she had felt from the innocent peasants in the marketplace, any more than the vision of the grass and the river and the castle and the cloudless sky.

"Your daughter is in the castle," said Lord Hugh. Rachel heard the words in a strange surrounding of quiet. She wondered if she might have missed something he had said before this, some way of catching up the years in which they had been so little to each other.

"Yosef has not been heard from for two years," she said, knowing as she said it that the statement was absurd. Of course the lord knew about Yosef. Even the blind beggarwoman knew about the husband of Rachel bat-Barzillai and his sad adventure at sea. Still, Rachel had never heard the lord of the castle of Mainz express his condolences, though she knew of the kindnesses extended to Deborah by the lord and his lady at the time of the disappearance; and how the lady especially urged Deborah to believe that Yosef was alive and would return to his family.

"I have asked her not to come to the castle," he continued, as if she had not spoken at all. "It is not she who has defied me, but Hugh, my son. I shall punish him, of course, but the fact remains that she is there, along with her cousin."

"Why is Deborah there? I forbade her to go there, even when Hugh begged me, apologizing for what you had said to her."

"She is there because she has twisted her ankle," said the lord.

"I would have had to raise my sword to my own son to force the girl from the castle. I am sure she will go when you ask her."

"What is wrong with her? How has she hurt herself?"

"It is a minor thing, a childish ache," said the lord. "I am sure you remember how one exaggerates the pains of childhood."

"There is no pain like a child's pain," said Rachel sharply. He had been the first to marry. When she had first seen the lady of the castle carried in pomp through the city, she had been astonished at her fresh-faced beauty. There had never been anyone else so pretty in Mainz. Even Rachel's mother's delicate features were coarse by comparison. Rachel understood at once that Hugh loved her the way one loved an angel, a perfect spirit. He had abandoned Rachel not because his lady was the daughter of a duke, but because she was sublimely beautiful; he had forgotten Rachel not because she was a Jewess, but because she was imperfect, ordinary.

"Do not tell me about a child's pain, or about any pain," he said. "Do not tell me anything at all. Simply collect your child, madam, and be gone."

"What is wrong with you, my lord?" said Rachel. She wanted to tell him a thousand things, because it had been so many years since they had spoken, and once, long ago, they had been the very best of friends. He had never spoken to her about Yosef, and she would have liked so much to be able to tell him about her husband, how she had fallen in love with him, how his character was strong and built around a faith in God that had allowed him to be fearless and forthright and admirable. She would have liked to tell her very old friend what it was like to lose the man she had loved and lived with, the man with whom she had brought a child into the world. She would have liked to tell him how it was to be close in the cold marriage bed, the heavy curtains hanging from the four posts unable to keep out the winds of memory and longing and desire. "You used to be my friend, and now you act like my enemy."

"Simply collect your child, madam," repeated the lord.

"Look at me," said Rachel. "I have come to look for you, because there is no one else to whom I can turn. I want to live, and I want my child to live, and I find you looking at me with hate, talking to me as if I am less than a serf. Even if I were no one to you but the daughter of my father, you owe me more than this. What is wrong with you? What is wrong with you, my lord, that you are so afraid of the great Count Emich that you turn on every Jew in your life?"

390

Rachel shut up her speech when she saw that his expression had not begun to change.

He was stone-faced, steady in his anger, looking at her as if she were a captured enemy, babbling to him in some language not only foreign, but repulsive as well. She looked at him for a moment longer, waiting for some sign that he would speak, that he would get to his knees and implore her forgiveness, that he would admit to his fear, his cowardice, and vanquish it in protecting her family with his last bit of earthly strength.

But Lord Hugh simply continued to look at her, as if words couldn't express the depth of his anger, as if her crimes were so great that he dared not begin to list them or his anger would become a murderous rage. Abruptly, she turned about, hardly knowing where she was, except that the castle was at her back, and she began to walk rapidly away, even forgetting in that agitated moment that her daughter was locked up in this madman's castle.

"Rachel," he said, and she felt his hand on her shoulder, stopping her with the lightest of touches. "Rachel, do you remember the Fourth Rule?"

Suddenly, she could feel the past open wide beneath her, an enormous chasm in the smooth earth of the present.

This was a surprise, but only for a moment.

Suddenly, she understood his anger, his hate, his fear.

A violent trembling began in her body. It was an eternity before she realized that he was touching her, and not with authority or belligerence. Lord Hugh had lightly placed his callused sword hand on her shoulder, where only the thinnest of silk separated their flesh, and whatever trembling refused to subside in her body yearned for the comfort promised in his own unsure hand.

"Don't," she said. "Don't, my lord."

But it was too late.

Of course she remembered the Laws of Love. It was all they had talked about at one time, the great complicated rules of love among the educated nobility of France and Italy and Germany—at least according to the exaggerations of the minstrels who sang their romantic tales.

The First Rule was that marriage cannot be used as an excuse for refusing to love someone else; the Second Rule was that a person who is unable to keep a secret is unable to be a lover; the Third Rule is that a person cannot love two people at the same time.

But Hugh had spoken of the Fourth Rule.

"Do you remember?" said the lord of the castle. He had increased the pressure on her shoulder, and she found herself turning around, looking into his face, with its tired eyes, exhausted from gazing into the past, measuring it endlessly against the present and future.

"Yes," she said. The Fourth Rule was simple enough: love never remains still. It either increases or decreases.

His anger was no anger, his hate was no hate.

She wanted to shout at him to stop, but knew that not one year or ten was propelling his lips toward her, but a lifetime; he had wanted her since he was a young boy, and his love had not diminished, it had increased. He didn't ask her if her love for him was still there or whether it had disappeared in the embrace of a husband. He simply took her in his arms, he pressed his lips toward her, and like a miracle, the fear that had been weighing on her for weeks and months suddenly vanished. Like a miracle she had found the memory of her first love, and had become eager and hungry and oblivious to the world.

Chapter 29

Rachel had not been inside the lord's castle since she was a child.

Though half the men and women of the village, even of the lowliest birth, visited the tower's great hall at least once a year, Rachel had never been past the interior gates since the lord had brought his lady home to Mainz. Just after the winter solstice, when Christians celebrated the birth of Jesus, she would watch the humble townsmen walk quietly up the streets of the city, eager to partake of the meat and wine and ale that the lord dispensed so freely. Rachel would have liked to join them, simple people in rough clothes, looking up at the bright silks and jewels and weapons of the castle dwellers. But she never did, not being simple or simply dressed. It would have been more than she could have borne to be noticed by Lord Hugh, her jealous face looking up at the spectacle of his family's bounty.

"You are certain that Deborah is well?" she said.

"My son is looking after her carefully." He smiled at this, as if he had told a joke, or was about to. "Even though I threatened him, he will look after her the way I will look after you."

Rachel feared the sound of these words.

What she had felt in his arms was sincere, and not the product of fear or delusion. But the solipsism engendered by the embrace was fading. She knew this man when he was a boy; what she knew of him now was built on memory, longing, wishes. She remembered the Jewish proverb: "In her sleep, it's not the lady who sins, but her dreams." But she was not dreaming now. She would try to live in the world-that-is-now, and not in the world-that-was or in the world-that-might-have-been.

As she and Lord Hugh walked the steep hill on which the wooden tower, or donjon, had been built a hundred years before, she remembered how awesome and invincible the castle and its grounds had once seemed; and by extension, how safe and privileged the charmed people were who lived within its unbreachable walls. But then Lord Hugh had himself seemed invincible, flawless. Whatever he promised her would be; even if it was to cajole the archbishop of Mainz to approve the love of Barzillai's daughter for a Christian knight; even if it was to convince Rabbi Kalonymus that nothing could be more sacred than the marriage of a Christian knight with a Jewess of priestly descent.

"The Fourteenth Rule," said Lord Hugh, extending his hand for her to hold as they climbed the steepest part of the hill. Here, horsemen had to dismount and stand under the inspection of the tower guards. Men with arrows and lances and boiling water and oil could defend the castle from a thousand men, she had always imagined. Even if they could get past the deep ditches that surrounded the three-story tower, they could hardly get a hand on the smooth walls, the iron gate, without being crushed by great stones.

Rachel shook her head, amazed that he would take up the game of their childhood, when they would challenge each other's memories with love rules that could have no bearing on a little Jewish girl of Mainz and her handsome young knight-to-be. What bearing could it possibly have on them now? On Lord Hugh, lay ruler of Mainz, and Rachel bat-Barzillai, a married Jewess of his city?

"You haven't forgotten?" said Lord Hugh.

"I remember," said Rachel, still under the spell of his kiss. It was nearly possible to forget that they were not alone, that knights watched their every move, that the lady of the castle was just across the little drawbridge, that the army of Emich was approaching with murder in their hearts.

"Tell me," said Lord Hugh.

"My lord," said Rachel. "We must talk of other things than the Rules of Love."

"I have talked of everything else since the last time we met," said the lord of the castle. "I've never had anyone else like you to talk to, to talk the way we did."

Rachel wanted to deny this, to mention his wife, her husband, the years they had spent without each other. But her lips betrayed her. Even if his embrace had come after years of coldness, after terrible minutes of harshness and hate, she felt comfortable in his presence. Surely all her feelings couldn't be false. He was her friend, and she was his.

Rachel said, "Yes. I've missed talking to you, my lord."

The drawbridge seemed less fine than her image of it, the gate behind it in sad need of paint, the walls of the tower pitted and peeling and groaning in the wind. Even if the tower could withstand a thousand men, she doubted it could hold back twice that; and Emich had far more than two thousand. His peasants and soldiers were so loosely organized, so vagabond an army, that half the countryside joined them as they approached a city simply to share in the joy of destruction. It took no great skill to pick up a stave or a pike and join a mob.

Knights in armor who were fearless and capable, in war or at tournaments, would be of little use in fighting such men. Used to rules, traditions, codes of combat, individual knights, or even small war parties on horseback, would be unhorsed by long pikes, their helmets yielding to the blows of a hundred clumsy staves. There were new castles, constructed of stone, manned by warriors experienced with Greek fire who could repel even the endless mobs of an army such as Emich's, not with death-dealing blows from knightly lances, but with the primitive terror invoked by flames. Greek fire was useful too against the siege towers and catapults said to be newly procured by Emich, but the lord had no such weapon, and all his men-at-arms were cut from the same cloth as he: fearless, reckless, ready to die rather than yield any point of honor. They would be as useless as his tower of wood. The castle of Mainz had become more a home than a fortress, more a comfortable seat from which the lord ruled the city by decrees and judgments than a place of destruction from which terrors sprang to control the country.

"Did you come to ask me for protection?"

"Yes."

"Did you think I would give it?"

"Yes, my lord."

"Of course," said Lord Hugh. "The Twenty-sixth Rule."

Rachel smiled in spite of herself. There were thirty-one Rules of Love, and she remembered them all; her heart had given them the importance of the Ten Commandments. "Rule Twenty-six," she said. " 'Love is incapable of denying anything to love.' "

"Good," said Lord Hugh. "And now, Rule Fourteen."

"My lord, this is very difficult for me."

"It is difficult too for me, Rachel."

For a moment, it seemed that he would return to his old anger, his false front of hatred and indifference. Rachel hoped that he was capable of moderation, that he would offer her something between a passion that was all encompassing and a loathing that would exclude her from his life.

"My lord, I must get away from this place. If you would help me, you will see to it that Deborah and I can leave the city before Count Emich arrives."

"You are not leaving," he said.

"My lord," said Rachel. "Our lives are in danger."

"My wife is going back to her parents," said Lord Hugh. "She has been brave, and she has borne me children, but she is going back to visit her family, and she will never return."

"I don't understand," said Rachel.

"You are not leaving," said Lord Hugh.

"I must leave," said Rachel. "I must get to Spain."

"Spain?" said Lord Hugh. He looked no less incredulous than the merchants of Mainz in the great synagogue. But she was still reeling from his words about his wife. Did he believe that she would usurp his wife's place in the castle, a Jewess taking on the robes of mistress and whore? She hoped the lady's leaving hadn't been prompted by the lord's revelation of a childhood romance. It seemed impossible that Rachel could be responsible for the destruction of anything so inviolate as the marriage contract. After all, if he had not spoken to her in the peasant's marketplace, she wouldn't have been able to open his heart to love. Certainly his wife must have good reason to leave him and her sons and daughters, reasons that were greater than their shared past.

Still, she must steel herself, must explain what she could be to him, wife or no wife. Whatever old love there was, she was the wife of a man who might still live, she was the mother of a daughter who must be protected and taken from this country to where it would be safe. No more than she would give in to religious fervor and wait for Emich's men to set the synagogue on fire, would she allow herself to live out childhood fantasies, while the Crusaders besieged the castle, demanding the lives of the Jews behind its walls.

"My lord," she began again, and when he gently insisted that she call him by his name, she repeated herself, more formally still. "My lord. I am very sorry. But what you or I may want for our lives may not be possible, may be just too hard."

Lord Hugh laughed at her, drawing her close to his side as they walked over the drawbridge under the eyes of the armored men at the open gate. "Rule Fourteen," he said. " 'A love too easily possessed makes the love contemptible. But to possess love after great difficulty makes love valuable, and of great price.' "

The lord and his family lived on the second floor of the wood castle, separated from retainers and servants by a wall of hanging silk. This private "solar room," so called because of its fortunate position facing south, where whatever sun reached Mainz in wintertime could filter through the small windows and tapestry-covered walls, was the exclusive retreat of the lord and his lady, their daughters and son, and whatever important guests took lodging in the castle. As Rachel made her way past odoriferous servants and the wall of heavy silk, she was struck by the sudden strength of the May sun, and by the harsh way it lit the lord's quarters. The very brightly painted walls were vulgar and garish; the south wall, outlined in gold paint, gave Rachel the feeling of a barbarian camp in one of her father's stories.

There were riches here, of course: chests filled with silks and furs; real glass in three of the windows; feather mattresses on the heavily curtained four-poster beds; cupboards built into the walls.

But the bright southern exposure revealed the poor craftsmanship of the beds, the benches, the tables, the tapestries. Yosef, and Barzillai before him, had labored to teach Rachel the value of the commodities with which they dealt. Iron and copperware, furs and honey, wax and wool and wine were all brought up the Rhine to Mainz, and Rachel had learned to select the best of these for trade to the east. The businessmen of Constantinople who sent her silks and brocades and spices and paper were no fools, and traded the best of their wares for the best of the wares of Germany and France. In this castle, which her childish imagination had always filled with the most sublime of treasures, were only rough edges, unpolished goods, a collection of all that evinced the clumsy materialism of the age. A rough pole allowed the lady's clothing the

397

chance to breathe, and Rachel could see at a glance how poorly sewn together, how inferior were the materials of each bright garment. The spindly chairs were without upholstery, the walls were damp and whistled in the wind, there was dirt underfoot, on the beds, in the clothing, ingrained in the bright paint of the walls. Worst of all was the stench rising up from the first floor. The latrine off the solar room simply drained its waste to the moat below. Even the poorer Jewish homes in the city used a cesspool system; and Jews rich enough to have servants did not allow them to sleep in filthy straw, breeding vermin a few paces from where the family slept.

Deborah sat on one of the beds, her left leg wrapped in a fur-lined coverlet.

"Mother, the lord says I must leave but Hugh won't let me, and I twisted my ankle, but it wasn't my fault. I wasn't running. Even Hugh said it was an accident that wasn't my fault, and you know how he always likes to think it's my fault. It's all my fault."

Rachel hushed her daughter and took her in her arms. Young Hugh was summoned into a corner by his father, who sharply whispered new commands in his ear.

"Where is your cousin?" said Rachel.

"Up in the turret," said Deborah. "Watching."

She didn't have to elaborate. Her mother wondered who else kept watch for the Crusaders from Speyer. She wondered when David would hurry down from the rickety ladders separating the upper story, with its high turrets, from the second floor. What good would it do to know that the men they feared had arrived, and were knocking on the gates of the city?

"Why is the lord so mean?" said Deborah. She whispered, though she had spoken in Hebrew.

"He is not mean," said Rachel. "There have been many troubles on his shoulders, and it has made him cross and unhappy. But he is not mean."

"But Hugh says that the city will be dangerous," insisted Deborah with the clear wisdom of childhood. "And his father wants me to leave, when here in the castle all will be safe and sound." But then the lord's son hurriedly broke from his father's embrace and stood before Rachel and her daughter. There was a look of triumph in his eyes, but also there was a sadness; as if he had vanquished one who had long been his hero.

"My father offers you the hospitality of his home, for as long as you wish to stay. No one will harm you here."

"But he wants me to go," said Deborah.

"No," said Hugh. "He wants you to stay."

Deborah didn't understand the change in the lord's attitude, but she was content to remain where she was on the bed, her mother's capable hands rubbing the pain out of her twisted ankle. Lord Hugh, resuming an imperious pose, left them in the solar room without a word of explanation. His son, however, had his own interpretation of Lord Hugh's behavior: "He's afraid of the Crusaders."

"Don't say such a thing," said Rachel.

"I've never seen him afraid before," said Hugh doggedly. "But he's afraid now. He said it's all right, but I still hate him. He was afraid to let me play with the Jews, he was afraid of the destruction they would bring to this castle, but I am not afraid. I am not afraid of anything. I will gladly die fighting those cowards, even though I am not yet a knight. I have never heard of a knight who violated the rules of hospitality by such cowardly behavior. I hate my father, and I will always hate him."

Rachel tried to quiet Hugh's anger, but even though the lord had rescinded his previous demand to remove Deborah from the castle, this didn't change Hugh's unhappy feelings toward his father. He had seen his hero tarnished, imperfect. He had believed him to be afraid of Emich's menace, and had seen him not grow in courage, but accept his own son's demands rather than draw blood between father and son. Young Hugh had always believed his father to be perfectly formed, perfectly disciplined, a true knight; but now he knew him to be less than this, something ordinary and vile. No matter that he could ride any wild horse to submission, that he had fought brave knights at a hundred tournaments, that the emperor thought him one of the best swordsmen in Germany. Young Hugh had seen him turn on his Jewish friends, had heard them be banished from his home, had witnessed the lord's inhospitable demands to a young girl with a twisted ankle: only the threat of being engulfed by the Crusaders could have changed his father so.

Rachel could have attempted to correct young Hugh, she could have told him why his father had acted the way he had: that his knowledge of the fate of the Jews hadn't hardened his heart, but on the contrary, had brought up to the surface of thought all the

399

feelings he had long held in check. Lord Hugh realized that he wanted to protect Rachel, her family, her loved ones, all the Jews of Mainz, to do more than was called for, more than any lay lord in any Rhineland city had done to protect their Jewish citizens; and he had realized what this meant, and then he had bridled against it.

In his mind, Rachel had betrayed him. Lord Hugh's marriage had been one of alliance, not of love. He had not wanted it, but he had accepted it, and in his young heart he had felt that he and Rachel would remain true to one another, just as lovers were supposed to according to the Rules of Love they both observed. Rule One was clear: marriage could never be pleaded as an excuse for refusing to love. Rule Eight was clear: no lover can be deprived of his lover without good cause, and marriage was not a good reason. When Rachel married Yosef, Lord Hugh retreated into his life with the loveless beautiful lady of the castle. He beat down his love, trying to force his feelings into submission the way he tamed a horse. But his love refused to dwindle to nothing. So he turned his love for Rachel inside out, until it was rage, until it was hate. Still, he couldn't remove her image from his mind. Whenever he saw Deborah, he saw in her Rachel's love for Yosef; whenever he saw Rachel, his love for her was so suddenly strong that all he could do to block it was to fill his heart with an overwhelming violence.

Dinner in the great hall was served five hours after daylight in springtime. In spite of all their troubles, they were hungry. Young Hugh teased Deborah about her penchant for marzipan. He said that he could hear her belly growling for food. Rachel followed Hugh and Deborah down the ladder to the main floor. The meal was already in progress, with the three courses all mixed into a mass of grabbing, greasy hands. This was not a time for feasting, though the great hall was crowded with knights, many of them wearing their chain mail, as if expecting to be called up to the defensive towers at any moment. Looking about at the coarse and vulgar men, Rachel felt the same kind of unease that had overcome her upon entering the solar room. These men weren't powerful, or sophisticated, or wise. They presented no greater strength than existed in the city, or just beyond its walls. Listening to the gruff talk, the rough oaths, the nervous jesting of those about to be put to a test of courage, Rachel felt no sense of safety. Only the lord of the castle and his son cared for her here, and ultimately, they would be less strong than the fear that could come from this mass of men.

As she began to move toward the raised platform at the end of the hall, where the lord sat with his lady, each of them staring at separate vistas down the center of the hall, young Hugh stopped her.

"Please, madam," said young Hugh, who rudely pushed his way onto a bench crowded with retainers of a lesser order. For a moment, he raised his eyes hatefully to where his father sat at the opposite end of the hall, as if to make a statement without the use of words. "Let us sit with the ordinary folk," he added, speaking in a Latin that was probably too good for anyone but Rachel and Deborah to understand. He took Rachel's hand and helped her to sit on the bench, and then he smiled at Deborah and added: "Come on, Growl-Belly, sit down."

"My belly does not growl," said Deborah sullenly, looking about her at the filthy men sharing their table, as if the sound of hunger had come from one of them and not her. Young Hugh stared fiercely at the men, most of whom were men-at-arms, unsophisticated villagers trained in the use of bow and arrow and not much else.

"Do not raise your eyes to this lady and her daughter," said Hugh.

"Yes, Master Hugh," said the biggest of the men, his eyes still rooted to Rachel's. He had never seen a woman so fresh-faced, with such strong clean teeth, with such luxuriant hair—certainly not one so old as this. Hugh slammed his fist on the table, and the man started, and looked away. "Yes, Master Hugh," he said again. Rachel watched as he lifted a half-gnawed hunk of meat from its resting place on a large flat bread and shoved it deep into his mouth. Smiling, he lifted his ale and drank, his eyes returning inexorably to Rachel's face.

"I still don't see David," said Rachel to Hugh.

"Perhaps he doesn't want to leave the turret," said the lord's son. "I would go there too, if not for you and Deborah." He acted as if were it not for him, the lord would have already thrown them across the drawbridge and harried them beyond the exterior walls of the city.

"Besides," said Hugh. "It's not the best place to see them come. They're not marching on the castle, after all. Not before they break

401

into the city. Not before they take the Jewish quarter and the archbishop's palace. About the only thing David might see from up there is fire."

"Why are they going to kill us all?" said Deborah.

"No one is going to kill us," said Rachel calmly. She had used just the same voice in telling her that she must never stop missing her father, and that she must always believe that God might bring him home.

"But what fire?" said Deborah. "What fire is David going to be able to see?"

Rachel looked at poor Hugh, as if to take him to task for frightening his ten-year-old friend. At fourteen, he was not so much her sweetheart as her playful antagonist, the lover-to-be masquerading behind the arrogance of four extra years of maturation.

"Look," said Hugh, directly to Deborah. "Listen to your mother. No one is going to harm you, either of you. And even if there's trouble in the city, you know that no one can ever get through to the castle. It hasn't been done. Not in a hundred years."

Rachel wondered if this were true. She knew that the castle, or its predecessor, had given rise to the present town as much as any cluster of merchant huts had. The ordinary Rhineland process was of a castle giving rise to a village to serve its needs; then the village growing bigger and more important than the castle from which it had come. Soon the resultant town would clamor for walls to protect itself—until the castle, surrounded by its own walls, perched on its own hill, was eventually surrounded both by a large population and a distant city. Still, the castle remained central. If the city itself had become a fortress, the castle was the inner fortress, the last refuge.

Because Mainz was a Roman town, the walls were more complicated. There were older walls closer to the center, newer walls surrounding the home of the archbishop and circling about within sight of the lord's castle. There was a part of Mainz that could be breached without disturbing the lord's sleep, even if a thousand men shouted in unison.

The castle was not so much a geographical center as a political and social one. If the walls of the castle were breached, Mainz was defeated; if not, it was yet free. The cathedral, the archbishop's house, the homes of the rich all clustered close to the castle, not so much seeking protection as seeking identification with the city's source of power.

"Do you think they'll burn the synagogue, Mother?" said Deborah. "Hugh said they were going to try and put all the Jews in the synagogue and set them on fire."

"Eat something, Deborah," said Rachel.

"What?" said the girl. "We can't eat their meat."

Hugh looked at her crossly, as he always did when she spoke Hebrew, excluding him from her thoughts. But Deborah hardly noticed Hugh, surrounded by so many people eating so many unclean things all at once. There was salted beef, and fresh pork and chicken; there were the remains of several pheasants, already considerably stripped of meat. The men of greater rank, at tables closer to the lord's platform, had sent the lesser orders their leavings.

"Eat the bread," said Rachel.

Deborah picked up a remnant of crude and discolored—but very fresh—rye bread. At the lord's table there would be "manchet," well-ground wheat bread, but here, at the lowlier tables, were breads made from peas, as well as from rye. The flat breads used as plates—shared by two or three men, all of whom left their bones in common on these stale "trenchers"—were tossed to the beggars at the end of every great dinner. There were not many of these here. Perhaps the servants had turned them away, for fear of siege.

"Do I say the regular blessing?" said Deborah. She had never tasted such poor bread before, and wondered if there was some less magniloquent way of thanking God for such a present.

"Yes," said Rachel. "You must thank God for whatever He grants you." She wondered what manner of bread she would be able to procure for her daughter in distant Spain, and absentmindedly touched the diamond against her neck.

" 'Blessed art Thou, oh Lord, King of the Universe,' " said Deborah softly. " 'Who brings bread from out of the earth.' "

Rachel's heart nearly broke as she watched her taste the bread. The men at the table drank their ale, wiping their thick lips on the tablecloth. They ate swiftly, endlessly, as if this might be their last meal. Mutton, rabbit, boiled geese were devoured; meat pies, roasted capons, soup with vegetables and meat were brought on by servants and attacked by the men-at-arms. Everything was floating in lard, so that everything was unclean. Even young Hugh began to look like an animal to Rachel as he methodically stuffed his mouth with meat and fat and gristle and bone. All hands were greasy, as the only utensil used was one's personal knife, and this only to cut the stubbornest of meat. Rachel drank some beer, but it was oversweet, worse even than the harsh cider. She allowed Deborah some fruit, floating in an awfully sweet syrup; but here at last was something not polluted by unclean meat or the fat of the pig.

Suddenly, a trumpet sounded, a quiet murmur against the din of boisterous men.

But a moment later, when the trumpet sounded again, it sang its pure note against an absolute silence.

All the coarse-mannered men had quieted. Even the dropping of their hunks of meat had been accomplished in silence. Without hesitation, they rose to their feet, and Rachel admitted to a feeling of shame: she recognized their courage like a reprimand to her heart. These men would protect her and hers; they would fight for the lives of any citizens under the lord's command.

"Is this the war?" said Deborah softly, but even so her words could be heard in the large silent space, and knights and men-at-arms awaited the command of their lord.

Lord Hugh had gotten to his feet, along with the rest of them, and stood high and tall above all the others from his place on the platform. But when he spoke, it was not to order the men up to their stations of battle. Instead, he addressed a man who had just entered the hall, accompanied by the lord's steward. This man wore battle armor, and when he removed his helmet, there was a bandage about his forehead. He walked toward the lord, his short frame ferociously erect.

"Welcome to Mainz," said Lord Hugh.

"Greetings and all God's good blessings," said the knight, a stranger to all those there, save for Rachel bat-Barzillai.

There was not yet a fire burning the synagogue of Mainz, but Count Emich of Leisingen had arrived outside the city walls; and here was his emissary, eager for money, arms, and the blood of the Jews.

Chapter
30

In the hours before midnight, Rachel slept in fits and starts. She tried not to move, she tried not to think. But her mind refused to quiet. And every memory of the last few hours gave rise to movement: winces, shakes, violent twistings. From the moment that Emich's emissary had appeared in the great hall, she had felt that the slightest motion would send her crashing through thin ice, would trip her wildly over a precipice, would rend the earth beneath her feet to a chasm where fires burned higher than mountains.

Deborah clung to her in sleep, and Rachel was afraid of hurting the child with the knife she held in her hands. But the knife was necessary. It was small, its ivory handle delicate, but its blade was sharp. If the emissary of Count Emich came to her, she would be ready for him. She would drive the point of the blade between the fourth and fifth rib, as Barzillai had long ago taught her; this was an easier target than the neck or the heart, and as deadly.

"You will go to the solar room," Lord Hugh had told her after the dinner was complete and the emissary had left the great hall in the presence of the lady of the castle, a priest, and the lord's two silent daughters. "You will stay there with your child, and you will do nothing until you hear from me."

And she had heard nothing further from him at all that day. She had remained dutifully, madly alone with Deborah in the private chambers of the lord's family, while all about was a cacophony of action, purpose.

Even David was allowed out, to run the ramparts with young Hugh in search of clarification of the hundred rumors of the day. From the highest points of the castle they could see the fire and smoke, they could hear the sudden explosion of sound coming from a thousand throats as they exulted in a victory or howled in cowardly retreat.

But even from the highest tower, no one could make sense of the terrible day.

One rumor had Count Emich rebuffed from the gates of Mainz, another had him escorted inside by a score of dignitaries. One story had the archbishop standing with a cross in his hands before the path of the count's approaching army, another had him inviting the count into his home. One tale had the count's emissary beseeching Lord Hugh for refuge, another had him demanding the surrender of the castle.

Every hour, every ten minutes, the rumors changed, like a river current unable to decide its true course. David and young Hugh had tried to keep Rachel informed, racing down the rickety ladders to the second floor, hurrying over and through the bodies of men-at-arms and their families, who continued to crowd in from the countryside to support their lord and seek refuge in his castle.

But as the day wore on, the rumors that persisted allowed for little hope. It was unclear whether Emich had been allowed into the city at once or whether his supporters within the walls had first staged a riot in the Jewish quarter. It was uncertain whether the Jewish community had gifted Archbishop Ruthard with two hundred marks of silver or whether his demands to keep Emich's army outside the walls were prompted by nothing other than friendship and moral rectitude. It was impossible to know whether the fact that a Christian died during the anti-Jewish riots hastened the opening of the gates to the anti-Jewish Crusaders or whether the riots never began until Emich's men were inside the city.

Even direct statements were clouded by the possibilities of falsehood.

Count Emich's emissary told Lord Hugh that the Jewish community had given his master seven gold pounds, paying mostly in Byzantine bezants, the most useful and valuable currency in the world. But the emissary was there to demand the heads of all the Jews under Lord Hugh's protection, suggesting that the seven pounds of gold had either been extorted under the false illusion that it would ensure the safety of the Jews or that the bribe had never taken place.

Rachel, who had witnessed the confusion and terror among the merchants early that morning, could believe that anything was possible: a bribe could have been volunteered or extorted; resistance could have been with force of arms or nonexistent; the Jews could have tried to flee the city en masse or huddled behind the shaky walls of their homes, waiting to be burned out or passed over, like Israelites among the Egyptians suffering God's wrath.

"Do you think they'll burn the synagogue?" Deborah had said, even before the count's emmisary had made his presence known to the gatekeepers of the castle. "Do you think they will put all the Jews in the synagogue and set them on fire?"

In spite of the question, the ten-year-old slept, and deeply.

In spite of the fact that Count Emich had already entered Mainz and was perhaps within sight of the castle surrounded by his own unruly mobs, Deborah slept. In spite of the fact that drunken men ran about the streets waving pikes and torches, setting up camp in the streets and the houses, before the walls of the archbishop's palace, in the courtyard of the great cathedral itself, Deborah slept.

Rachel hoped that the child dreamed of Spain, of warm-weather fruits and spicy foods and white stone buildings beating back the sun. She hoped that Deborah slept because she knew no evil in her own heart, and therefore expected only good things from life's adventure.

But what good, Rachel wondered, could she offer her child now? How could she get them out of the castle, past the lord's maniacal love, past the men of Emich, past a Rhineland filled with wild men? Knowing that Deborah slept, she heard the child speak, the words echoing in her mind.

"Do you think they will put all the Jews in the synagogue and set them on fire?"

"No, of course not," Rachel answered soundlessly, her eyes open to the dark curtain that surrounded their four-poster bed. "Why go to the trouble of taking them to the synagogue if they are all already assembled in the archbishop's palace?"

She didn't know that they were there, but she hoped for their safety and so imagined them in Ruthard's beautiful palace, in the cool cellars, the warmth of their bodies rising up to heat the entire house. Rachel could hear her voice grow harsh, though her words never left her lips and though Deborah never woke during the dialogue that never was. "The archbishop would never leave them in jeopardy. The Jews have made the village a city, have brought business and science and medicine to this place. Every book in the archbishop's library came about from Jewish translation from the Arabic. All the Latin classics he loves to quote would have been lost to him forever if the Jews of Mainz didn't bring them to him from halfway across the world."

"He will do no good, Mother," said Deborah's imaginary voice. "He is one man, no matter how good or how brave. The bishop of Speyer tried to help and they killed five hundred Jews there."

"We are a thousand and more here," said Rachel. "Not even Emich will slaughter that many."

But in the dark, she shuddered. She could see faint images of destruction: Ohel's body shielding that of his wife as a hundred men fell on them; the pillars of the great synagogue's sanctuary slowly succumbing to tongues of fire, allowing the collapse of the hand-carved roof; the archbishop's august figure dragged through the streets by a thousand Christians, reverting to paganism on waves of blood lust, money love, and hatred.

"Spain," she heard herself say, explaining it all to Deborah. "We will get to Spain." But then another voice called out, a voice not her own or Deborah's, and it frightened her. She wondered if it was that of Lord Hugh coming to her through the night, past the curtain, ignoring the rules of two sacred marriages, abiding only the Rules of Love.

"Rachel," she heard, and the voice was sweet and urgent, and she felt herself turning to it, with infinite patience, moving through an ether of her own design. What if Yosef was dead, and Lord Hugh's marriage was loveless, and this night was their last night in the world? Would God punish them for finding bliss before their lives would end under the sword or in the flames?

A tinge of sadness whispered through her now, so that the sound of her name was sharp, edged with pain. Lord Hugh's presence faded from the blackness about her, chased not by the fear of sin, but the memory of Yosef. He had loved her. If he had not been her first love, he had been her only husband, he had been gentle with her, drawing love from her stiff and awkward body with steady dedication. His passion was not that of a knight. He was not reckless in love, ready to topple a marriage the way one would unhorse a warrior. But Yosef knew passion. There was no other woman in his life but his wife, and not simply in the physical sense. Rachel knew his heart, remembered it, and it had been full of love for her and her only. Suddenly, she was ashamed, as if discovering that her heart had long been untrue, unfaithful. Now she missed him. She wanted him. She imagined that her eyes were closed tighter still and she prayed to the Lord God Most High that Yosef lived, that he awaited them on some sunny Spanish shore, that his innocent face had not become bitter or sad, that his youthful body remained firm and hale, that all his thoughts were for Rachel and Deborah.

"Rachel," she heard a voice say. Whether it was a third voice, or a second, or the first voice to break through sleep, she didn't know. Listening carefully, she tried to examine the blackness, wondering if her eyes were open, if she could have possibly fallen asleep after all.

"Aunt Rachel," she heard more clearly. The voice was dear and familiar. It reminded her of her nephew David's voice.

But suddenly this frightened her terribly. It was as if the voice was calling to her from the other side of the grave. He needed her help, and yet she couldn't bring herself to answer him. She couldn't see him through the dark, and she couldn't stop the terror that stilled her lips from speech. "Aunt Rachel," she heard again, more insistently now, and her sleeping body registered the shock of contact. But how could she be asleep, with all these thoughts, all these visions? She blinked with deliberation and could see at once that the curtain about the bed was slightly parted. For a moment, violence ran through her blood. No one would harm Deborah without feeling her mother's rage. The blade in her hand caught the tiny light of a hand-shielded candle, and Rachel clutched it tighter, feeling the presence of her daughter safe and warm against her breast.

"Aunt Rachel," said David, his curly head wagging insistently in the candlelight.

"I'm sorry," she said, apologizing in a whisper for having fallen asleep. In a second, her wild fear turned to shame. While Mainz burned, she had slept. While her daughter's life rested in her hands, she had shut her eyes to danger.

But the residue of fear stayed with her, in her body if not

409

her soul. Her heart pounded with such force that she was afraid of dying like a lady in a minstrel's story succumbing to a broken heart.

"Please, you must hurry," he was saying, as if he had already explained the urgency and named the place to which she must go.

"Have they come?" said Rachel.

"Who?" said David, then shaking his twelve-year-old's head with violence: "You must hurry."

"Deborah?"

"I will stay with Deborah."

"No," said Rachel. Without thought, she shook her daughter, softly at first, then more deliberately, calling out her name through the peace of sleep.

Deborah stirred, moving her lips as if tasting of something sweet in her dream. Then she said, "Rachel," and not "Mother," as if another spoke through her tongue, a spirit inhabiting her childish frame. But if this were so, it was a happy spirit. Rachel's child looked carefree, as if the thought of waking to a world of murderers had never occurred to her. Breathing the deep exhilarating colors of her dream, Deborah turned her shut eyes to her mother, so that Rachel had to shake her again.

"We must hurry," said David, and for a moment Rachel wondered if what they were hurrying to could be better than this: Deborah asleep, happy in her dreams, in the dark; Rachel aware that this moment, observing her daughter at peace, was more joyful than anything she could look forward to in this castle, about this city, in the long voyage from the Rhineland.

But the moment didn't last.

"Rachel," said Deborah again, opening her eyes and reaching for the diamond, the center stone of the three gems in Rachel's ancient necklace. "I dreamed of the diamond, and it was very bright, brighter than this one, brighter than the light of the sun."

Rachel had to steel herself against these words.

She had always felt a continuity of generations in the legacy of her name, but Deborah's talk about a diamond brighter than the sun seemed to pull her not backward to the women who had carried her name in the past, but to the women not yet born who would. Instinctively, she touched the diamond, pressing it closer to her neck.

"Come, child," said Rachel, babying her a bit, as she always did when waking her; but this time the way she caressed Deborah's forehead, the way she cupped the chin in her hand, the way she ran her fingers through the thick auburn hair had an urgency to it, as if all these actions must be completed before it would be too late to perform them at all.

"I had a dream," said Deborah, letting her mother swing her legs off the bed in the dark without question.

"I know," said Rachel. "You called me 'Rachel.' "

"In my dream?" said Deborah. "I don't remember."

"Later you can tell me about the dream."

"I want to tell you. You always like me to tell you."

"You have to be quiet, darling," said Rachel. Somewhere in the dark were the sleeping forms of the lord and his family and whatever guests were of high-enough station to join them in the solar room. But certainly anyone with ears would have already been torn from sleep by Deborah's chatter, if not by David's hushed commands.

"Should I put my boots on?"

"Yes," said Rachel thinking more like a mother than like an adventurer. On the rush-strewn floor was everything from animal droppings to unsheathed weapons. As Rachel lowered her head to put on her own boots, she felt a sudden racing of her heart, as if her body was responding to a terror yet unknown. She strained to see through the dark, to look into David's eyes, to hear through the quiet of the castle the sounds of violence. But all she could hear were the distant echoes of Deborah voicing the name "Rachel," as if the spirit who spoke through the child now spoke directly to the bearer of the name.

"I'm sleepy," said Deborah. "Are we going back home now?"

"I don't know where we're going," said Rachel, softly, so that Deborah couldn't hear. Rachel heard the spirit, or spirits, more clearly now, and she understood that they were calling to her, the way Ohel's parents and grandparents did—calling through time and death to remind one that nothing was more real than mortality, nothing more permanent than the passing of youth to age to the world-to-come.

She didn't know why these spirits called to her now, unless it was to intimate that death was near or to remind her that courage and conviction ran in her blood. In the stories of her ancestors, Rachel had learned that there were worse things than death; she hoped

411

she would have the strength to accept martyrdom before allowing herself to profane the Name.

"This way," said David, and as he retreated from the bed, Rachel saw him swallowed up by the dark.

She would go wherever he led; there was no doubt in her mind that this boy was part of the destiny she and Deborah would find. Quickly, she helped Deborah with her boots, took hold of her hand, and followed David away from their little island of privacy, past the hulking outlines of curtained beds, through the silk wall that set off the solar room from the rest of the second floor, and more carefully still, up the creaking ladder to the third floor.

Now her fear grew more quickly. Perhaps the spirits were not of the past, but of the future; they might be urging her to live, to bring future generations into the world. She remembered how the great martyr Amnon had hesitated before giving the bishop his refusal to convert; he had thought it over for three days. The twelve Jews murdered in Speyer met their deaths after refusing conversion. Did the Almighty prefer the decimation of His people to a lifesaving baptism? Did He approve of stiff-necked courage leading always to the same bloody end? Perhaps the rabbis were wrong. Perhaps the One God preferred life no matter how one was able to cling to it. Perhaps the sin was to assume that the voicing of an oath of faith to a new God was worse than death.

Besides, she was a mother.

Surely a mother had a different obligation. Did she have the right to let them cut her throat and Deborah's too in a sanctification of God's Name?

"I'll stay with Deborah," said David, his child's voice firm with purpose. They stood in the dark near scores of men sleeping on the floor. The men snored and whistled and groaned in a hundred odd ways, so that the vast space seemed to breathe a macabre music, a music of exhaustion and fear.

"Lord Hugh is waiting," said David, indicating the rough wall of crimson silk hanging behind the ladder to the turrets and towers above. A light burned behind this partition, and a soldier in a mail coat stood before this, looking at Rachel as if she might be a witch. She felt his wary eyes on her as she bent to kiss her daughter, and moved quickly forward, waiting for the man to pull back the silk.

"Rachel," said Lord Hugh, before her eyes had found him. She blinked against the light, remembering the tales of martyrdom she had ingested as a child: brave Hannah and her seven beautiful sons; Akiba and the Ten Martyrs: Hananiah, Mishael, and Azariah—each presented with a choice between life and death, between acquiescence and defiance, between profanation and sanctification of the Holy Name of God—chose sanctification, chose defiance, chose death.

"Rachel," said Lord Hugh. "Come close."

There were so many poorly made candles in the small space that the lord's stern face was framed in smoke. Behind his head were torches, blazing from sconces. He sat on a chair, dressed in a short tunic uncovered by mail. Lord Hugh was unarmed, but a danger emanated from him more clearly than if he had held a battle-ax. As she moved closer, she knew he was about to offer her a choice between life and death.

"I want you to live," said Lord Hugh, the words so closely akin to her thoughts that for a moment she was sure she had imagined them, part of the voices that had spoken to her without sound since David had pulled her from sleep. "Terrible things have happened today, but there is a way that you can live, and that no one can harm you or yours."

It was then that she noticed the two others in the room, seated at separate benches, each of them dressed in mail, their sheathed swords dangling from heavy belts to the floor: one was the lord's son, young Hugh, his face as stern and unyielding as his father's; the other was Emich's emissary, sitting very straight on the backless bench, his bloodstained head bandage the brightest thing in the bright and smoky room.

"What terrible things have happened, my lord?" Rachel found herself saying.

But she knew the answer to this. She saw fire and blood and suffering, and was afraid. "Have you heard of my brother? Is there any news from the archbishop? What does this man say about his master Emich? What does he plan to do with the Jews of the city?"

Lord Hugh had gotten out of his chair, and as she moved closer to him, she felt the violence of his nature grow in intensity, as if she were approaching a fire or a raging torrent. But behind the violence was something else, something weak and brittle, something that could shatter in an instant if one knew where to strike.

"I want you to live, Rachel," said the lord of the castle. He took her hands now, not as her lord or as her lover, but in an awkward pretense of friendship. "There is a way for you to live, and I honestly believe that way is the way of God."

He wanted to believe what he was saying, because he wanted her to live. But he was not good at dissembling. In place of the actor's mask, he exhibited anger and purpose. Still, Rachel could feel the words devour his throat. He was an honorable man, and his love for her was a love for a woman of valor. She knew he lied. This knight, her first love, could never believe that in compromise lay the way of God.

Behind him, she could feel the anger rising from his son like some irresistible force. She forced herself to concentrate on Lord Hugh's words, because an answer would soon be expected of her, an answer that was known only to God, Who knew everything.

Even if Lord Hugh hoped in his heart that she would spurn his offer, she must consider it. It was not his life that was at stake, but Deborah's, and David's and her own.

But first she must wait for the question, the choice.

"This man speaks in the name of Count Emich of Leisingen," said Lord Hugh. "Count Emich has ordered the death of all the Jews in the city. I have forbidden this, as has Archbishop Ruthard. But the killing is going on, a terrible murder of citizens for which I shall be responsible all the days of my life."

"Yes," said young Hugh, softly, getting to his feet behind his father. "Even if they had brought a thousand men, we would be responsible."

Rachel would have liked to interrupt the boy on behalf of her lover. Didn't young Hugh know that love could deny love nothing? Couldn't he see that behind his father's dull-metal facade was a fury a hundredfold greater than his own?

But Lord Hugh ignored his son. The pressure of his hands on hers lessened, and he seemed to be inclining toward her, as if he would like nothing better than to rest his handsome head on her shoulders. Rachel's heart went out to him. He was terribly tired. His world was in flames around him. His castle had defended the region well against scores of robber barons, bands of brigands without a country; it had allowed trade to pass freely for twenty-five miles over land and water in every direction. But Emich's hordes were not river pirates, nor were they simple bandits. They were an overwhelming force, a sea of men against whom there were no clear targets. They feasted on blood, they brought destruction

414

wherever they rested. Their hatred of the Jews was like a natural disaster, a hailstorm, an avalanche, against which reasonable action was no defense. Attacking them with a force of knights would be like fighting a plague of locusts with lances and swords; defending his city against the Crusaders would be like trying to hold back the rising Rhine after spring thaw.

"What killing?" said Rachel. "Where are my people?"

"God wills it," said the count's emissary, softly, but decisively echoing the Crusaders' credo. He too got up from his bench, his eyes alive with vengeance. "You will listen to Lord Hugh, madam," he said more firmly, unaware of young Hugh's anger, as young Hugh was unaware of his father's. "Lord Hugh has listened to reason and wants you to be saved, and there is only one way in the world that can be done."

Young Hugh was about to speak, but his body prevented this. He seemed to be jerked halfway across the room, like a clumsy puppet. All his energy was channeled into his limbs. When his mouth opened, no words came out; but there was blood about his nose, blood that ran as if he had been struck. But no one had touched him. He stepped before the count's man, and at fourteen he was half a head taller.

"Does your boy dispute the will of God?" said the count's man, measuring his words so that each syllable was heavy with disdain. "Does his father's adoration of the Jews extend to his own fledgling sense of knighthood?"

The emissary addressed the lord, and not his son, but young Hugh answered him, no longer hesitating. He drove the heel of his hand into the man's nose and, in the same forward movement, turned his mailed shoulder into the side of the man's head.

"Stop," said Lord Hugh, never taking his eyes from Rachel.

He was so much in pain that she nearly pulled him to her, her old friend, wild with love and remorse and guilt, wild with stifled action.

Young Hugh finally spoke, wiping the blood from his nose and the tears from his eyes, as the count's man staggered to the far wall of the room. "He insults you, Father. Can't you see how everything that he says about the Jews or Rachel or me all amounts to the same thing? He insults you."

"Yes," said Lord Hugh, answering his question. It was unnecessary to explain that young Hugh insulted his father in the same way, by taking action without permission, action that was indirectly forbidden until the lord himself initiated it. In the long preparations for knighthood, the value of restraint was as hard-learned as the impulse to violent force. Someday father would tell son how those moments of restraint in the small room were more difficult than any hours of combat he had ever known.

"Please, my lord," said Rachel, "if you know anything of the Jews of the city, tell me."

"The archbishop has given them refuge in the cellars of his palace," said Lord Hugh, his voice as methodical and uninflected as a messenger of the imperial court. "The men of Count Emich have violated the authority of the Church, as they violate the authority of the emperor and his vassals. They are murdering everyone they can find in the cellars. They are murdering all the Jews of Mainz."

That was not possible, Rachel knew. All the Jews of Mainz were more than a thousand people, women and children and men with gray beards, holy in their knowledge of Torah. Even if men were capable of such brutality, God wasn't capable of allowing such cruelty. And if such cruelty were possible in the mind of God, in the fabric of the world, it could not then coexist with what she felt in the touch of this man's hands. Such a knowledge of desire was a kind of peace, a peace made obscene by the fact of mass murder.

"What are you saying, Father?" said young Hugh. It was clear that he had not yet heard this news, that his anger was for the hundred ignominies offered before the calamity. The boy looked from Rachel to his father to the count's man, as if some explanation of the enormity of this horror must come from their lips. "What does this man want from us if he has shared in the murder of the Jews of our city?"

"How could men of the Holy Crusade enter the palace of the archbishop?" said Rachel, asking the question automatically, as if to delay the acceptance of what her heart had long since feared, what her dreams had long since shown. They had killed the Jews of Mainz, her brother, her family, her friends.

"Rachel," said Lord Hugh. "To live, to give life to yourself and your daughter, you need only agree to accept Jesus Christ."

Rachel didn't know that young Hugh seemed to stop breathing, seemed to be paused before an abyss. Not being able to see what Rachel saw, unable to feel what lay beneath his father's words, he heard only cowardice; he went so far as to imagine his own father sinking this low to protect not Rachel, but his own life as well.

416

"Please, Rachel," said Lord Hugh. "To accept Jesus Christ into your life means only to have faith in God, after all. You have faith in God, accept the God of the Rhineland, the God who rules over this place and will give you your life. Please, give yourself life."

His embrace was not violent now, his passion so twisted by sadness that it had been distilled to a sweetness; Rachel accepted the embrace as natural, and responded to it in kind. She wanted to hold this man, hold his warmth and friendship and life, remember in the strength of his arms their suddenly distant youth and love and dreams. Holding him, she could shut her eyes and feel the wild forces about her recede, so that there was no shouting in her mind, just the gentle insistence of waves in the sea, the slow erosion in time of a name etched in stone.

"Please," he said, more softly than before. "Please, darling."

Now the mask of anger was gone, and she could see the terrible kernel of truth in the large lie. He was pleading, and the words had so far taken charge of his soul that they were no longer completely false. This moved her more terribly than if he had never dissembled at all, than if he had always wanted her conversion, had expected it as sane and practical and life-giving.

"Please," he said, and she understood that he would not fault her for giving in to his pleas; he would love her and protect her and they would live together in an island of peace, even if it was a peace based on weakness.

Rachel felt a strength and a calm growing through her. Somehow her old lover had removed himself from the sphere of decisions. There were choices, but they were hers to make. There were examples before her, but they were examples from her heart and not his: the Jews who died in Speyer and in Worms, the martyrs of Jewish legend, the legacy of the women who bore her name throughout the history of her priestly family.

"You can live," whispered Lord Hugh, and she felt his chest heave, as if sobs threatened to burst from his warrior's chest. "You can live, you and your daughter can live in this world."

But it was not this world that she wanted, Rachel realized. Not a world in which she must profane the Name. Her God was not simply a figure floating through space, a white-bearded old man sitting amid clouds of glory. He was the God of her people. He was the God of her forefathers. He was the God of joy and sorrow, of persecution and glory, the God Who had made Jews an inspiration and a conscience for the world.

417

Rachel would not live in a world where she must deny her God. She did not want a world where Jews might not live. Not Mainz, not the Rhineland, not the land where the blood of the Jews ran like the river's water. There was a time for this country, a time when her family had sunk roots into this earth, but that time was over. She could no more stay here than a tropical bird could nest in the snow. There was no choice, no two-part path, no fork in the road. She had no fear. Not the ancestors of her family, but the descendants called to her. They would live, or she would not hear them. They would survive in the land that she would get to if she had to crawl a thousand miles on her hands and knees.

"No, Hugh," she said, still holding the embrace. She felt his taut body relax, open up like a flower. There was no anger from the lord of the castle. He was through pleading. There was a joy and release as he looked at her with love. "I will never renounce the God of my mother and father, and I will not stay here in Mainz. It is as I told you. I am going to Spain."

"Yes, of course," said Lord Hugh. He would help her. Love could deny love nothing. Rachel had chosen, and her choice had not been life ignobly led, nor had it been death eagerly embraced. Rachel had chosen courage; she had chosen truth.

"I am going to Spain," she said, and even the hate-filled Crusader could feel in her mad words the chance of success, even he could sense in her exhausted frame life ineluctable and free.

Chapter
31

Rachel learned that Archbishop Ruthard of Mainz was able to save twelve Jews of the city. These had hidden in the cathedral until the mass murder was done. Some Jews had fled before Emich had passed through the gates of Mainz, but these were few in number. Rabbi Kalonymus was able to get as far as Rudesheim with a half-dozen families, but all were slaughtered after refusing conversion.

As for the Jews hiding in the cellars of Archbishop Ruthard—all were murdered by Emich's Crusaders. There were a thousand men, women, and children, a number too vast to be readily imagined by the Jews of that time. But Rachel readily grasped the fact of Ohel's death, and the death of family, friends, servants.

From Mainz, the murderers went on to Cologne, where they burned the synagogue, but were able to find only two Jews to kill, as the Gentiles of that city hid them in their homes. In early summer, part of Count Emich's army began to follow the Main River toward Hungary and the east; but nearly half of his followers abandoned this route toward Jerusalem. Murder was more easily accomplished in the Moselle Valley. They had decided in their heart of hearts that they had not yet destroyed enough Jews. And so Emich's brave men swarmed down upon Trier and Metz, blasphemously invoking the name of their God to justify a thousand abominations. Battening on the blood of the Jews of the Moselle region, they returned to Cologne and the Rhineland, massacring Jews in Neuss, Wevelinghofen, Eller, and Xanten.

It is unclear how many of Emich's men ever left Europe for the Crusade against the infidels. Some made it to Hungary, fewer to the miserable Crusader encampments outside Constantinople, fewer still to the siege of Antioch. But surely that tiny number who eventually joined with Godfrey of Bouillon and shared in his glorious capture of Jerusalem in 1099 must have reveled in the slaughter of its inhabitants, Jewish and Moslem both. When they set the synagogues of that ancient Jewish capital on fire, it must have warmed their hearts; though their war was with Moslem infidels, they had learned on their travels that no opportunity to harass and murder the Jews should be left undone. Time was short in this world, and all good deeds would be called to mind before the Throne of Judgment.

As for Rachel bat-Barzillai-*ha-Cohen*, her daughter Deborah, and Rachel's nephew David, few details are known. Certainly, they went so far as Aachen, Charlemagne's old capital. Here that great emperor had built a church and a palace and established a tolerance far greater than any of the rulers who had followed him down to this time of bloodshed and disgrace. Apparently, young Hugh accompanied the three Jews, together with a party of his father's knights. The lord of the castle had relatives in Aachen, men of power and wealth, and somehow they were able to get Rachel and her daughter and nephew to Barcelona, in Spain.

Some legends suggest that young Hugh was knighted in Spain, and not in Germany, and that he married Deborah and served a score of Spanish princes with honor. More probably, young Hugh returned to Mainz, where his father defended his castle against the hordes of Emich. In the defense of Rachel, young Hugh had rediscovered his respect for his father.

Of course, in the telling out of tales, stranger things come to pass than the marriage of a knight of Mainz and a Jewess. It would be happy, and not impossible, to imagine other bits and pieces of story: that Yosef lived and awaited his family on the dock at Barcelona; that Ohel and Dinah survived the massacre and joined the rest of their family in Spain. But these things are so unlikely to have happened that they have never even entered the legends of the family.

More than likely, the three valuable stones—ruby, emerald, and diamond—were sold in Aachen, and the gold thus raised paid for an armed escort through Germany and France to Narbonne. Here,

Jewish traders of that city must have arranged for their passage to Barcelona by sea.

Even if the memory of the necklace's gemstones faded, the stronger legacy of the passing of Rachel's name remained. Family records haven't come down for the period of time in which Rachel must have lived and died in Barcelona, but the birth of a Rachel, daughter of David ben-Ohel, was recorded in 1120, according to a sixteenth-century document. David ben-Ohel must have gifted his daughter with the name after the death of his aunt. It is likely that David's descendants did likewise; following the death of a Rachel with the naming of a newborn girl and affirming the family's faith and history in a retelling of fact and legend. Surely no uprooting from Germany to Spain, no change of custom and language, no memory of horror or fear of the future could break a legacy begun in the ancient homeland of the Jews, in a time before destruction and murder and exile.

In 1420, three hundred years after the birth of David ben-Ohel's daughter Rachel, a great Jewish doctor was born to descendants of that family. His name was Abraham Cuheno. The family was related to other great families, ancestors with much longer roots in the soil of Spain. In the Cuheno family, the legend most often told was of a descent from King David, of Jewish ancestors in Spain since the time of the First Temple.

Still, Abraham's family acknowledged descent from other lands, immigrants from later times. Certainly they knew the Legend of the Brave Rachel, the young woman who defied Antiochus; and in the passing down of her name, they followed the form of the *ha-Cohen* family of Mainz. Indeed, among the Jews of Spain, it was the practice to name infants after the living, and not just the dead. The Cuheno family's most precious legacy, the passing down of Rachel's name only after the death of a Rachel, exhibited their mixed roots. They were not just of Spain, as they were not just of Germany or Byzantium or Rome. They were Jews of a thousand lands and times, a people loyal to the countries they inhabited, but loyal to their history, their legend, their faith. When Abraham's son Judah Cuheno brought home a magnificent diamond for his sister Rachel, he set in motion a physical legacy that was but a shadow of a far greater inheritance; something that could not be measured in length or breadth or weight. The diamond that would link later generations of the family down to our own day was only a reminder of what was pure, full of light, and delicate in its beauty; but also strong, enduring, harder than stone or steel. The name was what mattered, the tradition was what was passed down, the lives past and future, singing like a single gentle soul.

Whether the line from Rachel bat-Mordecai-*ha-Cohen*, born in 188 B.C. in Jerusalem, to Rachel, daughter of Abraham Cuheno, born in 1484 in Zaragoza, Spain, was straight, or whether it ran a crooked path between the centuries, adding the blood and tears of a thousand other human sources, made little difference. They were both Rachel. They were part of the story of their people, as their people were part of a larger story, the story of all mankind. All families are old, all men connect to ancient glories and tragedies, even if we no longer remember their names, even if at some moments in time we forget that all families, all men, all bloods are one.

Epilogue

Rachel Kane was on the ground.

There had been a moment when she had slipped out of her body, had been free to soar through every secret recess in her mind; it had been joyous and full of terror. She had been to places unknown, and places familiar, touched the surface of myth and found legends tangible as flesh and bone. But the moment passed, a mad moment, and her husband was there, tall and comforting, ignoring the women who urged him back to his side of the partition, even as they too rushed to help the young woman to her feet.

She looked up in amazement at the Western Wall.

"We'll just get you something to eat. It's nothing but hunger, fatigue and jet lag, and not listening to your husband."

Her husband had spoken, and though the words hadn't penetrated, she felt the love that prompted them. She had fainted. She had lost consciousness of her world. But in that tiny bit of time, she had heard words, syllables of sound as familiar and distant as her mother's womb.

Once before she'd fainted, nearly three years ago—on her wedding day. That was the day she'd been given the diamond worn by her ancestors, and something more than excitement had taken hold of her, something more than simple desire and longing.

"I heard music," she said.

"Ringing in your ears," said her husband. "We're going right back to the hotel. And I mean now."

And then the floodlights came on, and the ancient wall glowed with power. Rachel turned again to study its surface, to try and remember the music, to understand the words that had played through her feverish frame.

"I saw the Temple," she said.

"Please, darling," said her husband. "I don't like how you look, and I really insist that we go right now."

And then Rachel Kane smiled, even as the clear memory of the Temple faded, even as the music drifted back across the distant years. She chided herself. It had always been her way to imagine things that were not there. She had seen nothing, she had heard nothing, she had simply been overexcited, overtired. After all, her body contained the first stirrings of a new life.

But then the smile blew away against the evening wind, and with it, any certainty. There had been music—perhaps. And there was a vision—maybe. And the words might not have been many, but only one, and that was not a word precisely, but a name, the name of an ancestor, and when the name passed her lips even now, even on the arm of her husband under bright electric lights, she shuddered, in recognition, in kinship, with love.

"Rachel," she said, and the ancient name rang out like the shortest and dearest of songs.